*Watch for a brand-new historical romance
from JOAN WOLF*

*Coming August 2005
from MIRA Books*

JOAN WOLF

White Horses

MIRA

ISBN 0-7783-2097-9

WHITE HORSES

Copyright © 2004 by Joan Wolf.

www.MIRABooks.com

Printed in U.S.A.

This one's for Mike.

One

The sun was starting to shine through the fog when, dressed in civilian clothes, Colonel Leo Standish, Earl of Branford, passed through the front door of the Horse Guards building, home of the War Office. There was just the faintest trace of a limp in his walk, legacy of a wound he had taken at the siege of Burgos several months before.

Branford entered a functional room painted in a rich, dark green, with a desk, a glass-fronted bookcase and a large table with a map spread out upon it. Two men were sitting on either side of the desk, and when the earl walked in they both rose to their feet.

"My lord," John Herries, commissary-in-chief of the British Army, addressed him. "Thank you for coming. I don't believe you've met Mr. Nathan Rothschild."

"No, I have not. How do you do, Mr. Rothschild?" The earl came forward with an outstretched hand. He had certainly heard of Rothschild, the London scion of the industrious financial family, whose brothers were spread throughout Europe.

The short bald man was dressed in a flawless black coat, white necktie and buff pantaloons. He put his hand into the earl's large grasp. "It is an honor to meet you, my lord," he said.

The earl's blue-green eyes moved from Rothschild to Herries. "What's this all about, Herries?" he asked.

"Won't you have a seat, my lord?" the commissary-in-chief said. "We have a job for you and I'd like to explain it."

The earl drew his eyebrows together. "A job? I don't have time to do any jobs, Herries. I am returning to my regiment next week."

"If you would just let me explain, my lord..."

"Oh, all right." The earl folded his six-foot-two body onto one of the chairs. "Go on."

"I'm sure you are aware of the difficulties the Marquess of Wellington has been having with funds," Herries began.

The earl nodded. "He needs to feed and pay the troops, and the local Spanish and Portuguese bankers won't accept paper money anymore. He needs gold coin."

Herries continued. "Mr. Rothschild has managed to buy up for us several million newly minted *napoléon d'or* coins in Holland."

The earl's face broke into a rare smile. "Good for you, Mr. Rothschild. Well done."

Rothschild smiled back.

Herries went on. "Our only problem, my lord, is that we need a way to safely transport the gold to the army in Portugal."

"It's still in Holland?" the earl asked.

"Yes, and we need to get it through France to Wellington in Portugal. Needless to say, once the French government gets word of the sale of all those gold coins to Rothschild, they will be on the lookout for anything that might look like an English conveyance."

The earl arched an eyebrow. "By any chance, does this job you have for me have something to do with the transportation of these coins?"

"It does, my lord." Herries pulled at his lip, then turned to the other man. "I think I'll let Mr. Rothschild explain."

Rothschild looked earnestly at the tall, fair-haired man. "I have had some experience in this sort of thing, my lord. As you may or may not know, my family has transferred money around Europe all during the years of Napoléon's regime. One of the most trustworthy means we have found for doing this is a French circus, the Cirque Equestre. The circus owner, François Robichon, used to be Master of the Horse to Louis XVI, and he has no love for the Revolution or for Napoléon. The circus can travel anywhere without question, and Pierre has moved money for us successfully on a number of occasions."

"Two of the circus wagons have false bottoms where the gold can be stored," Herries put in.

The earl nodded. "It sounds like an excellent idea, but how does it involve me?"

Herries looked at the splendid young man who was sitting across from him. He had never met the Earl of Branford before, and faced with the man in person, a task that had once seemed reasonable now seemed highly improbable. He looked again at Nathan Rothschild.

Nathan continued. "Very unfortunately, François died several months ago and the circus is now headed by his daughter. I am hesitant to commit such a large sum of money to the care of so young a girl. I want her to have a British escort to make certain that the money gets safely to Portugal."

"And I want her to have a British escort to keep her

honest. We don't want little fingers dipping into the gold bags," Herries said bluntly.

Now both of the earl's eyebrows went up. "A British escort would most certainly draw French attention to the circus, exactly what you are trying to avoid."

"Not if the escort pretended to be a part of the circus," Rothschild reasoned bluntly.

There was a moment of silence. "And you want that escort to be me?" the earl asked at last.

Herries shifted on his chair. The earl hadn't changed his own position, but there was a dangerous look in his eyes. Herries cleared his throat. "That's right, my lord."

"May I ask whose idea it was to attach me to a *circus?*" the earl asked, his pleasant voice in contrast to the look in his eyes.

Herries could not bring himself to meet that blue-green gaze. "Lord Castlereagh put forth your name, my lord. As you can understand, he is quite anxious that the gold arrive as safely and as promptly as possible. Wellington will need it to finance his next campaign and his subsequent entry into France."

Silence. Finally the earl asked with awful courtesy, "Am I supposed to—*perform?*"

"Of course not, my lord," the two men chorused in horror.

The earl linked his long, manicured fingers together on his lap. "Then how are we to account for my sudden attachment to a circus? I speak French, but not like a Frenchman. And I'm not the sort of person who just blends into the background," he added ironically.

"We have thought about that problem, my lord, and we have come up with a solution," Herries assured him. "You will pretend to be Gabrielle Robichon's new husband."

This time the earl's eyebrows almost disappeared under the lock of golden hair that had fallen over his forehead. "What?"

Herries said earnestly, "It is the only way to disguise you, my lord, other than making you a performer. Mademoiselle Robichon's family will have to know the truth, but the rest of the circus performers will think you are married."

"I see," the earl said slowly. "I am to pretend to be the husband of a circus owner."

Herries and Rothschild exchanged glances. Neither one of them dared to answer.

There was a long silence.

"I suppose I shall have to do it," the earl finally said. "It's essential that the money get to the army."

For the first time Herries realized that he had been holding his breath. He let it out slowly.

Rothschild said, "Thank you, my lord. I realize that this duty may be distasteful to you, but we do feel it is necessary."

"And the girl is willing to pretend that I am her husband?"

Rothschild nodded decisively. "She agreed."

The earl asked, "What's in it for her? Are you paying her to carry the gold?"

Rothschild said with dignity, "Of course I will pay her, but she is also doing it because she knows her father would want her to. François Robichon was a royalist through and through."

The earl unlaced his fingers. "Where am I to meet this circus?"

Herries said, "I think it would be a good idea for you and Gabrielle to meet in Brussels. That is where you will tell people that you were married. Then you can return to the circus together.''

''Very well.'' The earl stood up. ''I imagine you would like me to get started as soon as possible.''

''Yes, my lord. Gabrielle will be waiting for you at the Hôtel Royale.''

''Is there any particular name I am to go by?''

Herries said, ''You could use your given name, my lord. I don't think anyone would recognize it.''

The earl smoothed one of his sleeves. ''Very well. I will meet this Gabrielle and go with her to the circus, where I will pretend to be her husband. What about the gold?''

''It will be loaded into the circus wagons before you get there, my lord. You should be able to start your journey immediately.''

''How long will it take us to get to Portugal?''

''If you get the gold to Biarritz, the army will take it over the Pyrenees to Wellington,'' Rothschild said. ''The journey from Lille to Biarritz should take about a month, my lord. The circus will have to make stops to perform. It would look suspicious if it didn't.''

The earl's finely chiseled lips settled into a grim line. ''The things I do for my country,'' he said. ''Very well. I will leave for Brussels tomorrow.''

''Thank you, my lord,'' both men chorused.

After the earl had gone and the door was closed behind him, both Herries and Rothschild looked at each other. ''Couldn't Castlereagh have gotten someone who was not quite so noticeable?'' Rothschild said.

Herries shook his head. ''He wanted Lord Branford. Said if anyone could get the money through, it was he.''

Rothschild said, ''I hope he was right, Herries. I hope he was right.''

* * *

Outside, the earl got into his chaise, tipped the boy who had been holding his grays and started the horses, driving through the city streets toward Grosvenor Square, where his town house was located. He pulled into the mews behind the house, relinquished his horse and carriage to one of his grooms, and went into the house from the back.

He was surprised by his eighteen-year-old sister in the hallway in front of the library.

"Oh, there you are, Leo," Dolly cried. "Mama and I have come to call on you."

"Have you?" he asked. "And whose idea was that?"

"Mine. Come into the drawing room and join us."

"I can't stay long, I have things to do. I am leaving for the Peninsula tomorrow."

"Tomorrow?" Dolly was clearly upset. "So soon?" Her gaze dropped to his injured leg.

"I am perfectly healthy. There's no reason for me to linger in England when my regiment needs me."

"But there is a reason," Dolly lamented. "I wanted you to help me with my come-out. I thought you could be my escort to Almacks when I make my first appearance there."

"Good God," the earl said. "Whatever put that into your head?"

"Well, there is one other thing you can do for me. Come along and talk to Mama," Dolly said, and, taking her brother's arm, steered him past the magnificent circular staircase into the marble-floored front hall and thence into the drawing room, which looked out onto Grosvenor Square. Sitting on a gold velvet sofa in front of an alabaster fireplace was a lovely middle-aged woman whose hair was so fair that it scarcely showed the white that had begun to streak it.

"Hello, Leo," she said quietly.

"Hello, Mama," he replied. He made no attempt to go to her. "This is a surprise."

"Dolly dragged me. We are planning her come-out and she has a question she wants to ask you."

His eyes, the same shade as his mother's, moved to his sister's animated face. "What question?" he asked.

His sister looked at him pleadingly. "Please, can we use the ballroom here at Standish House for my come-out ball? It would be so wonderful to have it here. If we have it at Jasper's house we will have to use the drawing room, and it isn't very big."

Jasper Marley, Lord Rivers, was Dolly and Leo's stepfather. Dolly, along with Leo's two young brothers and his half brother, lived with her mother and stepfather.

Leo looked at his mother. "Was this Dolly's idea or yours?"

"Believe it or not, the idea was Dolly's," she replied composedly.

"Yes, it was," Dolly said. "I think Papa would want me to have the best come-out, Leo. I think he would want me to use the ballroom."

He looked into his sister's anxious face. "I'm sure he would. Of course you may use the ballroom. But I won't be here for the great occasion." He turned his eyes back to his mother. "I am leaving tomorrow for the Peninsula."

Her fair eyebrows drew together with concern. "Must you go back, Leo? Surely you have done more than your share in this war. You're twenty-eight. It's time for you to be thinking of marrying and setting up your nursery. You have the succession to think of."

His mouth set. "I have two younger brothers, Mama. If something happens to me, the earldom will stay in the family. And I believe in finishing what I start. The war is not over yet."

She met and held his eyes. "You took a bullet in your leg. You may not be so lucky the next time."

He lifted an eyebrow. "Would you care?"

Her eyes watered. "Of course I would care! You're my son."

"Lucky me," he replied.

Dolly said anxiously, "I wish you wouldn't fight with Mama, Leo. I know you don't like Jasper, but he's not that bad. I think you and Mama should make up your quarrel before you go back to the war."

"We don't have a quarrel," the earl said. "Do we, Mama?"

She surprised him by answering, "Yes, we do. And I wish we could put it behind us, Leo. I hate to see you going into danger again." She stood up and clasped her hands in front of her. "Can't you forgive me?"

His face was hard as stone. "Some things can't be forgotten...or forgiven. And now, if there's nothing more you need me for, I have a number of things to do before I leave tomorrow."

A ripple of pain passed over his mother's face.

"Leo!" Dolly said sharply.

"You don't know what you're talking about, Dolly," he replied curtly. "You came here to get use of the ballroom—well, you've got it. Now, if you'll excuse me, I have things to do. Good afternoon." He turned and strode out of the room.

"Mama, are you all right?" Dolly flew to her mother's side.

"Yes, I'm fine." Tears were running down Lady Rivers's face.

"What is wrong?" Dolly asked in bewilderment. "Can Leo still be angry with you for marrying so soon after Papa died?"

"Leo has his reasons, Dolly. I don't blame him for his actions toward me. I just wish he had a little more charity in his heart, that's all."

She took out her handkerchief and wiped her eyes dry. "Come along, dear." She tried to smile. "Leo isn't the only one who has things to do."

Two

It was raining when Gabrielle Robichon's elderly carriage pulled up in front of the Hôtel Royale. She got out of the carriage and went to talk to the driver. "You can stable the horses in the mews in back of the hotel, Gerard. Make sure they are rubbed down and give them a bran mash."

"I know, Gabrielle," said the driver, who was almost as venerable as the carriage. "I've been taking care of horses for longer than you've been alive."

Gabrielle smiled at him.

Gabrielle's older companion appeared at her side. "For heavens sake, *chérie,* let's get out of this rain!"

"All right, Emma, all right," Gabrielle said. The two women hurried toward the door of the hotel, which was opened for them by a liveried doorman.

"Our bags are in the carriage," Emma said to the doorman. "Will you have them fetched, please?"

"Yes, *madame,*" the man replied. "I will have them sent up to your room."

"Thank you."

The two women approached the desk. "We are supposed to have a reservation, Emma," Gabrielle said.

The clerk behind the desk looked at them, and Emma said, "Madame Dumas and Madame Rieux. I believe we have a reservation."

The clerk looked at his book. "Yes, I see it here. I will have someone show you to your room, *mesdames*."

"Thank you."

The two women followed a livery-clad young man up the central staircase to a room on the second floor. Emma and Gabrielle looked around at the four-poster bed, the aged Oriental carpet, and the nightstand with a pitcher of water and a basin. When the young man had left, Emma said, "Well, here we are, ready to embark on this crazy scheme."

"It's not so crazy," Gabrielle said, taking off her bonnet. "Papa transferred gold for the Rothschilds many times."

Emma took off her own hat, baring her dyed red hair. "That may be true, but you never had to masquerade as the wife of a strange Englishman before!"

"Mr. Rothschild insisted. It's stupid, of course. He should know we can be trusted to get his gold to Biarritz without an English bodyguard to make us more noticeable." Gabrielle looked disgusted. "If Papa were still alive they would never have thought of doing this."

Emma said, "On the other hand, it will be nice to have someone along who will be responsible for the gold besides us." She put her bonnet on a walnut chest with a lace runner on the top. "If something bad happens, he can take the blame."

"Nothing bad is going to happen," Gabrielle said firmly. "Except I am going to have to pretend this *anglais* is my husband."

"I hope he is a gentleman," Emma said nervously. "Just think, Gabrielle, you may have to share your bedroom with him!"

"Don't worry, Emma, nothing is going to happen."

Gabrielle smiled. "I will keep my trusty knife handy, believe me. If he tries anything, I'll skewer him."

Emma shivered. "Please God it will not come to that."

"I doubt it will," Gabrielle said soothingly. "Mr. Rothschild said the man is a colonel on his way back to the army after being wounded. A colonel should be a gentleman."

"I hope so," Emma said

"There's a dining room downstairs," Gabrielle said. "Let's go and get something to eat. I'm starving."

Emma smiled in agreement. "We don't often get the chance to eat in a hotel of this quality."

The two women removed their pelisses, hung them in the wardrobe and went down to the dining room.

The earl arrived in Brussels the following afternoon to meet Gabrielle Robichon. He checked into his room at the hotel and was told that the ladies were out. He asked to be notified when they came back.

At five o'clock a hotel employee brought him word that Mesdames Rieux and Dumas had returned and would receive him in room 203. The earl, who was on the third floor, went down a flight of stairs and knocked at the designated door. It was opened by a middle-aged woman with dyed red hair and faintly slanted green eyes. She was wearing rouge.

"Good afternoon," the earl said pleasantly. "I am Colonel Leo Standish."

"Good heavens," the woman said, staring up at him. Then, visibly gathering her wits, she opened the door wider and said, "Come in, Colonel."

The earl stepped into the room. A charmingly husky voice said, "How do you do, Colonel. I am Gabrielle Robichon Rieux."

He turned slightly and looked into the huge brown eyes of one of the loveliest girls he had ever seen. Her shining brown hair was parted in the middle and drawn back into a single braid that went halfway down her back. Her nose was small and delicate and her lips were clear-cut and perfect. She was holding out her hand but she was not smiling. He crossed the floor to take her hand into his own. She was quite small; her head did not reach the top of his shoulder, but her handshake was as firm as a man's.

"You are married?" he said in surprise.

"I *was* married," she replied matter-of-factly. "Now I am a widow."

"You're very young to be a widow," he said. He was a little discomposed. He had not expected her to be so pretty.

She shrugged, a very Gallic gesture. "This stupid war has made widows of many young women. I am sure that is true in your country as well."

"Unfortunately, it is. Was your husband killed in the war?" he asked.

"No. He was kicked in the forehead by one of the circus horses." Her face was grave. "It was such a stupid accident. André lifted the horse's rear foot to clean it and Sandi kicked out—something he never does. It was just bad luck that he got André in the head."

"I'm sorry," he said.

"We had only been married for a few months. It was very sad," Gabrielle said. "And now let me introduce you to my companion, Madame Emma Dumas."

He turned to the older woman and held out his hand. "How do you do, Madame Dumas."

They shook hands and then he turned back to Gabrielle. "I appreciate the awkwardness of this situation for you, Madame Rieux. You are very generous, allowing me to masquerade as your husband.''

She shrugged again. ''I myself do not think it is necessary, but Monsieur Rothschild insisted. Frankly, Colonel, you are likely to call more attention to us than to be a help.''

He said stiffly, ''I will do the best I can to blend into the circus, *madame*. You are carrying a huge amount of money that is vital to the British forces. It is only natural that the army wants someone along to keep an eye on it.''

She bristled visibly. ''Monsieur Rothschild trusted Papa implicitly!''

''But your father is not here any longer,'' he pointed out. ''And even if he was, the army would probably want to have someone go along.''

She crossed her arms and eyed him up and down. ''You are not the sort of person who can easily blend in,'' she said.

He was annoyed. ''I will do the best that I can, *madame*.''

There was a little silence. Then she said, ''If we are to be married you must call me by my Christian name, Gabrielle.''

''And you must call me Leo,'' he said.

''Leo,'' she said. Then, briskly, ''It is too late to leave Brussels today. We should plan on leaving early tomorrow morning. That way we will make Lille before it gets dark.''

He asked, ''The circus is at Lille now?''

''Yes. We wintered there. We usually begin our tour in mid March, so we will be starting a little earlier than usual. But not so much earlier as to make us noticeable, I think.''

"Very well." He looked at Emma. "May I invite you ladies to have dinner with me this evening?"

"Thank you," Emma replied with dignity. "That will be very nice."

Gabrielle nodded.

"At seven o'clock, in the dining room?" he asked.

"That will be fine," Emma replied.

He gave the women a perfunctory smile and went to the door. It had not quite closed when he heard Emma say, "Whoever would have thought our escort would look like that?"

The door closed before he could hear Gabrielle's reply.

The dining room of the Hôtel Royale was small, with room for perhaps thirty people. When Gabrielle and Emma entered they saw Leo immediately; he was sitting at a table near the fireplace.

"Good evening, ladies," he said, rising to greet them.

"Good evening," the two women replied in unison.

A waiter held Gabrielle's chair and she seated herself, carefully arranging her plain yellow silk evening dress. Emma, who was dressed in emerald green, was seated as well.

Gabrielle looked at the man who was to pretend to be her husband for the next month. *André would be jealous,* she thought as she took in Leo's clean-cut features, his blue-green eyes and his thick golden hair. She noted the breadth of his shoulders underneath his black evening coat. This man was very different from André, who had been dark, whippet-slim and only a few inches taller than herself.

He's big enough to carry water and help with the tent, she thought. She looked at the unconsciously arrogant tilt of his head. *He'll probably think those tasks are beneath him, though.*

The waiter was standing by to take their order and she gave her attention to the menu. Once they had chosen, Leo looked at Gabrielle and said, "So tell me about your circus. How many people do you employ and what do they do?"

Gabrielle folded her hands in her yellow silk lap and replied, "It is called the Cirque Equestre because we feature horses. We have five Arabians who perform at liberty, we have a grand old fellow who is our rosinback, and we have two Lipizzaners that are trained to High School and who do a pas de deux. They also perform individually."

Leo held up his hand to stop her. "You have Lipizzaners trained in High School?" he asked incredulously.

"Yes. Two of them. Papa was able to buy them off the farm in Austria and he trained them himself."

"He trained them with your help, Gabrielle," Emma put in.

"Papa had the knowledge. I just followed what he said to do."

Leo said in amazement, "I had no idea you had horses of this quality."

Gabrielle was insulted. "Did you think we were just a carnival? I'll have you know that the Cirque Equestre is well-known for its horses."

Amusement glinted in his eyes. "I did not mean to denigrate you. Forgive me. It's just that I am very interested in classically trained horses. I had an opportunity to see some Lusitanos in Portugal and I thought they were marvelous."

Gabrielle didn't care for the amusement, but she accepted the apology by nodding gracefully. When she spoke she kept her voice cool. "Portugal has a wonderful history of classically trained horses. France, of course, did also, but the Revolution destroyed it. Papa was determined to keep alive the tradition as best he could. All of our horses are classically trained."

"That's wonderful. Who rides your Lipizzaners?"

"I do. And my brother Mathieu accompanies me in the pas de deux."

"I look forward to seeing them perform," he said with such obvious sincerity that Gabrielle was appeased.

She smiled at him. He did not smile back.

Very well, monsieur, she thought with annoyance. *If you want to be all business, then we will be all business.*

"How many people do you employ?" he asked.

"The part of the circus that is permanent is my family—myself and my brothers, Mathieu and Albert. Then there's Gerard, who is our ringmaster, and Emma and her dogs. That makes five. Then we have the acts that accompany us."

"And what acts are those?"

"First there is the circus band—that is four members. Then there is Luc Balzac, our equestrian, Henri and Franz and Carlotta Martin, who are rope dancers, and the Maronis, who are tumblers—there are four of them. Sully is our clown, and Paul Gronow, our juggler." She tilted her head a little. "How many is that? I have lost count."

"Fourteen plus the five permanent members," he said.

"Oh, and we employ two grooms."

He nodded. "Which of these people know about the gold?"

"Myself, my two brothers—" she smiled at her companion "—Emma and Gerard. The people who winter with us."

"What about the grooms?"

"Jean and Cesar don't winter with us. They report to the circus when we are ready to set out."

"So, five people. And everyone else will think that we are married?"

"Yes," she said. "I suppose it is good that you are so handsome. That will make it more believable that I should marry a noncircus man."

"Thank you," he said sarcastically.

She shrugged. "I speak the truth. You are going to be difficult to explain. You will have to work, though. You can't just stand around and do nothing. Everyone who knows me knows I would never marry a man like that."

Leo just looked at her.

"What do you think you could do?" she asked.

"I have no idea," he replied shortly. "Just don't expect me to perform. I'll help out with the labor end of things, but I'm not getting up in front of people and making an ass of myself."

Her eyes glittered. "Our performers are all trained artistes, *Leo*," she said. "I wouldn't dream of putting an amateur in our ring."

"Good," he said. "Then we understand each other. I'm here to get the gold to Wellington. If I have to work, I will. But not in public."

She folded her lips in a stern line. "Very well."

The first course was served.

What the hell can we talk about? he thought. *What do I have in common with circus people?*

Gabrielle said conversationally, "It looks as if we are seeing the last days of Napoléon. His *grande armée* was destroyed in Russia and soon your General Wellington will defeat his army in Spain."

The war was something Leo could always talk about and he responded appropriately. The war and international affairs carried them through dinner, and when he got up to escort the ladies out of the dining room, Leo was feeling slightly better. If he was going to have to spend the next month shackled to a female circus player, it was a help that she seemed to be intelligent.

Three

The following morning, Leo met his traveling companions in the hotel lobby, where they were waiting for their coach to be brought up. He was dressed in a rust-colored riding coat, breeches and high boots—an appropriate outfit for a circus, he thought.

Gabrielle frowned when she saw him. "Those clothes are all right for dress-up," she said, "but you can't dress like that around the circus."

He was dumbfounded. He had thought he was dressed *down*. "What do you suggest I wear?" he asked a trifle acerbically.

"Trousers, low boots, a shirt—without the tie—and I suppose you can wear that jacket to keep warm. We'll stop in a town along the way and do some shopping. I have a feeling that nothing you have with you is appropriate."

Leo looked at his portmanteau and said sarcastically, "Can I at least keep my underwear?"

He would never in a million years have mentioned underwear to an English lady.

But Gabrielle didn't blink. "Yes, you can keep your underwear. But I will pick your outerwear. It's important that you don't raise any suspicions. We can't do anything that may call attention to ourselves."

She was right, and he was annoyed that she was right.

He was also annoyed that she looked so pretty, standing there with the chandelier light shining off her beautiful silky brown hair.

"Where's your bonnet?" he asked abruptly.

"In the hatbox," she replied. "I hate wearing bonnets. They are so confining."

Emma, who was wearing a bonnet, said, "Nevertheless you should wear it, *chérie*."

"I made my impression coming into the hotel. Now that I am leaving I can do as I like."

Emma rolled her eyes. Gabrielle patted the circle of braids that crowned her head. "Besides, I can't fit a bonnet over these braids."

Leo said, "I was under the impression that short hair was in vogue for women."

"It's not in vogue for circus performers," Gabrielle informed him haughtily.

Leo was conscious of a fleeting feeling of approval. It would be a shame to cut off all that lovely hair. He found himself looking forward to seeing it down.

Good God, he thought in horror as he realized what he was thinking. *I can't become attracted to this circus girl. That would be disastrous.*

"Here is the carriage," he said crisply, grateful for the distraction. "Are you ready, ladies?"

Gerard stopped the carriage in front of the hotel door and the three of them went out to meet it.

Gabrielle's attempt to buy clothing for Leo was not very successful; he was too tall for any of the trousers they looked at, although they did manage to buy some plain white cotton shirts that were more appropriate than his own custom-tailored ones.

"I can make him some trousers," Emma finally said to Gabrielle, and so they bought material instead.

Leo found himself alternating between indignation and amusement at the way the two women treated him. *You would think I was five years old,* he thought, as Gabrielle held a shirt up in front of him and nodded that it would be all right. They made their purchases and returned to the carriage for the final leg of the journey into Lille.

The circus was gathered on the outskirts of the city, on the farm that Gabrielle's family had rented for the winter months. As they drove in, Leo saw a collection of a dozen or so wagons parked in a big field. Gerard drove past the wagons, however, and went directly to the farmhouse, where his passengers alighted.

A slender young man, who looked like a masculine copy of Gabrielle, came out to meet the carriage.

"Leo, this is my brother, Mathieu," Gabrielle said. "Mathieu, this is my new husband, Leo Standish."

"How do you do, Mathieu," Leo said.

Mathieu looked from Leo to Gabrielle. "He's going to be very hard to hide. He's so big—and he certainly doesn't look French."

"I know, but there's nothing we can do about it," Gabrielle said. "He's what Monsieur Rothschild sent us."

"What if we said he was Swedish?" Mathieu asked. "Would people know that his accent was English and not Swedish?"

"I don't think that's a good idea," Leo said flatly. He did not at all appreciate being talked about as if he wasn't there. "If someone does recognize my English accent they will wonder why you are attempting to disguise me."

Mathieu frowned, clearly not liking having his idea so summarily rejected.

"All circuses are international," Gabrielle said briskly. "The Maronis are Italian, after all, Mathieu, and the Cirque Barent has an English clown. It will be all right. Now, can we go into the house instead of standing here in the front yard?"

Leo had to duck his head as he went through the front door. The room that he found himself in was the main living room of the farmhouse. It was furnished with heavy oak furniture and on the walls were a series of rural landscapes. As if on cue, a fawn-colored greyhound came racing up to Gabrielle. She bent to caress the beautiful, deerlike head. "Colette, my darling. How are you? Did you miss me?"

The dog sniffed her clothes and her hands.

"She was a lost soul without you," Mathieu said. "You have her so spoiled, Gabrielle, that she just pines away when you are gone."

"Poor little girl," Gabrielle crooned. "I missed you, too."

Leo loved dogs. "What a beautiful animal," he said. The dog turned her head as if she had understood him. He snapped his fingers and she came to him, allowing him to caress her with royal grace. Then she returned to Gabrielle.

There was a rush at the door and more dogs came dashing in. *"Mes enfants!"* Emma cried. "Here you are!"

Leo looked at the six small terriers that were leaping around Emma. "Good heavens," he said.

Emma smiled at him. "These are my trained dogs. You will see them in action when we perform."

The room was very crowded with dogs. Emma said to Gabrielle, "I will take them outside and then upstairs to my room." She held the door open and the dogs scampered out, followed by Emma.

Gabrielle turned to her brother. "Where is Albert?"

"He went down to the barn to check on the horses. He'll be back soon," Mathieu said.

"Albert is your other brother?" Leo asked.

"Yes. He is two years younger than Mathieu."

"And how old are you, Mathieu?" Leo asked.

"Nineteen," the boy replied.

Leo's eyes went to Gabrielle, who was standing with one hand resting on her dog's head. "Who owns the circus?" he asked. "I thought it was you."

"My brothers and I own it together," she replied, "but Papa put me in charge because I am the eldest."

"How old are you?" Leo asked curiously.

"Twenty-two," she replied.

Emma said, "Here is Albert now."

A young boy who looked like Mathieu, but whose hair was several shades lighter, came into the room.

"Gabrielle!" He went to hug her. "Everything went all right?"

"Yes. Albert, this is Leo, my new husband."

The brown eyes that fixed themselves on Leo's face were a lighter shade than Mathieu's and Gabrielle's. "Hello," he said. "You are the English colonel?"

"That's right." Leo held out his hand. "I am pleased to meet you, Albert. But call me Leo."

"The horses are all right?" Gabrielle said.

Albert nodded.

"Good. Now, is there any food in the kitchen? We pushed on to make it here this evening and we missed dinner."

"I think there's some cold meat and bread," Mathieu said.

"I'll go and fix something," Gabrielle said. "In the meanwhile, you boys can show Leo to his room."

Both boys looked at her. Albert said, "Which room is his? There is no extra room."

"He's going to stay in my room," Gabrielle said. "It would look distinctly odd if he did not."

Both boys frowned and looked at Leo.

"Your sister will be perfectly safe," Leo said. "The only consequence she might suffer from this masquerade is a little embarrassment."

"I am never embarrassed," Gabrielle said. "Go along now and take him upstairs."

The two boys and Leo, who was carrying his portmanteau, went up the stairs with obedient alacrity.

Gabrielle fixed a plate of cold roast beef and sliced bread, which she set on the kitchen table. Emma was already sitting at the table when the boys and Leo joined them. Mathieu and Albert had already eaten, but they sat at the table, anyway, clearly wanting to hear whatever the conversation was going to be.

Gabrielle sat down and put some meat on her plate. She looked at her two brothers, then she looked at Leo. He was piling roast beef on his plain, slightly chipped white plate.

He looks down on us, she thought. *He is an English colonel and we are just circus folk. I foresee an uncomfortable four weeks ahead.*

Leo looked up from his meal. "Has the gold been loaded?"

Gabrielle looked at Mathieu. "Yes," he said. "Monsieur Rothschild's men came three days ago and transferred it into our wagons. No one saw them. The rest of the wagons only came yesterday."

"I would like to see the gold myself," Leo said.

Gabrielle was insulted. "Do you think we would lie to you?"

"Not at all. But since I have been charged with getting it safely to Portugal, I must see it."

He doesn't trust us, she thought. She said coolly, "Better to look tomorrow morning, when we are loading up to go. It will look strange to the rest of them if you start poking around the wagons now."

He looked annoyed. "Of course," he said in a clipped voice.

She pressed on. "As I believe I told you, my family, Emma and Gerard are the only ones who know about the gold. We don't want to do anything to raise suspicion in the others."

"I said I agreed with you." His annoyance showed in his voice. "I'll wait until tomorrow to check it."

Gabrielle was pleased. She had gotten under his guard. She rewarded him with a smile.

He stared back, his face impassive. He was the first man she had ever met who did not respond to her smile. The smile died away from her lips and she regarded him thoughtfully. Did he never smile himself? She could not remember seeing him smile once during that long dull ride from Brussels to Lille—he had not even smiled when they were buying clothes and he had looked so funny in the jacket he had tried on.

Was he always like this, or was it just because he was with people he thought were beneath him?

Don't brood about it, Gabrielle, she told herself. *You only have to put up with him for four weeks and then your duty will be done and he will go back to his regiment. Let him be as sour as he pleases. It can't bother you.*

"Everything is ready," Albert said. "Do you want to leave tomorrow?"

"Is everyone else ready?"

"Yes, we were just waiting for you," Mathieu said.

"There's no point in waiting, then," Gabrielle replied. "The sooner we leave the sooner we will get our cargo to its destination."

"What is your agenda?" Leo asked abruptly.

"Our first stop is Amiens," she said. "We will spend one day traveling and then two days in Amiens, where we will give four performances—one in the afternoons and one in the evenings. Vincent, our advance man, has gone ahead to Amiens to procure a field for us and to book lodgings."

He frowned. "You didn't mention Vincent."

She lifted a delicate eyebrow. "Didn't I? I suppose I forgot because he's our advance man, he doesn't travel with us, he travels ahead of us. We meet him at a designated spot and he takes us to the field he has rented and gives us directions to the lodgings he has procured."

"He puts our bills up all around town, too," Albert said eagerly. "Here, I'll show you one." He jumped up and went into the living room, coming back with a paper in his hand. Leo took it.

ROBICHON CIRQUE EQUESTRE

A GRAND EQUESTRIAN DISPLAY

STARRING
MLLE GABRIELLE ROBICHON

DANCING HORSES!
HORSES AT LIBERTY!
JUGGLING!
TIGHTROPE DANCING!

DARING FEATS OF HORSEMANSHIP!
M. LUC BALZAC!
M. SULLY, the Clown!
TUMBLING!
TRAINED DOGS!
THE COURIER OF ST. PETERSBURG!

Performances
12:00 and 4:00

"Very nice," Leo said, looking up from the circus bill. "But there is no direction."

"Vincent will write the direction on each bill before he posts it," Emma explained. "He'll also write the days of the week we will be performing."

Leo nodded and handed the bill back to Albert.

Emma stood abruptly. "There is a trundle bed in my room, Gabrielle. Shall I have one of the boys bring it into your room for Leo?"

Everyone stared at Leo as the thought of their sleeping arrangements was introduced.

Gabrielle suppressed the urge to laugh. "I own I would like to see the sight of Leo trying to sleep on a trundle bed."

"You forget I have been in the army for five years," he said imperturbably. "A trundle bed will look good compared to some of the places I have slept."

"Good," Emma said briskly. "Mathieu, come upstairs with me and we will move that bed."

Mathieu got to his feet. He looked at Leo suspiciously. "Where are you going to sleep when we are on the road? There will only be one bed in the room Vincent rents for you."

"If I have to sleep on the floor, I will," Leo said a little impatiently. "I've done it before."

Mathieu's brown eyes searched his face and seemed to be satisfied with what he saw there. He nodded and turned to follow Emma out of the room.

"I'm going to walk down to the barn to see the horses," Gabrielle said. "Would you like to come, Leo?"

"Yes, I would."

"Come along, then," she said. "Albert, if you will put the dishes in the sink, I will wash them when I get back."

Gabrielle picked up a lantern from beside the kitchen door and lighted it from a candle, her greyhound going immediately to her side. Gabrielle turned to Leo and gave him what she hoped was a superior look. "We can go out this way," she said. "Do try to keep up."

Four

The lantern threw a yellow light on the path before them and Leo took it from Gabrielle's hands, saying, "Let me carry that."

They crossed the yard, the dog leading the way, and went down a path that led to a large barn. When they had driven in earlier, Leo had seen that it looked rather ramshackle, but now in the dark it was simply a great looming building in front of them. The door was open and inside smelled like horses and hay.

He held up the lantern to illuminate the area.

"This way," Gabrielle said. "We'll say hello to the Lipizzaners first." Her voice softened. "Hello there, fellow."

Leo heard a soft nicker, and a white face loomed up out of the darkness of the stall. Gabrielle rubbed the white forehead and straightened a forelock. She gave the horse a piece of sugar, then opened his stall door to check if he had a full bucket of water.

"This is Sandi," she said. "Neapolitano Santuzza, to be formal about it."

"He's small," Leo said in surprise.

"Lipizzaners aren't tall, like thoroughbreds. They are built for collected work, not for running races. He has marvelous muscles, though. You will see them tomorrow."

"I'm looking forward to seeing him perform," Leo said sincerely. It was the one good thing he had heard about this circus. He might have to put up with tumblers and clowns, he thought, but at least he would get to see Lipizzaners in action.

Gabrielle moved to the next stall, the greyhound at her heels. "And this is Conversano Nobilia, also known as Noble."

Another white head appeared out of the darkness and another piece of sugar was snapped up. Once again Gabrielle checked the water.

"How old are they?" Leo asked.

"Sandi is twelve and Noble is thirteen. But Lipizzaners can work for a long time. Some of the horses that perform at the Spanish Riding School in Vienna are in their twenties."

"That is remarkable," Leo said. "Thoroughbreds can't match that."

"Thoroughbreds are beautiful animals, but they are no good for a circus. My father used to say all they are good for is going fast."

"But they do that extremely well."

He saw her white teeth gleam in the lantern light. "Yes, they do. I must say I have a wish to ride a thoroughbred one day. It must be like sitting on the wind."

"That's a good way of putting it," he said approvingly.

She moved gracefully across the aisle to another stall. "And these are our Arabians," she said. "They perform at liberty. You will be amazed at what they do."

He followed her to the next stall. "At liberty?" he asked.

"Yes, they have no bridle or saddle and they go by themselves in a circle, turning and reversing and circling at the slightest signal—without a hand touching them. It is an act Papa invented and it always gets a rapturous response from the audience."

"It sounds impressive," he said, noting the pride in her voice.

"This is Kania," she continued, offering sugar. She then went down the line, checking water and naming each horse as it came forward for its treat: "This is Shaitan, this is Sheiky, this is Fantan, and this is Dubai."

Each of the horses had the dished face and wide forehead of the true Arabian. All of the horses were pure white.

They recrossed the aisle to the Lipizzaner side of the barn. "And this is our darling Coco, our rosinback horse."

"What is a rosinback?" he asked curiously.

"Coco is the horse most of the trick riding is done on. We put rosin on his back so that the vaulters' slippers won't slide." She patted his white face. "He's part Percheron and he's a sweetheart."

When she spoke to her horses her voice was soft and full of love. For the first time, Leo found himself liking this circus girl.

"Are these all your performance horses?" he asked.

"Yes. The next horses in line are our wagon horses. They deserve a treat, too." They went along the line and fed eight more horses, who came as eagerly for their sugar as the elite horses had.

"I'm looking forward to seeing them all in the light of day," Leo said as he accompanied Gabrielle to the door. The greyhound preceded them out.

"They are lovely horses," she said. "My papa picked them all. He used to be Master of the Horse under the late king, you know."

"So Rothschild told me. He also told me that your father died recently. I am sorry for your loss."

"We miss him very much," she said softly. "It is a big responsibility for me, to try to run the circus the way he would have wanted. But I have the help of my brothers and Emma and Gerard."

He glanced down at the girl at his side. It *was* a lot of responsibility to rest on those slender shoulders, he thought. And she had had the courage to take on Rothschild's gold, too.

"Your brothers are very young."

"Yes, but Papa trained them well."

"I noticed that it was your name on the circus bill."

"I am the featured rider and trainer, yes. Mathieu and Albert are good riders, but not as good as I." She said this perfectly matter-of-factly. "I have Papa's touch with horses, you see."

They were approaching the door to the farmhouse kitchen and he held up the lantern to illuminate the doorknob.

"Who is Luc Balzac, the other equestrian mentioned on the bill?" he asked.

He noticed the faintest change in her voice as she answered. "Oh, Luc is a wonderful rider. You will have to see him to believe what he can do."

She pushed open the kitchen door and went inside, followed by Leo. As he extinguished the lantern she went to the sink. "I will just wash up these dishes," she said. "You can dry."

He looked up from the lantern. "I beg your pardon?"

"I said, you can dry these dishes after I wash them. Here is a towel."

He stared at the towel she was holding out as if it was a poisonous snake. She chuckled, a rich, husky sound that was thoroughly delightful. "Have you never dried dishes before?" she asked disbelievingly.

"No, I have not," he replied defensively.

"Well, now is a good time to start," she said. "In the circus we all have to do a little of everything."

He considered telling her to go to the devil, but then his common sense stepped in. *I suppose I must blend in,* he thought. *It's only for a month.*

He came forward and took the towel from her hand. He waited while she washed a plate in a pan of water and then he dried it.

"See?" she said, giving him a smile. "It's not so bad."

He looked back impassively. "It's a new experience," he said.

Her smile faded and she turned away, plunked another plate in the pan and washed it.

It was about ten o'clock at night when everyone went to bed. There was a tense silence as they all went up the stairs and Leo and Gabrielle went together into her room.

"I will be right next door if you need me," Mathieu told his sister meaningfully.

"I'm sure I won't," she replied. "Anyway, I have Colette. Get some sleep, Mathieu, and stop worrying about me."

"Good night, *chérie,*" Emma said, and kissed her on the cheek.

"Good night," Gabrielle replied. She opened the door to her bedroom. "Come along, Leo," she said, then went into the room, leaving the door open for him.

She talks to me exactly as if I was her dog, Leo thought indignantly as he followed her in, candle in hand.

The bedroom was not large. It had a four-poster bed,

and at its foot a narrow trundle bed had been made up with a quilt and a pillow. There was one nightstand and a wardrobe and a single straight chair in front of the fireplace.

Pretty dismal, Leo thought, thinking of his own sumptuous bedroom at home.

The dog jumped onto the bed and settled herself along the bottom. He looked at her for a moment before he turned to Gabrielle. "Is this your farm?" he asked.

"No, we rented it for the winter. It is not so easy to find a place for four months that has the stabling we require, so we have to take what we can get. We had this place last winter and I was lucky enough to get it again this year. They are looking to sell it, but the wartime economy is bad." She paused and gazed around the tiny room.

"Getting dressed and undressed is going to be a problem," she finally said. "There is no private dressing room in any of the places where we will be staying. If we turn our backs on each other can I trust you not to look?"

"Certainly," he said stiffly.

"All right. I will get undressed in front of the wardrobe and you can get undressed on the far side of the bed. Don't look until I say it's all right."

Leo said, "I had intended to sleep in my clothing."

"Don't be stupid," she replied. "You don't have that many changes and we don't have much chance to do laundry. Don't you have a nightshirt with you?"

He did not enjoy being called stupid and replied even more stiffly than before. "As a matter of fact, I do."

"Then put it on," she ordered. "I have been a married woman. I have seen a man in a nightshirt before. You won't shock me."

The humor of the situation suddenly struck him. He was sounding as if *he* was a virgin, he thought. His mouth quirked into a smile. Very well, he thought, if he wasn't going to scandalize her in his nightshirt he would be very much more comfortable than he would be sleeping in his clothes.

"All right," he said. He lifted his portmanteau onto the bed, extracted a nightshirt and turned his back. "I won't turn around until you tell me I can," he said.

"Good." He heard her walking toward the wardrobe.

Silence fell as he removed his clothing and slid the nightshirt over his head. The bedroom was cold and he moved quickly. It was about three minutes before he heard her say, "All right. You can look now."

He turned around and she was wearing a long white flannel gown with a collar and buttons. Her hair was still fixed into a coronet around her small head. "You can have the bed. I'll fit in the trundle bed much better than you."

"I wouldn't dream of taking your bed," he said with surprise. "No gentleman would consign a lady to a cot while he slept in comfort."

"You may be a gentleman, but I'm not a lady," Gabrielle said. "I'm a practical woman who works for her living. And it's ridiculous to fold you up on that bed when I shall be perfectly comfortable there."

As if to prove her point, she went over to the trundle and sat down. Then she reached up and began to remove the pins from her braids. "Go ahead," she said. "Get into bed. It's cold in this room and your legs are bare."

He was slightly scandalized. There was no other way to put it. Leo was far from being a virgin, but he was a little off balance with this girl who coped so matter-of-factly with their intimacy.

"What about the dog?" he asked.

"She always sleeps on the bed. She won't bother you. You have plenty of room."

Slowly he pulled the covers back from the bed and got in. He watched in silence as she unbraided her hair and let it fall loose around her shoulders and down her back. Then she took a ribbon and tied it at the nape of her neck.

She caught him looking at her. "Good night, Leo," she said pointedly.

"Good night...Gabrielle," he replied.

She nodded with satisfaction. "That is the first time you have said my name. It's not so bad, is it? Will you blow the candle out?"

He blew the candle out and listened to the small sounds she made as she pulled the covers up around her and settled herself to sleep.

Well, he thought, *the important thing is to get the gold to Wellington. If I have to put up with a snip of a girl ordering me around I suppose I can endure it.*

The bulk of Colette was warm against his chilly feet. He closed his eyes and went to sleep.

Gabrielle woke in the middle of the night, something that was unusual for her. For a moment she was disoriented, finding herself in a strange bed. Then she remembered that she was in the trundle bed and she also remembered who was sharing the room with her.

Leo. It suited him, she thought, a big golden lion of a man. And his eyes—never had she seen that shade of aquamarine. There was an aloof look in those eyes, however. She knew he was not happy to be joining a circus.

Perhaps he is the younger son of some great lord, she

thought. *Perhaps that is why he sought to make the army his career.*

She lay quietly and listened. The room was silent. If she listened very carefully she could hear Leo breathing.

He doesn't snore. That's nice. André used to snore and I would have to push him to turn him over.

Her thoughts turned to her dead husband and sadness overcame her. He had been so full of energy, André. It wasn't fair that life had been taken from him at such a young age.

Two years ago he was alive. Two years ago we shared a room together, and now I share it with this stranger, this cold Englishman who thinks he is better than the rest of us.

How he had looked when she told him to turn his back and undress! She swallowed a giggle. *The circus will take the starch out of him,* she thought. *I'll see to that.*

Five

When Gabrielle arose the following morning Leo heard her and sat up in bed. It was still dark.

"We need to be on the road early," she said. She lit a candle. "I want to be in Amiens by late afternoon. Turn your back so I can get dressed. Then I will get out of your way."

He obliged and listened to the sounds she made as she got into her clothes. Then she said, "All right."

He turned to look at her and found her clad in high boots, a brown divided skirt and a white, long-sleeved shirt. "Come downstairs when you are ready and Emma will prepare you breakfast," she said.

He watched her small, straight, slender back disappear out the door, followed by her dog, then he got up and opened the package of clothing they had bought yesterday. He took out a coarse cotton shirt and regarded it with distaste. It pulled on over the head and had a tie at the neck. He put the shirt on and then his breeches. The shirt was loose and billowed out of his tight breeches.

I must look a sight, he thought ruefully. *If Fitz and the others could see me now, how they would laugh.*

He pulled on his boots and went down to the kitchen to see what was for breakfast.

Emma was in the kitchen with her dogs when he entered. "Good morning, Leo," she said cheerfully. "Did you sleep well?"

"Yes, I did," he replied courteously.

Six dogs looked at him, but none came to sniff him. They remained where they were, curled up on an old quilt under the window.

Emma got up from her chair and went to the counter. "There is coffee and bread and butter," she said.

He was used to an English breakfast, with eggs and meat, and the proffered bread seemed rather paltry. But, "That will be fine" was all he said, and let her pour him his coffee and add milk in the French way. Then he took his plate and went to the table.

"Where is everyone else?" he asked as he took a long drink of the coffee.

"Getting the wagons ready," she replied.

"There looked to be quite a few wagons in the field," he remarked. "How many are in the caravan?"

"Let me think." She frowned slightly. "I have a wagon, the Robichons have two wagons, and the Martins—they are the tightrope dancers—have one. The Maroni brothers—they are the tumblers—have one, and Sully, our clown, shares a wagon with Paul Gronow, our juggler. Luc Balzac has a wagon. Then there is the bandwagon. That makes eight, I believe. Then we have two more wagons filled with hay and grain, and one for the tents and one for benches. So that makes twelve altogether."

"That's not a lot to house a whole circus."

"The horses are our chief performers, and they get tied behind the wagons."

The kitchen door opened and Mathieu and Albert came in. They were dressed in trousers, scuffed boots and knitted sweaters. "All that's left to do is to harness up the horses," Mathieu said. "Is there more coffee, Emma?"

"Where is your sister?" Leo asked Albert as Emma poured both boys a cup.

"She went back upstairs to pack her clothes."

"All the costumes are packed, I hope," Emma said.

Leo decided it was time to discuss their important cargo. "I would like to see the gold, if you please."

Mathieu scowled. "I can show you where it is," Albert offered. He stood up and started for the door. Leo followed him.

"Make sure there is no chance of anyone coming in on you, Albert," Mathieu warned.

"I know," the boy replied. "Come with me, Leo, and I will show you."

They exited the kitchen and began to walk across the field to where the wagons were parked in two lines. Most of the wagons had horses picketed next to them. The sun had come up and Leo was conscious of people looking at him curiously as he walked with Albert.

"How long has your sister's husband been dead?" he asked Albert. "Will people think it's odd that she has married again?"

"André has been dead for a year and a half," Albert said. "I don't think people will be surprised that Gabrielle has remarried, but they *will* be surprised to find she has married a noncircus man. We will have to find something for you to do so you don't look too odd."

"I can help with the horses," Leo said.

Albert cast him a dubious look. "We'll see," he said.

Leo was insulted. Evidently this slight boy didn't think he was fit to be trusted with circus horses. "I assure you that I am capable of looking after a horse," he said coldly. "I have been riding since I was four years old."

Albert said carefully, "You see, our horses are different from the horses you rode, Leo." By "different" it was clear that he meant "better." "And somehow I don't see you carrying manure, which is what helping out with the horses entails."

Leo hid his surprise. He hadn't envisioned himself carrying manure, either, but he was certainly capable of doing so, if necessary. He said grimly, "If you need me to carry manure, then I can do it."

"Let's see what Gabrielle says," Albert said. "She's the one who doles out the jobs."

They had reached the first wagon. "This is ours."

The wagon was painted white, with the words *Robichon Cirque Equestre* written on its side in red letters. There was a picture of two horses' heads painted under it.

Leo stopped to look at the picture. "The Lipizzaners?" he asked.

Albert nodded. "The one on the left is Sandi and the other one is Noble."

The two pictures were clearly painted by one who knew horses.

"It's a very good painting," Leo said slowly, leaning in for a closer look. "Who did it?"

"I did," Albert said.

Leo looked at him. "You have talent."

A faint flush stained Albert's cheeks. "I love to paint and draw," he said.

"Do you have other pictures?" Leo asked.

"Yes. I have pictures of some of the places that we've visited. And I have done many pictures of the circus and its horses."

"I'd like to see them," Leo said.

The boy's flush deepened. "I would be happy to show you."

They had come to the back of the wagon, which had two doors that opened outward. Albert opened the doors and climbed in, followed by Leo.

The wagon was lined with trunks. "Extra costumes and props," Albert explained. The center of the wagon was empty save for an old upholstered sofa and some large pillows. The floor was bare wooden boards. "Here," Albert said. He went to the front of the sofa and dropped to his hands and knees. "See, this board is loose." He took a knife out of his pocket, fitted it between the boards and pulled it up. "They were designed to fit together very tightly, but once you pry this one up, the rest of them can be lifted out." He removed a few more boards. "Come and see," he said.

Leo got down on his own knees and peered into the space that was revealed below the floorboards. "It's too dark to see anything," he said.

"Here, I'll get a candle." Albert rummaged through one of the trunks and took out a candle and a strike-a-light. He lit the candle and brought it back to Leo, who used it to illuminate the shallow space below.

He saw a brown canvas bag. He lifted it out and pulled it open. Inside was a large pile of gold *napoléon d'or* coins. He nodded with satisfaction. "Excellent," he said.

"Monsieur Rothschild had both our wagons fitted out like this. It is very clever, I think. The boards fit so closely together that they don't have to be nailed."

"Yes, it is clever," Leo agreed slowly.

"Are you satisfied?" Albert asked.

Leo replaced the moneybag. "I'd like to see the other wagon," he said.

Albert frowned. "It's just like this one."

"Nevertheless, I must verify that the gold is there."

"As you wish," Albert said stiffly, and led the way to the second wagon, which bore a picture of three horses all rearing in unison.

They both climbed into the wagon, which was loaded with saddles and bridles and more trunks. They repeated the same inspection that Leo had made of the other wagon, then replaced the floorboards and started back to the house.

"I take it your sister's husband was a circus man," Leo said easily as they walked side by side.

Albert looked up at him. "Oh, yes. André was a very great horseman. I have seen him jump two horses over four feet while he was standing on their backs."

"Good God," Leo said.

"Yes. Luc Balzac, who traveled with us last year, is a good equestrian, but he is not as good as André was."

"What a pity that he should die so young."

"It was terrible," Albert confided. "Gabrielle was distraught. They had only been married a few months."

"How sad," Leo said gravely.

"Yes. Gabrielle was sad for a long time. But over the winter she seemed to become happy again. Emma says that she has gotten over it."

They had reached the house and Leo did not reply. Albert opened the kitchen door and peered in. Leo heard Emma say, "Get yourself down to the barn, Albert. They need you to help harness the horses."

"All right, Emma," Albert said. He turned to Leo. "You can wait here with Emma and we'll call you when we're ready to go."

"I'll go down to the barn with you," Leo said. He looked down at the old building where Mathieu was putting a harness on two hefty-looking draft horses. "Perhaps I can help by holding a horse or two."

They arrived at the barn just as Gabrielle came out leading two more horses. "Albert," she called when she saw them. "Harness up Jacques and Tonton. Leo, you can help by leading the harnessed horses out to the wagons and hitching them up."

By eight o'clock they were ready to go. Gabrielle said to Leo, "Come with me and I will introduce you around before we leave."

She walked next to him as they approached three people standing beside a wagon. Gabrielle smiled at them nervously. "I have come to introduce my new husband. Leo, this is Henri and Carlotta Martin and Henri's brother, Franz, our rope dancers." Both men had black hair and the woman was blond, wearing a cotton dress with a large blue shawl draped over her shoulders.

"I am pleased to meet you," Leo said as genially as he could.

"A new husband?" Carlotta remarked. She arched a plucked brow. "And so handsome, Gabrielle."

"I have high standards," Gabrielle replied serenely.

Henri asked, "What do you do, Leo? You're awfully big to be an equestrian."

"I'm afraid I'm not a circus person," Leo said. "But I will be happy to pitch in and help in any way I can."

"Not a circus person?" Franz said. He could not have looked more shocked if Leo had announced he was a vampire.

Everyone looked at Gabrielle. "Where did you meet?" Carlotta asked.

"In Brussels," Gabrielle said easily. "It was quite a whirlwind romance, and here we are."

Carlotta gave Leo an arch smile. "Well, I can see why Gabrielle fell in love with you, Leo."

Leo did not smile back. "Thank you, *madame*," he said in an expressionless tone.

The smile faded from Carlotta's face. "Don't call me *'madame.'* Everyone in this circus is on a first-name basis with everyone else."

Evidently he had insulted her. Leo forced a smile to his face. "Then thank you, Carlotta," he said.

Her smile bloomed again. "Gabrielle is a very lucky girl."

"It is I who am the lucky one," Leo replied gallantly.

"Come along," Gabrielle said. "I want to introduce you to the others."

The rest of the introductions went much the same as the first. Leo met the four Maroni brothers, who were tumblers; the four band members Adolphe and Antonio Laurent, and Pierre Maheu and his wife, Jeanne. Paul Gronow, the juggler; and Sully, the clown. The only introduction that sounded a note of trouble to come was Leo's introduction to Luc Balzac, the equestrian.

"Married? When the hell did you get married?" he said angrily to Gabrielle when she introduced Leo.

Leo looked at him measuringly. He was a tall—though not nearly as tall as Leo—slender young man with black hair and blazing blue eyes.

"Quite recently," Gabrielle said. There were spots of color in her cheeks.

"I thought you were still mourning your precious André." There could be no doubt that the young man was furious. And hurt.

"I was, but then I met Leo and things changed. André wouldn't mind. He would want me to be happy."

Luc snorted and turned hostile eyes toward Leo. "So what do you do, pretty boy?"

Leo opened his mouth to give the antagonistic young man a scalding dressing down, but then he stopped himself. If he played the aristocrat he would betray his disguise. So he forced himself to reply dispassionately that he would be happy to help around the circus as best he could.

The angry blue eyes turned back to Gabrielle. "Christ, Gabrielle, you didn't even marry a rider!"

"Leo can ride very well," she said defensively. "He just does not perform."

"Then what good is he?" Luc demanded.

Leo said firmly, "I am good for Gabrielle and she is good for me. We love each other and the circus has nothing to do with it."

Good God, he thought. *Where did that come from?*

Gabrielle moved closer to him, so that he could feel her body actually touching his. "That is so, Luc, and you are just going to have to get used to it," she said firmly.

"You said that someday you would marry me!"

"I never said any such thing," she replied hotly. "I said I was not ready to marry again when you asked me. I never said anything about the future."

"Merde!" Luc said.

Leo had had enough. "Watch your tongue. There is a lady present."

Luc flicked him an angry blue glance. "Believe me, Gabrielle has heard much worse than that."

"Not in my company," Leo said grimly.

"What's done is done, Luc," Gabrielle said. "Now, we are ready to get moving so I suggest you get into your wagon." She touched Leo's arm with her hand. "Come along, Leo," she said.

Just like a dog, he thought again as he trailed after her across the field to their wagon.

"Just who is this Luc Balzac?" he asked when they had reached their destination. "He obviously feels he had strings tied to you."

She looked worried. "He wanted to marry me last year, but I put him off. I didn't want to say no outright because I was afraid he would leave the show."

"He loves you?"

"So he says. I wonder if he loves Papa's circus even more."

"You think he wants to marry you to get in on the circus?"

"The thought has crossed my mind," she admitted.

"And how do you feel about him?"

"I feel that he is a very good act that I would like to keep in my circus," she replied carefully. "So many of the truly great ones attach themselves to a stationary circus, like Astleys. I don't want to lose Luc."

"But not enough to marry him?"

"No, not enough to marry him. He has a dangerous temper. Not like my André, who was kind through and through."

They reached the first wagon where Leo had inspected the gold earlier and Gabrielle turned to survey the field. Everybody was in their wagons. She put her foot on the step and Leo automatically moved to help her. She cast him a scornful glance. "I am not helpless." She swung up to the seat, moved over and began to unwrap the reins. She glanced down at Leo. "Come up."

He followed her into the seat and looked at her small gloved hands competently holding the reins. "Do you drive this thing? Where are your brothers?"

"Driving the other wagons," she replied. She lifted

the reins and made a kissing noise to the two horses in front of her. Obediently, they started forward. Gabrielle turned to Leo with a brilliant smile. ''The start of another season. It is exciting, no?''

Leo didn't smile back. He said, ''I hope the season isn't exciting at all. I just want to get this money to Biarritz.''

''We will,'' Gabrielle said confidently. ''I know we will.''

Six

The other wagons fell in behind Gabrielle and drove out of the field and onto the road. They would pass through Lille and then take the road south to Amiens.

"I wish you would let me drive," Leo said. "I'm supposed to be helping out as best I can, remember?"

"You can drive when we get to the main road on the other side of Lille," she said.

It sounded to him as if she didn't trust him to get them through the city and Leo's mouth set. He refrained from comment, however, and instead tried to make his legs as comfortable as he could.

"So, Leo, tell me about yourself," Gabrielle said as they drove through the early-ploughed land on either side of them.

He looked at her. Her own eyes were on the road and her profile was so delicate and pretty that he was momentarily distracted. She turned her head to catch his eye and gave him an encouraging nod.

He had no intention of talking about himself to this girl. "There's nothing much to tell," he said stiffly. "I grew up, went to school, and when I got out I joined the army. End of story."

After a moment she said wryly, "It's a good thing you didn't want to become a novelist. You'd have trouble filling up the pages."

"What about you?" He tried turning the tables. "You must have led a far more exciting life than I."

She shook her head. "Oh, no, don't think you're going to get off that easy! Where did you grow up, the country or the city? What school did you go to? Why did you join the army?"

Those things are none of your business. He thought the words but restrained himself from speaking them. He would have to stay on good terms with this girl; it would look suspicious if they were at odds with each other. He said grudgingly, "I grew up in the country, in the part of England that is called Sussex. It's very pretty there, with rolling hills we call the Downs. My father had an estate and we had a lot of horses. I lived there until I was eight, then I went away to school."

She turned to him and her brown eyes were full of pity. "You English! It is terrible how you push your children off to school when they are so young. You must not like children very much."

He had never thought about such a thing. "I am sure English parents love their children quite as much as French parents," he said defensively.

"Then why do they send their children away to school so early?"

They had left the farmland and were now driving along a city roadway, with gray stone residences on either side. A man walking a dog stopped to watch as they went by. Gabrielle waved to him.

Leo answered, "For the education, of course. It would be impossible to get as good an education at home. Schools have masters who are experts in a variety of fields of study."

She clicked to the horses, which had turned their heads to observe a man painting an iron fence close to the road.

"That may be true for older children, but young children can learn all they need to know from a good tutor at home. Eight! *Mon Dieu*, that is outrageous."

Leo didn't think this remark merited a reply.

Gabrielle went on. "It is only the upper class who can afford to do such a thing, yes? Is your father a noble?"

He hesitated for a moment but could find no reason for not telling the truth. "Yes."

"Ah-ha!" She gave him a triumphant grin. "I guessed that you were the younger son of a noble. Wasn't I clever?"

"Very clever," replied the *eldest* son of an earl.

"Is that why you went into the army, to make a career for yourself?"

He frowned. Was this interrogation ever going to end? "Yes," he said shortly.

She nodded, as if satisfied.

He folded his arms. "Now it is your turn to tell me about yourself. Have you always traveled with the circus?"

"It has been my life for as long as I can remember. Papa had to find something to do when the king fell, and he didn't want to stay near Paris, where everyone knew he had been the king's horse master. A traveling equestrian circus seemed to be a good idea, and we have been very successful."

"And your father was against Napoléon?"

"Papa was a royalist, through and through. He himself was the grandson of a noble, you see."

"And you are a royalist as well?"

"Not like Papa was," she said. "I think too many people were poor under the ancien régime. But Napoléon is as bad. How many men did he lose in Russia? Half a million at least. And now his men are all over the country, conscripting a new army to go on fighting. Even the peasants are resisting this conscription—everyone is sick of war. We are sick of Napoléon, if the truth be known. A return of the monarchy would be better than what we have—if the monarchy was like the English one and responsible to a parliament."

A shock of hair had fallen across his forehead in the breeze and he pushed it back. He was impressed by her intelligence and conviction. "If Louis is restored it will be more of a constitutional monarchy—I'm sure of that."

"It had better be. To have gone through what France has gone through and to end up as we began—that would be a tragedy."

He, who had always thought it would be desirable if France returned to the old ways, thought for a minute about what she had said. Then he surprised himself by saying, "Yes, I suppose it would be."

They had been driving through the main part of Lille as they spoke and people on the sidewalk waved to them and called out greetings.

"I'm surprised you don't start your tour in Lille," Leo said.

"We end our tour in Lille," she explained, waving back to a little boy who was jumping up and down and crying, "Gabrielle! Gabrielle!"

Leo asked, "Do you go to the same places every year?"

"We have several different routes, and we have done the southern route before, so it won't look strange for us to be traveling toward Spain."

"That's good," Leo said. "The more normal this circus looks, the better." He looked around. "Where is Colette?"

"Inside the wagon sleeping on the sofa. That's how

she usually travels. I give her a good run before we leave and she runs again when we arrive, otherwise she sleeps.''

"She's a beautiful dog," he commented.

She smiled. "Shall I tell you a secret? She's not really a dog—she's a princess in disguise."

He laughed. It was the first time she had heard that sound and she turned her head to look at him. He looked younger when he smiled, she thought.

"How old are you, Leo?" she asked.

All of the amusement left his face. "I should have prepared a letter of introduction for you," he said.

She gave him an annoyed look. "I am trying to be polite and to make conversation. And I should know how old you are if we're supposed to be married."

"I am twenty-eight," he said evenly. "You seem young to have the responsibility for a circus like this." He tried to steer the conversation back to her.

"Yes, but I spent many years watching what Papa did. I can handle it." She looked at him. "That is, I can handle it if we don't come under suspicion for carrying this gold. Frankly, I think the English government was mad to insist I take a noble's son along on such a mission."

"I don't plan on telling people that I'm a noble's son," he said in annoyance.

"There's something about you...an air of authority...that makes you stand out. That could be dangerous."

"Nonsense," he said.

"It isn't nonsense. You saw the reaction of the rest of the circus members. You don't fit in."

He was aware of how clipped his voice had become.

"I am here to make certain that the gold gets delivered to Wellington and I intend to do my job."

"I know!" she exclaimed, not listening to what he had been saying. She turned to him and her large brown eyes were sparkling. "You can be our ringmaster!"

He looked at her as if she was insane. "I am not going to be a ringmaster—or anything else! I am not here to *perform* in your circus."

"But it would be such a clever disguise," she said excitedly. "You'd make an excellent ringmaster—there's that air of authority, you know. And it would be a great camouflage. It would make you part of the circus, not just a suspicious addition."

"I am not going to perform in your circus. You might as well get that through your head," he said in his coldest voice.

She looked at him with a combination of surprise and disappointment, then turned her head back to face the horses. They continued the journey in silence.

They reached the outskirts of Amiens at about five o'clock, and Vincent, the advance man, was waiting for them at the Coq d'Or inn on the main road. He came over to Gabrielle's wagon and told her that they had secured the same field as last year.

"Wonderful!" She turned to Leo. "This is Vincent Duplay, our advance man. Vincent, meet my new husband, Leo."

Vincent looked at Leo in surprise. "I didn't know that you had remarried, Gabrielle. When did this happen?"

"A few weeks ago," Leo said smoothly. "We are still newlyweds."

Gabrielle shot him a glance. His face was perfectly grave.

He is the most humorless man I have ever met, she thought. *I wonder if he is like this with people of his own class or is it just us peasants who rate that somber expression.*

She looked back at Vincent. "Where have you booked us to stay, Vincent?"

"The same place as last year. Is that all right?"

"Fine," she reassured him. "It was quite a decent hotel. Have you put notices around town?"

"Yes."

"Good, then you can help put up the tent."

"Yes, *madame*." He gave her a mock salute. "Nice to have met you," he said to Leo.

Leo nodded. Soberly.

Gabrielle sighed as she took the reins back from Leo's hands. "Better let me drive. I know where the field is."

It was large and flat, sparsely covered by grass and surrounded by trees.

"This is such a perfect place for us," Gabrielle explained to Leo as they arrived at the field. "There is a stream just inside the woods over there. We can bring the horses to the water instead of always having to drag the water to them."

She watched as Leo looked around. It looked like an ordinary field to him. "Very nice," he said.

Gabrielle said briskly, "Well, before we can go to our lodgings we have to make certain the horses are comfortable. Get down, Leo," she ordered. "There's work to do."

All of the wagons had emptied by the time Leo and Gabrielle reached the ground, and all the circus members gathered around her. She issued her orders.

"You know the routine," she began, looking at each

person in the group. "First we have to get the horses settled. Mathieu, Albert, Jean, Cesar, Leo and I can put up the corral. Then we'll unharness the horses and take them for water. The rest of you can help with the tents."

Most of the assembly turned and started to walk toward the wagon in which the tents were stored. Gabrielle went to open the back door of her wagon to let Colette out and her brothers and the grooms headed in the direction of the wagon Mathieu had been driving. After a moment's hesitation, Leo followed them.

Mathieu climbed up into the driver's seat and drove the wagon to a place a few hundred feet from where all the other wagons were parked. When he stopped, the two grooms jumped into the back of the wagon and started handing down long pointed wooden poles to the rest of the men who stood on the ground. When they had all been unloaded, they were followed by four heavy wooden mallets.

"We put the stakes into the ground and then we put up a rope to make a corral," Albert explained to Leo.

"Surely you can't put all the horses in the corral together?"

"The corral is only for our horses. The rest of the circus pickets their horses for the night under the stable tent. Gabrielle likes to give our horses a chance to lie down."

"They don't try to get out? A rope corral isn't that sturdy."

Albert shrugged. "If they wanted to get out they probably could, but the corral is where they are fed, and besides, they are used to it."

Something rustled in the trees and the greyhound was off like a shot.

"Good God," Leo exclaimed. "She moves like the wind."

"Colette can run," Albert agreed.

"I've never seen a greyhound run. They really are amazing."

"What kind of dogs did you have in England?"

"My family had mostly spaniels and retrievers—hunting dogs."

Albert said, "Greyhounds are hunters, too—they are sight hounds, not nose hounds—but Colette is a pet."

"Most of the ladies in England have little dogs for pets," Leo said. "Pugs or King Charles spaniels."

"Gabrielle has always liked big dogs. Colette is her second greyhound."

Mathieu came up to them and handed Leo a mallet. "Here you go, Leo," he said. "You look like you're strong. You can pound the stake while Albert holds it."

The men had pounded the stakes in the ground more quickly than Leo would have believed, then two lengths of thick rope were looped through holes that had been drilled in the posts.

"Very neat," Leo remarked, impressed despite himself.

Gabrielle came up to her brother and Leo. "Emma and I will start to untie the performance horses and take them down to the stream for water." she said.

She favored Leo with a brief smile. "See how you can make yourself useful?" she asked. "There is always something to be done in a circus."

He nodded but did not reply.

When the performance horses had been corralled, Leo helped unharness the wagon horses and take them for a drink. By the time they had finished with the horses, the circus tent was up. Leo looked at it and was impressed.

"I've never seen a tent like that," he said to Mathieu.

"It was Papa's invention, the round tent. It makes for good viewing from all sides and you can get more people in."

"And you put it up in so short a time!"

"It's simple, really," Mathieu said. "First we put up the center pole, then we lace the canvas pieces together and drape them over, then the quarter poles are put in to hold the tent out, and voilà, we have a tent."

"Very efficient," Leo said.

"Don't you have tents in the army?" Mathieu asked.

"Actually, Wellington has ordered tents for this last campaign. Until now the men have bivouacked in the open."

Mathieu said, "We have two more tents to put up, the stable tent and the dressing tent. Then we will be done for now."

Gabrielle came up to them, her greyhound at her heels. "We need to hay the horses," she said. "Leo, you can help Mathieu."

More orders. He replied as calmly as he could but knew his temper was showing. "Very well."

Gabrielle stood and watched as he went off with her brother, but not before he noted the speculative expression on her face.

Seven

"When were you married, Gabrielle?"

Leo could see Luc's question had taken her off guard. They had left the animals fed and watered back at the field, and were now piled into the Robichons' two painted wagons to make the short journey to their lodgings in town.

Leo ended up sharing a front seat with Luc Balzac and Gabrielle. Luc started asking questions as soon as Leo put the horses into motion.

"Oh, a few weeks ago," she replied, too nervously for Leo's taste. "It was quite a whirlwind romance, wasn't it, Leo?"

He looked at her. Her large brown eyes were anxious. "Yes," he said warmly, hoping to help the charade. "It was quite a romance."

"And what do you do, Leo—or what *did* you do before you had the luck to marry a circus owner?" Luc's voice was tinged with sarcasm.

Leo had already thought this out so his answer was prompt. "I bought and sold horses in England."

Gabrielle said with annoyance, "Leo would not have married *any* circus owner, Luc. He married me. Isn't that true, Leo?"

"Completely true, my sweet," he said, then took her hand in his and kissed it.

It was not the smooth, soft hand of a lady. It was a strong, competent little hand whose skin was slightly chapped. Touching it, he felt a shock streak from his lips to his loins. He dropped her hand as if it had burned his mouth.

Gabrielle looked startled. He didn't know if it was because he had dropped her hand so suddenly or because she, too, had felt the same shock that had leaped between them.

"You're English," Luc continued, not noticing Leo's reaction. "What were you doing in Brussels?"

"Selling a horse," Leo replied shortly.

"How did you meet Gabrielle?"

"Really, Luc," Gabrielle said. Her husky voice sounded a little breathless. "You sound as if you're conducting an inquisition. Leo and I met by chance and fell in love. That's the whole story."

Luc scowled. "I thought you were still mourning your beloved André."

The faintest flush bloomed on Gabrielle's cheeks. *She has beautiful skin,* Leo thought. It wasn't the rose and white of an English complexion; it was more like peaches and cream.

Gabrielle said tightly, "I will never forget André."

Leo sensed she was upset and forced a change of subject. "My wife tells me you are a superb horseman, Luc. Tell me about your act." He spoke with the unconscious authority of a man who has given orders all his life.

There was a pause, then Luc said sulkily, "You'll see it soon enough."

"I am looking forward to it," Leo replied. He glanced at Gabrielle to see if she had recovered herself. Her face looked composed.

As they were speaking, they had passed wagons filled

with produce and another wagon selling ice. Now they came abreast of a farm wagon with a man and a child on the front seat. "Look, Papa," the little boy called. "It's the circus lady!"

He started to wave frantically and Gabrielle smiled and waved back. "I hope we see you tomorrow," she called.

"Surely will," the farmer called back. "The lad's been talking of nothing else since he saw your poster."

"Wonderful." Gabrielle blew them a kiss.

"Was that necessary?" The words were out of Leo's mouth before he had a chance to think about their wisdom.

Gabrielle gave him a surprised look. "Was what necessary?",

Stupid, Leo thought. *She's a circus performer, not a lady. She drums up business however she can.*

"Nothing," he replied. "I spoke out of turn. I imagine you get a lot of children at your performances."

"We get people of all ages, from the very young to the very old. Luc, do you remember that woman last year who celebrated her eightieth birthday at one of our performances? It was amazing," Gabrielle said to Leo. "Eighty years old and she was sitting on a bench watching our show! Isn't that marvelous?"

Leo couldn't help but smile at her enthusiasm.

They had reached the town limits of Amiens and within a few minutes they pulled up in front of a stone building with a sign outside reading Hôtel de Champs.

"Here we are," Gabrielle said to Leo. "It's not fancy but it's clean and the beds are good."

Leo turned to Gabrielle to help her down, but all he saw of her was her back. A second later she had jumped to the ground unassisted.

She turned to look back at him. "Can you hand me my bag, Leo?" she asked.

He picked up the canvas bag that contained her clothes and handed it down to her. She continued to surprise him, he thought. Certainly she was nothing like any woman he'd ever known.

"Give me yours, too," she said.

He shook his head. "It's too heavy, I'll lift it down." He jumped to the ground himself and lifted down his leather portmanteau.

"The landlady will have supper for us," Gabrielle told him. "I don't know about you, but I'm hungry."

Leo looked down into her delicately lovely face. She looked as if she existed on champagne and strawberries. "Food sounds good," he said.

They all trooped inside the old hotel and settled around three tables in a large, shabby-looking dining room. Leo looked at the landscapes that hung on the wall. They were terrible.

A short, portly woman in a blue apron came bustling into the room. "*Bon soir,* Mademoiselle Robichon," she said. "It is good to see you again."

"*Bon soir,* Madame Gare," Gabrielle responded. "It is good to be here. What do you have to feed us with tonight?"

"Lamb stew," the landlady replied.

"Wonderful," Gabrielle said.

"I will serve it immediately," the woman said, and bustled out of the room.

"I thought you were Madame *Rieux,*" Leo said to Gabrielle. "Have you kept your own name for the circus?"

"Yes. Robichon is a well-known name in the areas we travel. Even when André was alive I was Mademoiselle Robichon in the circus."

"Gabrielle is famous," Albert said with pride. "Papa always said that of all the horsemen he had trained, she was the best."

Leo raised an eyebrow. "That is quite a compliment."

Gabrielle smiled modestly. "My father was prejudiced," she said.

"That's not true," Mathieu put in. "She has my father's touch."

Leo remembered Gabrielle had said that also. "What do you mean by 'touch'?" he asked curiously.

"She knows what a horse is thinking," Mathieu said.

"Horses can't really think," Leo scoffed.

"Perhaps not, but they feel," she insisted, "and they communicate what they are feeling through the reins. Unfortunately, few riders care to listen."

Something about Gabrielle's words and the certainty in her voice silenced Leo's argument. He thought about her theory as he ate his lamb stew, confounded again by her unusual ways.

The conversation at the table had gone on without him, and when he turned his attention back they were talking about the brutal conscription that was going on in France.

"A soldier came to the farm over the winter," Mathieu was saying. "Albert and I had to hide in the hayloft so he wouldn't find us."

"We had a scare, too," Carlotta said. "Henri and Franz had to bribe the conscripting officer to get off."

"Yes, it cost me a bundle," Henri said. "The peasants don't have the cash to hand over, though. Poor bastards. They're pushed into the army and they don't know the first thing about military matters."

"Napoléon lost a huge number of men in Russia," Leo said neutrally.

"Yes, and the rest of the army is tied up in Spain by

the English," Henri said. "It's time Napoléon made a deal with the Allies and agreed to give back all his conquered territory and rule within the boundaries of France."

"Do you think he would be content with that?" Leo asked curiously.

"No," answered Emma flatly. "That man will never give up his territories. The Allies will have to beat him on the battlefield. He will never give up voluntarily."

"Unfortunately, I think Emma is right," Franz said.

"Do you think that France would be content for Napoléon to rule it?" Leo asked.

"If he ruled in peace, yes," said Henri.

"After all, what's the alternative?" Carlotta asked. "The return of the king? Did we go through all that we have gone through just to see the Bourbons back on the throne again?"

"I hope not!" Henri said.

Gabrielle spoke up. "If the king ruled with a parliament, like in England, that would be all right, Henri."

"Perhaps," Henri said grudgingly. "But the history of the Bourbons doesn't suggest that they would be willing to do that."

"I think the Revolution changed things in France forever," Gabrielle said gravely. "No king will ever again have the power of Louis XVI."

"Napoléon has that kind of power," Henri pointed out.

"Napoléon is on his last legs," Gabrielle insisted. "The English are beating him in the Iberian Peninsula, and if he is going to march against Germany again, it will be with an army of raw recruits. I think we are in the days of a dying regime."

"I think so, too," said Franz soberly.

Leo was careful not to contribute much in case he inadvertently gave away clues to his real identity. He looked down now at his empty plate. Madame Gare came out of the kitchen. "How are we doing, eh? Finished? I have apple tart for dessert."

Gabrielle jumped up. "I'll help you clear, Madame Gare."

"Such a good girl," the landlady beamed.

Emma also got up and quietly went to the next table and began to collect plates. The two other women in the company, Carlotta and Jeanne Maheu, a band member, remained in their seats.

After dessert was finished, Gabrielle went into the kitchen and came out carrying a large bag. "Supper for Cesar and Jean," she said to Leo, referring to the two grooms who stayed behind to guard the horses. "I'll take it out to them tonight. It's the first night on the road for the horses and I want to make sure everything is all right."

Leo said, "Will they remain with the horses all night?"

"Yes," Gabrielle said. "Cesar has his two Alsatian dogs with him. They will sound an alarm if anyone tries to get near the horses."

"Are Cesar and Jean armed?" Leo asked.

"Yes," Gabrielle replied.

Leo nodded his approval.

"Shall I go with you, Gabrielle?" Luc asked.

Leo gave the equestrian a long, hard stare. "*I* will accompany my wife," he said.

My wife. The words sounded so strange rolling off his lips.

Gabrielle patted Luc on his sleeve. "Thank you, anyway, Luc."

Luc's handsome face looked grim.

"Come along, Leo," Gabrielle said, and without even glancing at him, she began to walk toward the door leaving him, along with her dog, to follow.

This has got to stop, Leo thought. *I am not her servant!* He wondered if she had treated André this way. *I pity the poor bastard if she did.*

Leo drove out to the field while Gabrielle held the food on her lap. Colette lay sprawled across her feet for the twenty-minute drive. Leo was silent and Gabrielle made no attempt to engage him in conversation. When they arrived they were greeted by two large black Alsatian dogs, which barked excitedly.

"Yes, yes," Gabrielle soothed them. "I am bringing your dinner, too."

Cesar approached them.

"Is everything quiet?" Gabrielle asked.

"Yes. The horses are all tired from the day's journey. No one has acted up."

"Good. I have lamb stew for you and Jean and the dogs."

"Wonderful. We're all hungry."

The two men had put out benches and Gabrielle began to set out their meal on one of them. They sat on the other and started eating. Gabrielle then went to the wagon and returned with two large dishes into which she poured the remainder of the lamb stew. The two Alsatians began to eat hungrily.

Colette stood and watched them, her ears pricked.

"Don't look like that—you just ate, you piggy," Gabrielle said affectionately.

Colette ignored her; she continued to watch the other dogs eat.

"Let's go look at the horses," Gabrielle said to Leo,

and they walked the twenty feet that divided them from the corral.

Inside, the Lipizzaners, the Arabians, Coco and four of Gabrielle's carriage horses were eating quietly from their separate piles of hay.

It was a mild, pleasant evening. Leo found himself very curious about Gabrielle's work. "What do you do when it's raining?" he asked. "Do they stay out in the rain?"

"I put them in the stable tent when the weather is inclement."

"And do you make a profit with this circus?"

"Papa did. I hope I can do the same."

"Is this your first season running the show?"

"I finished up the last weeks last year. This will be my first whole season." Leo thought she sounded a bit less assured than usual.

As they were speaking, one of the horses left his pile of hay, went over to another of the horses, nudged him out of the way and began to eat his hay.

"Jacques, don't be a bully," Gabrielle called.

The other horse stood looking sadly at his hay being devoured by Jacques. Gabrielle ducked through the ropes and went up to him. "Come along, Tonton," she said, and led him over to the pile of hay that Jacques had deserted. The horse lowered his head and promptly started to eat. Gabrielle came back to stand beside Leo.

"Poor Tonton," she said. "He is low man in the pecking order and I worry about him getting enough to eat."

"He looks fat enough," Leo said.

"That's because he was fed in his stall all winter."

As they watched, Jacques deserted Tonton's pile of hay and went over to reclaim his own. Once again Tonton was without food.

"Mon Dieu," Gabrielle said. "My poor Tonton." She went back to the wagon, and when she returned she was carrying a lead rope. "The corral opens over here," she said to Leo, pointing. "Hold it for me, and I'll bring Tonton out. He can eat out here with us."

She took down the rope and went in after the large bay horse. Leo watched, amused, as she led him out, handed him to Leo to hold and went back for Jacques's pile of hay. She brought the hay outside of the corral, dumped it on the ground and went to take Tonton's lead. She held the lead and Tonton lowered his head and began to eat.

"I'll have to tell Jean and Cesar to leave Tonton in the stall tent where the horses are tied. We did it last year—they must have forgot."

"You take good care of your horses," Leo said approvingly.

"They deserve good care," she returned. "They are the heart and soul of our show."

They stood quietly, side by side in the darkening light, as Tonton munched away on his hay. Leo suddenly found himself acutely aware of her presence. All of his nerve endings seemed to be attuned to her, and he scowled, not liking the feeling at all.

Gabrielle broke the silence and called to the grooms. "I am going to tie Tonton to the corral. Make sure you put him back inside when he has finished his hay."

Cesar came over to them. "I forgot about Tonton. Is Jacques still stealing his food?"

"Yes." Gabrielle was busy tying a knot in Tonton's lead rope.

Then she turned to Leo. "Let's get back to the hotel."

They walked back to their wagon, and as Gabrielle put her foot on the step to climb up, Leo put his hands around her slim waist and lifted her. She was light and buoyant as he swung her up to the seat.

"You don't have to do that," she said from her place above him. Her voice sounded a little breathless.

"A husband helps his wife," he returned as he went around to the other side of the wagon.

"Nevertheless, I can get into the wagon by myself."

He climbed into the seat beside her. "If we want to present the picture of a happily married couple, you are going to have to be less independent," he told her sternly. "I'm not the sort of man to stand by and let his wife climb into a wagon by herself."

With this, he pulled the reins from her hands and started the horses on their trip back to the hotel.

Eight

It was dark by the time Leo and Gabrielle got back to the hotel. Leo parked the wagon in the stable yard next to the other one. No groom appeared to unharness the horses, so he did it himself. Then he and Gabrielle put the horses into their stalls and returned to the stable yard.

Leo looked at the two wagons and said, "I'm wondering if I should plan to sleep on Colette's sofa. I don't like leaving the wagons unguarded for the night."

Gabrielle shook her head decisively. "Your job is to do everything you can to fit into this circus. If you start sleeping in one of the wagons, everyone will wonder what is going on."

"My job is to protect the gold," he corrected, "but I suppose you're right."

"I know I am, so come along."

Together they went into the hotel through the back door. They found Emma in the lounge, knitting, the Maroni brothers playing cards, and Mathieu and Albert playing chess.

"Here they are," Emma said, looking up over her spectacles.

"Everything all right with the horses?" Gianni Maroni asked.

"Everything's fine," Gabrielle reported. "Where is everyone else?"

"Gone to the café down the street," Mathieu reported.

Leo walked over to look at the chessboard. Mathieu was winning.

"Would you care to have a glass of wine before going to bed?" Gabrielle said to Leo. "We could walk down to the café if you like."

Leo agreed and Gabrielle said, "Let me change into something besides this skirt and boots." As Gabrielle left the room, he turned his attention to the chess game. "Whose turn is it?" he asked.

"Mine," Albert said. He picked up a piece and Leo said, "Are you sure you want to move that?"

Albert gave him a surprised look. "Why not?"

"Look at your bishop," Leo recommended.

Albert looked. "Oh," he said, and hastily moved his bishop out of danger.

When Gabrielle finally reappeared, Mathieu greeted her return with a disappointed "Oh, are you going to take Leo away? He is helping Albert and giving me a little bit of a challenge for a change."

"If I'm so terrible, then I won't play with you at all," Albert retorted. "It's no fun for me to get beaten all the time."

Leo looked at his supposed wife. She was wearing a long dark blue wool skirt with a matching jacket. It was a very simple outfit, with little trim, hardly fashionable, yet she managed to look very smart. Her hair was bundled into a loose chignon on the nape of her delicate neck.

"Stop quarrelling, boys," she said to her brothers. "Ready, Leo?"

"Ready." He followed her to the door and out onto the street. Colette went with them.

The café's outdoor patio was closed up for the night,

with chairs upended onto tables, but when they walked
inside they were greeted with brightness and the smell of
cooking oil. Most of the tables were taken, the largest
one by the circus people. Gabrielle and Leo went to join
them.

"Good," Carlotta exclaimed happily as they came up
to the table. "Another woman. Come and sit by me, Gabrielle."

"I'm sure Gabrielle will want to sit beside her new
husband, *chérie*," Henri said. "Bring over those chairs,
Leo, and you both can squeeze in here."

Leo dragged the chairs over and he and Gabrielle sat
down.

Sully asked, "I was wondering—why are we starting
out so early this year, Gabrielle? It's colder and the light
doesn't last as long. We usually don't start for another
two weeks."

Leo looked at the man who was the Cirque Equestre's
clown. Sully was a tall, thin man with mournful brown
eyes and a receding hairline. He didn't look at all jolly.

"I just thought it would be a good idea to get a head
start on the season," Gabrielle said easily. "The more
performances we put on, the more money we make.
No?"

Leo, who knew that they were starting early so they
could move the gold as quickly as possible, shot a swift
look around the table to see if Gabrielle's reason was
accepted. A few people nodded and the rest seemed indifferent. He relaxed.

Jeanne Maheu, one of the band members, smiled at
him. "Have you been to Astleys circus in London, Leo?"

Jeanne was an exotic-looking woman, with long black
hair and slanting brown eyes. She almost looked Oriental,
Leo thought.

"No, I have never had that privilege," he said.

"Have you ever seen any circuses at all?" she pressed.

He shook his head. "No, *madame*, I'm afraid I haven't."

"Jeanne," she corrected him. "We are all on a first-name basis in this circus, aren't we, Gabrielle?"

"Yes," Gabrielle replied.

"Never seen a circus?" Jeanne's husband, Pierre, was astonished.

Leo did his best to look genial. "I will remedy that omission tomorrow. And I'm looking forward to it."

Gabrielle said, "You have to fetch our drinks from the bar, Leo. I will have a glass of burgundy."

Leo stood up, annoyed to have taken orders from Gabrielle in front of the others, and went off to the bar. When he came back to the table the rest of them were discussing the next day's program.

"I am going by the order that Gabrielle gave me, and that's that," Gerard said hotly.

Luc said to Gabrielle, "I don't think I should come directly after you. That makes too many equestrian acts in a row."

"What's the matter, Luc?" teased Antonio Laurent, one of the band members. "Afraid of the competition?"

Luc's blue eyes glittered. "No!" he retorted.

"Let's go with what I have for tomorrow, Luc," Gabrielle said matter-of-factly. "If it needs changes I'll make them for the next day."

Luc did not look happy, but after a moment he nodded agreement.

The conversation veered to what they had all been doing over the winter, and Leo leaned back and watched the various faces around the table. The atmosphere among the group was comfortable. Everyone seemed to know everyone else and there was easy laughter when Adolphe Laurent told a funny story, which was then topped by his brother, Antonio.

They were a kind of people who were utterly foreign to Leo, but they seemed a pleasant-enough group. *This might not be so bad,* he thought. *I'll do what I have to do for four weeks, and then it will be over.*

"What kind of horses did you sell, Leo? Were they racehorses?"

He brought his attention to Jeanne's inquisitive face. "Hunters, mainly," he said. "There's a big market in England for reliable hunters."

"Oh, yes, the English and their hunting," Gerard commented. "Pierre Robichon used to say that the English passion for hunting has destroyed their horsemanship."

"How is that?" Carlotta asked.

"They have lost their seat. All they do is stand in their stirrups and gallop," Gerard said.

"I don't think it's quite as bad as that," Leo said mildly.

"Well that is what Pierre said."

"Papa meant that there is no manège training in England," Gabrielle explained.

"There isn't any in France any longer, either," Leo shot back.

"But there was before the Revolution and there will be again after Napoléon. There is a tradition in France of classical riding. There is no such tradition in England."

"The Duke of Newcastle was English and he trained in the classical way," Leo said.

"True, but Papa said no one in England studied the Duke of Newcastle any longer. The few Englishmen who were interested in learning to ride properly came to Papa when he was the king's Master of the Horse.''

Leo was annoyed. It was one thing for him to think his countrymen were not the best riders, but it was quite another to hear the same opinion from foreigners. "It takes a great deal of skill to ride a horse cross country," he said stiffly.

Gerard said, "It is easy to gallop a horse cross country. All you need is balance. Watch Gabrielle ride tomorrow, then you will see what real horsemanship is.''

Gabrielle smiled at Gerard. "Thank you, Gerard," she said.

Luc said scornfully, "However did you come to marry such a barbarian? Your father must be turning in his grave.''

Barbarian? Leo was outraged.

Gabrielle flushed. "Leo is not a barbarian," she said.

Leo did not find her defense overly enthusiastic.

Jeanne gave him a warm smile. "Don't pay any attention to Luc, Leo. He is just jealous because you married Gabrielle.''

"Not jealous, Jeanne—amazed," Luc said sarcastically.

Everything in Leo wanted to give this bunch of common people an icy dressing down. But he couldn't do it; it would alienate them and would make them wary of him. He forced a smile to his face. "Talk to me tomorrow, after I have seen your horses perform.''

"Good idea," Gabrielle said briskly. She stood up. "I am ready to go back to the hotel, Leo.''

He stood up also. He was really getting tired of her habit of issuing orders to him. It was a good thing she was so pretty, he thought, otherwise this assignment would be miserable.

They walked back to the hotel in silence. The only ones left in the lounge were the Maroni brothers, who were still playing cards. Gabrielle bade them good-night and started toward the stairs.

"I am just going to step out to the stable yard to check the wagons," Leo told her quietly.

She nodded. "I'll wait for you."

The stable yard was quiet. The moonlight illuminated the two wagons with the white horses painted on their sides. Leo pulled on the wagon doors, content that they were securely locked.

Christ, but I wish this journey was over, Leo thought. It stretched out before him like an eon of time. But it was only four weeks. Four weeks wasn't that long, Leo thought. Then the gold would be delivered and he would be free to rejoin his regiment. He looked up to the sky at the full moon. The same moon was shining on his compatriots in winter quarters in Portugal, he thought.

Four weeks, and he would be able to return to them.

He went back inside to rejoin Gabrielle, who was waiting in the lounge. Together they mounted the stairs to their bedroom.

Another plain, serviceable room, Leo thought as he walked in through the door after Gabrielle. It was furnished with one bed, one wardrobe, a bedside table with a lamp and another table with a basin of water. The floor was wide wooden planks with a small, thin rug just inside the door. Colette immediately jumped on the bed and established herself at the foot.

The floor looked very hard, Leo thought with discouragement.

"We will do the same as we did last night," Gabrielle said. "I will tell you when you can turn around."

Leo turned away and fished his nightshirt out of his

bag, which lay on the floor, and proceeded to take off his boots. Behind him he could hear the sounds Gabrielle made as she took off her own clothes, and he tried heroically not to envision how she would look naked. Her waist had been so slim and supple when he grasped it this evening....

Stop, he thought.

But it had been a long time since he had had a woman. Too long, he thought. That's why he was reacting to this circus girl, he reasoned.

"All right," Gabrielle said, and he turned around. She was wearing the same long nightgown as the night before, and her hair was loose around her shoulders and down her back. She had a brush in her hand, and as he watched she went over to the bed, sat on the edge of it and began to brush her hair.

He watched, fascinated, as the silken strands slid through the brush. "You have beautiful hair." The words were out before he could stop them.

"Thank you," she said, clearly surprised.

He cleared his throat. "Well, if you will lend me a blanket, I will bunk down on this rug."

She stopped brushing and looked at him. "You don't have to do that. You can share the bed with me—as long as you keep to your side."

He stared at her in astonishment. "Are you sure?"

"I am sure, but you must understand, Leo, that I am not inviting you to take liberties with me. I am simply allowing you to have a comfortable place to sleep." She looked at the rug. "That rug doesn't look too clean."

He looked at the bed. It was an ordinary double bed, the kind that a married couple would share comfortably. But they were not a married couple. He thought about what it would mean to lie so close beside her.

I might get more sleep on the floor.

But the rug definitely did look dirty. And the floor looked hard.

"All right," he said. "Thank you."

She nodded. "Is there a side that you particularly like? André always had to sleep on the left side of the bed."

"No," he said. "Either side is fine with me."

"*Bon.* You can have the left side, then. I am used to having the right."

He walked barefoot to the bed, feeling huge in his white nightshirt. She looked so delicate and so beautiful as she sat there brushing her hair.

He got in under the covers and watched as she finished brushing and took a ribbon and tied her hair at the nape of her neck. She stood up, folded back the covers and slipped into bed beside him.

"This is awkward, no?" she asked.

"Very awkward," he replied. He had to curl his legs because the dog took up the bottom of the bed.

"I am sorry that we seemed to denigrate your countrymen tonight," she said. "We of the Robichon circus tend to be very proud of the quality of our riding."

"So I gathered," he said.

"This disguise of you being my husband is very difficult," she said. "You saw tonight how astonished everyone was that I would marry a man who is not a good rider."

Leo sat up. "Wait a minute. Who said I wasn't a good rider?"

She looked up at him. "I don't mean to insult you, Leo...."

"Well you do insult me," he said hotly. "I'll have you know that I am a bloody good rider. You and your friends may know some circus tricks that I don't know, but..."

She also sat bolt upright. "Circus tricks! I am not talking about circus tricks! I'll bet you can't even ride a horse in shoulder-in."

"What the hell is shoulder-in?"

"Hah!" she cried. "Shoulder-in is the most basic training tool of all classical riding. And you haven't even heard of it!"

Why am I even arguing with this girl? He forced himself to calm down. "This is pointless," he said. "We should get some sleep."

"Certainly," she said. "There is no point in arguing with you. You are too ignorant."

It took all his discipline not to reply.

"Turn out the light," she said, then turned her back on him, pulled the covers up over her shoulders and shut her eyes.

She was giving him orders again. He set his jaw, leaned over to the lamp and turned it off. Her voice came through the darkness.

"Good night."

"Good night," he replied.

Silence fell on the room. He was acutely aware of her sleeping but two feet away from him. Under the same blankets. She breathed so lightly he could scarcely hear her. His pulse was racing from the argument, he told himself. *This is going to be a long night.*

Nine

When Gabrielle awoke the following morning Leo was still asleep. She watched him for a minute without moving.

His hair was tangled on the pillow, his lashes lay still on his cheeks. He looked like a god strayed from the shores of ancient Greece, she thought. She had a sudden impulse to bend over him and kiss him awake, an impulse that immediately horrified her.

Mon Dieu! What am I thinking? I cannot become attracted to this man. That would put us in a horribly awkward position.

As if he had heard her thought, his eyes opened. She looked into their aquamarine depths and said briskly, "Wake up, sleepyhead. It's time to go to work."

He blinked, as if trying to place her.

"It's Gabrielle," she said. "You're with the circus."

He looked annoyed and his serene godlike aspect faded. "I know who you are," he said.

"For a moment there you looked unsure."

His eyes glittered but he didn't reply. After a moment's silence he said, "Are you going to get up?"

"Yes. And I am going to get dressed. Gather your clothes together and turn your back."

She pushed the covers back and got out of bed, carefully pulling her nightgown down over her legs.

"Do you know, Gabrielle, I am getting rather tired of you issuing orders to me." His tone was pleasant, but she detected anger behind the words.

She turned to look at him in surprise. "How will you know what to do if I don't tell you?" she asked innocently.

He was sitting up in bed, the covers pulled to his waist. The open neck of his nightshirt showed his strong throat and chest. She looked at them, then quickly pulled her eyes away.

He said, "I am perfectly capable of figuring things out for myself."

"If I had joined you in the army, I would expect you to tell me what to do," she said reasonably. "You don't know anything about the circus. I am only trying to keep you from making a mistake. The last thing we need is someone suspecting that you are an English officer."

He folded his lips into a frown but didn't reply.

"*Bon,*" she said, pleased that she had put him in his place. "Now can we get dressed?"

People started arriving for the circus at eleven o'clock the following morning. Gabrielle had put Leo in charge of selling tickets, and he stood beside the wagon emblazoned with the circus name and collected money and handed out tickets.

The circus-goers were mainly families: mother, father and children. They looked like shopkeepers from the city and local farmers—solid, middle-class folk, the sort that Leo scarcely ever noticed so far were they below his own high head.

It was almost show time when Leo sold a ticket to an army lieutenant. He got a little shock when he saw the uniform but kept his face expressionless. "Come to enjoy some fun, Lieutenant?"

"I have come to see your circus," the lieutenant said. He looked closely at Leo. "You have an accent, *monsieur*. Are you English?"

Damn, Leo thought. *I should have kept my mouth shut.* "My wife's family owns this circus," he said, as genially as he could.

The lieutenant nodded, took his ticket and moved toward the tent.

There's nothing to worry about, Leo told himself. *The man has just come to see a circus.*

He waited at the wagon until he heard the band strike up and then he locked the ticket money in the wagon and moved toward the tent. He went around to the performer's entrance and outside he found Gabrielle with her five white Arabians. Their flowing manes were brushed and they wore a golden plume on their heads. They wore no other equipment and each was being held by a rope looped loosely around his neck. Gabrielle herself was dressed in male hunting attire: red coat, breeches and high boots. Her hair was pulled high on the back of her head and swung between her shoulders in a shining fall. She was not carrying a whip.

"Go and sit with the band," she said to him. He hesitated a moment, decided to wait until after the show to tell her about the lieutenant, and went into the tent. As he entered, Gerard, who was also dressed in hunting attire, announced to the audience, "Mademoiselle Gabrielle Robichon and her Liberty Horses!"

The band started a gay tune and the horses trotted through the door, followed by Gabrielle, who went immediately to the middle of the ring. The horses began to trot energetically around the ring, their tails flying high in true Arabian fashion.

The demonstration that followed had Leo as fascinated as the rest of the audience. Without a hand touching them, without a voice telling them, without even a noticeable signal from Gabrielle, the horses went around the ring, wheeling, turning, reversing and circling in perfect unison. They reared in unison, and went down on their knees at exactly the same time. At one point, Gabrielle put numbers on their backs, mixed them up in the ring, and they all found their exact places in order as they went back to circling the ring.

Toward the end of the performance, Leo began to watch Gabrielle closely. She *was* cueing them, he realized, but the motions were so minuscule as to be scarcely noticeable: a slight step forward, a step backward or sideways, the slight lift of a hand—all scarcely visible to the audience but obviously visible to the horses.

Leo was deeply impressed. He thought of some of the horses he had known, and their lack of obedience, and was even more impressed. And these were hot-blooded Arabian horses, not slugs.

As the horses trotted out of the arena, the audience applauded enthusiastically. Gabrielle bowed once to her left, once in front and once to her right, then exited after her horses. She passed Leo with a serious face and didn't acknowledge his presence.

Leo studied the faces in the crowd, looking for the lieutenant. Benches had been set up on three sides of the circus ring by laying planks over wooden trestles, and behind the benches people were standing. While Paul Gronow gave a dazzling display of juggling with plates and knives, Leo searched the audience. The juggling act was almost over when he finally located the lieutenant standing on the right side of the ring. He appeared to be watching Paul with interest.

The next act was the Maroni brothers' tumbling. They started off by somersaulting off a springboard and landing on a big mattress in the middle of the ring. Following this act, Coco was brought in and they somersaulted over his back. Then three of the Arabians were brought in and they somersaulted over the three horses' backs. After that, the last two Arabians were brought in and Gianni somersaulted over the six horses' backs. Then the horses were led out, the mattress brought closer, and each of the brothers followed each other in rapid succession from the springboard, throwing special twists and variations to a lively galloping tune from the band.

Next, a very tall man with an impassive face walked into the ring. He was wearing evening clothes with an elegant high hat. Sully, dressed as a rustic booby with a red wig and a ruddy face, came in also and spoke to the tall man, but the man didn't answer. After a few minutes of this, Sully, in irritation, knocked his hat off. To the delight of the audience, his head came off, too. The ringmaster brought out a coffin and Sully tried to stuff the headless corpse into it. After a few minutes of Sully's comical endeavors, the headless corpse got up and ran out of the ring.

The crowd roared.

Leo kept a careful eye on the lieutenant. He was not laughing.

At this point, Coco came into the ring wearing only a leather halter and a red plume. Gerard, as ringmaster, picked up a lunge whip and started him cantering around the ring. The old horse knew his business and immediately picked up a steady rhythmic gate. Then Mathieu and Albert came running into the ring to join Gerard and the horse.

The boys were dressed in white tights and spangles and they took turns vaulting onto Coco's back, jumping on and dismounting as the horse cantered steadily around the ring. Mathieu went around twice while standing on his hands, and at one point, Albert got onto Mathieu's shoulders and both of them went around at the same time. It was a pleasing display and the audience appreciated it.

After they had left the ring, Gerard raised his hand. The band music stopped. "Ladies and gentlemen," Gerard announced. "The Robichon Cirque Equestre is pleased to present Mademoiselle Gabrielle Robichon riding Conversano Nobilia in an equestrian display."

As Leo watched, Gabrielle and the Lipizzaner trotted into the ring. She rode astride, dressed in a long, full-skirted blue velvet jacket, and the white breeches and high boots she had worn for the Liberty act. Her hair was tied at the nape of her neck and over it she wore a tricorn hat.

As she and Noble halted—perfectly squarely—in the center of the ring, it was as if an intangible something swept through the audience. It was as if girl and horse were able to communicate a kind of finer energy just by their very presence.

The band started to play and Noble picked up a trot. They circled the ring a few times, warming up, and then, as Leo watched, scarcely breathing, the Lippizaner started to *passage,* a slow, floating trot that was so light, so airy that it seemed to defy gravity. Leo was riveted. Then the *passage* slowed and the horse stopped advancing at all, trotting in place in the *piaffe,* his neck arched, his hind legs tucked under him, his hocks bending in a seemingly effortless effort. Then the band tempo picked up and Noble trotted forward, flowing into a half pass, his legs crossing as he went diagonally from corner to corner of the ring.

Leo thought that girl and horse were the most beautiful things he had ever seen. She sat so straight and so still. There was no movement on her part to show that she was giving aids to the horse. They seemed to move together in perfect harmony, going through a series of movements that Leo had once seen executed in Lisbon, but not so perfectly as this.

She made it look so easy, but Leo was in no doubt about the difficulty of what he was seeing. A horse did not change canter leads on every stride easily, nor did he canter a circle keeping his hind legs in one place.

I want to be able to ride like that, Leo thought fiercely.

When the ride was over, the audience's applause was thunderous. Gabrielle was smiling as she rode by him on Noble.

In the ring, Gerard was announcing, "Next, Mademoiselle Gabrielle Robichon will demonstrate the Airs Above the Ground with Neapolitano Santuzza."

In a moment, Gabrielle was passing him again, this time leading Sandi, who was saddleless. Gabrielle held a long whip in one hand and a long rein leading to Sandi's bridle with the other. She was apparently going to guide Sandi from the ground.

Girl and horse established themselves in the middle of the ring and Gerard announced, "First the *pesade.*"

Gabrielle touched Sandi and he lifted his front two legs off the ground in what looked to Leo to be a controlled rear. The horse kept his hocks bent beneath him and his body formed an angle of forty-five degrees to the ground.

"Note the lowered hocks," Gerard commented for the audience. "If a horse lifts himself from the ground at an angle of more than forty-five degrees and does not bend his hind legs, he is not performing any classical movement, he is simply rearing up."

Leo applauded heartily.

"Next comes the *courbette*," Gerard continued. Once more Sandi rose to a *pesade*, then he jumped off the ground landing in *pesade* again, from which he jumped again and then again before his forelegs once more touched the ground.

Louder applause came from the audience.

"And last we have the most difficult jump of all," Gerard said. "The *capriole*. It demands a great deal of power and courage from the horse. And now, Neapolitano Santuzza and the *capriole*."

As Leo watched, the stallion leaped off the ground, and at the moment when he was at the height of his jump, his body perfectly horizontal to the ground, his forelegs well tucked in, he kicked out vigorously with his hind legs before he landed again on the same spot. The audience erupted in applause.

Leo couldn't tear his gaze from Gabrielle's face. The combination of beauty and intense concentration nearly overwhelmed him.

He forced himself to look toward the lieutenant. He was not applauding. *Damn the fellow, anyway,* Leo thought. *At least he is seeing that this is a legitimate circus.*

The next act to be announced was Luc Balzac's. He came in with Coco and proceeded to put on a demonstration that was far more exciting than the one given earlier by Mathieu and Albert. Luc Balzac could ride, Leo thought in reluctant admiration. He looked once more toward the lieutenant, but the man was no longer there.

Leo frowned. *I wonder if he's poking around the wagons?* A chill ran down his spine, and while Emma and her dogs came into the ring, Leo slipped out. The field was deserted. He hurried over to the two Robichon wagons and opened the doors to look inside. Nothing looked disturbed.

And no lieutenant.

He looked around again, then returned to the circus tent. Perhaps the lieutenant had just changed his place.

As Leo came in they were setting up the ring for the rope dancers. Sully was causing a bit of a commotion by trying to hang washing on the ropes, but once he had been chased away, the ropes and the safety net were put into position. While this was being done, Leo looked out at the audience.

The lieutenant was back in his old spot.

Maybe he just went out to relieve himself, Leo thought.

Leo watched the lieutenant on and off as Henri, Carlotta and Franz performed a variety of jumps and turns and backward somersaults on the ropes. Then the three of them did something Gerard called the Rivals. Carlotta danced coquettishly on one rope while the two men—rival lovers—struck attitudes, advanced and retired in a mock duel for her love on the other. At the end, Franz, the disappointed lover, fell dramatically off the rope and into the safety net.

The lieutenant kept his place all during the act, and he didn't move as Gabrielle and Mathieu came into the ring riding Noble and Sandi. While the band played dance music, the two horses performed a pas de deux, moving in perfect harmony with each other, moving together, then apart, each horse executing the same moves, each one a mirror image of the other. It was beautiful.

Next Coco came in and Gerard started him cantering

around the ring. As Leo watched, a drunken countryman suddenly lurched into the ring from the audience and proceeded to try to mount Coco's back.

Leo jumped to his feet, prepared to grab the fellow and throw him out. Antonio Laurent grabbed the skirt of his jacket and said, "*Non*, Leo. It is part of the act, it is all right."

Feeling more than slightly stupid, Leo sat down again.

As the finale for the show, Luc was joined by Gabrielle on Noble, Mathieu on Sandi and Albert on Shaitan. The four cantered around the ring to a rousing tune, waving at the audience, and when they left the ring the performance was over.

"How did you like it?" Pierre asked Leo, as the band put down its instruments.

"I thought the horses were amazing," Leo said honestly. "And all the performers are very talented."

Pierre smiled, pleased. "It is a very good little circus. We don't have the spectacular effects of the permanent circuses, but the quality of the acts is very high."

Albert came into the ring. "Oh, there you are, Leo. Gabrielle says you can help to clear the people out—you know, direct traffic for the wagons and such."

But Leo was already on his feet, heading outside to keep an eye on the lieutenant.

Ten

In between shows the horses were brushed and fed hay and the performers dined off wine and bread and cheese in the empty circus tent. Then the new audience came in and they did the whole thing all over again.

One of the things Leo noticed as the day advanced was the easy camaraderie that existed among the members of the circus. It was evident at lunch, as they talked about the performance, and it was evident in the way they helped each other out before the second performance started.

He commented on this to Gabrielle as they drove back to the hotel after the second show was over and all the animals had been attended to.

"We are like a big family," she said to him. "Many of the acts have been with us for years and we all know each other very well."

"Luc Balzac hasn't been with you that long."

"No. He took André's place when André was killed, so he has only been with us for a year and a half."

He found himself asking, "How long were you married?"

"We were married for eight months."

Her response was polite, but he got the definite impression that she did not want to talk about André. He could understand that. He was a private man himself. Yet he could not help feeling oddly jealous. He dismissed the thought. Obligingly he changed the subject. "Is the circus your only source of income?"

She shot him a look. "Yes."

"Except for the money you are receiving for transferring this gold."

"That money will go to send Albert to art school."

He didn't mask his surprise. "Are you planning to do that?"

"Yes." She sounded very determined. "Albert is very talented and he loves to draw above all else. He loves it more than he loves the circus. My father could never see that, but I do. Albert should go to art school. He may have it in him to be a great painter."

He said slowly, "You are a good sister."

She shrugged. "I am all Albert has left. I cannot fail him."

"You would miss him in the circus."

"Yes, but we will survive without him." Her tone signalled an end to the discussion.

He looked at the small, delicate figure sitting next to him on the wagon seat. She carried a large responsibility on those slender shoulders, he thought.

"Do you think I might get a chance to ride one of your Lipizzaners?" he asked.

It was her turn to look surprised. She turned her head to look at him. Then her large brown eyes were serious. "They are not easy to ride. They respond to the slightest shift of body weight. If you even increase the weight on one of your seat bones by a scintilla, you will get a reaction."

He thought about that for a while. Then he said, "How would I go about learning to ride like you?"

She gave him a brilliant smile and he found himself

wanting to smile back. She said, "You were impressed with my horses, yes?"

"Very impressed," he said. "And I was very impressed with you. You were so still. You didn't appear to be giving the horse any direction at all."

"That is how it should be," she said. "Horse and rider should be in such perfect harmony that they work as one. To be a centaur is the aim of all good classical riders."

He smiled faintly. "Were there female centaurs?"

"There must have been, otherwise there would have been no centaurs at all," she retorted.

"Well," he said, "actually, there weren't."

She laughed.

"But my question was serious," he said. "How would I go about learning to ride like you?"

"You would need to learn on a school horse. That is how Papa taught me. First, you need to be lunged so that you develop your seat. Papa would always lunge his pupils when he ran the king's manège. Even advanced riders got lunged sometimes."

He had returned his gaze to the horses in front of him. They appeared to be slowing down and he gave them a little chirrup.

"Do you have any school horses?" he asked.

"You could ride Coco, I suppose. But I don't like to give my horses any more work. They do enough with the circus. Coco especially goes around in a circle enough."

He sighed. "You're right, of course." He found himself more disappointed than he imagined.

She smiled at him again. "You really liked my Lipizzaners, didn't you?"

"They were the most beautiful things I have ever seen."

"Riding them is the highlight of my day."

"You are a wonderful rider."

She nodded, accepting her due. "Papa taught me well."

He looked at her thoughtfully.

"Here we are at the hotel," she said. "Let's get changed and eat. I'm starved!"

Gabrielle watched Leo as the dinner conversation swirled around her. He was not part of it. He answered courteously enough when a remark was addressed to him, but otherwise he was quiet. She thought that he carried himself as if there was a little space around him that no one could get into.

He sticks out in this circus, she thought worriedly. *He acts like an aristocrat. That could be dangerous.*

"You were very good today, *ma mie,*" Henri was telling Carlotta. "I was inspired to fight for you."

Carlotta smiled and turned to her brother-in-law. "That was a spectacular fall you took. I am glad you didn't break your neck."

Franz laughed. "The audience loves a spectacular fall."

"Gabrielle, I could jump over more horses than we're doing now," Gianni said. "Do you think we could bring my two carriage horses into the ring?"

She turned her attention away from Leo and thought for a minute. "If you put them last," she said finally. "If you don't make it I don't want you landing on my horses' backs."

"I'll make it," he said confidently. "I practiced over the winter."

"You're very quiet, Leo," Luc said a little truculently. "Surely you have something more to say about the circus than that it was very good."

Leo looked at him. "What more do you want me to say?"

"You could be a little more specific," Luc challenged.

"I thought all the acts were very accomplished," Leo said. "You are all very talented."

The words were all right, Gabrielle thought, but the polite, even tone was wrong.

"Thanks so much," Luc said sarcastically.

Gabrielle thought it was time to intervene. "Leo was so impressed that he wants to ride a Lipizzaner."

Mathieu, who was drinking a glass of wine, looked at him. "You have to be trained to ride one of ours."

"So Gabrielle told me."

"How well do you ride, Leo?" Albert asked.

Leo said, "I ride very well—for an Englishman."

Everyone laughed.

Gabrielle said with a smile, "Don't worry, I will teach you to ride over the winter, *chéri.*"

He gave her a quick look, her endearment clearly taking him by surprise. Then he smiled back. He had a wonderful smile. He should use it more often, Gabrielle thought.

"I will hold you to that promise," he said.

After dinner, most of the group decided to return to the café they had frequented the night before. Gabrielle and Leo went with them—Mathieu had brought the grooms their dinner earlier. It was a pleasant visit until it became obvious that Sully was drunk and getting drunker by the minute.

"Oh, dear," Gabrielle said with distress. "I was hoping he was over this."

"Frankly, I was surprised you had him back," Gianni said. "You can't rely on him."

"He has never missed a performance," Gabrielle said defensively.

"Maybe not," Pierre said. "But there's always a first time."

Gabrielle leaned over to look the clown in the face. "Sully, do you feel all right? Do you want to go back to the hotel?"

The clown turned his mournful brown eyes on Gabrielle. "Not feeling too good," he said.

"I bet he started before dinner," Pierre said. "He hasn't had that much to drink here."

"He was drinking in the wagon after the last performance," said Paul, who shared a wagon with Sully.

"We'll have to get him back to the hotel so he can sleep it off," Gabrielle said. "Sully, can you walk?"

"Walk? Shertainly." The clown tried to stand up but had to lean on the table to catch his balance.

"I'll take him, Gabrielle," Leo said, quickly reaching for Sully.

She gave him a grateful look. "Thank you, Leo. I'll come with you."

Leo put an arm across Sully's shoulders and under his arms and steadied him on his feet. Then he began to walk him toward the door. Gabrielle followed with Colette at her heels.

When they reached the hotel Gabrielle held the door open for Leo and Sully to go through.

"What's your room number, Sully?" Leo asked him.

Sully looked at him in confusion.

"I'll go and find out from the landlady," Gabrielle said.

When she came back with the number, Leo half carried Sully up the stairs, brought him into his room and dumped him on the bed.

Gabrielle started to take off his shoes.

"I'll do that," Leo said. "Why don't you go back to our room and wait for me?"

"Are you sure?"

"Yes."

Gabrielle went. She was sitting on the bed, her hands folded in her lap, a frown on her face, when Leo came in. Colette had already established herself at the foot of the bed.

"He's completely castaway," Leo said. "Does this happen often?"

She sighed. "At least once a week last year. I hope to God it doesn't happen more frequently this year. The others don't like it."

He sat down beside her. "Why did you hire him again if he has this problem?"

"What would happen to him if I didn't hire him? No one else would take him."

"Why should he be your responsibility?"

She looked at him in surprise. "Because he has worked for us for seven years. He is like family. You don't turn your back on your family, no matter what they do."

Leo gave her a strange, unreadable look. "I gather he was not always like this?"

What was that look about? Gabrielle thought. But his face had returned to normal and so she answered his question. "It started last year, after his daughter died. She was a pantomime actor with Astleys in Paris. Sully hasn't been the same since."

His striking blue-green eyes were regarding her gravely, and she was suddenly acutely conscious of this big male presence in her room. She said quickly, "Perhaps it will not happen so very often this year."

He looked skeptical but let her comment go unchallenged. Instead he asked, "Why did you call me *chéri?*"

She blinked at the change of subject. "We are supposed to be married. We should show some affection for each other, otherwise people will wonder."

He continued to look at her. *Mon Dieu, he is looking like a god again.* His cotton shirt was open at the throat and his russet jacket made his shoulders look very broad. A few strands of golden hair fell across his forehead.

"It is not easy," she said a little breathlessly, "trying to look intimate when we scarcely know each other."

A little silence fell, then he said, "I know this is awkward for you, but the government had to send someone along to keep an eye on the gold."

Her back stiffened and she stared straight ahead at the wardrobe door. "No one ever came with us when my father carried gold."

"Before you were carrying gold for the Rothschilds. Now you are carrying gold for the English government. It's not quite the same thing."

"No," she said sarcastically. "The Rothschilds trusted us and the English government doesn't."

She heard him sigh. "Let's not keep pointing fingers of blame at each other, all right? I was sent to guard the gold, and that is what I'm going to do. You must appreciate that. Keeping the gold safe means keeping you safe, too."

"Fine," she said, annoyed at herself for feeling disappointment at all his business talk. She was still not looking at him. "You can take care of the gold. I have enough to worry about without worrying about that, too."

"What do you have to worry about?" he asked. "The circus ran perfectly smoothly this afternoon."

She shrugged. "I must always worry that someone will

get hurt or that one of the horses will get hurt. We are a small circus. We need everyone to be healthy.''

"All of your performers seemed perfectly healthy to me."

"They are. But something bad can happen so quickly.'' She turned to look at him. "Look at what happened with André."

He met her eyes. "You don't appear to harbor a grudge against Sandi. I wouldn't blame you if you did."

She shook her head. "It wasn't Sandi's fault. André was standing right behind him and he bent suddenly to pick up Sandi's foot—he was going to pick it out, but Sandi didn't know he was there. That's why he kicked out. It was just a moment of carelessness on André's part, and he was dead." Her eyes were somber. "So you see, Leo, I know about accidents. That is why I worry."

He said, "Well, let me do the worrying about the gold."

Easily said, not so easily done, she thought. But she forced a smile. "It's too early to go to bed. Why don't you tell me more about yourself?"

Immediately, the blue-green eyes grew cold and distant. "I've already done that," he said.

That space around him has just got bigger, she thought. But she persevered.

"Tell me about your home. You said you were brought up in the country?"

"Yes." His voice sounded clipped. He was no longer looking at her.

"Does your home have a name?"

He hesitated and she didn't think he was going to answer, then he said, "Branford Abbey. It used to be an abbey before Henry VIII ceased to be a Catholic and dissolved the monasteries. That's when it came into my family—that was three hundred years ago.''

''Mon Dieu,'' she said. ''That is a long time.''

He nodded.

''I have always wanted a home,'' she said wistfully. ''A circus person is constantly on the move. The closest things to a home I have ever had are the farms we rented for the winter.''

A little of the coldness left his eyes. Clearly he was more comfortable talking about her. ''Have you always traveled with the circus?''

She replied readily, ''Since I was born. My *maman* had me while we were on the road—and the same with Mathieu and Albert.''

''Your mother is dead?''

''She died not long after she had Albert.''

''Then who took care of you?''

''Sometimes the women who traveled with the circus, sometimes nannies. But the nannies usually didn't like the traveling. I was the oldest so I took care of the boys the best I could.''

He frowned. ''Did none of you go to school?''

''Papa taught us.'' She thought of something and laughed. ''His choice of subject matter would probably not suit a regular teacher. I read Xenophon—the ancient Greek horse expert—when I was eight!''

''I have never read Xenophon,'' he remarked.

''You must. He is the foundation father of all good riding.''

He said curiously, ''Are you satisfied with the circus, Gabrielle? Is it something you want to do for the rest of your life?''

She shrugged. ''It's what I do. It's what I know how

to do. It's how I earn my living. I don't have a nice estate in the country to go back to. All I have is the circus.''

"I suppose that was a stupid question,'' he said quietly.

"Yes,'' she agreed, "it was.''

They were silent for a few moments, but it was a comfortable silence, not a strained one.

"Papa's family once had an estate,'' she began. "A small one, not like yours—but it was lost in the Revolution.'' She sighed. "The Revolution was a terrible thing. And now Napoléon has lost over half a million men in Russia and he is collecting another army of young men. France needs peace. That is one of the reasons why I am carrying this gold for General Wellington. He will help to stop Napoléon and give us peace.''

He nodded and said soberly, "He will do that, Gabrielle. I am sure of it.''

"Perhaps it is time for us to go to sleep.''

She could hear the smile in his voice as he replied, "All right, I know the drill. Just let me get my nightshirt and then I will turn my back and let you get undressed.''

She should be getting more comfortable getting undressed in the same room with him, Gabrielle thought, but instead she seemed to be getting more *un*comfortable. She was acutely aware of him moving behind her. She pictured him pulling his shirt over his head, then taking his breeches off.

Naked, he would really look like a Greek god.

She blushed at the thought. What was wrong with her? She shouldn't be thinking things like that! Hastily she pulled her nightgown over her head, then removed her undergarments under the shield of its voluminous folds. She folded her clothes on a chair and said, "I'm ready.''

"So am I.''

They turned around and regarded each other. Gabrielle hoped she was not blushing.

"Turn the lamp out," she said, and while he had his back turned she jumped into bed and pulled the covers up to her breast. He crossed the floor in the dark so she did not have to see his bare legs as he joined her in the bed.

They had looked long and muscular in his tight breeches. Good horseman's legs, she thought.

Colette stretched herself and groaned.

"Good night, Leo," Gabrielle said.

"Good night, Gabrielle," he replied. Then, in a voice that held more than a hint of irony, he said, "Good night, Colette."

She heard him turn over, seeking a comfortable position in which to sleep. She stayed as far as she could on her own side, not daring to risk any physical contact.

Eleven

Emma came to talk to Gabrielle the following morning as they were getting ready for the first show of the day.

"I hope we're not going to have trouble with Jeanne," she said.

Gabrielle was brushing Sheiky's tail and she continued with her even stroking motion as she looked up at Emma. "What do you mean?"

"After you left the café last night she started to flirt with Franz. Pierre didn't like it at all."

Jeanne was new to the circus; Pierre had married her over the winter.

"Mon Dieu," Gabrielle said. "They are newlyweds!"

"You wouldn't know she was wed at all, the way she was behaving last night."

"What was she doing?"

"She was only asking Franz questions about himself, but it was the way she did it. She kept touching his arm."

Gabrielle finished with Sheiky's tail and straightened up. "Maybe she was just being friendly."

"Well, as I said, Pierre didn't like it. He glowered for the whole time we were there."

"Then he will talk to her and it will not happen again."

"I hope so. We don't need sexual jealousy rearing its ugly head in our circus."

"Let's give Jeanne a chance, Emma. She's new and she was probably just trying to be friendly. I hope Pierre isn't going to be the kind of husband who won't let his wife talk to other men. We have so few women with this circus that if she can't talk to the men then she will be very isolated."

"Well, I just thought I should warn you."

Gabrielle reached out and gave Emma a hug. "You worry too much."

Emma smiled. "Perhaps."

Gabrielle watched as the older woman walked away. Then she turned to survey her domain.

It was a sunny morning and the field looked as if it was about to sprout some grass. The circus troupe was spread out among its wagons, some of them practicing, some of them just relaxing and playing cards. The big circular circus tent, with its flag flying off the center pole, looked bright and colorful in the early spring sunshine. She smiled as Paul tried bending forward and catching a plate behind his back.

"Bravo, Paul," she called, and he grinned and waved at her.

Everything looked peaceful and harmonious. She looked for Leo and found him with Mathieu just outside the horse corral. He was holding Kania while Mathieu brushed the horse's mane. Albert was sitting on a box nearby, sketching them.

I wonder if Leo could help Albert, she thought. He was an aristocrat. Perhaps he would be able to get Albert into a good art school—maybe even in England, where there had been no revolution to disrupt and destroy the arts.

I have to have Albert show Leo some of the drawings he has done. Leo likes horses. He will be very impressed with the way Albert can capture a horse in his drawing.

The more Gabrielle thought about this idea, the better she liked it. *If I have to be saddled with Leo for this trip, perhaps I can find a way for him to be useful. It sounds as if he comes from an important family in England. Surely he should be able to help Albert.*

She moved from Sheiky's rear and began to apply her brush to his long flowing mane. He stood quietly, with no one holding him.

She had just finished with the mane when she was approached by Sully.

"Gabrielle," he said, "may I have a word with you?"

"Certainly," she said. She patted Sheiky's arched white neck and snapped a lead rope on his halter. He lowered his head and looked hopefully for grass.

Sully said, "I'm sorry about last night."

"You should be. You promised me last year that you would stop drinking over the winter. Now here you are again, doing the very thing you promised you wouldn't do."

"I know. I'm sorry. It's just...when the blackness comes on me, I can't help myself."

"It's very unpleasant for everybody else. Leo had to put you to bed last night."

Sully's brown eyes looked even more mournful than usual. "I'm sorry."

Gabrielle's anger dissipated, "Sully, I know you are still grieving for your daughter, and I know the black feeling that you have. I lost my husband, remember. But I kept busy and I didn't give into it and it got better. Giving into it the way you do only makes it worse. It keeps you from healing."

"You're right. But you're young, Gabrielle. I'm not."

"You're hardly an old man. When you feel that black

mood coming on you, come and talk to me, Sully. Will you do that?''

He gave her a sad smile. ''All right.''

''I know I'm young, Sully, but I have known sorrow, too.''

He patted her shoulder. ''Yes, but you have a new husband. I can't get a new daughter.'' And he walked off.

Gabrielle stood looking after him. *I don't have a new husband, Sully,* she said in her head, but she could not say that to him.

Everyone in the circus must think she had forgotten André.

That's not true, André, she thought fiercely. *I will never forget you.*

They had been a perfect match: both young, both horse-mad, both circus people. Her father had thought André too irresponsible, but Gabrielle had liked his smile and his laugh and she liked the way he made her feel. He was young and handsome and she was nineteen years old. She fell in love and they married and her life had changed very little. Then he had died and for the first time in her memory she had known real sorrow.

Her life had gone on, however, and the constant flow of performances, caring for horses and her father's and her brothers' comforting presences had helped her get through. Then her father had died, and the whole burden of the circus and her brothers had fallen on her shoulders.

Now she was the one who had to pay the salaries; now she was the one who had to collect the ticket money and make sure it covered not only the salaries but the costs for the horses and for the hotels and food for her and her brothers. Now she was the one who had to worry what she would do if one of the horses got injured and could not travel. Now she had to worry about what would happen if Sully got too drunk to perform.

Oh, Papa, she thought. *Everything seemed so easy when you were alive.*

At the end of the first show, Gabrielle gave some of the collected ticket money to Leo and asked him to drive the hay wagon into town and pick up some bales at the feed store.

"What do you do with this money at night?" he asked. "You don't just leave it in the wagon, do you?"

"No, I take it to the hotel with me."

"Does everyone know you have it?"

"I suppose so. You're the first person who's asked what I do with it."

He frowned. "I don't like the idea of you carrying so much money. It's a temptation."

It took her a minute to understand what he was implying. "Do you think someone from the circus would steal from me?" she asked indignantly.

"You never know," he replied.

She stuck her chin in the air. "I don't know the kind of people you are accustomed to associating with, but I can assure you that no one in this circus would dream of stealing money from me. They get their salaries once a week, and I pay them quite nicely, thank you. There is no need for them to steal."

"I didn't mean to insult your circus," he said. "It's just that...you seem so young for all this responsibility."

How dare he! She had thought the same thing herself, but hearing him say it incensed her. "I have watched my father all my life and I know *exactly* what to do to run this circus! If I was a man you wouldn't be saying this."

He looked at her, his eyes grave. "Perhaps you are

right. I am not accustomed to seeing women in charge of businesses."

"That's your difficulty, not mine," she retorted.

"At least I hope you keep the money in a locked box," he said.

She kept the money in a box, but sometimes she forgot to lock it. "Of course," she said loftily.

"Someone from the hotel could get into your room and take it if you leave it unlocked."

"I keep it locked up," she repeated, and vowed that she would do so in the future. "Stop treating me as if I was a child."

He looked a little grim as he left to get her hay. "I don't think you're a child, Gabrielle. You don't have to worry about that."

Luc had too much to drink at the café that evening and spent his time trying to badger Leo. Leo, exercising tremendous self-control, did not respond. Gabrielle suggested that they go back to the hotel early, and Mathieu and Albert joined them.

"I'm sorry about that, Leo," Gabrielle said when they had got outside. "Luc was thinking he could replace André and he received a big shock when you came along."

"I'm sorry if I got in the way of your romance," he said.

"I had no plans to marry Luc," she insisted calmly.

Albert said, "He can be nice. He let me draw him the other day."

"He probably liked the attention," Mathieu said.

"I don't like the dissention that is creeping up in the circus," Gabrielle said in a worried voice. "First there was Sully, then Pierre got mad because Jeanne was talking to Franz, and now Luc is insulting Leo. We never had this kind of trouble before.''

Leo said easily, ''When people live as closely as your circus members do, there is bound to be some tension. It's just normal.''

''I don't need tension,'' Gabrielle said irritated. ''It's enough that I am responsible for all this gold.''

''*I* am responsible for the gold,'' Leo corrected. ''That's why I'm here.''

Gabrielle glared at him. ''I would not be having this trouble with Luc if it wasn't for you!''

''You would be having different trouble with Luc if I wasn't here,'' he retorted. ''He would be pressuring you to marry him.''

''I can handle Luc,'' she said.

''Then handle him and stop whining!'' he replied.

She was insulted. ''I have every intention of doing that.''

''Good.''

''Don't be mad with Gabrielle, Leo,'' Albert said tentatively.

''I think it is the other way around, Albert,'' Leo replied coldly.

Gabrielle stuck her chin in the air and didn't reply.

They finished their walk back to the hotel in silence.

Gabrielle said good-night to her brothers at the staircase and preceded Leo up the stairs to their room. She was fuming.

Whining! How dare he say that I was whining. I think I have been amazingly good natured about having him foisted on me. I have been nice to him! And he's useless. No, he's worse than useless. He's causing trouble. I should have refused to allow him to come along. I should have told Monsieur Rothschild that I wouldn't take the gold if he couldn't trust me to deliver it by myself. Now I am stuck with this pretend husband whom I can't get rid of. I don't even have the privacy of my own room anymore!

They entered their room and Gabrielle bent to pet Colette so she wouldn't have to look at Leo.

He said in a cold voice, "It's a little early for me to go to bed. I hope you won't mind if I read for a while."

Colette's fur was like silk under her fingers. "Fine," she said. "I would like to go to sleep, though. I am tired."

"Will the lamp disturb you?"

"What do you care?"

"I am asking you to be polite. Will the lamp disturb you?"

His voice was measured and that annoyed her even more. "No," she snapped. "It will not disturb me."

"Good. Let's get undressed, then."

Getting undressed was even more uncomfortable than it had been the night before. For the first time she found herself resenting his presence. For some reason, she just couldn't ignore him anymore.

He's too big, she thought. He takes up too much space in this room...in this bed. Poor Colette is squashed onto my side because of his big feet.

He plumped his pillows up to make a bed rest and opened a book. He looked perfectly comfortable, and she thought, *I should have made him sleep on the floor.*

He regarded her over the pages of his book. "Sleep well," he said.

"Humph," she replied, then turned away from him, pulled the covers over her shoulders and shut her eyes.

Twelve

It was raining hard in Paris when a small man was admitted into the office of François Nicholas Mollien, the French minister of the Public Treasury. He shook the raindrops off his coat, rather like a dog, and approached the desk of the minister.

"What is this news you have for me, Le Brun?" the minister asked.

"I've just learned through channels that Monsieur Nathan Rothschild has bought up millions of our newly minted *napoléon d'or* coins in Holland, Monsieur le Ministre. The sale took place about two weeks ago."

Mollien raised his thick black brows. "Nathan Rothschild?"

"Yes, Monsieur le Ministre."

"He's the Rothschild who lives in England?"

"Yes, Monsieur le Ministre."

"Damn."

Le Brun remained silent.

"He's going to try to get the money to Wellington. That must be it."

"It would look that way, Monsieur le Ministre."

There was a silence as the minister frowned into the distance. Then he returned his attention to his underling. "Very good, Le Brun," he said, dismissing him. "I will take care of this situation. Good job."

As soon as Le Brun had left, Mollien made his way to the office of Napoléon's ministre de la guerre, Alexandre Millerand. The war minister's reaction was the same as Mollien's. "That gold is for Wellington."

Mollien nodded. "That much gold is as good as another army. It must be stopped. Can you set up search points on the main north-south roads to try to intercept it?"

"Yes," Millerand said. He slammed his hand on his desk. "Damn the English. If they weren't tying up so many men in the Peninsula we would have a seasoned army to throw against the Prussians."

"Yes," Mollien agreed. "We need to defeat the English and drive them out of the Peninsula altogether. We do not need them reinforced by several million gold pieces."

"I wonder what Wellington is planning for his spring campaign," the war minister muttered.

The rain beat heavily against the window, and for a moment both men were silent. Then Mollien said, "It's a shame Napoléon himself can't take charge in Spain. He would have Wellington on the run in no time."

"Napoléon is getting ready to take on the Prussians and Russians. We will have to leave the command of the army in Spain in the hands of his brother, King Joseph."

"Joseph is no Napoléon," Mollien said gloomily.

"No one is the equal of Napoléon," Millerand declared. "Certainly not Wellington. But I will make certain that this gold does not reach the English. It was well done of you to have found out about this purchase."

"Thank you, Monsieur le Ministre," Mollien said.

As soon as the treasury minister had departed, the war

minister sent for one of his aides. Within a day the arrangements for checkpoints on the main roads into southwest France were finished. Within two days, the roadblocks would be in place.

Thirteen

A cold front blew in over the course of the night and Gabrielle, still asleep, gravitated naturally toward the warmth of the large body on the other side of her bed. Leo radiated heat and she settled in against him comfortably and drifted more deeply into sleep.

Leo awoke to feel a small round rump tucked up against his side. And he had an erection.

Dammit! he thought. *What the hell does she think she's doing?*

He had left the window partially open and a stream of cold air was blowing into the room. Cautiously he raised himself on his elbow. Colette, sleeping at the bottom of the bed, must have felt him move for she lifted her head.

He had to get Gabrielle to move away from him. If he didn't, then he would end up grabbing her and pulling up her nightdress. Gritting his teeth, he put his hand between her shoulder blades and pushed lightly. Nothing. He pushed again. She stirred a little. He pushed a third time and she said foggily, "André?"

"No," he replied. "It's Leo. You're on my half of the bed."

"Oh," she said. "Oh!" She scrambled away from him as if he was on fire. "I'm sorry," she said in a mortified voice.

Colette stood up on the end of the bed, stretched and changed the side she was lying on.

"The room is cold and you were looking to get warm." He pushed back his covers and got out of bed. "I'll shut the window."

She didn't say anything.

He got back into the bed and turned on his side to hide his arousal with his back to her. "Good night," he said. He had to keep his knees drawn up because the damn dog took up the bottom half of the bed.

He had been far more comfortable bivouacking on the ground than he was in this bed. He was acutely conscious of her lying less than a foot away. He wanted nothing more than to bury himself in her and he was furious with himself for feeling that way.

"Good night," she answered in a small voice.

Colette sighed.

Shit, he thought. *I'm never going to get any sleep.*

He was right. It was almost dawn before he finally drifted off again.

Gabrielle awoke before Leo, dressed quickly and went downstairs to breakfast. She was embarrassed to meet him.

I was curled up next to him, just as if he were André. How could I have done that?

His explanation about the cold room made sense, but it didn't make her feel any better. *I should have made him sleep on the floor. Now I'll be afraid to sleep because it might happen again.*

Albert was at the table when she came down and she sent him upstairs to make sure that Leo was awake. The circus was leaving early, aiming for the outskirts of

Rouen before nightfall. They would be giving two shows in Rouen tomorrow.

"It's cold this morning," Paul groused as he drank his coffee.

"At least it's not raining," Sully said.

"Perhaps we should have waited another two weeks before starting out," Henri said. "It feels as if the winter is still hanging on."

"If we extend the season we extend our income," Gabrielle said practically. "And we're going south. The weather should get better."

By eight o'clock the circus was ready to leave. Gabrielle sent Albert to ride with Leo while she drove the hay wagon. She was still too embarrassed about last night.

The day was cold, but the sun was out and the rolling farmland they passed through had just been put under the plough. Gabrielle wore her divided skirt and high boots with a wool coat over them and periodically leaned around the wagon to check that the horses that were following behind were all right.

Her mind was preoccupied by Leo.

She had been so warm and cozy last night when she had been so abruptly awakened. How had she felt comfortable enough with him to allow herself to let down her guard like that?

I was asleep, she told herself. *I couldn't help it.*

Am I going to cuddle up to him like that every night?

He hadn't liked it. He had tried to push her away.

Perversely, Gabrielle was insulted. She was not a great femme fatale, but she certainly was not accustomed to men pushing her away. André had definitely liked it when she cuddled up to him.

I am just a circus girl and he is an aristocrat. He does not want me to get too close.

Well, that was fine with her. She had no intention of getting too close to Monsieur le Colonel.

Maybe I should put Colette between us.

She smiled at the thought of the big dog trying to share the bed with Leo. *I'll bet he's never slept with a dog before.*

Another thought popped into her head. *At least he didn't try to take advantage of me.*

She hadn't thought of it that way before. Another man might have taken her action as an invitation. Leo had recognized the inadvertence of her gesture and taken steps to preserve her chastity.

Maybe he isn't that bad, she thought. *Maybe he was just being a gentleman.*

By the time they stopped for lunch, she was feeling much more charitable to Leo than she had when they set out.

They were five miles outside of Rouen when they were stopped. A cordon of French soldiers, dressed in blue uniforms, stepped into the road to halt the wagons. Gabrielle, who was still driving the hay wagon, felt her heart leap into her throat.

Leo was with Albert in the first wagon!

Should she go to the front immediately, or would that look suspicious? Her heart was slamming in her chest as she watched one of the soldiers walk up to the lead wagon. He stood there, talking to Leo for a few minutes.

Why are they stopping us? Can they be looking for the gold?

She sat frozen, not knowing what to do.

Then Leo swung down from the wagon and accompanied the soldier past the first few wagons, coming to a halt next to her.

"Darling," Leo said, "this is Lieutenant Amboise. His orders are to search all traffic on this road." He turned toward the lieutenant. "The circus belongs to my wife's family. It has been in existence for more than twenty years."

The lieutenant was a middle-aged man with a great hook for a nose and a pair of cynical brown eyes. Gabrielle gave him a brilliant smile. He didn't move a muscle. She said, "What are you looking for, Lieutenant?"

"Gold," the lieutenant replied. "English gold." He stared pointedly at Leo.

"Goodness," Gabrielle said a little breathlessly. "I can assure you, Lieutenant, that we are not carrying any gold."

"We'll see about that for ourselves, *madame*," the lieutenant said. "Will you pull the wagons off the road into that field, please?"

"Is this really necessary?" Gabrielle asked.

"Yes," the lieutenant replied.

Gabrielle watched as Leo walked back to the first wagon and put his horses into motion. The whole circus train followed him into the unplowed field at the side of the road.

The cadre of six soldiers spread out among the wagons and the lieutenant stayed with Leo. Gabrielle jumped down from the hay wagon and went to the first wagon, where half of the gold was hidden. Leo had just opened the rear door when she got there. They all looked at Colette, who was lying on the sofa.

"My dog rides in this wagon," Gabrielle said, trying to keep her voice from trembling. "Here, Colette," she called, and Colette got up, stretched and came to Gabrielle, jumping down from the wagon with graceful ease.

"What's in all of those trunks?" the lieutenant asked.

"Costumes mostly," Gabrielle said.

"Open them up."

Gabrielle glanced at Leo.

"Do as he asks, darling," Leo said calmly. "I'll help you." They climbed into the wagon, followed by Colette and Albert. Then, under the watchful eye of the lieutenant, they opened all of the trunks and showed him the contents. It took a while. Finally the lieutenant was satisfied.

"Move the sofa," he said next.

Gabrielle's heart leaped. The loose floorboards were not directly under the sofa, they were just in front of it. "Help me," Leo said to Albert, and the two of them moved the sofa so that it was standing over the secret compartment. The lieutenant looked at the floor that had been exposed, squatted and tried to pry up a board or two. Gabrielle felt as if she might faint. At last the lieutenant looked up.

"All right," he said. "Let's look at the next wagon."

Mathieu was standing next to the second wagon. "What is going on?" he asked.

The lieutenant ignored him. Gabrielle said, "They are looking for English gold. I don't know why they think we might have it, but they are welcome to look." She looked at the lieutenant. "Although, I hope that you will go as fast as you can, Lieutenant. We are overdue to meet our advance man."

"We'll take as long as necessary," the lieutenant said gruffly. "Now, open the back of this wagon, *madame*."

The search of the second wagon was much the same as the first. This wagon held the tack used in the show—

saddle and bridle racks were lined up along the walls and horse blankets were packed into several trunks. Gabrielle and her brothers also kept their everyday clothes and their personal effects in this wagon. Albert's paintings were stacked against one of the blanket trunks.

One of Gabrielle's fears was that the boys would do something to give them away. Both Mathieu and Albert looked pale and she smiled at them reassuringly.

It was somehow degrading to see the lieutenant go through their personal belongings, and if Gabrielle had not been so scared she would have been furious.

The lieutenant checked the floorboards in this wagon as well, missing the loose boards by inches. All of the blood drained from Gabrielle's head when she saw how close he was.

"Steady," Leo said in a low, warning voice, placing a hand on the small of her back. She gulped for air.

The lieutenant finally stood. "*Ça va.* The next wagon now."

It took the soldiers almost an hour to go through all of the wagons. Gabrielle could see how angry the circus folk were at having to open up their trunks and boxes for the inspection of the army. The soldiers didn't give them time to put things back in order and the wagons ended up looking as if a hurricane had hit them.

Finally they were done. The lieutenant said to Gabrielle, "Isn't it a little early to be starting your season, *madame?*"

They were standing next to the first wagon, with Leo and Mathieu and Albert looking on. The rest of the soldiers had gone back to their posts on the road.

"The longer the season, the more the money, Lieutenant," Gabrielle said lightly.

"When did you say you married this Englishman?"

"Over the winter," Gabrielle said.

"In January?"

"It was February," Leo interjected pleasantly. "I had brought some sale horses to Brussells for a client. My wife was visiting the city and we met and fell in love."

"How charming," the lieutenant said sourly. "And you gave up your horse business to join the circus?"

"My wife owns the circus," Leo repeated. "Her livelihood was more lucrative than mine."

"And do you do anything for this circus?" the lieutenant asked.

Gabrielle said hastily, "He collects the ticket money and helps out with the horses."

The lieutenant eyed Leo. "You don't look like a groom, *monsieur.*"

"I do whatever Gabrielle needs me to do," Leo said. "And I fail to see why I am being subjected to this interrogation."

A trace of aristocratic hauteur colored Leo's words and Gabrielle sent him an urgent mental message. *Don't make this man any more suspicious than he already is, Leo! Keep your temper. Please, please keep your temper.*

The lieutenant said, "I just find it a rather too convenient a coincidence that an Englishman should be traveling with a French circus that is going in the direction of Spain."

"What is suspicious about traveling toward Spain? This is a route we have taken many times in years past, Lieutenant," she said indignantly. "You can ask anybody. Besides, you searched my wagons and didn't find anything. Surely you should be satisfied that we do not have what you are looking for."

The lieutenant looked at her. "I've done what I could do," he said. "But I shall be making my report, *madame.*

Good day to you both.'' And then he left the field, re-joining his men on the road.

When he was well out of earshot, Gabrielle said, ''What did he mean by that, that he would be making his report?''

''I think it means we are not out of the woods yet,'' Leo said soberly. ''And the first thing I am going to do is to nail down those loose boards in the wagons. If we have to use a crowbar to pry them up when we get to Biarritz, then that's what we'll do.''

''He just missed the loose board in the second wagon,'' Gabrielle said faintly.

''I know.'' Leo gestured for silence as several of the circus folk were walking toward them.

''That was outrageous,'' Gianni said. ''My wagon is a mess.''

''Mine, too,'' said Antonio. ''Doesn't the army have better things to do than to harass innocent citizens?''

''The fellow who searched my wagon said that the government found out that the English were trying to smuggle gold to Wellington in Portugal. I suppose they thought a circus was a clever way to transport it,'' Luc said.

''That's just stupid,'' Antonio said. ''The Cirque Equestre has been around for years. We are a respectable institution, not a den of smugglers!''

''That's right,'' Gianni agreed.

''Apparently the soldiers had never heard of us. Well, the search is over and they found nothing. Let's get on to our meeting with Vincent. We can tidy up the wagons once we're parked for the night.'' Gabrielle struggled to keep her voice confident.

The men agreed and began to move away. ''Albert,'' Gabrielle said. ''Will you drive the hay wagon? I want to ride with Leo.'' She was suddenly grateful for his presence.

"Certainly," Albert replied.

The boys went to their respective wagons and Leo put his hands around Gabrielle's waist and swung her to the wagon seat.

"Leo!" Her cheeks were flushed. "I told you I can get into the wagon unassisted."

"This way is faster." He climbed into the seat next to her and picked up the reins.

"This is terrible," Gabrielle said. She twisted her hands together in distress. "Nothing like this ever happened when Papa carried gold for Monsieur Rothschild."

"This is a very different mission," Leo said grimly.

"I didn't realize..." Her voice was breathless. "I wouldn't have taken the gold if I had known how dangerous it was going to be."

"Calm down," Leo said. "They didn't find it."

"They almost did! When I think how close they came..."

"When we're parked for the night, I'll nail those boards down," he said.

"And he was suspicious of you. I knew it was a mistake to send an Englishman with us! You are only calling attention to us."

"Next time don't leave me with only Albert in the front wagon and I won't have to talk and betray myself."

She threw him an annoyed look but didn't answer.

It will be all right, she told herself. *Don't get yourself into a panic, Gabrielle. Everything is going to be all right.*

Vincent was waiting for the wagons at the designated place and took them to a field some two miles from the city of Rouen. The wagons lined up on the field in the same order in which they had stood in Amiens and all of the circus folk jumped out. They were still buzzing about the roadblock.

"Why did that soldier stop us?" Henri asked.

Luc repeated what he had heard from his soldier, that they were looking for gold being smuggled to Wellington.

"And they thought we might be carrying it?" Carlotta was indignant. "Everyone knows the Cirque Equestre. It's ridiculous to suspect us of doing something illegal."

"That's what I told the lieutenant," Gabrielle said.

"Where did the gold come from?" Jeanne asked curiously.

Leo replied, "He didn't say. There must be quite of lot of it, though, if they have the army out looking for it."

He sounded indifferent and Gabrielle shot him a glance. There was nothing on his face or in his eyes to indicate he found the situation anything other than a nuisance.

"Well, we have better things to do than to stand here talking about stolen gold," she said. "Let's get the tents set up, yes? The sooner everything is settled here, the sooner we can find our hotel."

The crowd scattered as each person went about his or her accustomed task, leaving Gabrielle and Leo alone. They looked at each other.

"I don't like this," Gabrielle said.

"I don't like it, either," Leo agreed. "We're traveling the main road. We'll probably run into more roadblocks."

"We always travel the main road. It would look suspicious for us to deviate from that."

His golden brows drew together.

She said, "We play good-size cities and towns. We don't play villages."

"I'll nail down those loose boards," he said again. "There's little chance of a search party prying up the floorboards."

Gabrielle said, "I have been thinking, Leo, and I still think it would be a good idea for you to study what Gerard does as ringmaster."

"What?" He stared at her in astonishment, his thick hair blowing in the breeze.

She said, "If you were our ringmaster your presence with the circus would not be so odd," she explained. "A circus draws its performers from many countries. The Maronis are from Italy."

"You're mad if you think I'm going to perform in this circus," he said flatly. "That subject is closed."

But she persisted. "All the ringmaster has to do is announce the acts and keep Coco going around the ring while the boys perform."

"Gabrielle, I am not going to make a fool of myself with this circus. Period. I am disguised as your husband. That should be enough to satisfy any French inquiries."

"It didn't satisfy that lieutenant. He definitely found it suspicious that you were present and that the circus was traveling toward Spain. You would be much more explainable if you were part of the circus."

He continued to frown.

"I'm right, Leo. You know I'm right."

He thrust his hand through his hair, "What would the others think if you suddenly replaced Gerard?"

"Gerard took over the ringmaster job when Papa died because there was no one else. He's not very good—his voice isn't loud enough and he doesn't have the commanding presence Papa had. You would do a better job. Everyone will see that.''

''Won't Gerard be hurt if you take his job away from him? I thought you wanted to keep all your circus members happy.''

''Gerard knows about the gold. He will understand why we are making the change.''

''Then what will Gerard do?''

''What he used to do—help with the horses. He worked for Papa when he was the king's Master of the Horse and he's been with the circus ever since it was formed. He helped train all our horses. He and Papa created the act with the Arabians. He's also a very good vet.''

Leo stared off toward where the tents were being unloaded from the wagons. ''I swore I wouldn't get involved with this circus—'' he began.

''You *are* involved, Leo,'' she pointed out. ''I didn't ask for an English escort and now it's up to you not to endanger us.''

There was a long silence. Then he said grimly, ''I'll tell you what we'll do. If we meet any more French roadblocks, you can introduce me as your ringmaster. The search party will never know if I actually perform or not.''

''But suppose one of them comes to a performance?''

He struggled within himself for an answer. The last thing he wanted to do in all this world was to perform for a circus. He would have to clown with Sully. He shuddered at the thought.

On the other hand, that damn lieutenant had been suspicious of him. There was no denying that.

"All right," he said grimly. "I'll study Gerard and if we meet any more French roadblocks, and you have to introduce me as your ringmaster, I'll do the two shows the following day."

Fourteen

Gabrielle pulled Gerard aside before dinner that evening and explained what she was going to do about the ringmaster's job. "The army is looking for us, Gerard," she said. "I'm scared."

They were standing by themselves in the vestibule of their hotel. The others had gone into the dining room. It was already dark outside and the lamp on the hotel desk cast a faint glow into the corner where they were standing.

He patted her arm. "That search was enough to scare anyone," he said.

"It was always so easy when Papa transported gold for Monsieur Rothschild. We followed our usual schedule, we gave our shows, and when we reached our destination, the gold was unloaded and that was that. I never thought that this would be any different."

"If you remember, I advised you not to accept this mission," he reminded her.

"I know, but I wanted the money to send Albert to art school, so when they insisted on sending Leo along, I agreed. I knew that he was coming with us to keep me honest, and I thought he would just be a nuisance."

"It's a good idea to have him be the ringmaster." Gerard smiled wryly. "How does he feel about it?"

"He's not happy, but he'll do it if he has to."

"He's all right, Gabrielle? He's not...bothering...you at all?"

"He's a gentleman, Gerard. Everything is all right."

"Good. I was not in favor of this masquerade, you know."

"I know. I didn't like it, either, but I didn't want to turn down this job. First of all, I thought Papa would want me to do it, and then there was the money for Albert."

"Your father would never have sent Albert to art school."

"I know. But he should go."

"He has talent, but he is a very good rider as well."

"He'll never be a *great* rider, Gerard, and he may well be a great painter. And that's where his heart is. I have to give him the chance."

He kissed her hand. "You're a good girl, Gabrielle. But after this, let's not carry any more gold!"

"I couldn't agree more," she replied fervently. "We'd better go into dinner—the others will be wondering what we are doing."

There was a seat vacant next to Leo and Gabrielle went to take it. Gerard sat next to Emma.

Antonio said, "What were you two cooking up?"

Gabrielle said, "Leo is going to understudy Gerard."

There was a moment of silence at the table. Gabrielle saw Leo's hand tighten around his glass.

"Is Leo going to take over as ringmaster?" Franz finally asked.

"May I have some wine?" Gabrielle said to Leo. Then, to the rest of the table, "Eventually."

Jeanne said with a smile, "Leo will look magnificent in the ring."

Pierre scowled at her.

Leo poured Gabrielle her wine and said, "For now I am just going to learn the job by watching Gerard."

"You don't mind, Gerard?" Henri asked.

"Not at all. I am too old to be the ringmaster. Leo will do a better job."

Luc said, "He has an accent."

"He has a slight accent, but he is perfectly fluent," Gabrielle said. "His accent will not be a problem."

"I think you will make a fine ringmaster, Leo," Sully declared. "And you will like being more a part of the circus."

"Yes," Leo said expressionlessly. "That will be nice."

"We will have to get Leo a costume, Gabrielle," Emma said.

Leo took a long drink of his wine.

"Yes. He will need a red huntsman's jacket and a top hat. He already has breeches and boots."

Emma said, "We'll go shopping in between shows tomorrow in Rouen."

"Good idea," Gabrielle said.

Leo drank some more wine.

How the hell did I get into this? Leo thought as he listened to Gabrielle and Emma talk. *I swore I wouldn't perform, and now here I am, auditioning for the role of ringmaster! Well, I'm not going to do it unless I feel the French are breathing down our necks.*

He wished he had Herries and Rothschild in front of him right now. He would give them a piece of his mind.

The only positive side to this new role of his was that it had evidently made Luc very unhappy. He sat scowling over his dinner, shooting dark, brooding glances at Gabrielle.

Leo was glad that Luc was unhappy. He did not like Luc. He did not like the way Luc continued to badger Gabrielle despite knowing she was a married woman and off limits.

Leo was grateful when Gerard changed the subject. "When those soldiers stopped us this afternoon I was afraid they might be looking to conscript for the army." The men began to complain about Napoléon's new drive to fill up his devastated ranks.

As soon as dinner was over, Leo excused himself and went out to the stable yard behind the hotel, where the wagons carrying the gold were parked. They looked completely undisturbed as they sat there in the dark. He would come back later, when everyone was in bed, and nail down those damn floorboards.

When he got back inside the circus party had moved from the dining room into the salon. When he appeared they were discussing what they would do with the rest of the evening.

"How about a game of chess?" Leo said to Mathieu.

Mathieu smiled. "Good—a challenge. Albert is too easy."

"Everyone is too easy for you," Albert said.

Mathieu said, "You would always rather draw than play chess, anyway."

"That's true. And I think I'll draw you and Leo while you play." Albert looked at Leo. "You won't mind, Leo?"

"Not at all."

"Come to the café with us, Gabrielle," Luc said. "There's nothing going on here for you."

"You can keep us company while we play," Leo said, wanting Gabrielle to keep away from Luc.

Gabrielle hesitated and glanced at Sully. "I think I will go to the café, Leo," she said.

Luc threw Leo a triumphant look. Leo was conscious of a desire to punch him in the nose.

After the café party had left, Leo realized that this would be a good time to work on the wagons. He told the boys what he was going to do and they offered to post themselves at the hotel's back door and intercept anyone who might be going into the stable yard.

It took Leo five minutes to hammer down the loose boards in both wagons, then he rejoined the boys and they went back into the salon. They set the chessboard up in front of the fireplace and Leo and Mathieu began to play.

At first Leo moved his pieces automatically, his mind on Gabrielle. About ten minutes into the game, when he lost a knight, he realized that Mathieu was not just a good player; he was a *very* good player. Leo began to pay attention to what he was doing.

They played for an hour, both of them absorbed in each move. It ended with Mathieu winning.

"Where did you learn to play chess like that?" Leo demanded as he watched Mathieu gather the pieces together.

"My papa was a very good player. We used to play all the time."

"Don't feel bad, Leo," Albert said. "He beats me all the time—and he gives me a handicap of two knights and a bishop!"

"This was fun," Mathieu said. "I haven't had a challenge like that since Papa died."

"Did you beat your father, too?" Leo asked.

"I started to beat him when I was fourteen," Mathieu said.

"Well, I am impressed," Leo said. "I must confess I never expected to lose."

Mathieu grinned. "I know."

He looked so like his sister when he smiled like that. Leo looked at the clock and said, "I think I will walk down to the café and see what's going on."

"They'll only be drinking wine and talking," Albert said. "That's what they always do."

"You don't sound very interested," Leo said.

"Oh, it's fine. But an evening like this is nicer. For a little while it was like Papa was back with us."

"Didn't your papa go to the café?"

"Sometimes he did. But he would stay with us most of the time, playing chess with Mathieu while I drew. Like tonight."

Leo asked curiously, "And what did Gabrielle do?"

"André always wanted to go to the café, so she would go with him."

"And before she married?"

"She would work on her book."

Leo looked from Albert to Mathieu. "Book? What book?"

"She wrote a book about Papa's training methods. He would work on it with her."

"What happened to this book? Did they finish it?"

"Oh, yes."

"And was it ever published?"

"No." Albert looked at Mathieu.

Mathieu said, "Papa always meant to take it to a publishing house in Paris, but he never got around to it. I think he was a little afraid to call attention to himself. Gabrielle said he was scarred by the Revolution."

"I would like to read it," Leo said.

"Gabrielle must have it somewhere," Mathieu said. "Ask her about it."

"I will."

Leo stood up. "Where is this café? Do you know? Is it one you went to last year?"

"It's one street down," Mathieu said. "Do you want me to go with you to show you?"

"That won't be necessary. I'll find it," Leo returned.

He left the two boys behind in the warmth of the salon and went out into the chilly night. The circus folk had pushed several tables together in the café and were laughing over something when he came in. He frowned as he noticed that Gabrielle was sitting next to Luc. As he stood in the door, Luc leaned over and said something into her ear and she turned to him with a smile on her face.

Leo stepped into the light of the café.

Jeanne saw him first. "Leo! How nice to see you. Bring a chair over and join us."

Leo forced himself to smile. "Thanks, I will."

Gabrielle looked at him. "How did the chess game go?"

"I lost," he said.

She gave him her wonderful smile. "Mathieu is a brilliant chess player. Papa used to say that if he could play chess for money he would be rich."

Leo brought a chair to the tables. Unfortunately there was no room next to Gabrielle and he was forced to place his chair next to Jeanne. She gave him a long look from her slanting black eyes and said, "Are you a good chess player, Leo?"

"I thought I was," Leo said.

"You have to be smart to play chess," Jeanne said admiringly.

"Mathieu must be a genius, then," Leo said.

"Mathieu is very smart," Gabrielle said. "He is particularly good at mathematics."

A boy like that should be in school, not traveling around with a circus, Leo thought.

"Are you good at mathematics, Leo?" Jeanne asked.

"Who cares what he's good at?" Pierre said harshly.

Gabrielle said quietly, "Jeanne was just asking a question, Pierre."

Pierre glowered at Gabrielle but didn't reply.

Leo said, "I have a feeling I'm not as good as Mathieu."

Emma changed the subject. "What do you think the weather is going to be like tomorrow, Sully?"

"Like today, I think," Sully said. "Clear but cold."

"Sully is our weatherman," Emma explained. "I don't know how he does it, but he always seems to know what's going to happen next."

"I feel it in my bones," Sully said.

Luc whispered something to Gabrielle and she nodded.

Leo frowned. "Are you ready to leave, Gabrielle?" he asked.

"But you haven't had anything to drink, Leo," Jeanne pointed out.

"I don't want anything," Leo said.

Gabrielle said, "It is getting late. Why don't you come back to the hotel with us, Sully?"

Sully gave her a sad smile. "Don't you trust me, Gabrielle?"

"It's not that. I just thought you might be ready to leave."

"Go along with her, Sully," Henri said. "You don't need another drink."

Sully sighed. "Oh, very well." He stood up. "Let's go, Gabrielle."

Leo stood up and Gabrielle followed. They all said their good-nights and exited out into the cold, dark street. Colette went with them.

"How do you know I don't have a bottle in my room?" Sully asked as they walked back toward the hotel.

Gabrielle's head whipped around. "Do you?"

"Not at the moment," Sully replied.

Leo said, "She's made herself vulnerable, bringing you back this year, Sully. Don't let her down by getting drunk again."

Sully was silent.

"Did you hear me?" Leo asked.

"Yes, I did. And I have told Gabrielle that I will try to stay sober."

"Everyone has something to be sad about," Leo said. "We have to learn to live with it."

"It's not always that easy," Sully said.

"I didn't say it was easy. I just said it had to be done."

Gabrielle went to peek into the salon when they reached the hotel, but Mathieu and Albert had gone to bed. Leo and Gabrielle said good-night to Sully in the lobby and went up the stairs to their bedroom.

"You could have been more sympathetic," Gabrielle said accusingly as soon as the door had closed behind them. "Poor Sully. He was devastated when his daughter died."

"Your husband died, but you didn't become a drunk," Leo said.

"I'm young. It's easier for the young to recover from a tragedy."

"I don't think it's good for the circus to have a drunk traveling with it," Leo said.

"I don't like drunks, either, but this is Sully. We should be trying to help him, not blame him."

"You won't help him by sympathizing with him," Leo said.

"Goodness," Gabrielle exclaimed. "I certainly wouldn't want to do anything to disappoint you. You're very unforgiving."

Leo froze. "What do you mean by that?"

She looked at him for a moment in silence. "I'm sorry. I didn't mean to say anything to hurt you."

"You didn't hurt me," he said coldly.

"Well, I think you're being too hard on poor Sully."

He said tensely, "You're the one who's worried he will have a bad effect on the rest of the circus members."

She waved her hand in dismissal. "Let's not talk about it anymore." She went to sit in the chair that was in front of the fireplace. "Do you think Jeanne was flirting with you tonight?"

He remained standing. "Why?"

"Pierre gets upset when she talks to other men, and I was just wondering if her conversation was innocent or if she was really flirting. What did you think?"

"I don't know," he said impatiently. "I wasn't paying much attention to her."

She rested her hands on the arms of the chair. "I should think you'd know if someone was flirting with you or not!"

"I know that Luc was flirting with you," he replied. "And I must say it doesn't do my ego any good to have my supposed wife flirting with another man. You might have some consideration for me, I think."

She glared at him. "I was not flirting with Luc!"

He walked over to the fireplace and leaned his shoulders against the wall next to it. "He was whispering in your ear."

"That's not flirting."

He arched his eyebrows skeptically. "Obviously you don't know what flirting is, then. Well, clearly you don't. You had to ask me if Jeanne was flirting with me."

"Well, you didn't know, either!"

They glared at each other. Colette came over to push her head into Gabrielle's lap. Gabrielle petted her and said, "It's all right, girl. No one is yelling at you."

"I was not yelling," Leo said.

"You scared Colette."

He took a step away from the wall. "I meant what I said, Gabrielle. I don't like the way Luc monopolizes you. What must the others think of me that I allow it?"

"What do you care what a bunch of circus folk think of you?" she shot back. "You're an aristocrat. We should feel lucky that you notice us at all."

This was so exactly what he had thought himself that he didn't know what to say. Then he was furious that she had read him so clearly.

He glared at her. She looked so lovely as she sat there, petting her dog. Her cheeks were flushed and her great brown eyes were sparkling with temper.

Why the hell does she have to be so damn pretty?

"If that's what you think of me, then I have nothing more to say to you," he said stiffly.

"It's just as well we stop talking, because you are making me angry," she replied.

He turned away and went to open the window.

"It's cold in here. We don't need the window opened," she said.

He replied over his shoulder, ''I always sleep with an opened window. It's healthy.''

''You didn't like what happened last night when I got cold in bed,'' she said sweetly. ''If you don't want a repetition of that incident, then I suggest you leave the window closed.''

He couldn't seem to win an argument with her. ''Fine,'' he said through his teeth, and slammed the window shut.

''Get your nightclothes and we'll get undressed,'' she said. Then, to the dog, ''Get up on the bed, Colette. It's time to go to sleep.''

''Can't that dog sleep on the floor?'' Leo asked. ''I have no room for my feet.''

''You're lucky *you're* not sleeping on the floor,'' she retorted.

''Did she sleep with you and your husband?'' he asked.

Gabrielle hesitated.

''Ha,'' he said. ''She didn't.''

''You're *not* my husband,'' she pointed out. ''I very nicely offered to let you share the bed with me. You're just going to have to put up with Colette!''

With that, they turned their backs on each other and proceeded to get into their nightclothes.

Fifteen

The bed felt very crowded. Between the bulk of Leo on one side and Colette at the bottom, Gabrielle felt as if there was no room left for her.

It didn't seem so crowded the first time we did this, she thought. *I wonder if this bed is smaller than the one in Amiens.*

It had looked the same size; this just felt smaller.

Leo was lying on his side, with his back turned to her. It was a nice, broad back and it radiated heat. *It would be lovely to cuddle up against that back,* she thought.

He would probably have a heart attack if I did that.

André had not had a back like that. André had been much slimmer than Leo. He had not taken up so much of the bed.

How dare Leo accuse her of flirting with Luc? It wasn't true. She was simply trying to be nice to Luc. She didn't want him quitting the circus in a fit of jealous temper. That would leave her in the lurch in regard to an equestrian. They had been tremendously lucky to pick up Luc so soon after André had died.

What will Luc say when he finds out that I wasn't married to Leo after all? How am I going to explain to the rest of them that Leo and I were only pretending to be married?

It hadn't seemed to be a big problem when she had

first agreed to the masquerade. She had thought she would confess to the rest of them that she had been carrying gold for Monsieur Rothschild and that Leo had been sent along as Monsieur Rothschild's representative.

But now the French army was involved.

She could be regarded as a traitor. Traitors were guillotined.

Gabrielle shivered and curled herself into a ball. *I was a fool to take on this responsibility. And now I am stuck with it.*

Perhaps Leo and I can pretend to have a fight and separate over it. Then no one will have to know that we were never married.

Restlessly, she shifted position.

"What's the matter?" Leo said out loud. "Can't you sleep?"

"I'm worried," she confided. "I wish I had never agreed to take this gold. If I am caught with it, I could be executed!"

He turned around so that he was facing her. He raised himself up on his elbow. The curtains that covered the window were thin and the moonlight shone through them, lighting the room. "Nobody is going to execute you," he said. "The gold is well hidden, Gabrielle. I nailed those boards down tonight. Even if the wagons are searched, they're not going to find the gold."

"You can't be sure of that. If they get suspicious enough, they might tear up the floorboards in our wagons."

"I don't think that will happen."

She let out a long, uneven breath. "I didn't think this through. All I saw was that Papa had carried gold before and that I would get money for Albert. I didn't realize that this was a very different kind of mission from the ones that Papa had taken on.''

He didn't say anything, just gazed down into her face.

"How are the English going to get the gold out of my wagons?" she asked.

"Don't worry. They'll do it in secret."

"That might not be so easy."

"They'll manage it. Don't worry," he said again.

"How can I help but worry? Then, on top of everything else, I have you accusing me of flirting with Luc!"

There was a moment of silence. Then he said, "Where did that come from?"

"From you. You said I was flirting with Luc. I don't flirt with people, Leo. I am simply trying to be nice to Luc so he won't get into a temper and leave the circus."

"Do you need him so much? Can't Mathieu and Albert take his place?"

"They are not as accomplished with tricks as he is."

She heard him sigh.

"It may not be important to you," she continued. "You are only with us for a month and then you will leave and go back to your own life. This *is* my life and I have to protect it. And I am not doing a very good job of that so far."

"You're doing fine," he said.

To her horror, she felt tears fill her eyes. Furiously, she blinked them back. She wanted to throw herself into his arms and have him hold her and comfort her. But all he would do would be to stiffen up against her, like he did this morning.

"That's what you think," she muttered.

"The circus members clearly hold you in great respect," he said. "No one is challenging your authority.

It seems to me that you are doing very well—you could be one of my captains any day.''

She gave a watery chuckle.

"Let me worry about the gold," he repeated. "That's what I'm here for. You concentrate on your circus."

She said in a small voice, "If you are caught with the gold you could be executed as a spy."

"What cheerful thoughts you are thinking," he said. "I think we have done a few things to shore up our situation in case we are stopped again. I will now be part of the circus, and thus less suspicious. And the gold is now better secured. No one is going to pull up those floorboards unless they have solid information against us."

She thought about that for a while. "You're right," she said at last. "I'll try to stop worrying."

"Good. Now, go to sleep or you won't be worth anything in the morning."

She cuddled down under her blankets. Colette felt nice and warm against her bare feet. "All right. And—thank you, Leo."

"You're welcome. Good night." He turned over and once more presented her with his back.

As Leo collected money for tickets the following morning, he noticed that Franz was deep in conversation with Jeanne in front of the rope walkers' wagon. As he watched, they were joined by Henri and Carlotta. After a few minutes' conversation, Jeanne walked away, toward the bandwagon where the Laurent brothers were shining their instruments. There was no sign of Jeanne's husband, Pierre.

Leo remembered Gabrielle's question about whether or not Jeanne had been flirting with him. He thought she had been, but he hadn't wanted to say so to Gabrielle. She had enough on her mind without having to worry about the love life of her employees.

Leo watched the show and grudgingly tried to memorize Gerard's act. He clenched his jaw as he watched Gerard chase Sully away from the tightrope on which he had just tried to hang washing.

Maybe I won't have to do this, he thought grimly. *Maybe we won't be stopped by any more roadblocks.*

But in his heart he knew that would happen. He knew the French would have the roads south covered and were going to be stopping any convoy as large as the circus.

He thought of what Gabrielle had said last night. *She's right. I'm an army officer out of uniform. If I'm caught carrying this gold I could be executed as a spy.*

On that cheerful thought he returned his attention to the ring, where Carlotta and Henri and Franz were dancing high above the ground on their tightropes.

Leo was seated with the band, and, as the rope dancers went out, he saw Franz wink at Jeanne, who was playing the horn. Leo's eyes went immediately to Pierre, but he was staring straight ahead and didn't appear to have noticed anything.

Leo frowned. Gabrielle didn't need a straying wife making trouble in her circus.

After the show was over, Gabrielle came to find him. The afternoon sun had warmed the air and she had changed into her blue skirt and jacket.

"Leo," she said, "I want you to come into town with me so we can get you a ringmaster costume."

He closed his eyes, then opened them again. "Is that really necessary?"

Her huge brown eyes regarded him with disfavor. "I thought we had been through all of this. Yes, if we are stopped again and questioned, we are going to introduce you as our ringmaster. You were supposed to be watching Gerard today to study the part.''

"I know. I did.'' A muscle twitched in his jaw. "I don't want to do this, Gabrielle.''

"I don't care what you want!'' she snapped. "All I care about is being safe. I thought we discussed all of this, Leo! You said you would do it.''

He could feel himself freezing up. "All right. I said I would do it and I will.''

She gave him a beautiful smile, which he did not respond to. "It will only be for a little while and then you can go away and forget all about us.''

He thought grimly that being a ringmaster in a circus was not something he'd ever forget.

"We'll have to take one of our wagons,'' she said.

He frowned. "I suppose the gold should be safe on the streets of Rouen.''

"Good,'' she said. "Come along, then. We have to be back in time for the second show.''

The first store they went into was a men's store in a narrow cobbled street not far from the cathedral. Leo left the wagon with Tonton and Jacques tied to a hitching post and they went into the store.

"May I help you, *monsieur?*'' the clerk said as he came up to them.

Leo was looking around the shop with disdain. "My husband is looking for a red hunting jacket, and we need it right away,'' Gabrielle told the clerk.

The clerk looked at Leo. "*Monsieur* is very large.''

"I know,'' Gabrielle said. "Do you have anything that you could alter to fit him?''

"I am afraid not, *madame*. I do very little business in

hunting jackets. You might try Flaubert's, which is just down the street. They cater more to that type of people.''

"What 'type of people' does he mean?" Leo asked as they exited the store.

"Rich people," Gabrielle said succinctly. "Only the rich can afford to chase around after poor little foxes."

They began to walk down the street toward the other shop.

"Those 'poor little foxes' are vermin who destroy crops," Leo retorted.

"Think of how he must feel," Gabrielle said. "A little fox, out on the land, happily going about being a fox, when all of a sudden he is attacked by a huge band of dogs, all baying at him, followed by all of these humans crashing after him on big horses. It doesn't seem fair to me."

Leo, who had hunted since he was ten, and who loved it, said, "You're being silly and sentimental."

"I am simply seeing things from the viewpoint of the fox," she said. "If everyone in the world was able to see things from the viewpoint of others, the world would be a much happier place to live in."

He had never thought such a thing before. He said slowly, "But if one always saw both sides of things, it would be impossible to act."

"That might not be a bad thing," she said. "There would certainly be fewer wars."

He looked at her. "Is this your own viewpoint or was it your father's?"

"It's mine," she said. "It seems to me that there is very little reverence for life in our world. When a half a million men can be killed in one military campaign—well, I think that's mad."

"I don't disagree with you," he said. "But that's very different from a fox."

"Reverence for life is reverence for life," she said. "It's one thing to kill an animal because you need to eat—that I understand. Animals kill one another in order to eat. But for sport? That is something different."

Leo searched for something to reply. He didn't agree with her about foxhunting, but he couldn't come up with an acceptable reason except that it was great fun. He didn't think she would be impressed by such an answer.

He looked down at the girl beside him. She was an interesting person, this girl. She was nothing at all like the carefully nurtured, hothouse flowers he had known in England. She had deeply felt opinions. She thought about things.

She lives in the real world, he thought.

Interesting that he would think such a thing about a girl who ran a circus.

They arrived in front of Flaubert's and went in.

Once more a clerk came to greet them and once more Gabrielle announced that they were in search of a hunt coat that would fit Leo.

This time they were lucky.

"I have such a coat that was made for one of our local landowners. He was a big—" the clerk gestured to indicate that he meant fat "—gentleman. Unfortunately, he died of a heart attack before he could claim the coat. We could try it."

"Good," said Gabrielle.

Leo looked around the shop as they waited for the coat to be brought. It looked marginally more prosperous than the previous shop.

Gabrielle said, "I hope it won't bring you bad luck, wearing the coat of a man who died."

He looked at her. "I'm so glad you brought that up."

The clerk came out with the coat and Leo tried it on. It was a little tight in the shoulders and quite large in the stomach.

"Can you fix it?" Gabrielle said. "If you can have it ready by tomorrow afternoon, I will pay you double."

The clerk looked at her curiously. "You do realize that hunting season is over, *madame?*"

Gabrielle gave him a sunny smile. "My husband is the ringmaster for our circus, the Cirque Equestre," she said. "His old coat was stained when paint fell on it and we need a new one quickly."

The clerk smiled back delightedly. It was amazing what she could accomplish with that smile of hers, Leo thought sourly.

"Oh, the circus!" the clerk said. "But of course, *madame.* We will have the coat ready for you tomorrow afternoon. It is just a matter of a little taking in and a little letting out."

"Thank you so much," Gabrielle said. Then, to Leo, "We had better be going or we'll be late for the second show."

The clerk bowed her out of the store as if she was royalty.

Once on the street, they looked toward where their wagon was parked. Gabrielle gasped.

The wagon was gone.

Sixteen

"**J**esus Christ," Leo said. It was more a prayer than an expletive.

"*Mon Dieu,*" said Gabrielle. "What has happened?"

"Someone has made off with the wagon," Leo said grimly.

Gabrielle grabbed his arm. "But who would have taken it? *Mon Dieu,* Leo, this is terrible!"

He struggled for composure. "Whoever has it can't have gotten far. We were only in that store for fifteen minutes."

"What should we do?" she asked fearfully.

"Find out who the authorities are in this town." He pulled away from her and went back into the shop. When he came out, the proprietor was with him.

"The gendarmes are four blocks from here," Leo said. "Let's go."

"We have been having some problems with mischief-making," the proprietor informed them. "Yours is not the first wagon to be taken."

"Did they get the other wagons back?" Gabrielle asked.

"Yes. The thieves go for a ride and then leave them. It's probably a group of boys. The gendarmes have been trying to catch them, but to no avail. Perhaps they will catch the ones who stole your wagon."

"I hope so," Gabrielle said, then ran after Leo, who had already started off.

Leo walked the four blocks to the gendarmes' station and Gabrielle skipped and ran next to him, trying to keep up. The station looked like a shop front and they entered to find a room with four different-size desks. Two of the desks were occupied. Leo approached the man who was closest to the door, "We have come to report a theft."

Both gendarmes looked up.

"What kind of a theft?" the one Leo had addressed asked.

Leo and Gabrielle moved to stand in front of his desk. "My wagon has been stolen," Leo said. "We are from the Cirque Equestre and it's a circus wagon. It has a picture of two horses painted on its side."

The gendarme rolled his eyes. "Just the kind of wagon our unknown ruffians would like."

"We have to get it back," Gabrielle said tensely. "It has our...*costumes* in it." She looked up at Leo. "Thank God I left Colette back at the circus."

He nodded, then said to the two men, "I understand you have had this problem before. Where do these wagons generally end up?"

The second gendarme answered, "Usually right here in town somewhere. The boys who steal them are evidently from Rouen."

"How do you know the thieves are boys?" Leo asked.

The gendarme shrugged his shoulders. "It's the sort of prank a boy would play. Let me assure you, *monsieur,* that none of the wagons or horses have been harmed. The thieves just take them for a little ride."

Gabrielle said urgently, "How long before you find them? I have a show starting in a little more than an hour."

"Sometimes we don't find them for a day or so, *madame*. But yours is a distinctive wagon. Perhaps someone will report it to us sooner."

"Listen, Gabrielle," Leo said. "I think you should go back to the circus. You have to perform. I will stay here at the station and wait for word on the wagon."

She pressed her lips together. She didn't want to leave, but she saw the sense of his words. "All right," she said reluctantly. "But how am I going to get out to the circus without a wagon?"

"We'll hire something for you." Leo turned back to the gendarmes. "Is there a livery stable nearby?"

He got directions to the stable, then he and Gabrielle left the station together.

"*Mon Dieu,* Leo," she said as they walked down the pavement. "This is just terrible."

"It's not good," he agreed, "but it could be worse. If this is just a youngster's trick, we should get the wagon back unharmed."

She shivered. "The thought of all that gold in the clutches of a group of silly boys—it makes my blood run cold."

"Mmm," he said.

"You don't think they would pull up the floorboards?" she asked anxiously.

"Why should they do that?"

She didn't answer.

"You have more chance of your costumes being pawed through," he said.

"My poor horses," she said. "If they hurt Jacques or Tonton, I will kill them."

"Is your costume in the wagon?"

"No. I hung it next to my saddle after the first show."

"Good. Then you can carry on."

"Leo," Gabrielle said urgently. "What if we don't get the wagon back? The gold—"

"We will get it back. It is very distinctive." He stopped and looked across the street. "There is the stable. Come along and we'll rent you a carriage."

Gabrielle drove back to the circus, her mind in a whirl, her stomach in a knot. She managed to get through the show, checking between each of her acts to see if Leo had returned. By the time the show was over, there was still no sign of him.

She had told the rest of the circus members about the wagon, and the small group of people who knew about the gold were worried sick. Leo had still not returned by the time all the animals had been fed and watered. Gabrielle said they should go to the hotel and hope that Leo was waiting for them there.

There was no Leo at the hotel. Gabrielle couldn't eat a bite of her dinner, and after the meal was over, she asked Mathieu and Albert to go with her to return the carriage to the livery stable. "Then we can walk over to the gendarmes' office," she said.

None of the Robichons spoke as Gabrielle drove the carriage back to the livery stable. Albert and Mathieu flanked their sister as they walked the five blocks to the gendarmes' office.

They found Leo sitting at one of the desks drinking coffee. He was alone.

"They haven't found it?" Gabrielle asked when she saw him. His hair was mussed, as if he had run his fingers through it, and the top of his shirt was open as if he was warm.

"Not yet," he said. "What are you doing here?"

"I came to find out about the wagon, of course," she answered impatiently.

"You shouldn't be walking around the streets of Rouen after dark."

"I had Mathieu and Albert with me," she said.

Leo didn't look as if that answer satisfied him.

Mathieu said, "I always carry a knife with me when I go out at night. Papa taught me how to use it."

Leo raised an eyebrow. "I seem to have underrated you, Mathieu."

"I can take care of Gabrielle," her brother said.

"Where are the gendarmes?" Gabrielle asked.

"Out looking for the wagon. I told them I would give a reward to the person who finds it. It was amazing how motivated they became."

"This is scary," Albert said. "What if they don't find it?"

"They will," Leo said positively. "They have had this kind of thing happen before, and the wagon has always turned up."

"How long did it take to find those wagons?" Mathieu asked.

A muscle twitched in Leo's jaw, showing that he was not as complacent as he sounded. "Usually only a day or so."

Gabrielle shivered. "We have a schedule to keep, Leo. Not just our performances but also the drop-off—"

"I know that," he said angrily. "That is why I posted the reward. Someone will find it, Gabrielle. I am certain of that. And there is no point in all of us missing a night's sleep. Go back to the hotel with the boys and try to get some rest. I will wait here for news."

"I won't sleep a wink," she said.

"Curl up with Colette and try," he said.

She looked around the room, which was dark and

dingy. "I hate to leave you here by yourself. I am responsible for the gold as well as you."

"I'm the one who was sent along to protect it, and I'm the one who lost it. I'll wait here, and you go back to the hotel."

"Leo is right," Mathieu said. "You can't do anything, Gabrielle. Let Leo wait. He will tell us as soon as he has news, won't you, Leo?"

"Yes."

"Well…all right." Gabrielle let herself be persuaded. She looked back once, as Mathieu held the door for her to leave, and Leo was watching her.

"It will be all right," he assured her.

She nodded and went through the door and into the street.

Gabrielle got into bed with Colette and looked at the empty side of the mattress.

I should take advantage of the blessing of having my bed to myself, she thought.

But her stomach was in a knot about the lost wagon. *What if the boys crashed it?* she thought. *What if the false bottom is smashed and the bags of gold fall out?*

Father in heaven, she prayed, *please bring the wagon back to us safely. I have put my whole circus in danger with my foolish decision to take the gold. If you will grant us a safe journey, I will never do anything so stupid again.*

The pillow was cool under her cheek and she rubbed her cold bare feet against the warmth of Colette. It was a long time before she finally fell asleep.

She remembered the lost wagon the moment she opened her eyes the following morning. As soon as she saw that Leo was not in the bed, she knew that the wagon had not been recovered.

She got out of bed and took Colette down to the stable yard, then brought her back into the kitchen to feed her. The dog followed her into the dining room as she went to get her own breakfast. The Martins were the only ones in the room and Gabrielle went to join them.

"Did the wagon turn up last night?" Henri asked Gabrielle.

"Not yet. Leo is waiting for news at the gendarmes' station."

"You must be worried about your horses," Franz said sympathetically.

"Yes," Gabrielle returned. She didn't want to talk about the theft, so she concentrated on eating her eggs.

After a few moments of silence Henri said to his brother, "You were paying particular attention to Jeanne at the café last night. If I were you, I would stay away from her. Pierre is jealous."

"All I've ever done is talk to the girl," Franz protested. "A little feminine conversation is nice. There are too many men in this circus."

"She is flirting with you," Carlotta said. "Henri is right. I don't like the way Pierre looks at you. Remember, she is a married woman."

"Well, she can't be a very happily married woman if she is flirting with other men only a few months into her marriage," Franz retorted.

Henri said, "It's none of your business whether she is happy or not. Stay away from her, Franz. She's trouble."

"She seeks me out," Franz said. "I can't be rude."

"You don't have to be rude," Henri said. "Just tell her that your friendship is disturbing Pierre and you think it would be best if she didn't talk to you anymore."

Gabrielle looked up from her eggs. "It's going to be difficult if we try to stop Jeanne from talking to any of the men in the circus."

"She's a troublemaker," Carlotta said. "I've seen her type before. Why ever did Pierre have to marry someone like that?"

Gabrielle felt a flash of conscience. "Perhaps we're misjudging her. Perhaps she is only trying to make friends."

"Hah," said Carlotta. "Has she tried to make a friend of you or me or Emma? You would think that she would try to be friendly to the only other women in the circus, but she has hardly given me any time at all."

"Actually, she has never said very much to me, either," Gabrielle admitted.

"You see?" Carlotta said to Franz. "We have never had division in this circus before. Don't be the one to bring it on us."

"I think you're all overreacting," Franz said. He stood up. "When are we leaving?" he asked Henri.

"In about fifteen minutes," he said.

Franz left and the three remaining at the table looked at one another. Gabrielle said, "Do you really think this is a problem?"

"You weren't at the café last night," Carlotta said. "Jeanne ignored Pierre and talked to Franz for most of the night. Pierre looked like thunder."

"What is wrong with that girl?" Gabrielle asked impatiently. She didn't have time for Jeanne with the worry about the stolen wagon on her mind.

Henri said grimly, "I don't know what's going on between her and Pierre, but I wish she wasn't involving my brother."

"I don't understand Franz," Carlotta said. "He is usually very sensible."

Henri said, "Jeanne is a very sensual woman. I can see how she could make a man forget his common sense."

The two women stared at him.

"What do you mean, she is a very sensual woman?" Carlotta asked. Her blue eyes were steely. "How would you know?"

"There's something about her," Henri replied. "Ask any man and he would tell you the same thing. Maybe it's those slanting eyes. But the fact of the matter is, she projects sensuality. And she's got her claws into my brother."

"I'll talk to Jeanne," Gabrielle said. "Perhaps I can make her see that she is causing trouble." She remembered how Jeanne had flirted with Leo. Did he find her sensual? Gabrielle wondered.

Carlotta rolled her blue eyes. "Good luck."

Gabrielle got to her feet. "I think I will walk over to the gendarmes' station and see how the search is coming along."

"It's still early," Henri said. "Take Mathieu with you."

"I'll take Colette," Gabrielle said. "She's big enough to be protection."

She excused herself from the table and went upstairs to put on her wool pelisse. Then she buckled Colette on a lead and the two of them went out into the cold, clear morning.

It was a twenty-minute walk to the gendarmes' station and the narrow streets of Rouen were crowded with farm wagons making deliveries to the various restaurants and greengrocers along the way. Gabrielle crossed the last street between a vegetable wagon and an ice wagon. The door into the station was unlocked and she pushed it open. Leo was sitting at the front desk, his eyes on the door as it opened.

"Nothing yet?" she asked him.

"No."

"*Mon Dieu,* Leo, what are we going to do?" she whispered. "I have been thinking—what if the boys overturned the wagon and the false bottom broke? The bags of gold would come tumbling out and we would be caught."

There was a thread of hysteria in her unusually high voice, and he got up from his chair and came to put an arm around her and pat her shoulder. "It's going to be all right, Gabrielle. I will stay here in Rouen until the wagon is recovered. I may have to catch up with you in Alençon, but that won't be a problem. You're scheduled to be there for two days."

She rested her head against his shoulder and closed her eyes. He sounded so calm. She leaned against him and tried to absorb some of that calm. "Do you really think it will be all right?"

"I do."

He sounded very positive and Gabrielle found herself feeling better.

It was a good thing she didn't see the bleak look in his eyes.

"Have you had breakfast?" she asked, opening her own eyes.

"Not yet."

"Then let me stay here and you go to the hotel for something to eat. You've been up all night. You must be exhausted."

"Don't worry about me, I'm fine. I'll get something

from one of the shops around here. You need to get out to the circus grounds and prepare the horses for the first show.''

His arm was still around her and she closed her eyes again. He was so big. He made her feel that everything would be all right. He made her feel safe.

At that moment a man burst through the door that Gabrielle had closed behind her. Leo dropped his arm.

''Monsieur,'' the man said loudly, ''we have found your wagon!''

''Oh, thank God,'' Gabrielle cried.

Leo turned to face the gendarme who was standing in the door. ''Where is it?''

''It was left under the trees in a little park on the outskirts of the city. We couldn't see it in the dark last night.''

''Where is it *now?*'' Leo said levelly.

''It is just outside, *monsieur.* I drove it here to show you.''

Leo strode toward the door, but he held it so that Gabrielle could precede him out.

There, at the curb, tied up to the hitching post, were Jacques and Tonton. Behind them was the wagon.

Tears began to roll down Gabrielle's face. ''My poor boys,'' she said, going up to pat the two horses. ''What a time you have had.''

Leo went around to the back of the wagon and climbed in. Gabrielle left the horses and followed him.

Some of the costume trunks had been opened and the costumes lay piled on the sofa. Otherwise the inside looked untouched.

Leo and Gabrielle looked at each other.

''We escaped with our lives that time,'' he said after a minute.

She nodded tremulously.

"Why don't we go directly to the circus grounds?" Leo said. "You'll want to feed Jacques and Tonton, and I confess that I want to get this wagon off the streets of Rouen."

"First we have to stop at the hotel so I can give the good news to the boys," she said.

They climbed down from the back of the wagon and Leo said, "Just a minute while I pay the gendarmes their reward money."

Gabrielle watched him go into the station as she petted Tonton's soft nose. Once they were on their way back to the hotel, she said, "How much reward did you post? I'll pay you back."

"That's not necessary," he said. "I was the one who lost the wagon, so I'm the one who should pay to have it found."

"We both lost the wagon," she said.

"Gabrielle." There was steel in his voice. "Don't bother me with importunities. I have paid the reward. The subject is closed."

"Fine," she said. She lifted her chin. "If that's the way you feel about it."

"It is."

Neither of them spoke again until they had reached the hotel to deliver the good news.

Seventeen

Now that the wagon had been recovered, Gabrielle was able to turn her attention to the breakfast conversation she had had with the Martins and her promise to speak to Jeanne. She picked a moment in between shows and went up to the girl, asking if she could talk to her for a moment. Jeanne looked surprised, but followed Gabrielle to a corner of the circus tent and sat down with her upon a bench.

Gabrielle said bluntly, "Your friendship with Franz is making your husband very unhappy. Don't you realize that?"

Jeanne stared at her and raised her slanting black eyebrows. "Since when is my marriage any business of yours?"

"It is my business if it causes trouble in my circus," Gabrielle replied. She didn't like Jeanne's tone and she tried to hold on to her temper. "You have been flirting with Franz and Pierre is very angry. Everyone can see this—why can't you?"

"I am friends with Franz, that is all. Surely I am allowed to make a friend? I don't know anyone in this circus and he has been kind to me. There's no need for you to have heart palpitations about it."

Gabrielle gritted her teeth. "You can make friends

with me and Carlotta and Emma. There is no need for you to make friends with a man."

Jeanne's dark eyes took on a mocking look. "I am not a woman for other women," she said. "I prefer men. That's just how I am."

Gabrielle stared at her. Jeanne's feline face was perfectly composed. She wasn't at all concerned by what Gabrielle was saying.

Gabrielle said, "Well, I am not talking to you as a woman, Jeanne, I am talking to you as the owner of this circus. I don't want you making trouble among my employees. Pierre has been with us for years, and there has never been any problem until he married you. I want you to remember that you are a married woman and I want you to leave the other men in the circus alone."

Jeanne looked at her scornfully. "This is about Leo, isn't it? You're jealous because Leo has paid attention to me."

"Leo hasn't paid attention to you, you've tried to flirt with him!" Gabrielle shot back.

"You *are* jealous," Jeanne said triumphantly. "That's what happens when a woman is in charge of something. She takes everything personally. You ought to put Leo in charge of the circus. *He* wouldn't make a big commotion over my friendship with Franz."

Gabrielle was speechless with fury.

Jeanne stood up. "If you've said what you have to say, I'll be on my way." Once again her eyebrows were raised. "Really, Gabrielle, I thought better of you."

And she walked away.

What a bitch! Gabrielle fumed. She didn't think anyone had ever been this rude to her in her life.

I should send her and Pierre packing, she thought.
But where would she get two more band members at

such a late date? They knew all the music. Plus, she couldn't do that to Pierre. He had been a faithful member of the circus for many years.

Damn, damn, damn, Gabrielle thought. It was her first season as head of the circus and things were not going as they had when her father was in charge.

She took a long, deep steadying breath and walked over to the stable tent to make sure the horses had been groomed and fed before the start of the next show.

At the hotel that evening, Leo paid a stable boy to stay with the wagons overnight. He was not taking a chance of losing one of them again.

After dinner, most of the circus folk went down to the café, but Leo said he wanted an early night and Gabrielle and the boys stayed with him.

"Why don't you show Leo your paintings?" Gabrielle suggested to Albert as they went into the salon.

Albert looked shyly at Leo.

"I would very much like to see them," Leo said.

Albert and Mathieu went out to the wagon to fetch the paintings, and Gabrielle said to Leo, "He is very good. You will see for yourself."

From what Leo had seen of Albert's drawing, he had known the boy had talent. But most of what Leo had seen were sketches. What Albert showed him now were three small oil canvases, one a painting of Sandi, one of an Arabian, and one of Gabrielle with Colette.

They were wonderful. Leo possessed several Stubbs paintings of thoroughbreds and he thought this boy possessed the same ability to show the magnificence of the animal without sentimentalizing him.

"Have you ever formally studied the anatomy of the horse?" he asked Albert slowly as he regarded the picture of Sandi. All of the proportions were exact; the joints were perfectly rendered, as were the muscles under the shining white coat.

"Papa knew everything there was to know about how a horse is put together," Albert said. "He taught me."

"Your father sounds like a remarkable man," Leo said, his eyes still on the picture.

"He was," all three Robichons chorused in reply.

Leo turned last to the picture of Gabrielle. She was wearing the outfit she rode Noble in, a long blue velvet coat, breeches and high boots, but her head was bare and her shining brown hair was fastened at her neck with a blue velvet ribbon. Her young face was grave and her hand rested on Colette's long, elegant neck. It was a lovely picture, posed outdoors against a rolling green field and blue sky.

Leo realized that it was a picture he would like to have for himself.

"I painted the three of them this past winter," Albert said. "I had tried oil paints before, but this is the best I have ever done. Gabrielle found someone in Lille to help me learn how to work with the paints, and he was a help."

"We have a painter in England named George Stubbs," Leo told Albert. "He died a few years ago, but he is famous for his paintings of horses. He was self-taught, like you, and he became one of the best painters in England during the last century. I have some of his paintings. You would appreciate them, I think."

Albert's face lit up. "He became famous for painting horses?"

"Very famous. All of the best people in England have his work hanging in their houses. He made a very good living painting portraits of people's favorite horses—

mostly racehorses—with their owners or their grooms. He did other kinds of paintings as well, but he was celebrated for his horse pictures."

"And he was able to earn a living doing this?" Gabrielle asked.

"A very good living," Leo replied.

"That is what I would like to do, Gabrielle," Albert said intensely. He turned back to Leo. "I wish I could see some of George Stubbs's pictures."

"When the war is over, you must come visit me in England and I will show them to you," Leo said, regretting the words as soon as they left his mouth.

Now, why did I make such a rash promise? Leo thought immediately as he looked into Albert's shining eyes.

"Do you mean that?" Albert asked.

"Yes," he replied. "But first we must dispose of Napoléon."

Later, when Gabrielle and Leo were alone in their bedroom, Gabrielle asked him about Albert. "Did you mean what you said to him about visiting you in England?" she demanded.

He didn't have the heart to renege on his offer. "Yes."

She pressed her hands together. "That is wonderful of you, Leo! I have been thinking, England might be a good place for Albert to go to school. Particularly if you already have a tradition of equestrian art."

He said honestly, "Albert will need a teacher to help him with the technical side of things, but he has his own vision, Gabrielle. You are right to encourage him in his art. He has great talent."

She smiled as if he had given her a fabulous present.

"Thank you, Leo. Your encouragement means a great deal to me."

He looked at her glowing face, at the finely sculpted cheekbones, the small, straight nose, the immense brown eyes. She looked so delicate, but there was strength in her determined chin and in the firm curves of her mouth.

I am becoming much too interested in this girl, he thought grimly. And he was finding it increasingly difficult to share a bed with her and get any sleep at all.

She continued to smile at him. "I am so happy about Albert. It will be a wonderful opportunity for him to go to England and study."

Her face was radiant. Leo thought, *How the hell did I get myself into this? Now not only is Albert visiting me to look at my paintings, he is staying to study art.* He gave a mental shrug. *No use worrying about it now*, he reasoned. *Once this trip is over and Wellington has the gold, I don't ever have to see anyone from this circus again.*

But this was not a thought that made him comfortable. He liked Albert. And the boy did have unquestionable talent.

I suppose I could find him someone to study with, Leo thought. *That shouldn't be too hard.*

"Thank you," Gabrielle said, and stood on tiptoe and kissed his cheek.

Leo stood frozen as her lips came into contact with his skin. They were soft yet firm as they rested against his slightly stubbly cheek. He felt her touch in every part of his body. He wanted to turn his face and capture her mouth with his, to feel it open under his kiss, to feel her surrender to him. At that moment he felt he wanted Gabrielle Robichon more than he had ever wanted anything in his life.

All this from a kiss on the cheek!

She stepped away from him, and it took him a moment before he could reply with a semblance of normality. "You're welcome," he managed.

After that kiss, getting into bed with her was harder than ever. All of that soft femininity was only a hand's breadth away from him, and he had to keep turned away from her, his knees drawn up because the damn dog had the bottom of the bed.

She should never have kissed him, he thought. It wasn't fair. She should know that; she had been a married woman. It wasn't natural for a man and a woman to live the way they were living and not have relations with each other. She should be trying to make the situation easier for him, not exacerbate it by kissing him!

The fresh smell of lemon drifted to his nostrils. It came from her hair, he knew. She must use lemon when she washed her hair.

He couldn't turn over, because Gabrielle was next to him, and he couldn't stretch out his legs because Colette was sleeping on the bottom of the bed.

I'm going to buy that dog a bed tomorrow, he thought. *I'm damned if I'll be more miserable than I have to be.*

The kiss on the cheek had affected Gabrielle strongly. She had done it impulsively, not expecting to be moved, but the feel of his skin, with its golden stubble of beard, had caused a ripple of sensation all the way down to her stomach.

I shouldn't be feeling this way about this Englishman, she thought. *About this English aristocrat. It was nice of him to take an interest in Albert, but he will never regard us as equal to him. He will never regard* me *as equal to* him. I have to remember that. I have to take care to keep him at a distance.

No more kisses on the cheek, Gabrielle, no matter how nice he may be! You're lucky he didn't misconstrue that innocent kiss and demand more.

Was it an innocent kiss? she wondered. *What had gotten into her to make her do such a thing?*

It was stupid, she thought. *I will take care not to do it again.*

Eighteen

Aside from the fact that Sully was obviously hungover, the two shows they gave on the following day went smoothly. Leo once more hired someone to stay with the wagons overnight, thus relieving them of the fear that someone may make off with them again.

Jeanne sat next to Leo at dinner and flirted with him throughout the meal. Gabrielle fumed silently. When Henri asked if she was going to accompany them to the café that evening, she said firmly, "I think Leo and I will stay home and play some cards with Mathieu and Albert."

Leo and the boys were amenable, and as the rest of the circus members left for the café, Gabrielle and the boys went into the salon while Leo went upstairs for the cards.

They played Hearts, Leo and Albert against Gabrielle and Mathieu.

Mathieu was a strong player, and Gabrielle concentrated hard so she wouldn't fail him. He knew exactly how many cards of each suit were out, and he knew who was likely to have what winner. When she made a mistake and played the wrong card, he frowned at her direfully.

"Didn't you know that Leo had the Jack?"

"No. I thought you had the Jack."

He rolled his eyes in exasperation. "How could you think that? Weren't you watching my discards?"

"No," she confessed, knowing her thoughts had drifted to Leo. "Should I have been?"

Albert said, "I'm glad I'm not playing with Mathieu. He always yells at me about something I've done wrong."

"You need to keep track of the cards to play this game," Mathieu grumbled.

Leo said, "Not everyone has the retentive mind that you have, Mathieu. You must have some tolerance for us lesser mortals."

Mathieu snorted. "*You* have counted all the cards."

"I play a lot of cards. A good part of soldiering is passing the time, you know. I have a lot of practice. Your sister obviously doesn't."

"That's because nobody wants to play with Mathieu!" Gabrielle said. "Albert is right. He gets angry if you make a mistake."

"Because it is so simple," Mathieu said.

"It is to you," Leo said. "Have you ever had any formal training in mathematics, Mathieu?"

Mathieu shrugged. "Papa taught me how to multiply and divide."

"You've never learned algebra?"

Mathieu shook his head.

"Would you like to try it? I think I can remember enough from my school days to give you a start."

Mathieu's smile was blinding. "I would like that very much!"

Leo smiled back. "Good. It will get me out of being defeated by you in chess for a while."

The card game broke up at about ten, and all four of them went out into the stable yard with Colette.

The wagons were parked where they had been left.

Leo talked with the boy he had hired to watch over them while Colette did her business. Then all four of them went back into the hotel and up the stairs to their bedrooms.

The first thing Gabrielle saw when she came into the room was a small mattress lying on the floor against the wall.

"What is that?" she asked with a frown.

"That is Colette's new bed," Leo replied. "It's a crib mattress I bought in town today. She should be very comfortable on it."

Gabrielle looked at the dog, who had just jumped on her bed. Colette looked back at her and wagged her long tail.

"She's very happy where she is," Gabrielle said.

"I have no doubt that she is, but I'm not happy," Leo said. "I'm tired of sleeping tucked up into a ball. I'm too big to sleep that way. It's time to give her her own bed."

Gabrielle folded her arms across her chest. "Colette slept with me before you did. If someone has to go it should be you."

She was irritated with Leo for letting Jeanne monopolize him at dinner, and not inclined to be conciliating.

"Be reasonable," Leo said. "When it was just you and Colette, there was room for the both of you. Besides, you're small. There is simply not room for the three of us—and I can't fit on a crib mattress."

Gabrielle had been feeling crowded also, but she didn't want to give him a victory. "I have been perfectly comfortable with the three of us," she lied.

"Well, I haven't been. I wake up every morning with cramps in my legs. You said you didn't have the dog in bed with you when you were sharing it with your husband.''

In fact, she had let Colette sleep on her bed only after André had died. It had made her feel less lonely.

"I don't think she'll go," Gabrielle said. "She's too accustomed to sleeping with me."

"I bought her a bone. Let's try it." He went over to the dresser and unwrapped a brown paper package. "Look, Colette," he said. "A bone for you."

The dog's ears went up and she lifted her head.

He brought it over to her so she could smell it, then he took it to the mattress on the floor and laid it down. "Look. For you."

Colette's ears flicked again, then she got her feet out from under her and stood up. She jumped off the bed and went over to the bone and picked it up in her mouth. She headed back toward the bed.

"No!" Leo said. He put a hand on her collar and guided her back to the mattress. He patted it invitingly. "Here. You can lie down here."

She stood for a moment, the bone in her mouth, and then she stepped on the mattress. Gabrielle watched with interest as the dog walked around it. Then, abruptly, she sank down onto her belly, stretched her legs out in front of her to take hold of the bone, and began to chew.

"See?" Leo said triumphantly. "That wasn't so hard."

"What are you going to do when the bone is gone and she tries to get back on the bed?"

"Take her back to the mattress," he said. "She's a smart dog. She'll soon get the idea."

"Well, this is your idea, so you can be the one to get up with her," Gabrielle said. "I don't feel like having my sleep constantly disturbed."

"I'll take care of her," Leo said. "All that's needed is some firmness."

Gabrielle went over to pet her dog. "Poor little girl," she said.

Leo snorted. "It seems to me she is a very lucky little girl. She has a nice warm room to sleep in, and a nice soft mattress."

"Greyhounds need to sleep on something soft," Gabrielle said. "They have so little flesh on their bones."

"Are you ready to get undressed?" Leo asked.

"Yes."

They performed their nightly ritual.

Once she was in bed, Gabrielle had to admit that it was much more comfortable without the dog. But Leo was still too close for comfort.

In fact, without Colette to distract her, she seemed to be even more aware of Leo than usual.

He leaned up to blow the candle out. This hotel did not have lamps in the bedrooms. "Ready?" he asked.

She looked at him. His hair hung loosely over his forehead and a stubble of beard had come back from his morning's shave. He was so beautiful.

"Yes," she said. "You can blow out the candle."

The room became dark and Gabrielle felt the mattress heave as Leo settled himself to sleep. "This is wonderful," he said. "I can stretch my legs out."

He sounded as if he was lying on his back.

She said before she thought, "You were certainly interested in what Jeanne had to say tonight."

"She got a hold of my ear and she wouldn't let go," he replied.

"What was she talking about?"

"A lot of nothing."

Gabrielle scowled into the darkness. He wasn't being

very helpful. "I think we might have a problem with Jeanne," she said. "Henri is concerned that she is flirting with Franz and that Pierre is angry."

He moved and it sounded as if he had turned toward her. The sound of Colette attacking her bone came from over by the wall. "She hardly said a word to Franz tonight," he said.

"That's because Henri made sure to sit between Franz and Jeanne, and she was sitting next to you."

"I think it's a lot of fuss over nothing, Gabrielle," he said impatiently. "If Pierre is annoyed with the way Jeanne is behaving, let him handle it."

"I don't know why he says nothing. He just sits there and looks like murder. Take a look at his face the next time we're all together and you'll see."

"Are you really worried about this?"

"Yes."

"Then talk to Jeanne."

"I tried to. She told me she was a woman for men, not for other women. And she told me to mind my own business."

She thought she heard a smile in his voice as he replied, "Maybe she's right. Don't borrow trouble, Gabrielle. When Pierre has had enough, he'll rein her in."

"Perhaps..." But Gabrielle was not so sure. For some reason, Pierre seemed to be handcuffed by Jeanne.

"She tried to flirt with Mathieu," she said indignantly. "He told me that she said he was handsome and that she bet all the girls loved him. She made him very uncomfortable."

"Mathieu is nineteen years old. He's going to have to get used to dealing with women sometime."

The warmth from his body was radiating toward her. It was so cozy in this bed, just the two of them.

I wonder what it would be like to be really married to Leo.

"You're no help at all," she said crossly.

"You can't seriously want *me* to lecture Jeanne?" he asked.

"Of course not!"

"Then let it alone, Gabrielle. You're not the mother of this circus—you're the owner. All of these people are grown-ups. Let them figure out their own problems."

She thought about that. "Perhaps you're right."

She heard him yawn. "Of course I'm right. Now, try to get some sleep. We have a long drive ahead of us tomorrow."

She sighed. "All right."

She drifted off to sleep to the sound of Colette chewing on her bone.

At about one in the morning, Colette tried to get on the bed. She landed with a thump on Gabrielle's feet and Gabrielle said foggily, "Leo?"

"No, no, Colette," he said firmly. Gabrielle heard him get out of bed. "Come with me."

Evidently, Colette resisted, for Leo repeated more loudly, "Come."

After a moment, the dog gave way and jumped off the bed. "Good girl," said Leo. "Come over here."

"Can you see?" Gabrielle asked.

"I'm going to open this shade," he said. He did so and a little light from the street lamp outside illuminated the room. Leo walked Colette to the mattress. "Lie down," he said. "There's a good girl."

Colette stood there looking at him.

Leo patted the bed. "Lie down."

Slowly she lowered herself to the mattress.

"Good girl." He rubbed her in front of her tail. "Now, stay."

He went back to the bed and got in next to Gabrielle.

Colette stayed where she was for a minute and then she got up.

"No," Leo said strongly. "Stay."

She looked at him, evidently trying to figure this out. Then she lowered herself to the mattress again.

"Good girl," Leo told her.

Gabrielle went back to sleep.

At two o'clock, Colette tried to get back into bed again and Leo repeated his training session.

"This would be much easier if we could tie her for a night," he muttered to Gabrielle as he got back into bed.

"You're not tying my dog," Gabrielle said indignantly.

"That's what I thought," he said.

At four o'clock, Colette made one last try to get back into the bed. Leo groaned as he got up.

"This was your idea," Gabrielle said. "We would have slept much better if we'd left her where she was."

"No, we wouldn't," he replied. "Once she realizes she has to sleep on the mattress, we'll be much better off. She'll be more comfortable, too. She can stretch out better than she could on the bed with us in her way."

They slept until six, when Gabrielle woke and saw the daylight coming in under the shade. She slipped out of bed and went to the window to peek out.

No rain.

Thank goodness, she thought. It was awful to travel in the rain.

Colette's tail thumped as she saw Gabrielle up. She went to pet the dog. "Did you sleep all right, sweet-

heart?'' she whispered. ''Did that big bad man push you
out of your bed?''

Colette's tail thumped harder.

Leo was still sleeping deeply. Gabrielle wanted to
stand there and look at him, but she forced herself to
walk away and get her clothes from the closet. She
dressed quickly and took Colette out for her morning visit
to the stable yard. Then she took her to the kitchen for
her morning meal.

Pierre was sitting in the dining room drinking a cup of
coffee when she went in with Colette at her heels. Gabrielle went to join him.

''Good morning, Pierre. Did you sleep well?''

He just looked at her. Then he grunted an affirmative.

Gabrielle sought for something to say. Pierre had always been quiet, but he had been pleasant. He didn't look
pleasant this morning. He looked grim.

''It looks as if it will be a nice day,'' Gabrielle said
brightly. ''Good traveling weather.''

Pierre grunted again.

She tried a different tack. ''The band is sounding very
good this year. Jeanne has replaced Philippe very well.''

He said nothing.

''I was a little dismayed when I heard that we were
losing Philippe, but you helped us out with that problem.
Jeanne is a very good musician.''

Pierre stood up. ''If you'll excuse me, Gabrielle, I have
some things I must do.''

Gabrielle watched as his sturdy body disappeared out
the door. She looked over at his coffee cup. It was still
half full.

Colette stood up as the maid came into the room with
Gabrielle's croissants. The dog was so tall that her head
topped the table and she looked with eagerness at the

bread in Gabrielle's hand. Gabrielle gave her a bit and broke off a piece for herself as she sipped her coffee.

Mathieu came into the room and joined his sister at the table.

"You look tired," he said to her.

She started to tell him about Leo's pushing Colette out of the bed, then stopped. The less she said to Mathieu about her sleeping arrangements with Leo, the better, she thought.

"I'm all right," she said instead.

"Do you think Leo meant what he said last night about teaching me algebra?" Mathieu asked anxiously.

"I'm sure he did. I don't think Leo says things he doesn't mean."

"I've always thought it would be wonderful to go to university and learn real mathematics," Mathieu said. "Perhaps Leo can even recommend some books for me."

Gabrielle looked at her brother. "You wouldn't want to leave the circus, would you, Mathieu?"

"For a chance to go to university, I would," Mathieu replied. "But I know that's impossible. It will be great just to work with Leo."

Gabrielle felt terrible. She had been scheming for Albert; it had never occurred to her that Mathieu might have needs of his own. He had always seemed content with circus life.

I can't lose the both of them, she thought a little wildly. *It would be awful to try to run the circus all by myself.*

She forced a smile. "I'm sure that Leo will be able to recommend some books."

At that moment, Leo himself came in the door.

"I didn't even hear you get up," he said to Gabrielle as he joined them at their table.

Colette's tail started to wag as Leo came up to them. He petted her and told her she was a good girl.

Gabrielle gave the dog some more of her croissant.

"I was talking to Pierre this morning—or I was trying to," she said to Leo and her brother. "That is a man with a lot on his mind."

"Remember what I said last night, and let him work his own problems out," Leo said.

"Good advice," Mathieu said. "Gabrielle tries to help people too much."

"Is that a bad thing?" she asked indignantly.

"Sometimes it can be," Leo said.

She could feel spots of color in her cheeks. "I think it's better to care about people too much than not enough."

"It may be good for the people you care about, but it isn't necessarily good for you," Leo said.

"That is the most cynical thing I've ever heard," Gabrielle said indignantly. "I think what God wants most from us is that we have a kind heart. If you're always thinking about yourself and your own feelings, you become a very selfish person."

Leo was looking at her. "Sometimes people can do things that are unforgivable," he said flatly.

She shook her head. "I don't believe that. The whole idea of Christianity is that everyone can be forgiven."

"By God, maybe," Leo said. "People are not always so large-hearted."

"That's true, but if we are Christians we are supposed to try."

Leo stood up. "Well, this is a very interesting conversation, but I have some things I must do. I'll see you at the wagon."

Gabrielle looked at his half-finished cup of coffee.

"That's the second man who's walked away from me this morning," she said to Mathieu. "Is my conversation that bad?"

He said seriously, "I think something you said may have touched Leo on a sore spot."

She thought about what Leo had said. *Sometimes people can do things that are unforgivable.* What did that mean?

Nineteen

Their trip to Alençon took them along the main north-south road in Normandy. The sun was shining brightly and the plowed fields stretched, rich and brown, on either side of the road. Traffic consisted mainly of farm wagons, with an occasional trap taking a husband and wife into a local town to shop. There was no sign of the French army.

The circus stopped for lunch at Bernay, at a café set next to a pond. The sun had warmed the day up considerably, and they took their lunch outside, where they could watch the ducks swimming around the pond.

Franz threw some bread to one of the ducks and they all rushed to cluster around the diners.

"Not a good idea, Franz," Henri said. "We are being attacked."

"They're cute," Jeanne said. She threw a piece of bread to the duck that was nearest to her.

"It looks like they're used to being fed by diners here," Gabrielle said.

Colette had been investigating another corner of the patio and now she came cantering up to the table. The ducks scattered when they saw the big dog.

"Good girl, Colette," Leo said.

"Surely you're not scared of a few ducks, Leo?" Carlotta said with amusement.

"I just want to eat my meal in peace," Leo returned. "Those ducks looked ready to pick the food right out of my mouth."

"I wonder if we'll be stopped by the army again?" Luc said.

Gabrielle stared at him. He was looking at Leo.

"I certainly hope we're not," she said. "Being searched is very time-consuming."

Luc seemed to ignore her. "They're searching for English gold. You wouldn't know anything about that, would you, Leo?"

Gabrielle's heart began to thump. *Mon Dieu*, she thought. *Luc suspects Leo!*

Leo met Luc's gaze steadily. "No," he said. "I wouldn't."

Luc looked skeptical.

"I hope Vincent gets us a different hotel from the one we had last year," Antonio said. "I didn't like that one at all. It was dirty."

Gratefully, Gabrielle turned to Antonio. "I told him to get us something different even if he had to book us into more than one place. I agree with you about last year's hotel."

"You played Alençon last year also?" Leo asked.

Henri nodded. "But we'll be taking a new route after Le Mans. Last year we went to Angers. This year we're going to Tours."

"We haven't been to Tours in a couple of years," Carlotta said.

Luc said, "Tours is directly on the route south, isn't it?"

"Yes," Gabrielle said briefly. "We decided to do the southern route this year."

Luc didn't reply but once more he looked at Leo with a knowing look in his eyes.

Gabrielle felt her heart sink.

They were ten miles outside Alençon when two soldiers pulled in front of the wagons on the road and raised their hands to stop them. Leo obediently pulled up. The wagons behind them rolled to a stop as well.

The two soldiers were young and Gabrielle gave them her best smile. "Is there something wrong?" she asked.

"We have orders to search all suspicious wagons on this road, *madame*," the soldier closest to the wagon said.

"Suspicious? *Mon Dieu*, what is suspicious about us? We are a circus!" Gabrielle said.

Leo looked on and said nothing.

"You have a great many wagons, *madame*," the soldier said. "It would be easy for you to conceal something."

"Don't tell me this is about that gold?" Gabrielle said. "Let me tell you, we have already been stopped and thoroughly searched, Sergeant. It happened before we got to Rouen. They made a mess of our wagons. I hope that is not going to happen again."

"I am sorry, *madame*. My orders are to search—"

Gabrielle cut in, "Yes, yes, I hear you. But we have already been searched, Sergeant. By a lieutenant with a great hook of a nose."

Both soldiers faces lit with recognition. "That must have been Avelard," one of them said.

They nodded at each other in agreement.

"All right," the sergeant said. "If Avelard searched you, then you must be all right. You may proceed."

Gabrielle had her hands folded in her lap to keep them from shaking. Once more she bestowed upon the two soldiers the glory of her smile. "Thank you," she said. "We are running a little late and another search would have been a great inconvenience."

"Perhaps we will come to your show," the sergeant said.

"Just tell the ticket taker that you are my guests," Gabrielle said generously. "I am Gabrielle Robichon, the owner."

"Thank you, *madame.*" Both young soldiers smiled happily.

"Bonjour," Gabrielle said, and Leo put the horses into motion.

When they were out of earshot, Leo said, "Thank God for your smile."

"It wasn't my smile, it was the mention of Avelard that did it," she returned.

"Your smile didn't hurt, believe me."

Her hands were still shaking. "How many more times do you think we'll be stopped?"

"We're on the main road," he said. "I think we'll be stopped again. At least this time they didn't tumble to the fact that I'm English."

"Yes, this time you had the sense to keep your mouth closed."

He shot her an annoyed look. "The last time you left me alone with Mathieu. I had to talk. It would have looked strange if a boy had done all the talking."

"I don't care how strange it may have looked, you should have kept quiet."

He didn't reply, but a muscle jumped in his jaw.

She changed the subject. "I hope you have the role of ringmaster down. You're going to have to play it tomorrow."

He turned his head. "What are you talking about?"

"You said you would be the ringmaster if we were stopped again. And those men are coming to the circus."

"I said you could *introduce* me as your ringmaster. But you didn't even have to do that. Those soldiers know nothing about me. There is absolutely no reason for me to play the ringmaster in tomorrow's shows."

She glared at him. "It isn't just the army that we have to fool, Leo. Did you hear Luc at lunchtime? He is suspicious of you."

He set his jaw. "Yes, I heard him."

"The last thing we need is Luc poking around in our wagons."

"I keep telling you, there is nothing to find in the wagons. The gold is well hidden under the floorboards."

"If you became our ringmaster it might help quell Luc's suspicions. It would look as if you were really interested in becoming a part of the circus."

He said between his teeth, "I am not going to be your ringmaster, Gabrielle. Will you please get that through your head?"

"You think you're too good for us, don't you?" she shot at him.

"I will not even deign to answer that remark."

"Because it's true!"

He didn't reply.

"Very well," Gabrielle said coldly. "If you want to ride in silence, then silence you shall have."

They neither of them said a word until they met Vincent on the outskirts of Alençon.

Vincent had engaged two hotels to put up the circus members, and Gabrielle, Leo, Mathieu, Albert, Emma, Gerard, Sully and Paul went to one, while the others went to a second hotel down the street. The hotel Gabrielle was staying at was small, so the circus party went to eat at a restaurant the concierge recommended.

Gabrielle thawed toward Leo as the good food made its way into her stomach, and she coaxed Sully to talk and tell them about his life in a circus in Austria. Paul also had some good stories—before he had joined the Cirque Equestre this year he had been a juggler with a traveling circus that went through Germany. That circus had actually had a tame tiger, and the boys had many questions about such a fabulous beast.

Circus folk certainly saw a lot of the world, Leo thought as he listened to the men talk. It was a hard life, with the constant traveling, but he supposed there could be worse. Sully and Paul certainly sounded as if they had enjoyed their adventures.

After dinner, they went back to the hotel and Mathieu asked Leo if he would have time to show him some algebra. Leo agreed, and he and Mathieu set up in the small salon that the hotel provided for its guests. Gabrielle elected to stay with them and read while Albert took out his ubiquitous drawing pad. Sully, Paul, Emma and Gerard decided to join the group from the other hotel at a café.

After half an hour, Leo looked up while Mathieu was studying a problem he had written out. Albert was concentrated on his drawing, and his eyes moved to Gabrielle, where she sat reading by the light of the fire. Her long hair fell in a single thick braid down her back, and the firelight glinted off her smooth cheek and brow and illuminated the long lashes that were lowered as she looked at the book in her lap.

She's just so damn beautiful, Leo thought.

As if she had felt his gaze, she looked up from her book. She smiled at him. "How is the lesson going?"

You could warm your hands at her smile, he thought.

"Very well," he answered. "What are you reading?"

"De la Guérinière's *School of Horsemanship*. It's my favorite book. Listen to this and you'll see how delicate the art of true horsemanship is." She looked back at the page and read, " 'The aid of putting weight onto the stirrups is the subtlest of all the aids; the legs then serve as counterweight to straighten the haunches and to hold the horse straight in the balance created by the rider's heel. This aid presupposes a high degree of obedience in the horse and much sensitivity, since by the mere act of putting more weight on one stirrup than the other, a horse is brought to respond to this movement.' "

Leo pursed his lips in a silent whistle. "Do you do that?"

"Yes."

He gave her a rueful smile. "I can see why you didn't think I was ready to ride your horses."

"You can learn," she said. "It just takes practice and the right instruction."

He said, "The boys tell me that you have written a book about equitation."

She looked surprised. Her great eyes shimmered in the firelight. "They told you that?"

"Yes. Are you ever going to publish it?"

She gave her customary shrug. "I am only a circus girl. Who is going to publish my book? When Papa was alive, perhaps he could have gotten it published, but he never got around to it."

"Perhaps I can get it published for you," he found himself saying.

Her eyes got even larger. "You?"

"I have some influence, Gabrielle. If you can't get it

published in France, perhaps I can have it published in England.''

''Someone would have to translate it. Although I speak English fairly well—we once had an English juggler travel with us and he taught me—I'm not knowledgeable enough to translate a book.''

''Getting it translated shouldn't be a difficulty.''

''But would the English be interested in it? Classical riding is not very popular in England anymore.''

He suddenly decided that he was going to make it his business to see her book get published. She was the best damn rider he had ever seen, and her thoughts on riding would be well worth reading.

He said decisively, ''We'll try to get it published in France first. Once Napoléon is defeated and the king restored, the atmosphere should be right for a book like yours.''

Her face glowed. She was beautiful at all times, but when she looked like this...

''That would be wonderful, Leo. It would make me so happy to know that Papa's great knowledge will be shared with others.''

Albert suddenly said, ''I'm glad that you came along with us on this trip, Leo. You have made us all very happy.''

Embarrassed, Leo glanced at Albert. The boy was looking very earnest. ''I wish you really were married to Gabrielle,'' he said.

Leo didn't know what to say.

Gabrielle answered for him. ''Don't be foolish, Albert. Leo is being nice to us because he is a nice man. There is no chance of us getting married.''

''Leo would be a better husband than André,'' Mathieu said. ''André was just a boy. Leo is a man.''

"Don't pay any attention to them, Leo," Gabrielle said, clearly embarrassed.

Leo cleared his throat and said to Albert, "I don't need to be married to Gabrielle to make certain her book is printed. Now, Mathieu, let's see what you have done with this problem."

He bent his head over Mathieu's work and Gabrielle went back to her book.

The boys went to bed at ten, but Gabrielle and Leo stayed up, waiting for Sully and Paul to return. Gabrielle wanted to make certain that Sully hadn't been drinking.

"What are you going to do if Sully ever becomes too inebriated to perform?" Leo asked her as they sat in front of the dying fire in the salon.

"That's never happened," she said.

"But if it does?"

"Even drunk, Sully could perform his part," she said.

The room was starting to get cold and Gabrielle stretched her feet out to the fire. Leo looked at those small feet, clad in sensible boots, and felt something give inside of him.

She was the loveliest girl he had ever seen. And the bravest. He suddenly realized that if he never made love to Gabrielle Robichon he would regret it all his life.

So much for his resolution to keep her at a distance.

She looked at him. "You must give me your dirty clothes, Leo. During the break between shows tomorrow I will take them to the laundry."

He almost laughed, so at odds were her thoughts to his. In an attempt to turn her thoughts, he asked, "Do you ever get lonely, Gabrielle?"

She turned to look at him. "What brought that question on?"

"I don't know. I was just thinking that you must miss having someone to share your life with."

She returned her gaze to the fire. "I missed André terribly at first, but it is not so bad now. I'm not alone, after all. I have my brothers."

"Brothers can't hold you in the middle of the night."

Her eyes widened. "Now you sound like Luc. That is just the sort of thing he is always saying to try to get me to marry him."

Well, that put me in my place, Leo thought wryly. The last thing he wanted was to sound like Luc. Nor was he thinking of marriage.

She leaned forward and poked the coals on the fire. "I think that being a little lonely is a fact of life. There's only so much you can share with another person. There's always a part of you that stays alone."

He thought that this was an interesting comment on her marriage.

She turned her head to him. "Do you get lonely, Leo?"

"Sometimes."

She nodded. "I can tell that about you. Even when you are in company, there is always a space around you. But perhaps that is because you know you don't belong here."

"Don't get started on my being an aristocrat," he said warningly. "I think I get along very well with your circus members. They all seem to like me."

"They do," she said. "But I don't think any of them would be surprised to learn that you are really an English aristocrat. You have that air about you." She gave him a brilliant smile. "It's why you will be such a good ringmaster."

He looked at her. Then he said slowly, "If I said I would be your ringmaster, would you kiss me?"

She stared at him, her eyes huge with astonishment. "Are you serious?"

He couldn't believe that he had said that. He needed to take it back. He opened his mouth and said, "Very serious."

She swallowed. "I don't think that would be a good idea."

"It might be very nice," he said.

"If I kissed you, you would really be our ringmaster?"

Say no, he thought. He heard his voice say "Yes."

"Well…" A small smile tugged at the corners of her mouth. "I'll do it," she said.

He stood up. "Not here. Upstairs, in our bedroom."

She looked a little uncertain.

"Come along," he said as he led her out of the room. "…It won't be so bad I promise."

Twenty

"**I** have to take Colette out first," she said as they stepped into the hallway.

"Fine. I want to check on the wagons, anyway."

They took a lantern and went out into the deserted stable yard, and while Colette did her business, Leo walked around the wagons.

"Why didn't you hire a boy to watch them tonight?" Gabrielle asked.

"It was understandable in Rouen, where there was a problem with wagons being stolen, but I doubt that Alençon shares that problem. I was afraid that if I seemed overly concerned with the wagons, people might wonder why."

"People like Luc," Gabrielle said.

"He doesn't like me and thinks he has reason to resent me. We don't want him spreading suspicion among the rest of the circus."

"That we don't," she agreed fervently.

"The wagons will be all right here in the stable yard," he said.

She thought he sounded as if he was trying to convince himself as well as her.

"They can't be stolen twice!" she said. "That would be unbelievable."

"Let's hope you're right."

Gabrielle called to Colette and together they walked back into the hotel and up the stairs to their bedroom. Once they were inside Colette went over to her mattress and they stopped and looked at each other. Leo lifted his hand and smoothed a finger over her cheekbone. "Do you have any idea how beautiful you are?" he said.

"You are not so bad yourself," she returned.

"This has got to be a serious kiss," he warned. "I'm not going to be ringmaster for just a peck."

Her eyes sparkled. "I keep my bargains," she replied.

"Good." He bent his head and kissed her.

Her mouth was the sweetest thing he had ever tasted. He held her against him, so he could feel the silhouette of her body, and moved his mouth over hers, asking her to open to him. After a moment, she did, and his tongue found hers and she answered him. He bent her back in his arms, and her arms came up to clasp him around the neck. The feel of her had him in a state of full arousal.

And yet, he tried to be gentle. She was so delicate, her bones were so small. He wanted nothing more than to rip her clothes off and slide into her, but he was still aware that this was Gabrielle, that she was trusting him, that he could never do anything that would hurt her. Alongside his lust bloomed the flower of tenderness, and when he straightened up and her arms remained around his neck and her feet came off the ground, he scooped her up and laid her gently on the bed, his mouth never once letting go of hers.

Maybe she'll let me...

He slid his mouth away from hers and rained kisses on her cheek all the way to her ear. "Gabrielle," he whispered. "How I have longed for you."

She made a tiny sound of acquiescence.

Suddenly a cold nose was poking at his face. "What the—" he said.

It was Colette, come to see what was going on. She whuffled a little and licked Gabrielle's cheek. Gabrielle's eyes flew open.

"Mon Dieu," she said. "What are we doing?"

Shit, Leo thought. If he could have strangled the dog right then, he would have done it.

Gabrielle sat up and Leo removed himself from the bed and looked at her. Colette tried to jump up on the bed to join Gabrielle. "No, no," Gabrielle said shakily. "You can't come up here, Colette."

"Come with me," Leo said to the dog. He put a hand on her collar and led her over to her mattress. Colette stood on the mattress and looked at Gabrielle, who was still sitting up in bed.

Leo petted the dog. "She's all right, Colette. She's fine. Now, lie down like a good girl and go to sleep."

The dog looked at him.

"Down, Colette," he said firmly.

The dog lowered herself to the mattress.

"Good girl."

He straightened up and turned to look at Gabrielle. "We seem to have gotten a little carried away," he said.

She swung her legs, clad in the blue skirt, over the side of the bed and stood up. "We certainly did," she replied. She was very flushed. "If it wasn't for Colette, I don't know what would have happened."

He gave the dog a grim look. "I know."

"This is terrible, Leo," she said. "How can we possibly share a bed after what just happened?"

I know how we can share a bed, he thought.

"I don't know what got into me," Gabrielle said.

"It was my fault," he said. "I just liked kissing you so much, I didn't want to stop."

She was already flushed and now a little more color washed into her cheeks. "I liked kissing you, too." She sounded mortified.

He walked over to her and took her hands in his. "Don't be upset. Nothing terrible has happened except you kissed me and now I have to be your ringmaster."

Her brown eyes looked troubled. "Is that all?"

"Certainly."

"And you think we can continue to share the same bed? You won't mind?"

It would be hell, but he wasn't about to let himself be kicked out now. He had every intention of following up on the start he had made tonight.

"It will be fine," he said.

She bit her lip. He looked at her white teeth as they sank into the softness of her lower lip, and something inside him clenched.

He wasn't going to get a wink of sleep tonight.

"All right," she said. "I suppose we can go on as usual."

He raised one of her hands to his mouth and kissed it. "That's a good girl."

Colette got off her bed and came to thrust her head between them.

"How the hell did you ever become intimate with your husband with her around?" Leo growled.

Gabrielle smiled. "It's an art," she said, and, putting her hand on Colette's collar, led her back to her bed.

Gabrielle curled up on the edge of the bed, as far away from Leo as she could manage.

Whatever got into me? she thought. *God knows what would have happened if Colette hadn't interfered.*

She had known she was attracted to him. Well, he was a gorgeous man. And he had been very kind to her brothers. But it was more than that. There was something in him that appealed to her very much; that sense of loneliness, perhaps, that made her want to get close to him and ease it.

Obviously he was attracted to her. But Gabrielle didn't fool herself about his intentions. He would like her to sleep with him, but he wasn't going to marry her. The social gap between them was too great.

If she let him make love to her, she would fall in love with him.

That way lies only heartache, she told herself. *I would be a fool to put myself through that.*

This business of our sharing the same bed is dangerous.

But she didn't know how to change it. At this point, she didn't have the heart to make him sleep on the floor. Plus, he probably wouldn't go.

Somehow, Leo had established himself as something very big in her life—and in her brothers' lives, too. She thought of Albert's wish that they were really married.

That would be nice, she thought. Leo was so big, so competent. She wouldn't have to worry and struggle alone if she was married to him.

She wondered what his life was like when he lived in England. Did he live on the estate where he had grown up, or did that belong to his older brother? Did he have a piece of property of his own?

It would be nice to settle down on her own farm in the country, to have a stable where her horses could live all the time. Gabrielle had always loved the winter, when the circus was off and they had lived in various rented farms and trained their horses. They had lived as a family, then, her father and brothers and Emma and Gerard.

But the circus was fun, too, she thought loyally.

In truth, it had been more fun when her father was alive, and she had not had to assume the responsibility of running it. Then she had just done her own acts and taken care of her own horses and left all the worrying to him.

It would be good to marry a man who would help assume the responsibility of the circus, she thought.

André had not been such a man. André had been fun, but responsibility had not been a big part of his character.

Leo may not be going to marry me, but he is still going to help me, she thought. He was going to make arrangements for Albert to establish himself as a painter. He was going to get her book published. These were significant things.

I have much to be grateful to him for. Another thought struck her and she smiled. *He is even going to be our ringmaster.*

He must have wanted to kiss her very much, if he had made such a sacrifice to do it.

He had wanted to kiss her; he had told her that he longed for her. *Maybe he loves me a little bit.* And on that thought, she finally drifted off to sleep.

''Let me spend one more day watching Gerard, and then I will be the ringmaster tomorrow,'' Leo said to Gabrielle the following morning.

He was looking grim, and she forcibly quelled her impulse to let him off the hook altogether. It would be safer for them all if Leo would become more a part of the circus. She agreed to let him watch for one more day.

Leo was sitting with the band during the afternoon performance. Luc had finished the Courier of St. Petersburg, and Henri and Franz put up the ropes for their performance while Sully stood on a small ladder and tried to hang washing on them. Gerard chased Sully away and the last thing Henri and Franz did was secure the safety net that they always used.

The rope-dancing routine began and Leo watched it absently, his mind on Gabrielle and what had happened between them last night. *That damn dog,* he thought for the hundredth time. God knew he was a dog lover, but it was hard to have good feelings about Colette this afternoon.

Up above him, the Martins began their act, the Rivals. Carlotta postured coquettishly as Henri and Franz pretended to fight over her. Finally Henri prevailed, and Franz took his usual dive downward.

The net didn't hold.

The crowd gave a loud cry, and Leo raced into the ring to go to Franz, who was lying very still in the middle of the collapsed net.

When Leo got to him, Franz's eyes opened. *Thank God,* Leo thought.

"What happened?" Franz asked slowly.

"Lie still," Leo said. He knelt beside him. "The net broke. How do you feel?"

"I hurt all over," Franz said.

"That's good," Leo said. "It would be worse if you didn't feel anything."

At this point, Henri and Carlotta appeared and knelt on the other side of Franz. "Are you all right?" Henri asked urgently.

"I don't know," Franz replied.

The volume of noise from the crowd had increased and

people were standing on their benches trying to see what was going on. Gerard came running up to Franz.

"Tell everyone to stay in their seats, Gerard," Leo ordered. "Tell them that we'll attend to Franz and everything will be all right."

Gerard nodded and went to do Leo's bidding.

Gabrielle came running up and looked down at Franz. She was very white. "How could this have happened?" she asked.

"I don't know," a distraught Henri replied.

Leo said, "Can you move your legs, Franz?"

There was a moment of tense silence as Franz tried. "Yes," he said. His lips were white.

"How about your arms?"

Once more silence prevailed as Franz tried. "Yes," he groaned.

"Try to move your head from side to side."

Franz did it, turning his head stiffly.

Leo looked at Henri. "It doesn't look as if he's broken his back or his neck."

"Thank God," Henri said.

Leo turned to Gabrielle. "He needs to see a doctor immediately. He may have some broken bones, and he probably has a concussion. Get a litter rigged up and we'll take him back to the hotel and I'll get a doctor."

As Gabrielle raced off, Leo said to Franz, "Do you have bad pain anywhere in particular?"

"My right leg and my right arm," Franz said. "I must have landed on them."

"All right. Gabrielle's getting a litter and we'll get you back to the hotel and get you a doctor. Just hold on."

"You're going to be all right, Franz," Henri said.

The noise from the crowd had subsided into a steady murmur. Leo stood up, went to the edge of the ring and looked out at the assembled faces. "Who can tell me where's the nearest doctor? Raise your hands."

Dozens of hands went up. Leo went to the closest man and got directions. The Maroni brothers came into the ring with a litter and two of them lifted Franz onto it. The crowd went silent as he was carried out.

Leo had stopped two of the Maronis from following the litter. Now he said to Julius, "Pick up the net and put it into my wagon. I want to have a look at it."

A flash of understanding flickered in Julius's dark eyes. *"Sì,"* he said. "We will do that, Leo."

Leo turned to Gerard. "Tell the audience that the show will resume in a few minutes."

Gerard nodded and Leo went out of the tent to look for Gabrielle. He saw her standing next to the Martins' wagon, where they were loading Franz, and went over to join her.

"I told Gerard to announce the next act," he said.

She looked up at him, her eyes deeply troubled. "Yes, we have only my pas de deux with Mathieu left, anyway. We'll perform it and get these people on their way." She shut her eyes briefly. "Please God, let Franz be all right."

"I'll collect the doctor and, hopefully, have him at the hotel by the time Franz arrives," he assured her.

"You could ride Tonton," she said. "He will go under saddle."

He nodded. "Good. That would be faster than taking the wagon."

"I'll tell Albert to help you saddle up," she said. "I have to perform."

"I'll find Albert," he said. "You and Mathieu just try to settle down the audience."

He started to turn away, but she put a hand on his arm

and said in a troubled voice, "Leo…do you think someone could have tampered with the net?"

She's thinking the same thing I am, he thought.

"I told Julius to put the net in our wagon," he said.
"I'll take a look at it as soon as I can."

"*Dieu,*" she said, and touched her hand to her forehead.

He hated to see her so worried. "Don't look like that,
sweetheart," he said. "It was probably just an accident."

"I hope so." But she did not sound convinced.

He was probably even more skeptical than she was,
but he smiled encouragingly. "Go ahead, collect Noble
and do your act."

She drew a deep, long breath. "All right."

He watched her walk away, her slender back straight
as an iron rod. She would make a good soldier, Gabrielle,
he thought.

Leo was fortunate to find the doctor at home, and he
tied Tonton to the back of the doctor's trap and went
with him to the hotel. The doctor examined Franz and
found that he had a broken arm, a broken leg and a broken collarbone, all on his right side.

"It's fortunate that he landed on his side," the doctor
said. "If he had landed on his back, he may have had
more serious injuries."

He splinted the arm and the leg but left the collarbone
to heal on its own. He also thought Franz probably had
a concussion.

"It could have been much worse," the doctor said to
Henri and Carlotta. "From what you have told me, the
net probably did break his fall a little." He shook his
head. "Dangerous stunts you folks do."

Henri said, "The net is there to keep it from being too

dangerous." He looked at Leo. "I don't understand how it gave way like that. It has been fine."

Leo said, "Do you check it before all your performances?"

Henri shook his head. "No. We have never had trouble with it before."

"Something might have frayed," Leo said. "I had it put in my wagon and I'll look it over and let you know."

Henri nodded. Unlike Gabrielle, he did not seem to suspect an outside hand. "I should have checked it," he said. "It was careless not to."

Leo left the Martins at their hotel and rode Tonton back to the circus field, passing some leftover circus traffic on the road as he went. As he rode into the field, he was surrounded by the remaining circus members, all wanting to know how Franz was doing.

Pierre was not among the group.

He reported on Franz's injuries, then he and Gabrielle went back to their wagon.

"Wait until the others are occupied and then we'll take the net out and examine it," Leo said.

Gabrielle nodded.

Mathieu and Albert arrived at the wagon.

"Poor Franz," Mathieu said. "What a miserable thing to happen to him. Didn't they check the net?"

"Apparently not," Leo replied. "I asked Henri and he confessed that he just put it up without looking at it."

"That's so stupid!" Gabrielle said passionately. "How could he be so careless with such an important piece of equipment? Franz took a dive into that net every performance!"

Leo shrugged. "Sometimes it takes an accident like this to open people's eyes, sweetheart. It's too bad."

The four of them were standing outside the back of

the wagon and now Colette got up off her sofa, stretched and walked around the net to jump out the back and join them. Gabrielle bent to hug her and she licked Gabrielle's cheek.

Albert said soberly, "What is going to happen to the rope-dancing act? Will Henri and Carlotta still perform? Will Franz be able to travel with us?"

Gabrielle shut her eyes. "I don't know, Albert."

Mathieu said, "Every circus has a rope-dancing act."

"I know," Gabrielle sighed.

Leo said, "Henri and Carlotta will need their salaries—even more, with Franz injured. I can't see them just throwing away their jobs to stay here and nurse Franz."

Gabrielle brightened. "That's true."

Leo said, "Perhaps we can find a family that will take Franz in and nurse him until he is able to rejoin the circus. I'm sure the doctor must know someone who would be happy to earn some extra money."

Gabrielle brightened even more. "That's a wonderful idea, Leo! I will tell Henri that I will continue to pay Franz his salary, and he can use it to pay for Franz's care."

"How much salary does he make?" Leo asked.

She told him.

"Excellent," said Leo, who privately thought that he would have to subsidize Franz's salary to get the kind of care he was thinking of. But if he did that, he wasn't going to let Gabrielle know.

She said, "Maybe I should go into town now and talk to Henri and Carlotta. Then we can talk to the doctor." She looked into the wagon, toward the place where the gold was hidden. "Unfortunately, we can't afford to fall behind schedule. Otherwise I would suggest we stay an extra day at Alençon."

"Why don't you let me talk to the doctor first?" Leo said. "If we can find someone to take Franz, it would be easier to bring the idea to the Martins with all the details in place. And I have the whole afternoon. I don't have to get ready for a show."

"Would you really do that, Leo?" Gabrielle asked.

"Of course."

"Leo will arrange it, Gabrielle. Don't worry. Everyone will do as he says," Albert said with simple faith.

Gabrielle smiled wryly. "Leo does have a way of getting what he wants."

Colette rejoined the group by the wagon. She pushed her head under Leo's hand for him to pet her. Gabrielle looked first at the dog, then at him. He raised his eyebrows and she smiled.

"Let's get the net out and look at it," Mathieu said. "I wonder what could have happened."

It didn't take them long to find the broken spot in one of the main supports. Leo looked at it closely. The edges of the rope on both sides of the break were frayed.

Gabrielle said, with relief in her voice, "It broke because it's worn."

"Yes," Mathieu said. "Shame on Henri and Franz. They should have looked after this. We check our bridles and our stirrup leathers and our girths all the time."

Leo said nothing. He knew it wasn't impossible for someone to have cut the rope, then frayed the ends by hand. As a matter of fact, it looked to him as if that might be what had happened. But he did not want to alarm Gabrielle.

"Can someone fix this rope before the evening performance?" he asked.

"Gerard can," Gabrielle said. "Do you think Henri and Carlotta will perform later?"

"There's not much they can do sitting around the hotel while Franz sleeps," Leo returned. "And isn't there a tradition in circuses that the performance must go on?"

Gabrielle smiled. "There is."

He nodded. "Then why don't I go back into town, talk to the doctor about finding a family, talk to Henri and Carlotta, and see what I can arrange."

"Thank you, Leo," Gabrielle said simply. "You are very good."

Sully and Paul came wandering up. "What was wrong with the net?" Sully asked.

"One of the main supports was frayed," Leo replied. "It finally gave way when Franz's weight hit it this afternoon."

"What a shame," Sully said.

Paul said, "Henri and Franz should have kept better watch on their equipment."

Leo nodded agreement.

"What's going to happen to the rope-dancing act with Franz gone?" Sully asked.

"I'm going to see about that," Leo returned. "If you all will excuse me, I'll be on my way."

He could feel them all watching him as he walked toward the stable tent.

Twenty-One

Leo went back to the doctor's house, but he had to wait because the doctor was out on another call. When he returned, he and Leo sat down in his small surgery and Leo explained what he wanted.

"I'm assuming he can't travel in his condition," Leo said.

"Certainly not right at this moment," the doctor replied. He was a small, slim man with a large mustache. "He is in a great deal of pain, plus we can't take a chance of those bones being jarred."

"Well, is there someone in the neighborhood with whom we could leave him?" Leo asked. "I am willing to pay well for good care."

"How well?" the doctor asked bluntly.

"Very well, if the situation is a good one."

The doctor thought for a minute. Then he said slowly, "I have an extra bedroom in my house. If it would be all right with my wife, he could stay with me."

"That would be perfect," Leo said vigorously. "None of us would worry about Franz if he was under the constant supervision of a doctor."

"I would have to speak to my wife."

"If you would like to invite her in here, I would be happy to explain our situation," Leo said. He smiled. "Perhaps I can appeal to her charitable instincts."

When Madame joined them, however, it became clear that the instincts Leo was going to have to appeal to were mercenary rather than charitable. She dickered like a fishwife and Leo had to promise a considerable amount of his own money in addition to Franz's salary.

It was worth it, he thought, to keep Gabrielle from worrying.

From the doctor's house he went to the hotel, where he found Carlotta and Henri sitting together in the salon, looking distraught.

"Did you look at the net?" Henri asked as Leo came into the room.

"Yes. One of the main ropes was frayed. Evidently it gave way when Franz's weight hit it."

Henri struck himself on the forehead. "Stupid! How could I have been so stupid not to check the net?"

"Franz didn't check it, either," Carlotta pointed out.

"I am the elder. It was my responsibility."

Leo pulled a chair up close to the old brocade sofa they were sitting on. "I have made some tentative arrangements for Franz, if they meet with your approval," he said, and went on to explain his agreement with the doctor.

"This way, Franz will be well looked after, and you can continue on tour with the circus," he concluded. "He can rejoin us when he is able."

Henri said, "And Gabrielle will continue to pay Franz his salary, so he can pay the doctor?"

"That's right."

"That's very nice of Gabrielle," Carlotta said.

"She is concerned about Franz."

Henri and Carlotta looked at each other. "It sounds good," Henri said.

"Yes," Carlotta agreed. "I think it is the best solution to a nasty situation."

Leo said, "Can the two of you perform the rope-dancing act without Franz?"

"We'll have to," Henri said grimly.

Carlotta said, "I can write to my cousin Philippe. Remember how over the winter he was afraid that his act was breaking up? Perhaps he would like to join us."

Henri said, "Then what do we do with Philippe when Franz comes back? Can Gabrielle afford to keep paying an extra rope dancer?"

Leo said, "It may be a while before Franz is well enough to perform again. Why not write to this Philippe and see if he is interested in coming on a temporary basis, with the possibility of a permanent job?"

Henri nodded slowly. "It wouldn't hurt to try."

"Good," Carlotta said. "I'll write immediately."

Leo stood up. "Gabrielle is expecting you to be at the circus for the evening performance. Is your wagon still here?"

"Yes," Henri said. He ran his fingers through his thinning black hair. "It is going to be a very improvised performance."

"I'm sure you'll do fine," Leo said encouragingly.

"We'll come up with something," Carlotta said. "Tell Gabrielle not to worry. We'll be back in time for the show."

They got through the evening performance in good form. Henri and Carlotta added some more somersaults and twists and turns to lengthen their act, and though it was not as good as when Franz was with them, it was better than nothing.

The rest of the circus had been very relieved when

Henri and Carlotta showed up, and they were even more relieved when Leo explained the arrangements that had been made for Franz's care. Paul and Sully had already spread the word about the frayed rope, so it was a fairly comfortable group of people who drove back to town from the circus grounds that evening.

After dinner at the small hotel where they were staying, Paul and Sully and Emma and Gerard decided to go to the café with the group from the other hotel.

"I'll go with you," Gabrielle said.

Mathieu and Albert looked at her in surprise. "I thought we were all going to play cards," Mathieu said.

But Gabrielle had decided that she didn't want to spend the evening in such close company with Leo. She was beginning to feel as if she *was* married to him, she was with him so much. And such a feeling was not safe. *God knows what it would lead to,* she thought.

"I've changed my mind," she said to her brother. "I think it would be good for me to be with the others tonight. We have all had a very painful day."

Mathieu turned to Leo. "Perhaps we could play chess, Leo." The hopeful look on his face hurt Gabrielle.

We are all becoming much too attached to Leo, she thought.

Leo looked from Mathieu to Gabrielle. She could see clearly that he wanted to go with her. He opened his mouth to speak, looked back to Mathieu and stopped. Then he said quietly, "Chess would be fine. My brain is in need of some sharpening."

Mathieu grinned. "I can help you with that."

Albert said to his sister, "Perhaps I will come with you for a while."

She smiled at him. "That would be nice, Albert."

The evening at the café was not at all pleasant, however. Jeanne flirted with Luc all evening and Pierre steamed. "I wish Pierre had never married Jeanne," Albert said as he and Gabrielle walked back to the hotel.

Gabrielle sighed. "I do, too. She is surely causing a lot of trouble."

"He should just leave her," Albert said. "We would do fine with a three-piece band."

"It's not as easy as that. There is a legal bond between them that's not so simple to break."

"Jeanne doesn't act as if there's a bond between her and Pierre. She was flirting with Luc all night."

The voices of Sully and Paul floated back to them as they walked on ahead.

"I know," Gabrielle said. "I don't know what's wrong with her, Albert. I don't know what possessed Pierre to marry her, but he did, and now we're stuck with her."

"I don't think she's pretty at all," Albert said. "She's not half as pretty as you, Gabrielle."

Gabrielle reached her arm around Albert's thin, boyish shoulders and gave him a hug. "Thank you."

"Leo thinks you're pretty," Albert said. "He watches you. I've seen him."

Gabrielle thought it was a good thing that the dark kept Albert from seeing the flush that rose to her cheeks. "Leo is just concerned that we get the gold delivered. He is not interested in me, Albert."

"I think he is," Albert said stoutly. "I like Leo, Gabrielle. He's a good man. It would be a good thing if you married him."

"Don't talk like that," Gabrielle said sharply. "Leo is an aristocrat in his own country. There is no way he is going to marry a circus girl. Please don't pin your hopes on such a thing happening, Albert, because it won't."

There was silence as they walked along. The hotel entrance was halfway down the street. Albert said, "He said he would help me with my art."

"And I believe he will do that," Gabrielle said. She squeezed his arm. "He does not have to marry me in order to help you, Albert. He will help you because he likes you and because he sees that you have talent."

"Do you really think so?"

"I am sure of it."

They had reached the hotel door. Gerard and Emma had already gone in and Sully was holding it open for them. Colette bounded in first, followed by Gabrielle and Albert. The two of them went to look in the salon to see if Mathieu and Leo were still there, but the room was empty.

"Gone to bed," Gabrielle said.

"Do you like Leo, Gabrielle?" Albert asked.

"Yes, of course I like Leo. He has been very kind to us. But I meant what I said before, Albert," she said impatiently. "Don't be imagining that something is going to happen between us, because it won't."

"If you say so." But he didn't look as if he believed her.

"It's time for you to go to bed," she said.

He started toward the stairs, then stopped and turned when she didn't follow. "Aren't you coming?"

"In a moment. I am going to take Colette to the kitchen to see if she wants a drink. Go ahead, I'll be up in a minute."

Albert nodded. "Good night, Gabrielle."

"Good night," she replied.

She clucked to Colette and started toward the kitchen. After Colette had lapped up some water from a bowl,

Gabrielle went back into the hallway, hesitated, then went into the salon and sat on the hard sofa.

She was afraid to go upstairs. She was afraid to be alone with Leo.

He had been so wonderful today. He had taken charge of the whole Franz situation and resolved what had seemed to her at the time to be an unsolvable problem. André would never have done that. But then, André had been a boy. Leo was a man.

What would it be like to make love with Leo?

She shivered and wrapped her arms around herself. Colette came over and pushed her face into Gabrielle's lap. "If it wasn't for you, I would have found out last night what it was like to make love to Leo," Gabrielle said.

Colette gazed up at her with adoring brown eyes.

Gabrielle kissed the top of her head. "I love you, too." She sighed.

What am I going to do?

Leo's kiss had shaken her to her very marrow and she knew what she wanted to do. She also knew it wasn't the wise thing to do.

She could get some of the herbs that all the circus women used to prevent pregnancy from Carlotta. She had used them the whole time she had been married to André, and they had worked.

We could have an affair. My brothers wouldn't have to know.

She petted Colette's sleek, fawn-colored head and let her thoughts dwell on what it would be like to have an affair with Leo. She shivered again.

What would I do when it was over? she thought. *I've already had my heart broken once. Do I want to go through that again?*

Twenty-Two

Leo was sitting up in bed reading when she came into the room. When he saw her, he closed the book, put it on the table next to him and said, "You've been a while. I heard the others come down the hall about fifteen minutes ago."

He was wearing his nightshirt, with the covers pulled up to his waist. The nightshirt was open at the neck and showed his strong throat and part of his chest. His eyes looked like twin aquamarines. Her stomach turned to jelly just looking at him.

"I took Colette to the kitchen for a drink," she said. "She was thirsty."

Colette looked at Leo, then padded over to the mattress against the wall and lay down.

"Good girl," Gabrielle said.

Leo didn't say anything; he just looked at her.

"Who won the chess game?" she asked, trying to make her voice light.

"Mathieu won easily," he replied. "I was a little distracted."

"Yes," she said. She hadn't moved from her place just inside the door. "It has certainly been a distracting kind of day. I cannot thank you enough for all of your help, Leo. You were wonderful."

"I don't want your thanks," he said. His voice sounded a little harsh. "I just didn't want you worried."

She swallowed and told herself to act naturally. She took off her blue jacket and hung it in the wardrobe. Then she turned around to face him once more. "What a night we had at the café," she said. "Jeanne started to flirt with Luc, then Pierre got mad and tried to make her leave with him. She wouldn't and Luc stood up for her and Pierre stormed out, furious." She shook her head. "Now that Franz is out of the picture, apparently she is going to set her sights on Luc."

He frowned. "I thought Luc was in love with you."

"Luc thinks I'm married and out of his reach," she pointed out. "He didn't seem at all averse to a flirtation with Jeanne."

"Damn," he said. "Someone should rein that girl in."

"Pierre tried tonight. He told her to come back to the hotel with him. But she said there was nothing there for her. What do you think she could mean by that, Leo?"

He shrugged his shoulders. "It could be anything."

She began to undo the long braid that hung down between her shoulders. When she had finished, she went to the table where she had laid out her things and picked up a brush. "Gianni had some ideas for adding to his act. I thought they sounded good. The rope-dancing act is going to be shorter without Franz."

"Did I tell you that Carlotta was going to write to a cousin of hers, to see if he could fill in until Franz is able to come back?" he asked.

She stopped brushing her hair. "No, you didn't tell me. Carlotta and Henri didn't tell me. They didn't *ask* me."

"I told them to go ahead," Leo said.

The hand holding the brush fell to her side. Her hair

was hanging all around the shoulders of her white shirt. She glared at him. "You didn't have the authority to do that! I have said I would pay Franz his salary. How can I afford to pay an extra man as well?"

"You need to have a good rope-dancing act. Carlotta and Henri by themselves will not do the job. You saw how it was this evening. You need at least three people."

Her nostrils quivered. "You don't know what my costs are. It is very expensive to feed all of the horses as well as pay out salaries. I have to have enough money left over to keep us over the winter, when we are not performing."

He said softly, "I have plenty of money. I would be happy to pay for this extra rope dancer."

She went rigid. "No! I am not taking any money from you, Leo. The circus is my responsibility, not yours."

"Then use some of the money that you are getting for delivering the gold."

"That money is for Albert."

"I am going to take care of Albert. He can live with me for free, and I will make sure he gets the proper instruction. I will also introduce him to the people who will commission paintings from him."

She stared at him, her eyes wide. "Why are you doing this?" she whispered.

"I am doing it because I like Albert and I think he has a very great talent. It is a big thing for you and Albert, Gabrielle, but it is not a big thing for me. For me, it will be easy. Truly."

After a moment the tension went out of her and she nodded. "Well then, I suppose I can pay this extra person and keep the money from the gold to make sure we can get through the winter."

He smiled at her. "Of course you can."

The jelly in her stomach got a little mushier. She said starkly, "The reason I stayed downstairs was that I was afraid to be alone with you."

His face became very sober. "Afraid?"

"Afraid of how you make me feel," she said, boldly meeting his eyes.

There was silence as they looked at each other. Then he said, "You make me feel that way, too."

She folded her lips. "I know."

"I want to make love to you, Gabrielle, but not unless you want it, too."

I owe him so much, she thought. *He took care of Franz today, and he is going to take care of Albert. I should show him gratitude, not rejection.*

"There is an herb I took when I was married to keep from getting with child. I need to get some from Carlotta before we can do anything."

His blue-green eyes glinted. "A good idea."

She raised her chin. "Now, turn your back while I get undressed. I'm tired and I want to go to sleep."

Obediently, he turned his face away from her and she quickly disrobed, pulling her nightgown over her head. Then she went over to the bed, turned back the covers on her side and got in.

He rolled toward her, reached for her hand and kissed it. "Good night, sweetheart," he said.

"Good night," she whispered in reply. Briefly she met his eyes. She looked away, pulled the covers up over her shoulder and curled up to sleep.

She had said she was tired, but she lay awake for a long time with many thoughts going through her head. Uppermost in her mind was the thought that gratitude alone decreed that she give Leo what he wanted. She held on to that thought, using it to justify what she was going to do, using it as a shield to hide the deeper, more troubling truth from herself—that, foolish as it may be, making love to Leo was what she most profoundly wanted to do.

There was a thunderstorm in the middle of the night. Gabrielle was made aware of it by Colette, who landed on her feet at three o'clock in the morning.

"What the..." Leo said, and sat up.

Gabrielle was on her knees, petting the dog. "Colette is afraid of thunder. Look, she's trembling." Her voice softened. "It's all right, baby. Nothing can hurt you. I'm right here."

Colette began to scramble up the bed so she could get between Gabrielle and Leo.

Leo said, "This is ridiculous. If we let her back in now, we'll never get rid of her."

"She's scared, Leo," Gabrielle said.

"She's enormous!" he said. "She has to weigh eighty pounds. There is no room for her in this bed with you and me."

"You're mean," Gabrielle said.

"Get her back on her mattress and I'll sit with her until the storm is over," he said. He did not sound happy.

Gabrielle said, "Colette, I'm afraid that the days when it was just you and me in the bed are over. Come on, girl. I'll stay with you until the storm is over."

"You don't have to do that," Leo said irritably. "I said I'd do it."

"She wants me, not you," Gabrielle said. "Come on, *chérie*." She got out of bed and coaxed the dog to follow her. Then she took her over to her mattress. Colette stood on it, looking at her. Another flash of lightning came through the open window and Gabrielle rubbed the dog's head. "It's all right, baby. It's all right, girl."

The thunder rolled and Colette jumped.

Leo came over with the quilt off the bed folded up. He put it on the floor next to Colette's mattress and said to Gabrielle, "Here, sit on this. Perhaps she'll lie down if you're sitting."

Gabrielle did as he said, all the time talking to Colette in a soothing voice. Slowly, Colette lowered herself to the mattress.

"Good girl," Gabrielle said.

"I'll get you your jacket. You're going to be cold sitting there in your nightdress," Leo said. He went to the wardrobe and returned with her blue jacket, which Gabrielle put on.

Lightning flashed again, then the thunder. Colette flinched, but she didn't get up. Gabrielle continued to pet her.

"Get back into bed," she said to Leo. "There's no point in us both losing sleep over this."

"Actually," he said, "my feet are freezing on this floor. Is there room on that quilt for me, too?"

"I think so," she said. "But you don't have to do this, Leo. She's not your dog."

He didn't answer, but lowered himself to sit beside her.

Colette poked her nose in his direction and he smoothed his hand over her forehead. "What a lot of trouble you are, little girl," he said. But his voice was soft.

The thunder rumbled again, and Colette was quiet.

"She's all right as long as she's not alone," Gabrielle said.

"Has she always been afraid of thunder?"

"Since I got her, when she was eight months old."

There was silence as they both listened to the storm.

He said, "When I was a boy I had a dog named Regent—he was afraid of thunder, too. He was a foxhound who wouldn't hunt."

"What did you do with him when it stormed?" she asked.

She could hear the smile in his voice as he answered, "I let him in the bed with me."

"Aha," she said, and laughed.

"My parents would have had palpitations if they had known. I always worried about him when I went away to school, wondering if anyone was taking care of him when it stormed."

"Was it hard to leave your family and home and go away to school?"

"At first it was, then I got used to it."

"Are your parents alive, Leo?"

There was a long silence. Then he said, "My mother is alive, my father is dead."

"I'm sorry," she said. "I know how terrible it is to lose a father."

The thunder rolled again, but it sounded as if it was moving away.

He said, "My father had some kind of a disease that ate away at his insides. He was in a lot of pain for a long time."

"How terrible," she said. She spoke quietly, not wanting to disturb the mood of confidence that had come across him. "Terrible for him, but also terrible for your mother and you to have to watch him."

He said in a hard voice, "My mother didn't care. She was having an affair with another man the whole time it was happening."

"*Mon Dieu,*" she breathed.

He gave a harsh laugh. "Pretty disgusting, isn't it?"

"That's awful," she replied. "Did your father know?"

"No. She was there at his bedside like a good wife. He didn't know what she was doing when she was gone."

"But you knew?"

"I caught them," he said flatly. "He was a neighbor of ours, you see, and I caught them in the fishing house out by the lake."

"Oh, Leo," she said with pity. "How awful for you. How old were you?"

"Sixteen," he replied.

"I'm so sorry," she said. "That is an ugly thing for you to carry around."

"I've never told anyone about this," he said. He looked at her and frowned in puzzlement. "Until now."

"Sometimes it helps to share a burden," she said. "If it helps you at all, I am glad you told me."

"I've never forgiven her," he said. "I know you preach forgiveness and charity, Gabrielle, but there are some things that just can't be forgiven."

"She did a very bad thing," Gabrielle said. "Is she sorry for it, do you think?"

"A year after my father was dead, she married the other man. I wouldn't say that she was sorry in the least," he said.

"It sounds as if she loved this other man," Gabrielle said.

"She *slept* with him, Gabrielle, while my father was dying." His voice was deeply bitter. "Christ, all they had to do was wait a few months."

The thunder seemed to have stopped. The only sound in the room now was the rain beating against the window.

Gabrielle rested her head against his arm. "I'm not trying to defend her, Leo. What she did is not defensible."

He put his arm around her and drew her close. "I was actually glad when she got married. It got her out of the house so I could go home again."

"No one else knew?"

"I never told anyone."

"That was good," Gabrielle said. "So you are still estranged?"

"Yes."

"Does this make her unhappy?"

She felt him shrug. "Insofar as it reminds her of what she did, I suppose it does. I don't care."

Gabrielle thought that he did care. She thought that part of his mission in life was never to let his mother forget what she had done. She thought that it could not be easy to be Leo's mother.

She was not going to say this to Leo, however.

"Did you love your father?" she asked softly.

"My father was a wonderful man. That's what makes the whole thing so sordid."

On the mattress, Colette began to close her eyes.

"Look," Gabrielle said. "Colette is going to sleep."

"Why don't we follow her example and do the same?" He stood up and Gabrielle followed him. He bent, picked up the quilt and once more spread it on the bed. Then they each went to their own side of the bed and got in, Gabrielle first taking off her jacket.

"You must be cold," she said. "You had only your nightshirt on."

"How about coming over here and warming me up?" he asked.

"I told you about the herbs...."

"I just want to hold you," he said. "Nothing more."

"Well, all right." She moved in his direction and was taken into a warm embrace. "Mmm," she said, resting her head against his chest. "You don't feel cold at all. You feel warm."

"My feet are cold."

"Well, keep them to yourself," she warned. "I was sitting on mine and they are warm. I want to keep them that way."

"All right," he said pitifully. "I'll just let them freeze away."

"We could always get Colette to lie on them," she said. "That would warm them up."

"No, thank you, sweetheart!" he said forcefully. "I'm sure they'll warm up on their own."

She chuckled sleepily. She could hear his heart beating steadily under her cheek and it was oddly soporific.

"Good night, Leo," she said.

"Good night, Gabrielle."

In no time at all, she was asleep.

Twenty-Three

François Nicholas Mollien, the French minister of the Public Treasury, was sitting at his desk when the war minister came into his office. Mollien looked up from his figures.

"I have had a report from one of the teams that is searching for the Rothschild gold," the war minister said.

"Oh?" Mollien raised one of his thick black eyebrows.

"The officer I put in charge of organizing the roadblocks had a report from the lieutenant who is stationed outside Rouen. He reports that he stopped and searched a circus."

"So?" Mollien said. "What is so strange about a circus?"

"This one is traveling toward Spain. And it had an Englishman with it. An Englishman who had just been married to the circus owner. In Brussels."

"Ah," Mollien said. "Now, that is interesting. Did the search turn up anything?"

"No. But all those wagons... It would not be difficult to conceal the gold somewhere in those wagons, I think."

Mollien sat back in his chair. "What are you going to do?"

"I think it would be worthwhile to send a man to accompany this circus. If it is carrying the gold they will have to transfer it into the hands of the English. It will be difficult to do that with a French army officer looking on.''

"Can you spare a man?"

"We'll pull one of the men off the roadblock and assign him to the circus."

"Good idea," Mollien said.

The war minister nodded. "I'll send the order out right away."

Twenty-Four

The twelve o'clock show was Leo's first turn as ringmaster. *How did I ever get myself into this?* he thought grimly as he dressed in the back of the wagon with Colette looking on. She had given up following Gabrielle around a few minutes earlier and had come back to flop on her sofa.

He knew the answer to that question, all right. He had bribed Gabrielle into giving him a kiss by promising to fill in as ringmaster. And thanks to that kiss, it looked as if he was going to get a lot more.

It was worth it, he told himself as he slid his arms into the red hunting jacket, which was too small across his shoulders. The thought of the coming night filled his mind and he felt his manhood stir.

Better control my thoughts, he told himself. *I don't want to make more of a spectacle of myself than I already am.*

Colette let out a long sigh, and as he turned to look at her, the events of last night came back to his mind.

Whatever possessed me to tell all of that to Gabrielle? I haven't had such a loose tongue since...since it happened.

Yet he wasn't sorry he had told her about his mother. For some reason, that heavy secret seemed lighter this morning. Perhaps it was true what Gabrielle had said, perhaps it helped to share a burden. And Gabrielle certainly wasn't going to tell anyone. She didn't know any of the people involved, and would never know them, so his secret was safe with her. Besides, she wasn't the type of person to betray a confidence. He thought he knew her well enough to know that.

He wondered why she had changed her mind and agreed to sleep with him. *Did it have something to do with the way I helped her out with Franz? Is this her way of showing gratitude?*

If it was, a gentleman wouldn't take advantage of it, he thought. But he had every intention of taking advantage of whatever impulse it might have been that had caused Gabrielle to acquiesce to him. He had never met a woman who appealed to him the way she did. Her unique mixture of strength and vulnerability; her loyalty to her young brothers; her magic touch with animals; her gallantry in taking on the burden of the circus after her father had died—all of these things drew him to her as he had never been drawn to anyone before. And she was so beautiful. It stirred him just to look at her.

He wanted her more than he had ever wanted anything in his life.

And tonight she would be his.

His eyes fell on Colette. "What are we going to do with you?" he asked.

Tie her, he thought.

I have to remember to bring some rope back to the hotel tonight. Gabrielle can't object to tying her up for an hour. She can stay perfectly comfortably on her mattress while we…do what we want to do.

It wouldn't be a bad idea to go and look for a piece of rope while he was thinking of it. He didn't want to get back to the hotel room tonight and find that he had forgotten this most important piece of equipment.

I'll get some baling twine from the hay wagon, he thought, then finished buttoning up his coat and jumped out of the wagon to do his errand.

When Leo stepped into the ring and the audience applauded, he had to restrain himself from turning and walking out.

God, if any of my fellow officers could see me now! he thought as he waited for the applause to die down. He couldn't believe that he was about to make a fool of himself in front of a bunch of farmers and shopkeepers.

"Good afternoon, *mesdames et messieurs,*" he said in the voice that could carry across a battlefield. "The Cirque Equestre welcomes you to our show. We will start off today with Mademoiselle Gabrielle Robichon and her Liberty Horses."

He made a motion toward the performer's door and Fantan trotted in, followed by Kania, Shaitan, Sheiky and Dubai. The horses began to circle the ring and Gabrielle took the center. Leo ducked out the door.

Mathieu and Albert were standing outside.

"You were good, Leo," Albert said. "Nice and loud. Gerard isn't loud enough sometimes."

"Thank you," Leo said woodenly.

He grew marginally more comfortable as the circus progressed. The worst part was when he had to chase Sully away from the tightrope and out of the ring. He thought that had to stand as the single most humiliating moment of his life.

The circus members were full of compliments when the show was over and Leo tried to be gracious with his thanks. After all, they couldn't know how degraded he felt out there in front of the kind of people who would come to the back door of Branford Abbey.

The second show started promptly at four and trouble arose right away. Two young men, obviously drunk, started calling out to Gabrielle as she worked the Liberty Horses. Leo heard them and, angered at the insult to Gabrielle, strode up the aisle to where the men were sitting and told them in a low voice that if they didn't quiet down, he would throw them out.

The next few acts went by without interruption, but when Gabrielle entered on Noble, the two young men began to call out again.

"Come out with us after the show, Gabrielle, and we'll show you a good time."

"Come and meet some real men, not these circus mountebanks."

That's it, Leo thought grimly, and he came back into the ring. When he reached the benches, he turned to Gabrielle and held up a hand. "Start over when I have removed these miserable nuisances," he told her. Then, to the rest of the audience, "Sorry for the interruption."

"We're not leaving," one of the men said. "We paid for our tickets just like everyone else."

"I'll refund your money, but you are going. Now," Leo said.

One of the young men crossed his arms. "No, we're not."

"Excuse me," Leo said pleasantly to the family on the end of the bench where the troublemakers were sitting. They got up and let him through. He moved in to tower over the two young men.

"You can leave on your own feet, or I can knock you out and carry you," he said. "The choice is yours." His voice was still pleasant, but the undernote in it was dangerous. He was furious that Gabrielle had to be subjected to these drunks.

One of the young men stood up. There was a flash of something, and a knife appeared in his hand.

The audience audibly caught its breath.

Quicker than the eye could see, Leo's own hand shot out and knocked the knife out of the other man's grasp. It clattered to the floor and Leo grabbed it.

"Correction," he said. The edge in his voice was sharp as the knife he held in his hand. "I will *not* give you your money back. Now, move."

Sullenly, the two men began to edge their way out of the seats as Leo followed. When he got to the aisle, he spoke to the audience.

"*Mesdames et messieurs,* I apologize for this interruption. If you will return your attention to the ring, Mademoiselle Gabrielle Robichon will now ride Conversano Nobilia in an exhibition of the highest level of equitation."

That said, he escorted the two drunken men out of the tent. They swung around to stare sullenly at him once they were outside. Both men had the sturdy build of peasants.

"How did you get here?" Leo asked.

One of them kicked the brown grass and the other said after a moment, "We walked."

"Well, you can start walking again," Leo told them. "I want you off these grounds, and if you try to come back I'll shoot you for trespassing."

Both men looked at each other. "We didn't mean any harm," one of them mumbled.

"You pulled a knife on me in front of hundreds of people," Leo said. "If I have to shoot you, there will be plenty of witnesses to say that I had cause."

At this point, Gerard came around the curve of the tent and walked up to Leo. "Is everything all right?"

"Yes. These men are leaving. I want you to stand right here, Gerard, and watch them leave. If they show any signs of lingering, come and get me."

Gerard nodded. "All right, Leo."

Leo looked at the young men, who had visibly sobered up during the last few minutes. "Do you understand what I have just said to you?"

They nodded.

"Good. Then go."

With droopy shoulders and hanging heads, the two young men walked off.

Leo said to Gerard, "If they show any sign at all of returning, come and get me immediately."

"All right, Leo," Gerard repeated.

Leo went back into the tent in time to watch the end of Gabrielle's act with Noble.

The rest of the show went smoothly, and Leo was less focused on the humiliation of his role than he had been earlier. Instead his mind was on the two drunks and the insult to Gabrielle.

"Does something like this happen often?" he asked Sully as they stood talking next to Gabrielle's wagon after the show.

"Not often, but it does happen. Some of the time we just try to ignore the disturbance and continue on, but you did a great job of getting rid of the problem today, Leo."

"I am not putting up with any lack of respect for Gabrielle," Leo said grimly.

Sully patted him on the shoulder. "You're a good husband, Leo. Gabrielle is lucky to have you."

Leo didn't know what to say. He watched as a bird

landed on the top of the wagon and finally replied, "Thank you. I'm lucky to have her, too."

"You are," Sully replied. "I've known Gabrielle since she was a little girl and there has always been something special about her. She has great compassion, Gabrielle. It is not a trait that is in abundant supply in today's world."

"True," Leo said. "She has compassion for you, Sully, which is why you should not disappoint her and give in to your own demons."

Sully sighed and rubbed his high forehead. "I know. But it is hard, Leo."

"When you feel like drinking, come to me and I will stay with you. A man in a situation like yours needs a friend, Sully."

"Paul is a friend, but he feels sorry for me and lets me drink."

Leo shook his head decisively. "That's not the kind of friend you need. You need someone who will be understanding but tough. Come to me, Sully, and I'll try to help."

"Gabrielle said the same thing to me, but I can't burden her with my problems."

"My shoulders are much broader than Gabrielle's."

Sully gave him a faint smile. "You are very good, Leo. I'll try."

Leo didn't get a chance to talk privately to Gabrielle until they were together on the front seat of her wagon, driving back to town.

She turned to him with a smile. "You certainly got your baptism by fire today! Only your second show and you had to throw people out."

"I hope that sort of thing doesn't happen often," he said.

"Not often, but when it does it's extremely disagreeable. It spoils things for the audience as well as the performers."

He frowned. "I didn't like it that they picked on you."

She sighed. "I hate it, too. Thank you for defending me." She gave a little laugh. "Sometimes the audience even throws the hecklers out. That has happened more than once."

His frown deepened. "What would you have done if Gerard had been your ringmaster and I hadn't been here?"

She wrinkled her nose. "We probably would have tried to ignore them and gone on with the show. Papa was more like you—he would evict anyone who got too rambunctious. But Gerard is not up to such things."

He said soberly, "You need someone younger to be your ringmaster."

"I know. I was hoping that we could make do with Gerard until Mathieu gets old enough to take over the job, but perhaps I should start to look around for someone to fill in in the meantime."

He said carefully, "Does Mathieu want to become the ringmaster?"

"Let me have the whip for a moment," she said. He gave it to her and she flicked a fly off Jacques's back. She gave him back the whip and turned her attention to his question.

"Papa always said that Mathieu would be the next ringmaster after him. Of course, he didn't expect to die so soon. Mathieu needs a few more years before he can take over that kind of a job."

"That's not what I asked you," he said. "Your father may have wanted Mathieu to be ringmaster, but what about Mathieu?"

She didn't look at him. "The circus is Mathieu's life, like it is mine. Why shouldn't he want to be ringmaster?"

"I rather think Mathieu would prefer to be a mathematician," he replied.

Her face was blank and she still was not meeting his eyes. "That is not possible," she said. "It is possible for Albert to support himself by art, but Mathieu cannot support himself by doing mathematics."

"So he is tied to the circus."

"He likes the circus," she said defensively. "As do I. We are fortunate to have a means of supporting ourselves. Many people in this day and age do not."

They drove in silence for a few minutes. The dark of evening was closing in and Gabrielle pulled her jacket around her a little more closely.

Finally Leo said, "If you could do whatever you wanted to do, Gabrielle, what would it be?"

"What do you mean?" she asked.

"If you didn't have to worry about money, if you could choose whatever life you wanted, what would it be?"

"I would like to have my own horse farm," she answered immediately. "I would like to breed and train Lipizzaners. Someday, when the king is restored, the Royal Riding School will be restored also, and they will need horses. I could supply them."

"You sound as if you have given this some thought."

She laughed. "It is a dream, Leo, that is all. I think about it when I feel badly that I have to drag my horses all over France for eight months out of every year. It is a hard life for them."

"It's not exactly an easy life for you," he said.

She shrugged. "Oh, I don't mind it. Really. I have a

good troupe of people to be my companions. It would just be better if Papa were still with us.''

''If he was, then Albert would not be getting a chance to be an artist.''

''That's true,'' she admitted. ''Papa was very strong on keeping the family together.''

There was a little silence as they drove over a wooden bridge. Ducks floated on the stream beneath them. Then Leo asked, ''Did your father like your husband?''

''He liked it that André was a member of our circus. And he liked André—well, it was impossible not to like André. He was very personable. But he wasn't someone to take charge of things. He wasn't like you.''

Houses started to appear on the road on either side of them as they came closer to the city.

Gabrielle said, ''We will have to say farewell to Franz this evening. I hope the doctor doesn't mind us coming in.''

He'd better not, Leo thought. *I'm paying him a fortune.*

''I'm sure it will be all right,'' he said.

She smiled up at him. ''You have been my guardian angel these last two days, Leo.''

He smiled back at her and thought: *Tonight.*

Twenty-Five

Leo, Gabrielle, Mathieu and Albert had dinner at a restaurant close to their hotel and then walked over to the doctor's house to say goodbye to Franz. His room was crowded and they didn't stay long. They returned to their hotel and Leo set out some algebra for Mathieu to do while Gabrielle and Albert played cards.

"Another few lessons and you will surpass me," Leo was saying to Mathieu when Julius ran into the salon.

"Leo," he said breathlessly, "Pierre has been arrested."

Gabrielle shot to her feet, knocking a few cards off the table. "*Mon Dieu*. What happened?"

Julius gave her an uneasy look. "I think I had better tell Leo about it, Gabrielle."

"This is my circus," she said fiercely. "If there is a problem, I want to know about it."

Julius looked at Leo, who nodded, then back to Gabrielle. "Well…apparently Pierre went to a…house of ill repute tonight and got into a fight. Alençon has a local gendarme and he arrested Pierre and threw him into jail."

"A house of ill repute," Gabrielle shrieked. "What was he thinking of?"

Leo said dryly, "Living with Jeanne probably drove him to it. Who did he get into a fight with?"

"I'm not sure," Julius said. "Pierre paid the gendarme

to send someone to get one of us. As soon as I heard, I came to tell you."

Leo mumbled something under his breath.

"We are leaving Alençon tomorrow morning," Mathieu said.

"It doesn't look as if Pierre is coming with us," Julius added.

Leo stood up. Everyone looked at him. He said, "I will go and talk to this gendarme," he said. "Where is the jail, Julius?"

"I have the directions," Julius said. "I'll go with you."

"Good," Leo said. He looked at Gabrielle. "Don't worry, I'll take care of this. The gendarme probably wants a fine paid."

She stood up as well. "I will go with you."

"That's not necessary," he said. "I'll take care of it, Gabrielle."

"It's my circus," she said.

Julius said, "Leo is your husband, Gabrielle. He will deal with this for you. Your father would not like you to be visiting a jail."

She lifted her chin stubbornly.

"Julius is right, Gabrielle," Mathieu said. "This sounds sordid. Papa would not like you to get involved."

"But it's *my* circus," she repeated.

Mathieu stood up. "It's my circus, too. I will go with Leo. You stay here with Albert."

She looked at him. Suddenly, it seemed as if he was taller. Older.

"All right, Mathieu," she said. "Thank you."

He nodded.

Leo said, "Let's go, then," and the three of them left the room.

* * *

Gabrielle and Albert continued to play cards for a while, waiting for the others to return. When Albert had yawned for the fifth time, Gabrielle said, "Why don't you go to bed? You're tired."

He shook his head. "I'm not leaving you alone down here." He yawned again.

Gabrielle stood up. "Then I'll go upstairs as well."

Albert accompanied her out to the stable yard with Colette, then they both went up the stairs to their separate bedrooms.

Gabrielle changed into her nightgown and got into bed. She didn't lie down, however, but pushed her pillows up against the headboard and sat up, waiting for Leo to return. She had been in bed for fifteen minutes when she heard his step outside the door. Then the door opened and he was there.

She had left the lamp on the bedside table burning and she saw him clearly, from his slightly untidy hair to the tips of his well-made black boots. His presence seemed to fill the room. Once more her stomach turned to jelly.

"What happened?" she said.

He came over to the bed and sat next to her. "Pierre evidently went berserk and tore up the whorehouse," he said.

She stared at him in shock.

"Don't look like that, sweetheart. It was mostly a matter of some broken mirrors and lamps."

"But what could have gotten into him?" she breathed.

There was silence as he looked at her. Then he said, "I don't know."

She searched his face. She had a feeling that he did know but wasn't going to tell her.

"What is going to happen?" she asked.

"Pierre has to pay for the damages, and he has to pay a fine for disturbing the peace. They won't let him out until he does that."

"Can he make those payments?"

"He can if you will advance him his next month's salary."

"I suppose I can do that," she said, slowly.

"I've been thinking, and I'm not so sure that it's a good idea," Leo said.

His blue-green eyes were very grave. She frowned. "I don't understand."

"The way things stand now, Pierre is bringing you nothing but trouble," he said. "This might be a good way to be rid of him."

"You mean leave him stuck in jail?"

He shrugged.

Her eyes widened. "That would be a terrible thing to do, Leo. Pierre may be having his problems, but I can't just leave him to rot in jail!"

He sighed. "I was afraid that was what you would say."

"Has anyone talked to Jeanne?" she said.

"She was at the café when the messenger came with news of Pierre's arrest. She must have gone back to the hotel. She certainly wasn't at the jail."

Gabrielle said forcefully, "All of Pierre's problems started when he married Jeanne. If there's anyone we should get rid of, it's her."

"Pierre is the one who is going to have to make that decision, Gabrielle."

She shut her eyes. "Oh, Leo, none of these things happened when Papa was running the circus. Why are they happening to me?"

"You've had some bad luck, that's all," he said encouragingly. "It will get better."

"The Pierre-Jeanne situation isn't going to get better."

"Then why don't you dismiss them both? Surely it won't be too difficult to replace musicians."

"They know all our music."

"A new musician will be able to pick up your music very quickly."

There was a long silence. Then she said in a small voice, "I just feel as if I can't turn my back on Pierre when he is in such trouble. Especially when I don't think that it's his fault." She looked up. "What will happen to him, Leo, if I let them go? I must admit that I don't care much what happens to Jeanne, but I have known Pierre for years. There are not many steady jobs for musicians these days."

He lifted his hands and smoothed his thumbs along her cheekbones. "Your heart is too kind. That's your problem."

"No one can ever be too kind," she said breathlessly, his touch electrifying her.

"Kiss me," he said, and lowered his head.

At the touch of his mouth, she melted. His large body bent over hers and she let him push her back against her pillows. His kiss was deep and intensely erotic. She reached up to put her arms around his neck and her fingers caressed the golden hair on his nape.

Time stopped. Thinking stopped. All she could do was feel this kiss, feel the heat from his body, the crispness of his hair between her fingers.

Then, as had happened before, an inquisitive black nose poked itself onto the pillow next to her face.

Colette, Gabrielle thought dizzily.

"Damn," Leo said. He sat up and Gabrielle blinked

at him. "I brought a little something home to take care of this problem," he told her huskily. He went to the wardrobe and pulled out a piece of baling twine, which he slipped around Colette's collar. Gabrielle sat up and watched as he walked Colette back to her mattress, then fastened the other end of the twine around the leg of the wardrobe.

"There," he said. "That should take care of her for a while."

Colette pulled against the twine and couldn't move. Leo came back to the bed and the both of them watched the dog as she attempted once more to move away from the mattress. When it became apparent that she couldn't do so, she laid down, put her face between her paws and looked resigned.

"Good girl," Gabrielle said.

Colette's ears flicked but she didn't move.

"When did you get that twine?" Gabrielle asked.

"This afternoon," he replied. "I was thinking ahead."

She laughed.

He turned to her, and slowly and deliberately, he unfastened the small buttons at the neck of her nightdress. "Do you know that you have the most beautiful neck?" he said. "I have been wanting to kiss it forever."

She felt his lips on her throat and closed her eyes. "Oh, Leo," she said huskily. "Oh, Leo."

His hand came up and covered her right breast. She could feel her nipple stand up under his touch. His mouth moved up her neck, to her jaw, to her cheek, then once again to her mouth. His hand caressed her breast. She felt a sweet sensation tremble between her legs.

He said against her mouth, "I am going to get out of these clothes."

He stood up and she watched with dilated eyes as he

removed his jacket and shirt, then his boots and breeches. He looked like one of the Greek gods she had once seen depicted in the Louvre, clean-limbed and strong and pure.

Then he was back beside her on the bed and she spread her hand over his chest, which was covered in fine golden hairs.

He kissed her until she was quivering, and when he suggested that she remove her nightgown, she pulled it up and let him take it off over her head. Then he slid her down on the bed so that she was lying flat, and he began to kiss her breasts. She buried her hands in his thick hair and gave herself up to pure sensation.

When his hands caressed her thighs, and then moved higher to touch her most vulnerable spot, she inhaled raggedly. It had been a long time since she had felt like this; in fact, she knew she had never felt *quite* like this before. His fingers moved back and forth, and she spread her legs wider to give him better access.

When finally he poised himself above her to enter, she was straining toward him, looking for him to release the incredible tension he had built inside her. When he entered her, she had to stretch to take him, and for a moment she was uncomfortable. Then he began to move, and the tension inside her ratcheted higher. She lifted her legs and encircled his waist. Finally it came, searing bolts of pleasure that seemed to shoot all the way down her legs and up her back. She actually cried out loud, the sensation was so powerful.

She heard him cry out as well as he found his own release. For a long moment they clung tightly together, two people in one body, giving and taking pleasure from each other. Then, slowly, they relaxed into tenderness.

"Gabrielle," he murmured against her hair. "That was...unbelievable."

"Yes," she said in a hushed voice. She had enjoyed sex with André, but it had never been as stunning as this.

His arms were around her and her head was resting against his chest. His skin was moist with sweat. She felt so safe in his arms, so cherished. She shut her eyes and listened to the slowing of his heartbeat.

His lips touched her hair. "It's like silk, your hair," he said. "It's the prettiest hair I've ever seen."

She smiled. "It's just brown hair, Leo."

"It shines." He breathed deeply. "And it smells like lemon."

They were quiet, still wrapped in each other's arms. Then Gabrielle said, "When first I met you I never dreamed we'd end up like this."

"When first I met you I thought you were the most beautiful girl I had ever seen."

"Did you really?"

"Yes, I did really."

"You also thought I was bossy."

"You *are* bossy, but you are still beautiful."

She chuckled.

Gabrielle said, "Thank you for going to the jail tonight to see about Pierre. I'll bring him the money early tomorrow morning so he can leave for Le Mans with us."

"If you're sure that's what you want to do."

"I'm sure."

Once more she felt his lips touch her hair. "Beautiful and kind," he said. "Not too many women have that combination, sweetheart."

She said, "I like it when you call me 'sweetheart.' It is an English endearment?"

"Yes," he said.

"It's nice."

He didn't say anything.

Colette stood up and looked at them.

"I think she is uncomfortable," Gabrielle said. She pulled away from Leo and sat up. "I'll untie her."

She got out of bed, pulled her nightgown over her head and went over to the dog. Colette stood quietly as she untied the twine from her collar.

Gabrielle went back to the bed and got in. "I suppose I should be grateful that you don't insist on housing your horses with us," he joked.

"That would be a little excessive." She pulled the covers up to her breast. "But I wish I had a nice barn, with big airy stalls, that they could live in. And big green pastures where they could graze."

He said, "You take very good care of your horses, Gabrielle. They seem to be quite content with the life they have."

She turned to give him a radiant smile. "Thank you, Leo. It makes me happy to hear that."

His face was grave as he said, "Go to sleep. We have an early start tomorrow."

She snuggled her head into her pillow, content for the first time in ages. "Good night, Leo."

Twenty-Six

When Leo awoke the following morning, Gabrielle was still asleep. He propped himself up on his elbow and watched her face: the delicately molded lips, the fine cheekbones, the long dark lashes lying so gently on her cheeks.

He wanted her. He glanced at the window, at the light coming in under the partially drawn shade, and sighed.

How nice it would be to get Gabrielle all to himself—no dogs, no circus, nobody except the two of them. He would make love to her every morning, every afternoon and every night. He didn't think he would ever get tired of making love to her.

She stirred, as if she felt his gaze, and her lashes fluttered. For a moment, he tensed, wondering if she would say her husband's name.

"Leo," she said, and he smiled.

"Good morning, sweetheart. Unfortunately we have to get up and go rescue Pierre before we can leave for Le Mans." He bent his head, kissed her slightly parted lips and said huskily, "I can think of something I would much rather do."

She gave him a sleepy smile.

He straightened away from her and got out of bed. Colette, who was stretched out in almost the identical position she had been last night, didn't move.

Leo had almost finished dressing when he said, "If you will give me Pierre's money, Gabrielle, I will go and bail him out."

She turned to look at him. She was wearing her divided skirt and a white shirt, tucked in. Her hair was loose and her feet were bare. Her expression was troubled. "I think I should do that, Leo."

"Don't let's start with that 'my circus' business again," he said. "We all know it's your circus. You don't have to keep proving it."

A faint frown drew her brows together. "It isn't that."

He sat down to pull his boots on. "Then what is it?"

"I think I'm getting too dependent on you," she said. "I was thinking about it last night after you left to go to the jail. We're not really married, after all. You will be leaving after we deliver the gold. It isn't good for me to grow too used to having you around to deal with my problems. I have to deal with them myself."

He pulled his first boot on and looked at her. She was so brave, and sweet and beautiful. She shouldn't have to be dealing with drunken louts and employees who smashed up whorehouses.

"While I'm here, you might as well make use of me."

She shook her head. "It isn't good for me. And it isn't good that all the others are looking to you for leadership. I am the one who must hold this circus together. Papa left the responsibility to me."

"As Mathieu said last night, the circus belongs to him, too."

"Yes, it does. And it will be good if Mathieu can help me. But I don't think that you should help me anymore, Leo. I think I have to manage on my own."

"Damn it," he said angrily. "I can't stand by and

watch you cope with things I'm much better equipped to deal with.''

"I have to learn to cope," she argued. "I should have thought about asking the doctor to keep Franz until he is well. If something like that happens again, though, at least I will know what to do. I must thank you for that.''

Leo thought of all the extra money it had cost to make that arrangement. But he couldn't tell Gabrielle about that.

"The others all think we are married," he reasoned. "It is natural for them to look to the man for leadership, Gabrielle. Why don't we just leave things as they are, and when I am gone they will go back to looking to you?''

Her big troubled brown eyes clung to his face.

He wanted to catch her in his arms and tell her that everything would be all right, that he would make everything all right for her. But he couldn't do that. She was right; he would be rejoining his regiment once the gold was delivered.

"We can both go and negotiate Pierre's release," he suggested. "How about that?''

"I thought I might go with Mathieu," she said.

He shook his head decisively. "It will look strange to the others if you do that. You don't want to start gossip, do you?''

Slowly she shook her own head. "No, I don't want to do that.''

"Fine, then the two of us will go to the jail together and collect Pierre. That way it won't just be me. You will be part of it, too.''

She sighed. "Oh, all right, Leo. I suppose that will do.''

"Good. Now finish dressing and we'll get some breakfast before we bring Pierre his money."

Pierre was silent and grim when he was released from the jail. He didn't say a word as he, Gabrielle and Leo got into the front seat of the wagon to drive back to the circus grounds.

They were on the outskirts of town when Gabrielle finally asked, "Are you all right, Pierre?"

"Yes," he said. "I'm all right."

"Gabrielle was the one who insisted on rescuing you, you know," Leo told him. "I wasn't so sure it was a good idea."

Pierre turned his head to stare at Leo, who was driving. "What do you mean?" he said.

"I mean we don't want trouble in this circus, Pierre. If you and Jeanne have marital problems, then take care of them between the two of you. I don't want any harm coming to the circus because Gabrielle was kind enough to advance you money you have not yet earned."

Pierre scowled. "I'm not bringing any harm to the circus."

Leo turned his head and met his eyes. "I hope not. But if we have any more injuries, Pierre, I will know where to look."

Pierre turned to stare straight ahead. "I don't know what you're talking about."

"I think you do. And I mean what I say. I am not a good man to cross, Pierre. I think you should know that."

Gabrielle, who was sitting between the two men, looked anxiously at Leo. She didn't say anything.

Leo said, "Gabrielle feels loyalty to you because you have been with the circus for a long time. I hope you feel the same loyalty to her."

Pierre mumbled something indistinguishable.

"Do I make myself clear?" Leo said.

"Yes," Pierre said harshly.

"Good."

The rest of the ride passed in silence. After they had reached the circus grounds and Pierre had departed to go to his own wagon, Gabrielle turned to Leo, who was standing beside her watching Pierre go.

"What was that all about?" she asked.

He kept his eyes on Pierre. "What do you mean?"

"You know what I mean. You were warning Pierre. Do you suspect him of something, Leo?"

He turned to her and hesitated. He didn't want to burden her with his suspicions about Pierre, but on the other hand she should be warned. He would not always be here to help her.

"I am not entirely sure that Pierre wasn't responsible for Franz's accident," he said carefully.

Her brown eyes widened. "But the rope was frayed from wear!"

"It was frayed pretty evenly, Gabrielle. I'm not saying that it wasn't an accident, but I definitely plan to keep an eye on Pierre."

"Mon Dieu," she breathed.

It was a sunny morning and her complexion as she turned to face him was flawless. Her brown eyes were huge. "Why didn't you tell me your suspicions before this?"

"I didn't want to worry you. But what you said to me this morning makes some sense. You should be warned to watch out for Pierre."

"But you have no proof?" she said anxiously.

"No. The rope was definitely frayed. It could have

been an accident. I am just not completely comfortable about it.''

"This is why you wanted me to get rid of him?"

"Yes. And it's still not too late to do that."

"I need some time to hire new musicians. Plus, Pierre may be innocent. I would feel terrible dismissing him on a false suspicion."

He put a finger under her chin and leaned down to lightly kiss her lips. "If everyone had a heart like yours, the world would be a wonderful place to live. I've warned him—he knows I'm suspicious. That may be enough to quell any desire he has to do anything else."

"I'll keep an eye on him," she said soberly.

He hated to see her look this way. "I shouldn't have told you. I've knocked the smile right off your face."

She shook her head. "You were right to tell me, Leo. I know you don't like me to keep saying this, but it is my circus. I have to be aware of any potential danger."

He sighed. "That's why I told you."

Paul approached them. "I think one of my wheels is about to break, Leo. Would you take a look at it?"

"Certainly," Leo replied, and the two men walked across the winter-brown grass to Paul and Sully's wagon.

From their place by the horse corral, Mathieu and Albert watched Gabrielle and Leo pull up with Pierre. They watched as Pierre walked away and Gabrielle and Leo talked. They watched as Leo leaned down to kiss Gabrielle on the mouth. They looked at each other.

Albert said, "I think something is going on between Gabrielle and Leo."

Mathieu said, "It looks like it, doesn't it?"

"It would be perfect if they married for real," Albert

said. "Leo would take care of Gabrielle—and he would take care of us, too."

"He has promised to take care of you, no matter what," Mathieu said.

Albert pushed his light brown hair away from his eyes. "I have been thinking—I don't know if I should go away and leave you and Gabrielle to run the circus alone."

Mathieu raised his brows. "Don't be stupid. Leo is offering you a great opportunity, Albert. You would be a fool not to take it."

"I don't know," Albert repeated. "I would feel as if I was deserting you and Gabrielle."

"Gabrielle wants this for you. The reason she agreed to take the gold was so that she would have the money to send you to art school." When Albert looked surprised, Mathieu smiled faintly. "You didn't know that, did you?"

Albert shook his head and Mathieu went on. "Well, now that you have an even better opportunity—and it won't cost Gabrielle anything—you can't refuse it."

Albert regarded his brother solemnly. "And what about you, Mathieu? You have gobbled up these mathematic sessions with Leo. Wouldn't you like a chance to go to university and study mathematics?"

Mathieu laughed harshly. "That's impossible. Even if I could find the money to go to university, what would I do with myself after I got out?"

"Perhaps you could teach."

"I don't think so, Albert. I'm sure I make far more money in the circus than I would teaching farmers' sons in some dreary provincial school."

Albert looked at him out of troubled golden-brown eyes.

Mathieu patted him on the shoulder. "One day, if you

become a great painter and make a lot of money, you can pay for me to go to university and become a mathematician.''

"Maybe Leo would pay for you," Albert said. "He likes you a lot."

"Leo is going to take on your education. We can hardly ask him to take on mine as well. Besides, I couldn't leave Gabrielle all by herself with the circus.''

Albert sighed. "Everything would be so perfect if Leo would marry Gabrielle. She is so beautiful, and so good. How could he not fall in love with her?''

Mathieu said soberly, "He may fall in love with her, but that doesn't mean he'll marry her. Remember, he is an aristocrat in his own country, and the English are very conscious of the differences between the classes. They did not have a revolution like we did.''

"But he kissed her," Albert said.

"Do you know what I am afraid of?'' Mathieu said. "I am afraid that Gabrielle will fall in love with Leo, and when he leaves, her heart will be broken. I would hate to see her the way she was after André died.''

"Do you think they are sleeping together?''

"I don't know, and if they are, it's Gabrielle's business, not ours.''

Albert was silent for a long minute. Then he said, "I am going to pray that Leo falls in love with Gabrielle and marries her.''

Mathieu gave his brother's shoulders a brief hug. "You do that, Albert. You do that.''

Twenty-Seven

There was a definite crack in Paul and Sully's wheel and they had to drive into town to get a new one. Gabrielle told them to follow the circus to Le Mans and the rest of them were on the road by nine o'clock.

The day was warm and sunny, a portent of spring. Gabrielle sat beside Leo in the wagon, her face turned up to the sun, her eyes closed.

He smiled at her. "You look like a flower soaking in the sunshine," he said. "Ladies in England hide from the sun under bonnets and parasols."

"Ladies in England are so fair they have to watch their skin," she returned. Her eyes were still closed and her face uplifted. Her peaches-and-cream complexion had turned a very faint golden tan.

My golden girl, Leo thought.

They drove for a long while in comfortable silence, Leo occasionally thinking how pleasant it was to find a woman who didn't feel it necessary to talk all the time.

They had lunch at Beaumont-sur-Sarthe, in a small restaurant on the river, where Colette had fun scattering the geese. Then they resumed their journey, going through the town of Le Mans and stopping just to the south of it, where they were to meet Vincent to find out about their arrangements.

When they reached the meeting site they found that

Vincent was not alone. A soldier dressed in the uniform of an army sergeant was standing with him. Gabrielle's heart began to pound.

"Shit," Leo said as they approached the wagon.

The sergeant was a man of medium height and medium age. His eyes were so dark they were almost black, and his features were sharp.

"Good afternoon, Vincent," Gabrielle said as calmly as she could.

"Good afternoon, Leo, Gabrielle," Vincent returned. "This sergeant has been waiting to see you."

Leo remained prudently silent. Gabrielle lifted an inquisitive eyebrow. "To what do we owe the honor of this attention, Sergeant?"

"I am Sergeant Gaston Jordan, *madame,* and I have been assigned to travel with your circus," the man announced in a crisp voice. "The War Ministry is desirous of keeping close watch on all convoys traveling from the north of France toward Spain."

Gabrielle could feel the color drain from her face. "This is ridiculous," she snapped. "We are a perfectly innocent circus. We don't deserve to have a spy foisted on us!"

"As I said, *madame,* the War Ministry is keeping close watch on all vehicles that might possibly be transporting gold." He paused and looked meaningfully at Leo. "Your circus is of particular interest because you are carrying an Englishman."

Leo said to Gabrielle. "I am sorry, *chérie,* that I have brought this nuisance upon you. When you agreed to marry me I had no idea that something like this would happen."

She smiled at him. "You're right. It is a nuisance, that

is all.'' She returned her gaze to the sergeant. ''You are going to ride with us until we reach Biarritz?''

''Yes, *madame,* those are my orders.''

''I suppose you will want to ride in one of our wagons.''

''Yes, *madame.*''

''Very well,'' Gabrielle said tightly. ''My brother is driving the wagon just behind us. You can ride with him to the field that Vincent has found for us.''

''Thank you, *madame.*''

The sergeant moved off. When he was out of earshot, Vincent said, ''I couldn't get rid of him, Gabrielle. He was at the hotel I booked for you and he's stuck to me like glue ever since.''

''Don't worry about it, Vincent,'' Leo said. ''It's an annoyance, but we'll deal with it.''

''Go back to your carriage,'' Gabrielle said. ''We'll follow you to the field.''

The field was closer to the city than last year's field had been, and Gabrielle expressed her approval. Once they arrived, the circus folk set about raising the tents and tending to the horses while the sergeant stood around and watched.

Everybody wanted to know why there was an army sergeant watching them, and a representative from each act approached Gabrielle with the question. She told each one that the War Ministry was keeping close watch on all wagons traveling from the north of France toward Spain.

''It's that gold they're looking for, isn't it?'' Henri asked.

''It seems so,'' said Gabrielle. She fixed a feed bag over Shaitan's face and the horse began to gobble his grain.

"Still," Henri said, "we're an established circus. I'm surprised we would fall under suspicion."

Luc had just joined them and now he said, "It's Leo. Not only are we traveling from the north, but we have an Englishman with us—an Englishman who joined us only a short while ago."

Henri frowned. "We told them that Leo is married to Gabrielle. Surely that is explanation enough."

"You would think so," Gabrielle replied, hoping she sounded calmer than she felt. She affixed another feed bag on the eager Fantan. "The War Ministry is being overly zealous, that's all."

"I hope this man isn't going to search our wagons again," Henri said indignantly.

Gabrielle said, "I don't know what he's going to do, but I think we should try to cooperate with him. We don't want to add any fuel to his suspicion."

There was a little silence in which the only sound was that of the horses chewing their grain. Then Henri said, "You're right, Gabrielle. I will tell Carlotta what you've said."

"Thanks, Henri," Gabrielle said.

Henri walked away but Luc remained, waiting for Henri to be out of earshot. "If you're carrying that gold you're putting everyone in this circus in jeopardy," Luc said.

"I am *not* carrying any gold," Gabrielle said evenly.

"Then explain Leo."

"I have already explained Leo," she said fiercely. "We fell in love and got married. Our relationship has nothing to do with any gold."

Luc looked into her eyes for a long minute. "I don't think I believe you, Gabrielle."

"I don't care what you believe," she said. "I have told you the truth."

At this point, Paul came up to them. "What is that sergeant doing here?" he asked Gabrielle.

Grateful for the interruption, she began her explanation again as Luc walked away.

Leo didn't have a chance to talk to Gabrielle until they were alone in their bedroom before dinner. Leo closed the door behind them and Gabrielle turned to him, her eyes filled with worry.

"*Mon Dieu*, Leo," she said. "What are we going to do about the soldier?"

"Work around him," Leo said. "We don't have much choice."

"But *how?* How are we going to transfer the gold from my wagons to the custody of the English without that man knowing? I asked him if he wanted us to book him a room in the hotel and he said no, that he was going to be staying with the wagons! He will eat and sleep with the grooms. That's what he told me, Leo! What are we going to do?"

"Sweetheart, calm yourself. We'll find a way."

"What way?"

He took her cold hands into his big, warm grasp. "For one thing, the two wagons that matter come to the hotel with us."

She was silent, but her hands returned his clasp. "That's true," she said at last.

"Your job is not to worry about transferring the gold. Your job is to get it to Biarritz. It's the job of the British army to get it from your wagons to Wellington. And the British army is very good at its job, Gabrielle. So stop worrying. I hate to see you with that anxious look in your eyes.''

She said tensely, ''Luc thinks we have the gold. He told me that today.''

''He can think what he likes, but he can't do anything. Don't worry about Luc.''

''There's more about Luc,'' she said. She withdrew her hands from his and went to sit on the side of the bed. ''Emma told me today. You know how you said Jeanne never showed up at the jail last night?''

''Yes.''

''Well, she apparently spent the night in Luc's room.'' Gabrielle gripped her hands in her lap. ''If Pierre finds out, there will be mayhem.''

He walked over to sit beside her. ''Dismiss her, Gabrielle,'' he said firmly. ''Give her a month's wages and dismiss her. She is bringing you nothing but trouble.''

''What about Pierre?''

''Give Pierre a choice. Either he can stay with the circus or he can leave with his wife. But I strongly recommend you get rid of Jeanne.''

Gabrielle bit her lip and stared at her lap. ''But, Leo, how can I dismiss Jeanne for doing what I am doing myself?''

He put his hand over the small clenched hands in her lap. ''It's not the same at all, sweetheart. You're not married, so you're not betraying any vows. Jeanne is.''

Gabrielle didn't look at him. He continued to cover her hands with his. Finally she said in a low voice, ''I feel as if I am betraying André.''

Shit, Leo thought. This was the last thing he wanted. He slipped off the bed and knelt in front of her so he could look in her face. ''André has been dead for a year and a half. Do you really think he would want to deprive you of any happiness you can find?''

''I think he would approve of my getting married again. I don't think he would approve of this.''

''Gabrielle, I admire your bravery for taking on the circus. I admire the way you have shouldered responsibility for your brothers. I admire the way you ride. I care about you very much.''

There was a long silence. Then she lifted her head and gave him a smile that did not reach her eyes. ''All right, Leo,'' she said. ''But I don't want anyone else to know what we are doing. We must be careful when we are around other people. Don't kiss me like you did today.''

''We're supposed to be husband and wife. Don't you want to convince the sergeant of that?''

''I don't care about the sergeant,'' she said. ''The most important people, the people I care about, my brothers and Emma and Gerard, know we're not married. I want to keep their respect. So we have to be careful.''

He sighed. ''All right. I will behave to you in public as if you were my sister.''

''Good,'' she said. ''Now, let's go down to the salon to meet the others. We have to decide on a restaurant to eat in. This hotel does not serve meals.''

For Leo, the dinner was interminable. So was the aftermath, at the café where Gabrielle had insisted on going to keep an eye on Jeanne and Pierre. Pierre did not join them at the café, however, and the rest of them had to endure the sight of Jeanne flirting with a very cooperative Luc all night long.

Leo and Gabrielle left the restaurant with the others to return to the hotel. Emma and Gerard walked in front of them and Gabrielle watched as Gerard tripped a little, then righted himself and walked on.

"I worry about Gerard," she said softly. "He is getting old for this kind of a life. He should have a nice chair by a nice fireplace, with grandchildren coming to visit."

"Was he ever married?" Leo asked curiously.

"No. He was the chief groom under Papa at the king's manège, and when Papa started the circus, he asked Gerard to come along. I don't think Gerard has ever been in any place for long enough to woo a woman."

"What about the wintertime?"

"He always winters with us, and helps to take care of and school the horses. He never meets many eligible women."

To Leo it sounded like a grim kind of a life. "Not even through the circus?"

"No. Papa never seemed to hire many women. There was always Emma, of course, but all of Emma's devotion goes to her dogs and to me and my brothers. Gerard is just a friend to her."

Leo asked curiously, "What will he do when he is too old to travel with the circus?"

"I don't know." She whistled to Colette, who had gotten too far ahead of them.

Leo watched as the big, elegant dog cantered back to them. "What was your father going to do about Gerard?"

"I don't know. Papa died so suddenly, he didn't have a chance to give me advice."

"How did your father die?" Leo asked gently.

"He had an apoplexy. It was awful. One minute he was talking to me, the next minute he was on the floor, completely unconscious. He died within two hours."

"I am so very sorry," he said.

"It was pretty grim," she said, "especially since I had lost André not that long before."

He wanted to gather her in his arms, to reassure her, to comfort her. But what could he say? That he would give her the money to retire Gerard? He would be happy to give it to her, but he knew she wouldn't accept it. And he knew he must take care not to get too close.

He might be able to do something about Pierre and Jeanne, however. "Listen, Gabrielle, Le Mans is a pretty big city. If you hang up posters around town, advertising that you need two new band members, I'm certain you would get some replies. Hire two new people and tell Jeanne and Pierre that they are dismissed."

She was silent for a while. Then she said, "I'm just not ready to do that to Pierre yet, Leo. I own I would like to get rid of Jeanne, but I can't get into the middle of a marriage. It wouldn't be right. If Pierre wants to be rid of Jeanne, then he has to be the one to make that decision."

They reached the hotel and most of the circus folk went up the stairs to bed. Leo said to Gabrielle, "You go up first. I'm just going to check the wagons in the stable yard."

When Leo came back into the hotel, the lobby was empty and dim, with only one lamp burning. Then he heard the sound of shouting coming from the salon to the right of the entrance hall. Leo thought it sounded like Pierre and Jeanne and went to look through the open door.

The two of them were standing in the middle of the room, facing each other. Pierre was shouting in his deepest voice, "I was in jail and you slept with Luc! Can you deny that?"

"I'm not denying anything to you," Jeanne screamed

back. "If you can't be a man to me yourself, then I will find a man who can be." The contempt in her voice was excoriating. "What happened at the whorehouse, Pierre? I'll wager you couldn't get it up there, either."

Pierre's answer was the sound of an open hand going across human flesh. Leo strode into the salon and they both turned to look at him. There was the mark of a handprint on Jeanne's face.

"See, Leo," she said in a trembling voice. "You see how he treats me. He is a wife-abuser."

Pierre's furious dark eyes met Leo's. Leo said, "How do you know she slept with Luc?"

Pierre replied truculently, "Sully told me, as well as Henri. As soon as the news came that I had been arrested, she and Luc went back to the hotel. Well, what would you think?"

Exactly what you're thinking, Leo thought. Out loud he said, "Under the circumstances, Pierre, do you want to keep her with the circus? Gabrielle is worried about this situation, and I don't like to see my wife worry. Frankly, I recommended that she dismiss both of you, but you know Gabrielle—she has a heart of gold. She wouldn't do it. But if there is going to be this constant strife between you two, she may change her mind."

"Gabrielle has a man for a husband," Jeanne said sullenly. "She should have pity on me, for I don't."

Pierre flushed a deep brick red from his neck to his hairline.

"Sleeping with a bitch like you would put any man off his stroke, Jeanne," Leo said neutrally.

She stared at him in speechless astonishment. Then, finally, "How dare you speak to me like that?"

"I dare because my wife owns this circus, and as things stand, you are both liabilities we don't need."

They both of them looked at the ground.

"Had he been alive, Gabrielle's father would have fired you while we were in Alençon, but she has a softer heart," he continued. "So I am giving you one more chance. Jeanne, if I catch you flirting with any man but your husband, you'll be dismissed. Is that clear?"

Her slanting dark eyes flashed. "What about Pierre? He hit me, Leo!"

"He won't hit you if you behave yourself" came the calm rejoinder. Leo looked from Jeanne to Pierre then back again to Jeanne. "Am I clear?"

"Yes," Pierre mumbled. "Very clear."

"Jeanne?" Leo asked.

"It's not fair," Jeanne said. "I can at least talk to men, can't I?"

"If you can manage to talk without flirting." He turned to Pierre. "If you want us to dismiss Jeanne and keep you, we will do that."

Pierre gave Jeanne a look of baffled fury and longing. Then he mumbled, "No. Tell Gabrielle that we will be on our best behavior from now on."

"All right," Leo said dubiously. "But I expect you both to adhere to your words."

"We will, Leo," Pierre said.

A tight-lipped Jeanne nodded.

Leo left them together in the salon, hoping that would be the end of one more distraction.

Twenty-Eight

Gabrielle was standing by the wardrobe, still in her clothes, when Leo came into the room. He had been hoping to find her in bed.

"Why haven't you changed?" he asked.

"I was petting Colette," she said. "She loves to have her belly rubbed, and I have been so busy with you lately that I have been neglecting her."

"She is the least neglected dog that I know," Leo laughed. He went over to where Colette was lying on her mattress, squatted on his heels and stroked her head. She gazed up at him with serene brown eyes.

Gabrielle said, "Did you see Pierre at all?"

He waited a moment, then he said, "I saw both him and Jeanne in the salon a few minutes ago. Sully and Henri apparently told him that Jeanne had slept with Luc and they were having a fight."

The anxious frown he hated to see came across her forehead. "Did you say anything to them?"

"As a matter of fact, I did. I told Jeanne that if I caught her flirting with a man other than her husband, you would dismiss her."

"What did Pierre say to that?"

"He went along with it."

She crossed her arms over her breasts. "But what is *wrong* with Jeanne? They have only been married for a few months. You saw how she was with Luc all the time we were at the café tonight. And Luc is not helping matters by encouraging her advances.''

He stopped petting the dog and stood up. *Better tell her,* he thought. He drew a deep breath and said, ''I think the problem is that Pierre has not been able to perform sexually with Jeanne.''

Her brown eyes grew to twice their normal size. *''Mon Dieu,''* she said.

''When I came into the room, Jeanne was screaming at him, 'If you can't be a man to me yourself, then I will find a man who can be.''' Leo lifted one golden eyebrow. ''What does that sound like to you?''

''It sounds like a problem that neither of us can fix,'' she returned. ''And Jeanne is certainly going about it in the wrong way. Pierre needs reassurance that she loves him. He does not need to be whipped into a frenzy picturing his wife with other men.''

He left the dog and crossed the room to gather her in his arms. ''Most women aren't as compassionate as you are, sweetheart. Or as wise.''

She rested her head against his shoulder. ''What a nice compliment. Thank you.''

He bent his head and touched his lips to her hair. ''The hell with Jeanne and Pierre,'' he said. ''Let's concentrate on us.''

''That's fine with me,'' she said, her voice a little muffled by his shoulder.

He kissed her head, then loosened his arms. ''First let me get my trusty piece of rope.''

When he had finished tying Colette to the wardrobe, he turned around and found Gabrielle taking off her shirt. As he watched, she next pulled her camisole over her head.

The swell of her breasts was beautiful. He had seen many beautiful women in his life, but none were more beautiful for him. Never for him.

She took off her skirt and carefully hung it in the wardrobe.

Leo had to restrain the temptation to spring on her, like his namesake, the lion. He wanted to pounce on her and devour her, to ravish her with his desire.

He strode across the room, took her into his arms and pulled her against him.

"Leo!" She was half flustered and half laughing.

He bent his head and kissed her long and deep. She melted under his touch, melted into him so that the whole length of her slender body was pressed against him. He felt her breasts against his rib cage, and when he put one hand on her waist, it almost encircled it halfway.

"Gabrielle," he said hoarsely. "Let's go to bed."

"Yes," she said. Such a simple word, but right now it was the world to him.

He managed to get out of his clothes without too much fumbling, although he had a hard time with his boots. As he was pulling at them, he looked up to see Gabrielle lying on the bed, waiting for him. If he had had a knife handy, he would have cut the damn boots right off his feet.

Finally they were off, though, and he quickly removed his breeches and drawers and went on bare feet toward the bed where she awaited him.

She lifted her arms as he sat on the bed and he rolled over to gather her close.

I have to take my time, he told himself. *I can't rush.*

And, in truth, he didn't want to rush. He wanted to savor every moment of this encounter. He wanted to kiss her all over, to fill his mouth with her breasts, to slide his hands through her loose hair, to feel under his hands her rib cage and the gentle swell of her hips. And she touched him, too, running her hands over the muscles in his arms and back, ruffling the soft hair on his chest. At last he kissed the perfect shell of her ear and whispered, "Ready?"

"Yes," she said. "Oh, yes."

He raised himself on his hands and, for a moment, hovered over her, admiring her body. Then he plunged.

He made a little choking sound. God, it felt wonderful to be inside her. She was so warm, so wet.

She was so perfect.

"Gabrielle," he cried.

"Leo," she managed in response.

He began to move inside her, in and out, and as he moved he felt the tissue around him begin to soften. Gabrielle arched her back, moving to meet him, to urge him along. He drove faster and harder, and she met him all the way, until the moment when orgasm swept through her and she rippled all around him. She cried out with the intensity of the pleasure he was bringing her, and when he heard that, he let go the control he had been exerting on himself and drove twice more, deep into the heart of her. His release was shattering.

They lay pressed together, naked flesh to naked flesh, heartbeat to heartbeat. Leo did not think he had ever been this happy before in his life.

"Oh, my," Gabrielle whispered after a while. "That was *formidable*."

He wanted to ask her if she had had the same experience when she had made love with her husband, but he thought that this was not an auspicious time to bring up André.

There's no need to be jealous of André, he thought.

André is dead and I am the one who is here with Gabrielle.

The thought brought a smile to his lips.

They lay peacefully together for a little while, then Colette barked, causing the two of them to jump. "Good God," Leo said.

Gabrielle pulled away from him and sat up. She put her nightgown on over her head and went to check on the dog. "What's the matter, *chérie?* Don't you feel all right?"

Colette was standing up, pulling against the rope.

Leo swung his feet out of bed and picked up his breeches. "I'll take her out, sweetheart. You go back to bed. It's getting late."

"I'll take her out," Gabrielle said. "She's my dog."

Leo frowned. He wished she would not keep saying the word *my*—*my circus, my dog*—it made it so difficult for him to help her.

He said, "You already have your nightgown on, and all I have to do is put on these breeches and throw a coat on. I will take her."

He spoke authoritatively, in the voice his subordinates in the army always obeyed instantly.

Gabrielle set her jaw and said, "She is *my* dog and I will take her out. If you want to come along, I can't stop you—although it is silly for us both to miss sleep." And she marched to the wardrobe and took out her long gray pelisse, which she put on over her nightgown. Next she shoved her small feet into a pair of low boots and untied Colette. "Come along, love. Let's go."

Without another word, Leo pulled his jacket over his bare torso, lit a candle from the lamp and joined her as she left the room.

The hotel was very dark and they went down the stairs

by candlelight, into the kitchen and out the back door to the stable yard. Colette immediately went to sniff the ground and Leo and Gabrielle stood together near the door and watched her.

Leo said, "It's very frustrating, the way you won't let me help you."

"We have already discussed this, Leo," Gabrielle replied. It was chilly in the yard and she crossed her arms. "You know my feelings on this matter. It is very kind of you to want to help, but I think it is better if I do things myself."

Colette finally found the spot she wanted and squatted.

"Good girl," Gabrielle cooed.

"What a come-down," Leo said humorously. "I've just had the best sex I ever had in my life, and twenty minutes later I'm standing in the cold with a dog."

She turned to look up at him. The candlelight showed him her face and her sparkling eyes. "Was it the best?" she asked.

"Definitely," he replied.

She smiled at him. "Oh, Leo, for me, too."

That smile of hers played havoc with his heart. All he could manage to say in reply was "I'm glad."

Colette came over to them and Leo patted her on the head. Then the three of them went back into the house and up the stairs to bed.

When they arrived at the circus field the following morning, Sergeant Jordan was waiting for them.

"Do you always take these wagons into town for the evening?" he asked Gabrielle.

"Yes," said Gabrielle.

The sergeant looked at Leo, then turned his black eyes

back to Gabrielle. "They are your wagons? I see that they are painted with the sign for your circus."

"They are my wagons," Gabrielle agreed. "We have always used them for transportation back and forth to our hotel."

"I think it would be better for you to use other wagons from now on," the sergeant said.

"Why?" Gabrielle demanded. "We have used these wagons for years."

"I want them where I can see them," the sergeant said. He looked around the field. "Use two of the wagons belonging to your troupe. I want all of your wagons to stay at the field."

Gabrielle looked as if she was going to argue, but Leo cut in. "Very well. If that is what you want, Sergeant, that is what we'll do."

The sergeant regarded him with barely concealed suspicion. "What do you do in this circus, *monsieur?*"

"I am the ringmaster," Leo replied amiably.

Sergeant Jordan looked surprised.

"Yes," Gabrielle said. "My husband has assumed that duty. He has been a great help to us."

"I am going to search these wagons while you are doing your shows today," the sergeant said.

There was a beat of silence, then Gabrielle said, "You are welcome to look through them, but please leave them in the same condition as you found them. The last search left us in chaos."

The sergeant scowled.

"Come along, Gabrielle," Leo said. "Let the sergeant do his job. We have to get the horses ready."

She hesitated, then went reluctantly. The two of them walked away from the sergeant and headed toward the horse corral.

"What are we going to do now?" Gabrielle said in a low, despairing voice. "He has the whole afternoon to search our wagons."

"We'll be all right," Leo said. "I doubt that he will want to pull up the floorboards."

"He isn't letting us take the wagons into town," Gabrielle said. "How are we going to turn the gold over if he is watching the wagons all the time?"

"The army will think of something," Leo said.

"They don't even know about the sergeant!" she cried. "Do you have a way of getting in touch with them?"

"No," he admitted.

"Then it seems to me you should be just as worried as I am," Gabrielle said.

Leo's mouth set into a grim line and he didn't answer.

The noontime show was Leo's third performance as ringmaster, and he approached this show differently from the way he had approached the others. Before he had felt humiliated performing in front of people so far below his own social station. Today all he could think about was Sergeant Jordan searching the wagons.

He had spoken soothing words to Gabrielle, but he was worried. The sergeant had singled out the two Robichon wagons for his special attention. What if he decided to pull up the floorboards?

After the show had concluded, Leo went directly to the first wagon to see what was happening. The soldier was standing outside the wagon, with his arms crossed over his chest.

"Are you finished?" Leo asked. The back door to the wagon was open and he went to look inside. It was as orderly as it had looked when he left it. He turned to the sergeant. "Thank you for being so neat. We appreciate it."

The sergeant said, "Do you have a hammer? I want to pry up some of these floorboards."

Leo's heart thudded in his chest. "What?" he demanded. "We have tried to be cooperative, Sergeant, but this is going too far. I won't allow you to destroy our wagon."

His voice had taken on the tone of authority that was natural to him. The sergeant shifted from one foot to the other. "I'm not going to pull up all the floorboards," he said, "but I want to see the ones that are under that sofa."

Shit, Leo thought. *That's too close to the gold.*

He saw Gabrielle approaching the wagon.

Her face will give us away, he thought. He said quickly to the sergeant, "My wife will know where there's a hammer," and he moved hastily to intercept Gabrielle before she reached the wagon.

"Can you find us a hammer, sweetheart?" he asked loudly as he came up to her.

She looked up at him in surprise.

He moved so that she would have her back to the sergeant.

"Sergeant Jordan wants to pull up a few floorboards in the wagon," he said. "We need a hammer."

She went white as a sheet.

Leo went on, "Apparently he thinks we have hidden gold under the sofa. It's ridiculous, but I suppose we will have to go along with him."

She raised her chin and said sharply, "I'm not going to let him damage my wagon."

"I don't think we have a choice," Leo said calmly.

"I know it's a nuisance, but the sergeant has the right. We must go along with him, Gabrielle."

She didn't say anything; she just looked at him with huge brown eyes.

"It will be all right," he said. "Can you get us the hammer?"

She stood there looking at him for ten more seconds, then she turned and walked to the second wagon, where the tack was stored.

"If you will excuse me, I will assist my wife," Leo called to the sergeant.

Jordan nodded and Leo followed Gabrielle to the second wagon. She was lifting a hammer out of a box when he climbed in to join her.

"*Mon Dieu,* Leo." Her face was still very pale. "We can't let him do this!"

"If he just looks at the boards directly under the sofa we'll be all right," Leo said.

"What if he doesn't? What if he looks in front of the sofa?"

Leo opened his coat so that she could see the small pistol that was thrust into the waistband of his breeches. "Then we have to get rid of him," he said.

Her eyes became even larger. "You will shoot him?"

"Only if I have to," Leo said.

"*Mon Dieu,*" Gabrielle said. "And how will we explain *that* to the rest of them?"

"We'll say that the sergeant found my pistol and was holding it when it went off."

"*Mon Dieu,*" Gabrielle cried again.

"Do you have a hammer?"

"Yes."

"Then give it to me. You stay here. Your face will give us away."

She handed him the hammer. He took it and went back to the wagon where the sergeant was awaiting him.

"Good," the sergeant said, and held out his hand.

"I'll do it," Leo said. "I'll be more careful than you. I don't want the floorboards ruined."

"Fine," the sergeant said. "First, help me to move this sofa."

Leo took one end of the sofa and the sergeant took the other. Leo lifted it first and the sergeant followed. Together they moved it so that it was now standing directly over the gold.

Leo inserted the claw end of the hammer and began to pry up floorboards. There was nothing underneath. The only way to access the hidden bottom was through the floorboards that were now hidden by the sofa.

When all the floorboards that had stood under the sofa were pulled up, Leo put down the hammer. "I am not going to destroy this whole floor," he said to the sergeant. "Surely you can see that there's nothing here."

The sergeant scowled. After a long moment of silence, he said, "All right. Put the floorboards back. This wagon seems to be clear."

"I could have told you that," Leo said. "We are just a circus, Sergeant. There is no gold hidden here."

"Maybe," the sergeant said. "But I still want these wagons left at the field."

"If you insist," Leo said. "We will use two of the other wagons to get back and forth to town."

He moved toward the back wagon door. "I'm going to get some nails so I can put these floorboards back."

The sergeant scowled again. He was clearly very disappointed that he had not found gold under the sofa.

Leo went directly to the wagon where Gabrielle was

waiting for him. He opened the door, climbed inside and said, "It's all right. He didn't find anything."

Gabrielle was sitting on one of the tack trunks. "Thank God," she said fervently. "I was so afraid."

"It was a close call," Leo agreed. He sat next to her and put his arm around her shoulders. "Were you praying?"

"I certainly was," she said emphatically.

"Well, your prayers were answered. He only looked under where the sofa stands."

She put her head on his shoulder. "Would you really have killed him?"

"I didn't have to make that choice," he said.

She leaned into his warmth and strength and didn't pursue the question any further.

Twenty-Nine

The two shows went smoothly the following day, and Leo actually found himself starting to feel comfortable in his ringmaster role. When the second show had finished, the job of taking down the tents and preparing the horses for the night began. Everyone was so busy that it was a while before they missed Jeanne and Luc.

It was Antonio who first noticed that they were missing. Then word spread among the rest of the workers. Everyone stopped what they were doing and gathered around Leo and Gabrielle. Pierre was there as well and everyone studiously refrained from looking at him.

Gabrielle said in a calm voice, "Has anyone seen them?"

Antonio said, "She left the tent with us after the last performance, but I haven't seen her since."

"I'll go and check Luc's wagon," Leo said.

"I'll go with you," Pierre said.

Leo looked at him. Pierre's square face was flushed with anger. "Perhaps you'd better stay here," Leo said.

"She's my wife. I'm coming."

Leo glanced at Gabrielle. She looked pale and worried.

"All right, but don't lose your temper," Leo said. "Let me handle this."

"She's my wife," Pierre said again.

After a moment, Leo nodded briefly. "All right. Let's go."

The two men strode across the field, the shorter Pierre having to scramble to keep up with Leo's longer legs. When they reached Luc's wagon, the back door was closed.

Pierre wrenched it open.

Luc and Jeanne were inside, lying on a quilt that had been spread on the open area of floor. They were both partially disrobed.

Luc sat up and cursed as he saw Pierre in the doorway. "I told you it was too late in the day," he said to Jeanne.

Jeanne pulled down her skirt and sat up as well.

"You cheating little whore," Pierre said to his wife. His voice came out as a growl. "This is it. I'm done with you. You can find another dupe to live off of. I'm finished."

"You can't blame your wife for looking for a man to satisfy her," Luc said while pulling on his pants. "Evidently, you can't."

"You bastard," Pierre said through his teeth, and put his foot on the back of the wagon, ready to leap at Luc.

Leo grabbed his shoulder. "Steady, Pierre. You have every right to be angry, but we'll handle this without a fight. Gabrielle can't afford for either of you to get hurt."

He could feel Pierre quivering under his grip.

Pierre turned to snarl at Leo, "You don't know how this feels! You have a wife who is faithful."

"You're not my husband," Jeanne screamed at Pierre. "You can't even get it up for me!"

If Leo had not had a firm hold on him, Pierre would have gone for her.

"Steady, Pierre," Leo said. Then, to Jeanne, "A bitch like you would take the manhood from anyone."

"I didn't take it from Luc," Jeanne said defiantly.

Pierre looked furiously at Luc. "Why don't you find another place to work and leave Jeanne with us?" Luc taunted. "Your marriage is clearly a failure. Gabrielle can replace you in the band."

Pierre surged forward again, but Leo held on to him. "If we are going to replace anyone, Luc, it will be Jeanne, not Pierre. Pierre has been with this circus for many years and Gabrielle feels some loyalty to him." She looked at Jeanne. "She doesn't feel any loyalty toward you, however. And she cannot put up with your disruptive behavior any longer. We'll give you a month's salary, Jeanne, and when we pull out of Le Mans tomorrow, we're leaving you behind." He looked at Pierre. "Is that all right with you?"

"Yes," Pierre said grimly. "I don't care what happens to her. I'm finished."

Jeanne stared at Leo in astonishment. "You can't mean that."

"I couldn't mean it more," he said.

Jeanne said, "If you dismiss me, then you'll be dismissing Luc as well." She turned to the equestrian. "Isn't that so, *chéri?*"

But Luc wasn't looking at her, he was looking at Leo. "You don't have the authority to dismiss anyone, Leo. This is Gabrielle's circus, not yours."

"I can get Gabrielle over here, if you wish," Leo said. "But first I think you both should get your clothes on."

"Go and get her," Luc said.

Leo looked at Pierre. "Can I leave you alone with them for a few minutes?"

"Yes," Pierre said from between clenched teeth.

"Get dressed," Leo said to Luc and Jeanne, and hurried to get Gabrielle.

She was angry but not surprised when he told her what had happened. The rest of the circus folk, who were still crowded around her, felt the same way. Sergeant Jordan, who had come over to see what was going on, looked from Leo to Gabrielle and didn't say anything.

"I told Jeanne that we would not be taking her with us when we leave for Tours," Leo said. "She is trying to get Luc to leave the circus with her. That's when he said he wanted to see you."

"I will come," Gabrielle said, and set off briskly in the direction of Luc's wagon. For a moment it looked as if the rest of the crowd would follow her, but Leo told them to stay where they were. Then he strode off to catch up with Gabrielle.

She said, "I cannot afford to lose Luc, Leo!"

"I know that, sweetheart, and I don't think you will. You may need him, but he also needs you. He's not going to leave a steady job with good pay for a whore like Jeanne. Believe me, you will have nothing to lose and everything to gain if you get rid of Jeanne."

"I have to get rid of her," Gabrielle said. "I can't put up with this kind of behavior. Papa would have dismissed her. I know he would have."

"Then all you have to do is be firm. Luc isn't going to go with her, no matter what he may say. Don't let them bluff you, Gabrielle."

"I *hate* this," she muttered. "I never understood how much Papa had to put up with to keep the circus going."

Leo said sympathetically, "You're dealing with people, sweetheart. It's like apples—there are some rotten ones in every barrel."

"I suppose so," she said gloomily. "Jeanne certainly qualifies as rotten. And Luc does, too. He knew Jeanne was a married woman. He should have stayed away from her."

"I agree. But the fact of the matter is that you need Luc and you don't need Jeanne."

"You said I would give her a month's wages?"

"That's right. And I will pay them."

She opened her mouth to say something, and he forestalled her. "Don't you dare say that phrase again. I know it's your circus, but I'm the one who decided to dismiss her and I'm the one who will pay the wages. I only said I would do so because I knew you would never send her away without any money. She deserves it, but you wouldn't do it. So I will pay the month's wages—and that is the end of this subject, Gabrielle."

They had reached the wagon and the three people who were waiting for them. Jeanne and Luc had gotten dressed and were now standing with Pierre. Everyone was looking at Gabrielle.

"Jeanne," she began. "I want you to pack your things and be gone from this circus by tomorrow morning. I will give you a month's wages. That will be enough for you to be able to return to Paris, where I'm sure a woman of your—talents—will be able to find work." Her voice dripped scorn.

Leo smothered a smile at her comment about the talents.

"If you dismiss me, then you lose Luc, too," Jeanne said.

Gabrielle looked at Luc. "Is that true, Luc?"

Luc's greenish eyes looked boldly back. "Yes, that's true."

"I am sorry to hear that," Gabrielle said pleasantly. "Then I expect you will be gone tomorrow morning along with Jeanne."

Luc looked stunned. "You can't lose me! Next to you, I'm your main equestrian act!"

"Mathieu and Albert can fill in until I find someone else," Gabrielle said.

"They can't do what I do! You know that, Gabrielle. Neither one of them could do the Courier of St. Petersburg."

"I think Mathieu could do it if he practiced enough."

"He can't," Luc said flatly.

Gabrielle said, "I am not dismissing you, Luc. I don't approve of what you have done here, but you're right in that I need you more than I need Jeanne. I will be happy if you wish to stay on. But Jeanne goes. It is strictly your decision whether or not you will go with her."

Jeanne took Luc's arm. "He will come with me, won't you, *chéri?*"

Luc pulled his arm away. "No, Jeanne, I am not coming with you. If I have to choose between my job and you, I'm afraid that the job wins."

Her mouth fell open. "Luc! You can't mean that!"

"Oh, but I do. Leo is right. You're a whore. And I am not giving up a good job for a whore." He stared into her furious face. "Sorry, but there it is."

"You bastard," she screamed.

He shrugged. "Call me what names you will. It won't change my mind."

Finally, Pierre spoke. "Get your things out of the wagon. I want rid of you as soon as possible."

"This is not fair!" Jeanne said. Then, to Gabrielle: "You're a woman. It isn't fair that the woman should be the only one punished here."

"I gave you a chance, Jeanne," Gabrielle said. "I spoke to you about your flirting and you told me you were a woman who likes men. Well, like them somewhere else. I don't want you in my circus."

Leo said to both Luc and Jeanne, "You wanted to hear what Gabrielle had to say. Well, now you have heard it. Pierre and Luc, go with Henri to the hotel." He turned to Jeanne. "As for you, I will help you clean out whatever is yours from this wagon and then I'll drive you into Le Mans, to a different hotel from the one we are staying in. After that, you're on your own."

"Fine!" she said defiantly. "I don't need your stupid circus, and I certainly don't need a husband who can't be a man to me."

"A real man wouldn't want to have anything to do with you," Gabrielle shot back, trying to defend Pierre. "It will be a much more pleasant place around here with you gone." She gestured to Luc and Pierre. "Come with me. It's dinnertime and everyone is hungry."

Without a single look at Jeanne, the two men moved off with Gabrielle.

"Now," said Leo, "if you will show me what is yours, I'll help you move it."

Jeanne looked at Leo out of her long, slanting eyes. "Leo," she pleaded, "can't you help me?"

"I have just said I would help you," Leo said.

"I don't mean by moving my things!"

"That is the only help you are going to get from me," Leo said calmly. "Don't think to try your tricks on me, Jeanne. I am the one who told Gabrielle she had to get rid of you."

Jeanne bent down, picked up a stone and threw it at Leo. He ducked, eluding it easily. "Let's get started, Jeanne," he said. "Your time with this circus is over."

The circus members all ate in the same restaurant that evening, with Jeanne conspicuously absent. They ate at four different tables, with Pierre and Luc sitting as far away from each other as was possible. Sergeant Jordan was not with them. He took his dinner with the grooms so he would not have to be out of sight of the wagons.

Before they had left for the restaurant, Gabrielle had announced that Jeanne would not be with them any longer.

"Good riddance," Carlotta had said. It had been the only comment made.

Leo, Gabrielle, Albert and Mathieu sat together at one table, and when the meal was over, Antonio came over to pull a chair next to Gabrielle. "If you are looking for someone to take Jeanne's place, I have a suggestion for you, Gabrielle," he offered.

"Oh, do you know someone?" she responded. "That's wonderful, Antonio."

"It's my cousin's daughter. She's very accomplished—she plays a number of instruments. She could easily fill Jeanne's spot. I would be happy to teach her our music. She'd probably be able to learn it in a day."

"Where is she now?" Gabrielle asked.

Antonio smiled. "This is what is so wonderful. She's at my cousin's home in Bressuire. If I send her a letter tomorrow, she should be able to meet us in Angoulême."

"Has she ever played for a circus before?" Gabrielle asked.

"Not permanently. She is only eighteen, Gabrielle. Her mother would let her come to the Cirque Equestre because Adolphe and I are here to look after her. She can travel with us."

Gabrielle said, "Eighteen is awfully young, Antonio."

"I know Isabel. She's a good girl, Gabrielle. You will like her."

Gabrielle looked at Leo, as if to ask his opinion. Then she changed her mind and looked back to Antonio. ''All right,'' she said crisply. ''Send for her. But if she doesn't work out, she will be your responsibility.''

''She'll work out,'' he said confidently. ''Thank you, Gabrielle.''

He stood up, picked up the chair he had brought over and moved away.

Leo said, ''It seems that all of your circus members have cousins who are in the business. First there was Carlotta and now Antonio.''

''It's not unusual,'' Gabrielle said. ''The circus runs in families.''

Albert said, ''Has Carlotta heard from her cousin yet?''

Gabrielle nodded. ''He's going to meet us at Bordeaux.''

People were getting up from the other tables and moving out of the dining room. Mathieu said eagerly, ''Do you think we could do some algebra tonight, Leo?''

''It depends.'' Leo looked at Gabrielle. ''What do you want to do?'' he asked.

''Stay home, put my feet up and read a book,'' she said. ''I hate confrontations. They exhaust me.''

Albert said, ''I'll draw you, Gabrielle.''

Leo looked at Mathieu. ''I guess it's algebra for us.''

Mathieu beamed.

''What a day,'' Gabrielle said to Leo as they reached the privacy of their bedroom several hours later.

''It wasn't pleasant, but I think Luc did us a favor by giving us a reason to get rid of Jeanne. She was a troublemaker right from the start.''

''She certainly was.'' She looked anxiously at Leo.

"Do you think she'll be all right? She might have to live for a long time on the money you gave her."

"Women like Jeanne can take care of themselves," he said. "Don't bother yourself worrying about her, sweetheart. She'll be fine. I don't know if I can say the same about Pierre."

"Poor Pierre," she said. "I hope Luc doesn't spread the news of his impotence around the whole circus."

"I had a little talk with Luc," Leo said. "I don't think he'll be opening his mouth on that subject."

She looked at him and almost reprimanded him for once more butting into circus business. But then she thought of herself having to talk to Luc about such a subject and decided that she was glad Leo had taken the initiative.

It's going to be so hard when he goes, she thought dismally.

He read the unhappy look on her face. "What's wrong?" he asked.

What's wrong is that I don't want you to leave me.

She said instead, "I'm a little worried about having an eighteen-year-old girl in my charge. She's awfully young."

"Albert is seventeen and Mathieu is nineteen. You yourself are only twenty-two. And besides, she's not in your charge. She will be in the custody of Antonio and Adolphe."

To hide her face she went over to Colette and bent to pet her. "That's true," she said.

"Gabrielle," he said. "Are you all right?"

"I'm all right. But we can't make love tonight, Leo. It's not the right time of the month for me."

He crossed the floor to pull her up and take her in his

arms. "It's all right. I can wait. It's just that we don't have much more time. We reach Biarritz in two weeks."

"I know," she said sadly.

He looked down at her, but she buried her face in his shoulder so he couldn't see it. "I meant what I said about helping Albert," he said. "As soon as this war is over—and I think that is going to be a matter of months, not years—I will contact you. You must give me an itinerary of your stops."

"I will," she said.

He bent his head, pressed his lips against her hair and said, "Every time I smell a lemon, I'll think of you."

You're breaking my heart, Leo, she thought. *Stupid, stupid me for letting you do it.*

She said, "Let's get into bed and you can hold me for a while."

"All right," he said, then bent down and scooped her up in his arms. "You're like a feather," he said. "It always amazes me that you can control such powerful animals as Sandi and Noble."

"It's all in the back," she replied.

He deposited her on the bed. "Next winter I am going to come and visit you and you can teach me how to ride like you."

She smiled up at him from her pillow. "Leo, it took years and years for me to learn to ride the way I do now."

He went around to his side of the bed and got in. "You had to start someplace. I'm serious, Gabrielle," he said. "I really want to learn your kind of riding."

She looked up into his blue-green eyes. He did look serious. "Fine," she said. "Come and stay with us and I will teach you."

He smiled. "Come here and let me hold you."

Leo, Leo, she thought as she moved into his arms. *I should say goodbye to you and never see you again. You should go home and marry a girl of your own class and I should get on with my life as owner of the Cirque Equestre. I don't need to keep the heartache fresh.*

She closed her eyes and rested her cheek against his shoulder and knew that if he insisted on coming to visit during the winter, she would let him. Her heart may break, but life without Leo was too bleak to contemplate.

I love you, she thought.

But she couldn't say that to him. She couldn't put him on the spot like that. He cared about her, perhaps he even loved her a little. But the gap between them was too wide for love to leap across.

Her stomach cramped and she felt tears come to her eyes.

Stop it, Gabrielle, she ordered herself. *You are acting like a baby. You have your own life, and you must learn to be satisfied with that. Many women have to carry on with a lot less than you have.*

After half an hour she fell asleep in the comforting warmth of his arms.

Thirty

The circus made its uninterrupted way to Tours and then from Tours to Poitiers. They weren't stopped on the road again, but as they grew closer to their destination, Leo became more and more concerned about how they were going to get the gold out from under the eyes of Sergeant Jordan. His biggest concern was that they do it in a way that would not incriminate Gabrielle. He tried to hide his concern from her—she was worried enough already—but the problem preyed on his mind.

Another problem that kept him awake at night was his own imminent disappearance from the circus. How was Gabrielle going to explain that? Everyone in the circus knew that the army was looking for the gold. What would they think when he simply disappeared at Biarritz? Luc was already suspicious of him. It wouldn't take much for Luc to put two and two together.

She should never have agreed to carry this gold, Leo thought as he went over the situation for the hundredth time in his mind. *Rothschild was wrong to ask it of her. She's a baby when it comes to the business of smuggling.*

It was up to Leo to make certain that Gabrielle wasn't hurt. *I wish to God I could make contact with the English command,* he thought. *They need to know about this bloody sergeant we have traveling with us. They have to come up with a plan to retrieve the gold without alerting Jordan.*

The army could always shoot Jordan, but that would only point the finger of suspicion at Gabrielle. He would demand that they find another way.

These were the thoughts that were running through Leo's mind as he lay awake next to Gabrielle on the night before the circus left Poitiers to go to Angoulême. He and Gabrielle had made love and now she was sleeping while he lay awake and worried.

She stirred a little in her sleep and he turned and looked at her.

She is so beautiful, he thought. *And so good. I wonder if she would let me buy her that farm she wants so much for her horses. I hate to think of her burdened by this circus. She isn't tough enough to make the hard decisions. She is too prone to see the good in people.*

He rolled over on his back and stared up into the darkness. *When the war is over, I'll figure something out for her,* he thought. The idea of Gabrielle on a farm, where he could visit her whenever he wanted, was very appealing.

He should be thrilled by the prospect of returning to the army. He had thought of little else all during his convalescence. Why was it that he felt so unenthusiastic now?

I've done what I swore I wouldn't do, he thought. *I've let her get under my skin.*

It's good that I will be returning to my regiment. I need to get back to my old life, to put my feelings into perspective.

He would feel much better about going once he was sure that Gabrielle was going to be safe.

* * *

Isabel Laurent joined the circus at Angoulême, bringing the band size back to four. She was a very pretty girl with lovely blue eyes, and Mathieu took one look at her and was smitten. Gabrielle was tenderly amused by her brother's infatuation, and that evening, when Sully proposed playing a game of chess with Leo, she suggested that Isabel might like to play cards with her, Albert and Mathieu.

Isabel asked Antonio, who gave his permission, so it was a cozy group who gathered in the salon after dinner. Mathieu was Isabel's partner, and, to Albert's astonishment, he never once chided her for making a mistake.

As everyone was getting ready to go upstairs, Sully said in a low voice, "Thank you, Leo. I was very tempted to get drunk tonight and you helped me."

"I told you before that I would be here for you," Leo replied. He clapped Sully on the shoulder. "You'll be a hero, Sully, if you conquer this. And, if you are determined enough, you will."

Sully nodded, started to say something, then just shook his head. "I'll see you in the morning."

Leo and Gabrielle said good-night to the others on the stair landing and turned to go into their room. As Leo closed the door behind him, Gabrielle went to the wardrobe and hung up her blue jacket.

Leo said, "That is a very pretty blue outfit you have, but don't you have any other clothes?"

"I don't need many clothes," she said. "I wear my circus costume most of the time."

She made that plain blue outfit look stylish, Leo thought. He imagined what she could do for some really nice clothes. He would love to take her shopping, but he knew without asking that she would never let him do that.

He admired that ferocious independence of hers, but it annoyed him as well. He could be of so much help to her if only she'd let him. He crossed the floor until he was standing behind her, then he put his arms around her waist. She leaned against him.

"We leave the day after tomorrow for Bordeaux," she said.

"I know." He rested his chin on the top of her head. "And we'll probably be stopped again. I'm sure the army will be on the hunt on that particular piece of road."

"Perhaps they won't search us again. Perhaps the presence of Sergeant Jordan will put them off."

"Just the opposite, I think. The sergeant will probably encourage them to search."

She pulled away and turned to face him. "The closer I get to Biarritz, the more worried I get. I wish I knew what the army's plan was."

"Someone will make contact with us," Leo said positively.

She looked up into his face and said in a low voice, "Are you going to leave with the army and the gold?"

He sighed. "Come and sit beside me on the bed."

He picked up her hand and held it in her lap. "That was what I planned to do, but if the sergeant stays with the circus it will look suspicious at the very least. At the most it will convince him that you had the gold and have gotten rid of it."

"Could they arrest me?" she asked.

He tightened his grip on her hand. "I won't let things come to that. But I have to confess, I'm not quite sure how to do this. I need to rejoin my regiment, Gabrielle."

"I have been thinking." Her voice was so low that he had to bend his head a little to hear her. "What if you stay with the circus beyond Biarritz? Pau will be our next stop after that and I doubt that the sergeant will accompany us that far. Pau is still close to the border with Spain, but it is much farther east—a good distance from Portugal. And the gold is going to Wellington in Portugal. The sergeant will think that if we are indeed carrying the gold, we will have to unload it in Biarritz.''

He ran his thumb caressingly over her hand. ''You're right about Pau—it is out of the way for getting the gold to Wellington. But it is out of the way for me to get to Wellington as well.''

''The English can't be planning to start their campaign in March,'' Gabrielle said. ''In the mountains it will still be too cold. You will have time to backtrack to Portugal.''

There was a little silence. ''It's a good idea,'' he said at last.

He put his arm around her and she rested her head on his shoulder. ''Have you by any chance thought up a story to tell the circus to account for my leaving?'' he asked.

She nestled a little closer. ''I thought we could tell them that you had received word from England that your father was dying. It would only make sense that you would want to go to his side.'' She went on, ''Then, when you don't come back, I'll tell the others that you inherited property from your father and want to stay in England, but I don't want to give up the circus to join you.''

He felt the softness of her against him and tightened his arm. He didn't reply.

''What do you think?'' she asked, lifting her head away from his shoulder and twisting so she could see his face.

''I think it's a perfect story,'' he said. ''When did you think it up?''

"I have been racking my brain for weeks trying to come up with a story that would account for your leaving," she said. "This one came to me in the middle of the night. I woke up and it was there."

"I have been racking my brain as well, but to no avail," he said. "I suppose I'm not as inventive as you."

"You mean you're not as good a liar," she retorted.

He shook his head. "I didn't mean that at all."

She sighed. "Well, it is a lie. But your whole masquerade with the circus has been a lie, so we might as well top it off with the biggest lie of all."

"But I will be back," he said. "Remember, I'm coming this winter to learn how to ride."

"The story won't matter then. The other circus acts don't winter with us and everyone who does knows the truth."

They both fell silent. The only sound in the room came from Colette, settling herself more comfortably on her bed.

He said, "Let me take the braid out of your hair."

She blinked, then she smiled. "Well, that is certainly a change of subject."

"I love to touch your hair," he said. "It's so silky."

"All right, go ahead and unbraid it." She turned her back to give him easy access to the long smoothly plaited braid.

He took the tie off the bottom and unplaited the braid until her hair was free on her back. Then he ran his fingers through the loose, shining strands. She closed her eyes, clearly enjoying the touch of his hand.

He slid his hand under her hair until it was cupping the nape of her neck. "Everything about you is so delicate and fragile," he said. "And yet you ride and control thousand-pound horses."

"I would be an even better rider if I were bigger," she said. "Papa could get leverage just from the length of his torso. I can't."

"I'm glad you're not bigger," he murmured. "I like you just the way you are."

"I like you the way you are, too." She turned to face him and he bent his head to hers. They kissed deeply.

"Let's go to bed," he said huskily.

"Good idea," she replied.

They both shed their clothes with swift efficiency and Gabrielle was the first to crawl in under the warmth of the covers.

He came to his side of the bed and pulled the covers back. "I like to see you," he said.

"Too bad," she replied, snatching the blankets back. "It's too cold. You'll just have to maneuver under them."

"Oh, all right," he grumbled as he pulled the covers up around himself.

She smiled up at him. "I'll make it up to you."

"Mmm," he said. "I'll take you up on that offer."

She moved into his arms and he ran his hand down her back and over the curve of her hip. She touched his ear, his cheek, his mouth. "Kiss me," he said, and they joined together in a long, deeply erotic kiss.

Finally he lifted his head. "I could eat you up," he growled.

During the course of the journey they had learned how to please each other, and now they slowly and tantalizingly built up their passion until it was glowing white-hot and irresistible. When Gabrielle whimpered and lifted her hips toward him, Leo knew the time had come. As he entered her he thought that nothing he had ever done in his life could ever compare with the bliss of being inside Gabrielle Robichon.

She lifted her legs to encircle his waist and hung on to him with her hands on his shoulders. He drove into her wet, slippery heat and felt her soften around him. He groaned.

I love you. He wanted to say it, but the words just wouldn't come out. They were words he had never said to a living creature since the day he had caught his mother with their next-door neighbor.

"Leo," she cried. "Oh, Leo."

Her fingers were digging into his shoulders and he drove again and again into the heart of her until he felt her spasms again and again in the shuddering ecstasy of orgasm. He increased his own movement until the moment of his own release came, and he cried out loud with the power of the sensation.

When it was over they stayed joined together for a long time, clasped in each other's arms. Once again Leo had the urge to tell her he loved her, but once again he bit the words back.

After all, she had never said them to him.

"I feel much warmer now," Gabrielle murmured.

He felt a pang of sadness as he withdrew from her and rolled away. "I hate to let you go," he said.

She leaned back against her pillows and smiled at him. Oh, the glory of Gabrielle's smile.

"Will you get me my nightgown?" she asked. "It is in the first drawer in the wardrobe."

He got out of bed, went over to the wardrobe and withdrew her nightgown. He brought it back to the bed and handed it to her.

"Thank you," she said, and immediately pulled it over her head.

Leo went to his bag for his own nightshirt. It *was* a little chilly walking around this room with no clothes on. He put the nightshirt on and returned to his side of the bed, passing Colette who was asleep on her mattress.

He got in next to Gabrielle and she scooted over to rest against his shoulder. He put his arm around her.

"I think Mathieu is in love," she said.

"Really? With the Laurent girl?"

"Yes. She was his partner at cards tonight and he never once corrected her or yelled at her. Albert couldn't believe it."

Leo chuckled. "Well it was bound to happen sooner or later. Matthew is nineteen, after all."

"She seems like a nice girl," Gabrielle said. "Henri told me they expect Carlotta's cousin to join us tomorrow, so the rope-dancing act will be at full strength."

"Good," he said.

"I will miss having you to talk to at night," she said sadly.

He bent his head and pressed his lips to her hair. "Don't think about that. Let's just concentrate on the pleasures of the moment."

"I think it is easier for a man to do that than a woman," Gabrielle said soberly.

He said, "You mean a great deal to me, sweetheart."

She sighed. "I am glad to hear that, Leo." She pulled away from him. "Now I think we should try to sleep."

"All right." He adjusted his pillows the way he liked them, and waited until she was lying on her side, the way she liked to sleep. Then he blew out the lamp.

Thirty-One

The first half of the next day's noon show went very well. The audience was particularly responsive to Gabrielle's exhibitions with Noble and Sandi, and Leo found himself smiling from ear to ear as the tent erupted in loud applause for the small, erect figure who commanded the attention of horse and audience with such seeming effortlessness.

She's amazing, Leo thought as he watched her disappear out of the tent. *I could watch her ride all day long, she's so beautiful.*

The next act was Luc's and Leo ducked out of the tent to collect Coco from Albert, who was holding him. Pierre exited with Leo, muttering that he had to relieve himself. Leo brought Coco into the tent and started him cantering in a circle around the ring. Coco, who knew his job, did not need Leo to encourage him much with the whip. He cantered like a rocking horse around the ring, his cadence steady and even.

The three players left in the band struck up the music, and Luc came running lightly into the ring dressed in tights and spangles.

The act started out well, with Luc vaulting easily on and off the cantering Coco. The accident happened when Luc was standing on Coco's back and attempting a somersault. The minute his feet left the horse's back, Coco squealed and reared straight up. Luc had no place to land except the ninety-degree angle of Coco's back. He slid down the horse's back and slammed into the ground. Coco squealed again and this time he kicked out, mercifully missing Luc, who was sprawled on the ground. Then Coco began to gallop madly around the ring.

The crowd was on its feet, those in the back standing on their benches to get a better view of Luc, who was starting to move. Leo decided it was more important to get control of the horse before he did any more damage and started to speak soothingly to the excited Coco. Antonio and Adolphe came running from their positions in the band to bend over Luc, who was still on the ground.

Emma, whose act was next, came running to Luc as well.

The noise from the crowd as everyone exclaimed and talked was making it difficult for Leo to get control of Coco, and he turned, faced the benches and called loudly, "Silence, please."

Abruptly, silence fell.

By the time Gabrielle came into the ring, Coco had slowed to a trot. She went straight to Luc, who was sitting up now but had not attempted to rise. He was holding his right shoulder.

Shit, Leo thought. *If Luc is out of commission, Gabrielle will be in trouble.*

Finally Coco slowed to a walk, then to a halt. As Leo came up to him he could see the horse was trembling. "It's all right," Leo said soothingly. "It's all right, big fellow. You're fine." He patted the horse's neck. It was damp with sweat.

"Here, Leo." Albert held out a lead rope. Leo got the lead onto Coco's halter and patted him again.

"What happened?" Albert asked. He was as white as Sandi.

"I don't know. All of a sudden Coco squealed and reared up. Luc was in the middle of a somersault and came crashing to the ground. It was very strange."

"Mon Dieu," Albert said. "What will we do if Luc is too badly hurt to perform?"

"I don't know," Leo said grimly.

They both watched as Luc got to his feet. Seeing him rise, the audience burst into applause. Luc managed to lift his left hand in acknowledgement. Then he walked out of the ring, accompanied by Gabrielle. The two Laurents went to rejoin Isabel in the band. Leo noted that Pierre had returned to his band station as well.

He remembered meeting Pierre going out as he was coming into the ring. *Pierre has never had to leave during a performance before,* he thought.

He pictured in his mind the way Coco had squealed, as if something had hurt him. The words *It was almost as if he was stung by a bee* popped into his head.

He let this thought percolate in his mind. There were no bees inside the tent; he could pretty much swear to that.

What could have made Coco, who was as rock solid as they came, behave like something had hurt him?

Something did hurt him, Leo thought. *Something* must *have hurt him.*

A dart. Someone could have shot a dart at him. Or a BB.

The crowd was beginning to grow restless and Leo announced, "*Mesdames* and *messieurs,* if you will be patient for a little longer, the Martins, our world-famous rope dancers, will perform for you. Thank you for your good nature."

He turned to leave the ring, and as he was passing the band he said to Antonio, "Play something!"

He heard the band start up as he exited into the afternoon sunshine.

Everyone was clustered around Luc.

"Henri," Leo said sharply. "I have just announced that your act will be next. Get moving, will you, please?"

Henri nodded. "Come along, Gerard," he said. "You can help me set up the ropes.

Leo went over to Luc. "How are you?" he asked.

Luc looked pale. "I landed on my shoulder. It hurts pretty bad."

Gabrielle said, "Paul is going to take Luc into town to see a doctor."

Leo nodded, then said, "Gabrielle, can I see you in private for a moment?"

She gave him a worried look, then nodded. The two of them walked a little distance away from the group and Leo said in a low tone, "I think someone should go over Coco thoroughly. I suspect that he was hit by something—most probably a small dart. It's the only thing that would account for his squealing and rearing like that."

Her big brown eyes widened. "You can't be serious," she said in horror.

"Pierre was not with the band when it happened. I passed him when I was going into the ring. He said he had to relieve himself."

Gabrielle's hands flew to her mouth. "*Mon Dieu!* You think that Pierre shot a dart at Coco?"

"I think it is a distinct possibility," Leo said grimly.

"This is terrible," Gabrielle said.

"It's not good," Leo admitted. "Especially since we will have a hard time proving that Pierre did anything."

Gabrielle glanced over Leo's shoulder and saw Sergeant Jordan watching them with interest. She turned her back so he could not see her face and said, "I will go over Coco with a fine-tooth comb once the show is finished. But I need him right now."

"Gabrielle, Luc is not going to be able to perform. What do you need Coco for?"

"Mathieu and Albert will do some more trick riding to fill up Luke's spot. I need him for that. Then I will do the Courier of St. Petersburg with the Arabians."

He stared at her, appalled. "You can't do that! It's a totally different kind of riding from what you do." He had seen Luc perform the trick once before. "You have to straddle galloping horses while other horses pass beneath you! You have to lie down across horses' backs! That's not your kind of riding."

"When I was a child I used to do trick riding," she said calmly. "I did it for fun, not for show, but I think I can manage to do most of the act. I'm going to try, at any rate. I don't want to have to refund all of the money we collected. We advertise the Courier of St. Petersburg, remember?"

"You can't do it," Leo repeated. "I won't let you."

She lifted her eyebrows. "You can't stop me, Leo. I am my own person. I don't have to answer to you."

He stared at her in angry frustration.

"Let Mathieu do it," he argued. "He is accustomed to trick riding."

"I am a better rider than Mathieu. I don't want him getting hurt trying to do too much."

"What if *you* get hurt? You are the main attraction in this circus. We can't afford to lose you!"

He never even noticed his use of the word *we* when he spoke of the circus.

Gabrielle smiled at him and patted his arm. "I won't get hurt, Leo."

"I don't like this," Leo said.

"I don't like it, either, but I like even less losing the money we collected today."

"You don't have to refund their money. They have still seen a pretty good show."

"I like even less leaving my customers thinking they have been cheated," Gabrielle retorted. "That is not the way to be successful, Leo. People talk and word gets around."

"The people here today will understand that it is not your fault if you have to give an abbreviated performance."

She shook her head. "You had better get back into the ring. Announce more trick riding from Mathieu and Albert, then we'll have the Courier of St Petersburg and we'll finish off with Emma's dogs and my pas de deux with Mathieu."

He didn't move and she gave him a little shove. "Go on, Leo! We'll talk about Coco when the show is finished."

Reluctantly he did as she asked and went back into the ring.

When the show was over, Leo and Gabrielle collected Coco, gave him a pile of hay and proceeded to go over him from head to tail. It was Gabrielle who found the small wound in his right shoulder. Then she found another in his right flank.

"Look at these," she said to Leo.

Leo came around the horse and regarded the small, round perforations in Coco's skin.

"Darts," he said.

"That's what it looks like."

Gabrielle patted Coco's neck, which was stretched down toward the hay.

"It must have been Pierre," she said.

"I can't think of anyone else who would do such a thing."

Her delectable mouth set in a grim line. "Neither can I."

"You have to dismiss him, Gabrielle. He's dangerous. Luc could have been killed."

"I know," she said. "I know."

Henri came over to stand next to them. "What happened to Coco that made him do such a thing? In all the years I've been with this circus, he has never behaved as he did today."

Gabrielle said, "Look at this, Henri." And she showed him Coco's two wounds.

"Mon Dieu," Henri said. "What could have happened?"

"We think someone shot darts at him," Gabrielle said.

There was a moment of silence. Then Henri said, "Where was Pierre when Coco was performing?"

Gabrielle and Leo looked at each other. Then Gabrielle said, "He had excused himself. He was leaving the ring as Leo was coming in."

"Merde," Henri exclaimed. He thought a moment, then said in dawning fury, "Do you think he is responsible for Franz's accident as well?"

When Gabrielle did not reply, Leo said, "Perhaps. I always thought that the rope had frayed too evenly."

Henri flushed. "Let me get my hands on the bastard. I'd like to kill him!"

Leo put a hand on Henri's arm. "Hold on, Henri. There are other ways of dealing with this."

Henri said, looking at Leo, "I hope you are going to dismiss him."

Leo said, "That will be up to Gabrielle. It's her circus."

Henri switched his burning gaze to Gabrielle. "Don't be softhearted over this, Gabrielle. He's dangerous."

Gabrielle straightened her spine. Leo saw the movement and his heart went out to her. *She shouldn't have to make these kinds of decisions. It's too hard on her,* he thought.

Gabrielle said, "I will dismiss him. I don't see that I have any choice."

"You don't," Leo said.

She nodded. "Henri, would you ask Pierre to come and speak to me?"

"Let me go," Leo said hastily. He looked at Henri, who was still flushed with anger. "We don't want Henri knocking him down. We need Pierre in good enough shape to walk away from us."

Henri smiled sourly.

"All right," Gabrielle said. "Let Leo go, Henri."

"I want to be here when you dismiss the bastard," Henri said.

"I don't think we need you," Gabrielle said.

Henri folded his arms over his chest. "I'm not moving until I see that bastard dismissed."

Gabrielle sighed and looked at Leo. He shrugged.

"All right," Gabrielle said. "But behave yourself, Henri."

"I will," Henri said. He looked grim.

Gabrielle and Leo exchanged another look, then Leo

said, "I will go get Pierre and send him to you, Gabrielle."

"Thank you," she said. Then, as an afterthought, "Do you think you could go through his things, Leo? To see if he has a dart blower?"

"I'll look," Leo said.

He went across the field in the direction of the band's tent, leaving Gabrielle and Henri to wait in silence.

Thirty-Two

Pierre blustered and protested, and Gabrielle had twinges of conscience about perhaps being wrong, but just as she was on the verge of wavering, Leo came up with the dart blower he had found in Pierre's trunk. That did it. Gabrielle told him to pack up his things and be gone by the next performance.

"That little bastard slept with my wife!" Pierre snarled when it became apparent that Gabrielle meant what she had said. "It would serve him right if he never rode again."

Henri said too quietly, "Did you damage our safety net?"

Pierre looked at the dangerous expression on Henri's face. "No!" he said vehemently.

No one believed him.

"I want you away from my circus, Pierre," Gabrielle said. "You have almost ruined us. I never want to see you again. Do you understand me?"

"I understand you," he mumbled. "I never meant to hurt *you,* Gabrielle."

"Well, you have hurt me. What hurts my circus hurts me. Now, go away, please, Pierre, and don't come back."

White-faced, Pierre turned on his heel and headed back toward his wagon.

Henri said, "I'd feel better if he was in another town from us."

"We're off to Bordeaux the day after tomorrow," Leo said. "Anyway, I think we're safe. He's been found out. He won't try anything else."

Gabrielle said in a small voice, "I wonder how badly Luc is hurt."

Leo said, "Come along with me and we'll find the doctor and check on Luc."

"All right," Gabrielle said. She turned to Henri. "Will you tell the Laurents that they are going to have to play without Pierre?"

"I'll tell them," Henri said. "I'm sure they'll do fine. What luck, though, that Isabel arrived when she did."

"Yes," Gabrielle said. "But if we have lost Luc, I don't know what I am going to do."

"You handled the Courier of St. Petersburg very well," Henri said encouragingly.

"Thank you," Gabrielle said. "But Luc does more than the Courier."

Henri said, "Mathieu and Albert will have to step up and do more. Your father always wanted them to be classical riders and he underestimated what they could do as trick riders. They can take over for Luc, Gabrielle, if you give them the chance."

Gabrielle looked dubious.

Leo said, "Henri is right. There is no reason why Mathieu can't do the Courier. And Albert can do the drunken-man act. They both have wonderful balance on a horse."

Gabrielle looked at him anxiously. "Do you really think so?"

"Yes, I really think so."

"I don't want them to get hurt."

"They won't get hurt, sweetheart. They're young. If they take a fall, they'll bounce."

"Well...I'll talk to them and see how they feel."

"You do that," Leo said encouragingly. "Now, come along and let's see how badly Luc is hurt."

Luc had dislocated his shoulder and would not be performing for at least a few weeks. When Gabrielle approached Mathieu and Albert about taking over his acts, the boys responded enthusiastically. They knew Luc's acts from having watched them so often and both felt that, with a little practice, they would be able to step in and perform.

So Gabrielle canceled the first show the following day, which gave Mathieu and Albert the whole morning and most of the afternoon to practice. By the time the four o'clock show came around they had their acts memorized. The show went very well; the boys left out a few of Luc's more daring tricks, but their acts were exciting and well received by the audience. At Leo's and Mathieu's insistence, Mathieu did the Courier of St. Petersburg and he did it well.

Mathieu had another reason for wanting to shine other than helping out the circus. Isabel's large blue eyes had been full of admiration when he had come out of the ring after each of his acts, and he had given her a nonchalant wave to signify his acknowledgement of her appreciation.

As they left the ring after their last appearance together, Albert said teasingly, "I think Mathieu is in love."

"Be quiet," Mathieu said furiously.

"You are! You are!" Albert cried delightedly.

"You don't know what you're talking about," Mathieu said.

Gabrielle came up to them where they were standing just outside the tent where Emma was performing with her dogs. "That was wonderful, boys. The skipping-rope trick was a huge success, Mathieu."

Albert said, "Mathieu is in love with Isabel, Gabrielle."

Gabrielle looked at Albert's elated face. "Don't tease your brother," she said.

"But he is!" Albert said. "He waves to her every time he comes out of the ring."

Gabrielle said seriously, "Mathieu's feelings are none of your business, Albert. Leave him alone."

Some of the pleasure left Albert's face.

"I mean it," Gabrielle said.

"Oh, all right," Albert said reluctantly.

"Thank you, Gabrielle," Mathieu said in a stifled voice.

She patted his arm. "You are doing brilliantly," she said. "Are you ready for the Courier?"

"Yes, I am."

Albert opened his mouth to say something, met Gabrielle's stern eyes and closed it again. She said to him, "You should get ready for the drunken-man act. You need to be sitting in the audience before it begins."

"I know," Albert said. "I'm going."

Mathieu said, "I'm glad you gave me and Albert this chance to show you what we can do, Gabrielle. I'm happy you didn't try to do it all yourself."

Thanks to Leo, she thought. Gabrielle smiled at him. "I am, too," she said.

Gabrielle elected to go out with the rest of the circus members to a café that night.

"I think it's important that we be together tonight,"

she said to Mathieu when he reminded her of her promise
to invite Isabel to play cards in the hotel.

"Gabrielle is right." Leo was standing behind Mathieu
and he stepped in to support Gabrielle. "We've been
wounded and it's important that we show some solidarity
tonight."

So everyone went to the café and Mathieu managed to
seat himself next to Isabel. Luc was seated next to Gabrielle.

After the wineglasses had been filled, Gabrielle raised
hers. "I want to thank everyone for pulling together today. I especially want to thank Mathieu and Albert for
filling in for Luc, which was a difficult task." She gave
Luc a quick smile. "And I thank Antonio, Adolphe and
Isabel for the good work they did as a three-piece band.
You were superb."

Everyone clapped and Gabrielle sat down.

"What are you going to do until your shoulder heals,
Luc?" Sully asked.

"I am going to Paris," Luc replied. "When my shoulder heals, I am going to try to get taken on by Astleys."

The table went silent as Gabrielle turned to Luc. "I
didn't know that! What about us?"

"Mathieu and Albert did a wonderful job today."
There was a trace of sulkiness in Luc's voice. "You don't
need me anymore."

"Of course we need you, Luc," Gabrielle said with
distress. "You are our featured equestrian."

"No—*you* are our featured equestrian," Luc returned.
"And now that Mathieu and Albert have become such
heroes, there isn't any room here for me."

Gabrielle looked even more upset. "Albert is going to
art school next year, Luc," Mathieu said. "He won't be
here. There will be plenty of room for you."

Luc looked surprised, but then he shook his head. "It doesn't matter. This is something I've been thinking about for a while. If there isn't any room for me at Astleys and I need a job, I'll come looking for you."

"Nice of you," Mathieu muttered under his breath.

"I will pay your salary if you stay with us, Luc, but if you have no commitment to us then I can't pay you," Gabrielle said.

He shrugged. "I know that. That's why I'm telling you now what I'm going to do. I don't want to take your money, Gabrielle, and then walk out on you."

"But what will you live on?"

Mathieu said roughly, "That's Luc's business, Gabrielle, not yours."

"I have family in Paris," Luc said. "I will be all right."

"We wish you luck, Luc," Leo said firmly.

"Yes," Sully said. "Good luck and good fortune."

Everyone lifted their wineglasses and toasted Luc.

Gabrielle got through the rest of the evening with outward calm, but when she and Leo were back in their hotel room she turned to him. "Luc wouldn't have left if he didn't think I was married to you," she said accusingly. "He saw that his chance to marry into the circus was gone—that's the main reason he is leaving!"

"You may be right," Leo said mildly.

Gabrielle threw her jacket onto a chair. "You have caused me to lose one of my most important acts, Leo!"

"You weren't going to marry him, so he wouldn't have stayed forever," Leo pointed out.

She sat on the bed and clasped her hands tensely in her lap. "Everything is going wrong this year. Nothing like this ever happened when Papa was in charge."

"Stop blaming yourself, sweetheart," he said. "All of

your problems have come from the Jeanne situation, which was not your fault. The same things would have happened no matter who was in charge.''

''I should have dismissed Pierre sooner. You warned me about him.''

He sat beside her on the bed and put his arm around her. She stiffened against him, refusing comfort. ''Don't fret about what you could or could not have done. You did what you thought was right at the time.''

''But it wasn't right,'' she said.

''You wanted to give Pierre another chance and it didn't work out. That's all that happened.''

Her hands tightened even more. He was so big and warm next to her, but she wouldn't give in and lean against him. ''What happened was that I lost my main equestrian act!''

''Luc was right—you don't need him. Mathieu and Albert did a wonderful job today.''

''They are not as good as Luc.''

''Give them time and they will be.''

''But Albert is going to be an artist.''

''Mathieu will grow into Luc's role by himself.''

''Don't you see?'' she asked impatiently. ''If Mathieu and Albert do Luc's acts, then who will do Mathieu and Albert's acts? The circus will be too short!''

His arm was still around her shoulders, not demandingly, just there, offering comfort if she wanted to take it. ''Ask Sully to increase his role. The audience always loves Sully. I'm sure he can come up with some more routines.''

She thought for a few minutes. ''I could do that. Papa always limited Sully because he wanted the circus to be more equestrian than comic.''

Leo said, ''How about teaching one of the horses to

count? I saw that trick done once in London when I was a boy. And I remember a horse that played dead, too.''

She turned to him in excitement. ''Shaitan could do that! He loves to perform and he's very intelligent.''

''That could be another act.''

She looked up at him, smiling in relief. ''Those are good ideas, Leo. I should have thought of them. I'm the circus person, not you.''

''You're too upset to think straight right now.''

She finally relaxed against him and leaned her head against his shoulder. ''I feel better now. You've been a help.''

He rested his cheek against the top of her head. ''I'm glad. I hate to see you worried and distressed.''

They were quiet for a while. Then she said, ''I would be feeling fine if it wasn't for that gold. I wish I knew how the army was going to remove it from my wagons. That sergeant never lets them out of his sight!''

''I wish I could tell you something,'' he said.

She turned to look at him. ''What precisely do you know?''

''Not much,'' he admitted. ''I was told to get the gold to Biarritz. What happens when we do that was not discussed with me.''

Gabrielle said soberly, ''I have made many mistakes this last month, but my biggest mistake was agreeing to carry that gold.''

Leo's arm tightened around her. ''If you hadn't carried the gold, then you never would have met me.''

Gabrielle didn't say anything for a while. Finally she said in a low voice, ''Meeting you was the worst mistake of all.''

She felt him stiffen. ''What do you mean by that?'' he asked.

Don't tell him, Gabrielle, she thought fiercely. *Don't make him feel guilty. It's not his fault that you have fallen in love with him.*

She managed to make her voice light. "I mean that we will miss you as ringmaster when you leave," she lied.

"That's not what you meant," he said.

"I will miss your good advice," she said. "You have helped me a great deal, Leo."

He hesitated, as if he would say something else, then he said merely, "I will miss you, too."

Tears stung behind her eyes and she fought them back. *Don't let him see you cry,* she told herself. She gritted her teeth and forced the tears back. *Don't you dare let him see you cry.*

She cleared her throat. "This is wonderful," she said. "We are carrying two wagonloads of gold and neither of us knows how we are going to get rid of it."

"That's about it," he said.

They sat in silence, Gabrielle luxuriating in the feel of his arm around her shoulders, the warmth of his shoulder under her cheek.

"I have been thinking," she said. "If we do get caught with the gold, will you say that I am the only one who knows about it? I don't want Mathieu and Albert involved. If you swear that I am the only one involved, then perhaps everyone else will be all right."

"You are not going to get caught," he said roughly.

"I hope not, but I would be foolish not to plan for that possibility. Promise me, Leo, that you will not involve anyone but me."

He didn't answer.

"Promise me!"

"I promise," he said in a low voice.

She closed her eyes and snuggled her cheek more deeply into his shoulder.

"I'll get you out of this mess, Gabrielle," he said. "I promise you that also. Neither you nor your circus will be hurt by this bloody gold."

"Bloody," she repeated thoughtfully. "Isn't that a swear word in English?"

He laughed a little painfully. "Yes, it is. Don't ever say it yourself. It's not a word that ladies use."

"I am not a lady," she pointed out.

He turned her so that she was facing him, then he looked down into her eyes and said very seriously, "You are the greatest lady I have ever met."

Her smile trembled. "You sound as if you mean that."

"I do," he said. And bent his head and kissed her.

Thirty-Three

The circus was stopped when they were ten miles outside of Bordeaux.

"Damn," Leo said to Gabrielle when they saw the line of soldiers blocking the road. "I was afraid this was going to happen."

One of the soldiers approached the wagon. "We are searching all vehicles passing along this road, *monsieur,*" he said to Leo. "I am going to have to ask you to pull your wagons to the side so we can go through them."

"We have already been searched," Gabrielle said coldly. "And the soldiers made a mess of our wagons. I fail to see why we should be subjected to this ordeal again."

At this point they were joined by Sergeant Jordan, who had jumped down from his wagon at the sight of the roadblock. He introduced himself to the other sergeant. "I have been assigned to keep an eye on this circus. The government is suspicious that they might be carrying the gold we are looking for. I have been waiting to meet just such a roadblock. I think a thorough search of these wagons is definitely called for."

"Well that's what we're here for," the sergeant said. "I'll have my men get started."

"You want to concentrate on the wagons that belong to the Robichons," Jordan said. "These two wagons with the circus name on them, the wagons with the tents and the poles and the wagon with the hay and grain. Look particularly at the sacks of grain. I have thought that they could easily be hiding gold in those."

"Very well," the sergeant said. "What about the other wagons?"

"Look in them, by all means, but concentrate on the Robichon wagons."

"Very good. Do you want to help us?"

"By all means." Jordan looked positively enthusiastic at the thought of going through the wagons.

It was mid afternoon when the soldiers started the search and it was almost dark by the time they had finished. Gabrielle was livid. They had looked into every trunk and wantonly scattered the contents around the wagons. They had ripped open her sacks of grain so that it was spilled all over the place, and they had removed the bales of hay from the wagon and left them lying on the road. The rest of the circus members had not fared much better. They all stood in a group, cursing the soldiers, as the search of the wagons was completed.

"This is outrageous," Henri steamed to Sergeant Jordan who was standing with them as the soldiers regrouped. "Our costumes have been pulled out of our trunks and not put back. The same is true of my personal belongings. As a French citizen, I am outraged. We have done nothing to deserve such treatment."

"Someone is carrying gold to the English," Sergeant Jordan said. "It is my responsibility as a French soldier to try to recover it before it can reach its destination."

Gabrielle said, "This is the second time we have been searched. How many more times do you have to do it before you are convinced that we are not carrying the wretched gold?"

The sergeant's black eyes went over the faces that were gathered in front of him. "It is true that we have not uncovered the gold, but that doesn't mean you aren't concealing it somewhere we haven't looked. And let me be clear about one thing. These wagons will not be out of my sight while you are moving south. I don't care how often your belongings are disturbed. Our actions are necessary for the safety of France!" And on this grandiose statement he strode away to talk to his fellow sergeant.

"What an idiot," Henri fumed.

Gabrielle, whose heart had been pounding all during the search, pulled herself together enough to say, "Don't worry about putting your wagons to rights until tomorrow. We are hours late to meet Vincent. He will be wondering what happened to us."

"All right," Henri grumbled and the others agreed. Within ten minutes of the conclusion of the search they were back in their wagons and headed toward Bordeaux.

The circus stayed in Bordeaux for three days and during that time Gabrielle kept hoping that someone from the British army would get into contact with them. Their next stop would be Biarritz, and she was convinced that the whole French army would be waiting to pounce on her once they entered the city limits.

To add to her extreme tension about getting rid of the gold, she was dealing with the nearness of Leo's departure. She tried to treasure in her heart all of the moments that she spent with him. She would watch him as he played chess with Mathieu, or groomed a horse, or stood in the middle of the ring keeping Coco to an even canter. At night, in his arms, she responded to his ardor with all the sweetness that was in her, giving her body to him generously even as her heart ached with the knowledge that their time together was almost over.

The night before they left Bordeaux, when they were alone in their bedroom, Leo told her that someone had finally contacted him immediately after the second show.

"He was dressed like a workingman and he watched the show like the rest of the audience," Leo said. "He spoke to me very casually. I don't think anyone noticed."

"What did he say?" Gabrielle demanded. Leo was sitting on the bed and she was standing in front of him, between his legs. They were holding hands.

"It wasn't what he said so much as what I said," Leo returned. "I told him we had a French sergeant traveling with us and keeping a constant eye on the wagons. I told him which wagons contained the gold and that they were left on the circus grounds at night under the watchful eye of two grooms, two dogs and Sergeant Jordan."

Gabrielle clutched his hands more tightly. "What did he say to that?"

"He said he would check with his superiors and get back to me."

"But when?" Gabrielle said. "When will he get back to you? We are leaving for Biarritz tomorrow morning!"

"Don't panic, sweetheart. The army will come up with a plan."

"I'm not panicking," she said, "but I think I have a right to be concerned. I have done my part by getting the gold across France. Now the British army must do its part and remove it from my wagons without anyone knowing that I have been carrying it."

"I'm sure they will do that, sweetheart."

Gabrielle was not so sanguine.

There was an urgency to their lovemaking that night that had not been there before. Both of them realized that the end of their time together was coming, and the tenderness that had been so much a part of their lovemaking in the past was almost absent. Tonight was about need.

When it was over and Leo was asleep, Gabrielle lay awake next to him, dry-eyed and suffering. _This is terrible,_ she thought. _This is almost as bad as when André died._ But Leo was not going to die; he was not even going to disappear from her life altogether. He would come during the winter. He had said that he would. She clung to that thought like a drowning person to a lifeline.

I think he does love me, she thought. _Perhaps when he comes...perhaps everything will turn out all right._

The circus set off for Biarritz at eight o'clock the next morning, and at eleven o'clock they met a farm wagon that had broken down by the side of the road. Leo pulled up, jumped down from his high seat and went to see if he could be of help. All of the wagons stopped behind him.

Gabrielle watched curiously as Leo stopped in front of the farmer, who was standing on the road next to his wagon. As she continued to watch, the farmer handed something to Leo, who immediately put it inside his coat.

Gabrielle's heart began to thunder as she waited to see Sergeant Jordan appear, demanding to know what Leo had just received. But nothing happened. She was tempted to peer around the side of the wagon to see what was going on behind her, but she didn't want to do anything that might call attention to Leo. She looked at him again, and this time she realized that he had positioned himself so that his broad back and shoulders were blocking the sergeant's view of the so-called farmer. No one in the second wagon would have seen that package passed from one set of hands to the other.

Leo returned to the wagon and climbed up to the seat beside her. He picked up the reins and put the horses in motion. The wagons behind followed suit. They were perhaps five hundred feet from the broken-down wagon when Gabrielle said in a low voice, "What did that man give you?"

He glanced sideways at her, surprised. "You saw it?"

"Yes. But I don't think they saw it from the second wagon. You were blocking their view."

"God, I hope so," he said.

"You can be sure that if Sergeant Jordan had seen it, he would have been on you immediately, demanding to know what you had received."

He nodded. His profile looked stern. "I think you're right."

"But what *is* it?" Gabrielle asked.

He turned his eyes her way. "Drugs," he said. "We're to give them to Jordan, the grooms and the dogs in their dinner. The farmer who gave them to me said they were guaranteed to keep them all out for the duration of the night."

"Mon Dieu," she said.

"I should have figured they'd do something like this," Leo said. "The chap whom I met at the circus yesterday asked me how the grooms and Jordan got their dinner and I said one of the boys usually brought it out to them. He told me to stop for the farmer today."

"So the army will come while everyone is sleeping and take away the gold?"

"Yes. They have a fishing boat in the harbor that will take it to Santander, which is Wellington's supply port on the Bay of Biscay. It's controlled by the English."

"Mon Dieu," she said again. "But what will happen

when Jordan and the grooms wake up and realize they have been drugged?''

''Why should they think that? It's more likely that they will think they all had a good night's sleep.''

''But if Jordan suspects he was drugged?''

''He may suspect but he will have no proof,'' Leo said. ''And the gold will be gone.''

''What about the floorboards? They will have to tear up the floorboards in our wagon? What if…''

''Calm down,'' he said. He pulled her toward him until she was sitting on his knee. ''I told the man by the wagon about the floorboards and I told him that they would have to be replaced before they left. He promised me he would see to it that that was done.''

She went over the scheme in her head. ''We have to mix the drugs into their dinners?''

''Yes. He even gave me a separate, smaller portion for the dogs.''

''I see. Well, it seems as if they have covered everything.''

''I think it's a good plan, sweetheart.''

''When will they do it? Tomorrow?''

''Yes. We'll have Mathieu pick up the food and he can mix in the drugs before he delivers it. It might be a good idea to request that the hotel make stew for dinner.''

''Won't you want to take care of the drugs yourself?''

He shook his head. ''I haven't brought the grooms their dinner since that first night. We want to keep everything as normal as possible. Mathieu will do a good job.''

She buried her face in his shoulder. ''It's going to be all right, sweetheart,'' he said soothingly.

''I'm so frightened, Leo,'' she said. ''I don't think my heart is going to slow down until that damn gold is out of my wagons!''

"Only another day and you can relax."

He smoothed his hand over her hair and she closed her eyes, inhaling the scent of him, the strength of him.

It's going to be all right, she told herself. *It's going to be all right.*

The next day, the circus members went about their usual chores following the second show. About forty-five minutes before they all left for their hotel, Mathieu hitched up the empty tent wagon and went to collect the dinners for the grooms and Sergeant Jordan. The cook had them ready for him, a covered basket along with some meat and two bones in a pail for the dogs.

Halfway to the field, Mathieu pulled off the road, took out the package that Leo had given to him and emptied the powder into the stew that was the meal. He used his finger to stir it into the thick gravy, and then did the same thing with the portion for the dogs. Mathieu's heart was pounding but his hand was steady as he doctored the dinners. Then he picked up the reins and continued on his way.

By the time Mathieu reached the field, the others were ready to leave for town. He delivered the meals to the grooms and the sergeant, who were at their usual posts close to the corral and the horse tent. The men received them with gratitude and professed themselves ready to tuck right in.

"Bon appetite," Mathieu said cheerfully, and went hastily to crawl into the back of Henri's wagon for the ride to the hotel.

Gabrielle didn't sleep that night. She made love with Leo, then lay awake, listening to his breathing and picturing in her mind what was happening out at the circus field.

What if someone wakes up?

It was her greatest fear. What if one of the supposedly drugged men had not been hungry? What if one of them was awake? What would happen when they heard the noise of hammering in the night? Or what if the dogs didn't eat their meal? Wouldn't the noise of the dogs barking wake the grooms and Jordan, no matter how much they'd been drugged?

Slowly the hours slipped by and everything remained quiet. There was no Sergeant Jordan pounding on her door, demanding that she account for the gold that had been removed from her wagon. No gendarmes came to arrest her. When she finally fell asleep near dawn, she was thankfully sure that the venture had been a success and the gold was gone.

Thirty-Four

Everything was quiet when the circus arrived back at the field in the morning. Gabrielle was relieved to see the dogs come to greet the wagons, as they usually did. Apparently the drugs had been strong enough to put them to sleep for the night, but not strong enough to keep them from waking up at a decent time in the morning.

Thank you, God, Gabrielle thought with huge relief.

Their second day in Biarritz went smoothly and Gabrielle felt as if a huge burden had been lifted from her back. The gold was gone and she had not been discovered or arrested. The floorboards in the two wagons had been nailed back down and there was no visible sign that anything had ever been in those wagons except their circus equipment.

That night, as she and Leo lay in bed together, she said, "You were right. The army was clever in the way they removed the gold. I didn't have to worry so much after all."

"I don't want you worrying at all," he said. He was leaning up on his elbow, his eyes on her face. "I want you to be happy."

How can I be happy when you are leaving? she thought, but she made an effort to smile bravely.

"Once we have pushed the French out of Spain," he continued, "I will take leave and come to see you. You gave me your itinerary for the rest of the season, so I shouldn't have any trouble finding you. We will have a reunion.''

She produced the smile once more.

''I meant what I said about taking care of Albert, but I'd rather wait until the war is ended to collect him. Is that all right?''

''That will be fine,'' she managed. ''Thank you.''

''I also meant what I said about visiting during the winter for riding lessons, too. I hope the war will be over by then.''

''I hope so, too.''

He turned to gather her into his arms. ''I'll miss you,'' he whispered in her ear.

Oh, Leo, she thought, pressing her face against his chest. *You are breaking my heart.*

''Kiss me,'' he whispered fiercely.

She lifted her face and met his fiery kiss. His mouth pressed her head back into the pillow and his body followed. He kissed her throat and reached around to the neck of her nightgown to open it.

''Damn nightgown,'' he muttered, fumbling.

Gabrielle sat up and smiled, stripping the full cotton gown over her head.

''You are so beautiful,'' he said.

He flicked his tongue over her nipples and passion shot like a bolt of lightening down to her loins. She whimpered.

His hands were all over her, running over the gentle curve of her hips, trailing down her thighs, then up to the secret place where the heart of her desire lodged. She opened to him, urging him onward, beckoning him in so he could assuage the rising passion that was building inside of her.

He came in a rush, deep and hard, filling her, stretching her, thrusting in and out of her quivering flesh, driving her up the bed until her head was pressed against the headboard. Then the climax came, an excruciating wave of intense jolts of pleasure that caused her whole body to spasm while he himself gave a shout of triumph and completion as his seed spilled into her body.

Afterward they lay together, naked and glistening, body pressed to body. "My God, how I will miss you," Leo said.

"Will you miss me or will you miss this?" she couldn't help asking.

He tried to hold her closer. "I can't have this without you. It's not the same with anybody else."

"Me, too," she said.

"Listen to me, Gabrielle," he said. "I am going to give you my address at home and in the army. If something happens—if you need money, for example—I want you to contact me."

The beat of his heart was slowing. "That's nice of you, Leo, but we will be all right." She did not want his charity, she thought.

"Listen, Gabrielle. I need to tell you who I am." Leo sat up and looked at her with a troubled expression. "You know that I am an aristocrat, as you say, but I am not a younger son as you believe. I am the Earl of Branford, and the estate I have talked about belongs to me. I have a great deal of money, and if I can help you at all, I want to do it."

A great quietness descended upon her heart. "An earl?" she said. "We do not have earls in France."

"It is like a count," he said. "In England we don't have counts, we have earls."

It seemed as if her heart stopped. This was worse than

she could ever imagine. An English earl! She had thought he was above her reach before, although at this moment she realized that deep in her heart she had always believed in the possibility that he might love her enough… But now, now all hope was dead. There was no way that an earl could marry a circus girl.

"Gabrielle?" he said. "Are you listening?"

"I don't want your money, Leo," she said. "If you will help Albert, I will be grateful. But I don't want your money."

"I want to help you," he said.

"It will make me feel like a kept woman to accept money from you," she said shortly. "Please don't speak of this anymore."

His arms tightened so much that they hurt. "Don't say that about yourself!"

"What else would I be?" she asked.

"You are someone I care about."

"No, Leo," she said firmly. She shut her eyes and called on all of her resources. "In fact, I think that when you leave us in Pau we should say goodbye. I need to get on with my life. It isn't fair to me to have you hanging around. Come for Albert, but don't plan on staying. If you want lessons in riding, go to Lisbon. Or to Vienna. You can learn there everything you want to know."

He started to protest, but she shook her head.

"No," she said. The pain in her heart was terrible. "These few weeks have been magical. I will never forget them. But it is over, Leo. You are a great lord and I am a circus girl. There can be nothing permanent between us, and I cannot bear to keep up a relationship that is only temporary. It isn't good for me, Leo. Please respect my wishes in this matter and don't make it harder for me than it already is."

He loosened his arms so he could look into her face. "I can't believe that you are doing this to us," he said disbelievingly.

"Leo," she said. Her heart was aching. "Please!"

He heard the pain. "All right." His own voice was rough. His eyes bored into hers. "If you're sure this is what you want."

She sustained his gaze steadily. "It's not what I want, it's what has to be."

"But it's not goodbye, Gabrielle. I will come for Albert."

"Come for Albert. But you can't stay, Leo. I can't go through this again."

He flung himself back on his pillow. "I never should have told you the truth," he said grimly.

Tears flowed down into her loose hair. "I'm glad you did," she said calmly. "It made our situation clearer to me. We are from different worlds, Leo. For this little time our worlds have meshed, but it won't happen again. You must go back to your world and I must learn to live without you in mine."

"Very well." His voice was suddenly cold. "If you are determined to kick me out of your life, I suppose there's nothing I can do about it."

"That's right," she said. "There isn't."

He got out of bed to untie Colette and to pick up his nightshirt. Gabrielle lay and watched him, watched the golden body that was so powerful yet so lithe, watched the hard set of his mouth and the hurt look he was trying to conceal in his eyes. And her heart bled and bled and bled.

The following morning the circus left Biarritz to go east to Pau. Sergeant Jordan rode with them, but when they reached Pau he announced to Gabrielle that he was leaving the circus and returning to Paris. Apparently he was finally convinced they were not carrying the gold.

"Finally, we're rid of him," Gabrielle said to Leo. "Now we can pretend to get a letter from England for you."

"We'd better wait until tomorrow," he said. "Give Jordan a chance to get away."

It was clear to Leo that she wanted him gone as quickly as possible. He didn't want to betray how deeply her change in attitude had hurt him, so he tried for a tone that was matter-of-fact. "We can pretend to get the message in the morning and I will hire a horse and be gone before evening. You won't have to put up with me for much longer, Gabrielle."

She didn't answer. She just nodded her agreement.

That night Leo wanted to stay home and make love to Gabrielle, but she insisted on going to the café with the others. When they got home she stayed up talking to Mathieu and Isabel until almost midnight.

Clearly, she did not want to be alone with him.

Fine, he thought as he sat silently in one of the salon chairs and listened to the three-way conversation. *If that's the way she wants to handle things, then that's the way they'll be. She knew all along that I was going to leave. What else did she expect me to do?*

Mathieu and Isabel finally went to bed and Leo said grimly, "I think you've run out of excuses, Gabrielle. You're going to have to come upstairs with me."

She gave him a look that was almost hostile. "We can share a bed, Leo, but I am not going to make love with you. All that is finished between us."

"Gabrielle." He crossed the floor, ready to take her in his arms. "I don't want us to end like this."

She took a step backward. ''I can't take any more goodbyes, Leo.'' She sounded almost desperate. ''It has to be this way. I'm sorry.''

''But why have you changed so suddenly?'' He was truly bewildered. ''You always knew I was going to have to rejoin my regiment.''

''It isn't that,'' she said.

''Then what is it? I don't understand.''

She shrugged. The gesture was so familiar that it hurt him to see it. ''I have been deluding myself, Leo,'' she said. ''I let myself forget the way this affair would have to end. I just went on, day after day, never letting myself look ahead. Well, I can't do that anymore. You are leaving and I can't hide from the truth of our relationship any longer. We had what we had, but it's over, Leo. As I told you before, you aren't good for me.''

''But I'm not leaving you forever, Gabrielle! I have told you that I would come and spend the winter with you.''

She shook her head. She was very pale. ''I can't be your mistress, Leo. I have a responsibility to be a good example to the boys. And I have my own self-respect to think about, too. What you have to offer me just isn't good enough, Leo. That's what this is all about.''

He was angry. He never thought of her as his mistress. He had thought that what they had between them was something rare and special. But evidently she didn't think the same way.

''Fine,'' he said in a hard voice. ''If that's the way you want it.''

They went up the stairs in silence, and without exchanging a word, they turned their backs on each other and got undressed.

I can't believe we are back to where we started, Leo

thought. Then, with anger at his own stupidity, *I never should have told her I'm an earl.*

At breakfast the following morning, Leo told everyone that a message from home had been delivered to his room informing him that his father was dying.

"I must go at once," he said.

Everyone understood and offered their sympathies.

"We will miss you," Henri said. "You are a good ringmaster and a good person, Leo. I hope your father recovers. I will pray for him."

Leo looked into Henri's sincere brown eyes and felt guilty for lying to him. He said gruffly, "Look out for Gabrielle for me."

"Of course, my friend," Henri said.

Albert was almost in tears. "We will miss you, Leo," he said. "I'll pray for your safety."

"I'll miss you, too," Leo said. And he realized that he would miss these two young brothers of Gabrielle. He had grown quite fond of them during his time with the circus.

Mathieu shook his hand firmly. "Goodbye, Leo," he said. "I'll pray for your safety as well."

Leo shook hands all around. Then he said to Gabrielle, "Come upstairs with me while I get my clothes together."

She looked at him, knowing there was no way she could refuse his request with everyone looking on. Silently the two of them left the breakfast room and climbed the stairs to their bedroom. Once they were inside, he thrust a piece of paper at her. "Take this," Leo said. "It has my address at home and in the army. I want you to have it—just in case something happens."

She looked at his outstretched hand. "Nothing is going to happen."

"Please," he said, "do me this last favor. Take it. I will feel better knowing you can contact me if you find it necessary."

"Nothing will happen," she repeated.

"Suppose Carlotta's herbs didn't work," he said quietly.

She stared at him, her brown eyes huge.

"Take it," he said.

Slowly she reached out her hand and took the folded paper from him.

He reached out, caught her to him and lowered his mouth to hers. His kiss was full of passion. He raised his head. "Goodbye, Gabrielle," he said.

"Goodbye, Leo," she returned. She had tears in her eyes.

He hesitated, as if he would pull her into his arms once more, then he turned and left the room, never looking back.

Thirty-Five

Wellington himself sent for Leo when he arrived at the British camp in Freinada, Portugal, just outside Ciudad Rodrigo in Spain. The general looked up from some papers on his desk when Leo walked in. "The troops are five months in arrears," he began. "The staff has not been paid since February and the muleteers not since June 1811. We are in debt in all parts of the country. Your contribution in getting this coin to us is inestimable, Lord Branford."

"Thank you, sir," Leo said. "We owe a great debt of thanks to the brave owner of the Cirque Equestre who carried it through France for us."

"Good job," the commander-in-chief said brusquely. "Good job by all. Now I can pay my troops and get on with the business of pushing the French out of Spain for good."

The campaign was to begin in six weeks' time. Leo knew that Wellington had hoped to move forward in the first weeks of May, but the crops were late and without grass the horses would starve on the advance. So Leo and the rest of Wellington's officers remained at the decaying town of Freinada, where the streets were immense masses of stone and holes, with dung all around, and where houses were nothing but farm kitchens with stables underneath. But Freinada was in the middle of good foxhunting country, and Leo and his friends passed the time chasing Portuguese foxes and taking occasional trips to Oporto to buy pipes of port for their families back at home.

Leo should have been happy. He was where he had wanted to be ever since his injury, back with his comrades. They were on the brink of the biggest event of the entire Peninsula War—the major advance that would push the French troops under Napoléon's brother, King Joseph, finally and forever out of the Iberian Peninsula and pave the way for Wellington's triumphant entry into France. The mood of the officers and the troops was exuberant. But Leo's mind was somewhere else.

How was Gabrielle faring without him?

She did well enough before you came along, he told himself. But he remembered the money he was paying the doctor in Rouen to take care of Franz; he remembered the time he had chased the hecklers out of the circus tent; he remembered going to the jail to bail out Pierre. Who knew what other incidents would occur, and he wouldn't be there to help her with them.

She needs a husband, he thought.

But he couldn't bear to picture Gabrielle with anyone but him.

Outwardly, Leo was the same man who had left the army with an injury sustained at Burgos. He galloped over the countryside with his friends, speculated with them on Wellington's plans, looked forward with enthusiasm to the upcoming campaign.

Inwardly, however, he was quite a different person. Inwardly, he belonged to Gabrielle.

On May 22, the long-awaited advance into Spain finally began. The French believed that any English thrust would have to be made through central Spain, so Wellington fostered that assumption by sending an army under General Hill in the direction of Salamanca. Hill's advance guard was six brigades of cavalry and Leo was in charge of two of them. Behind the cavalry, however, there was an army of only 30,000 men. The rest of Wellington's men, numbering some 66,000, were ascending into the mountains to the north, to outflank and swing down behind the French defensive line while it was drawing up to face the advancing General Hill.

The plan worked perfectly, and by June 19 both arms of Wellington's army were just a short distance from Vitoria, which Wellington had chosen to be the venue for this decisive battle.

The battlefield of Vitoria lay along the floor of the valley of the Zadorra, some six miles wide and ten miles in length. The eastern end of this valley was open and led to the town of Vitoria itself, while the other three sides of the valley consisted of mountains. The river Zadorra wound from the southwest corner of the valley to the north, where it ran along the foot of the mountains. The river was crossed by four bridges to the west of the valley and four more to the north.

Wellington divided his army into four columns. Hill's column on the right was to secure the defile of La Puebla and drive up the main road toward Vitoria. To do this, Hill was allotted the First and Fifth Divisions, two independent Portuguese brigades, five battalions of light infantry, and two cavalry brigades under Leo.

On the extreme left Thomas Graham, with a column of similar strength, was to strike in behind Vitoria by the Bilbao road. The left center column under the Earl of Dalhousie was to cross the rugged Monte Arato and cross the Zadorra by one of the bridges. Wellington himself commanded the right center column, with the remaining four brigades of cavalry.

The battle began with an advance by Hill. He started by sending a brigade up the steep hillside beside the main road to secure the defile of La Puebla high above them. The hill was steep and overgrown in many places with underbrush and trees. After a short time, Hill reinforced the first brigade with a second, and the men eventually established themselves on the crest of the hill, seemingly securing the road beneath.

To Leo, waiting with the cavalry, it looked as if the road to Vitoria was now open, but a French commander, seeing what was happening, sent a cadre of troops to challenge the Englishmen on the heights. All of a sudden there was a firefight going on above them, and seeing what was happening, Hill ordered Leo to the heights to support the men who were under attack.

Leo was in front as the cavalry took to the hill. As they ascended the French opened a tremendous fire from the rocks above and men and horses started to fall around him. As Leo and his men pushed furiously on through the undergrowth on the hillside, the French began to retreat before the horses, from rock to rock, still keeping up a destructive fire. Men were falling left and right when Leo perceived that a French column was trying to outflank Captain Hall's company on the far side of the defile. As he turned around on his horse to give orders to his men to reinforce Hall, he was struck from behind by a ball from a French *chaseur* and toppled from his horse.

The pain was excruciating. Two of his men dismounted and came to his assistance as he was lying on the ground.

"Leave me and go on," he said to them from between his teeth.

"You were hit pretty badly, sir," one of the men said. "I think we better get you back to the hospital tent."

"Finish this up first," Leo gritted out. "Come back for me when it's over."

The two men, who couldn't have been more than twenty-two, looked at each other.

"Go," Leo ordered.

"You go," one of them said to the other. "I'll get the colonel off the mountain and then come back."

Leo was sweating and the pain was making him dizzy. "I'll be all right," he managed to say.

"Can you sit up, sir?" one of the youngsters asked.

"Certainly," Leo said. One of the boys put an arm around him and tried to boost him to a sitting position. His arm hit the wound in Leo's back and Leo's world went black.

The battle that day was a brilliant success for Wellington and his allied forces. Hill's division cleared the Puebla heights after withstanding a furious French counterattack. With this done, the other three columns began their attack. Gradually, all avenues of escape for the French were closed down as they were herded back to the village of Vitoria. Finally King Joseph gave the order for a withdrawal along the Pamplona road. The whole French army took to its heels, abandoning not only its heavy equipment but in many cases its personal arms and accoutrements. The withdrawal quickly turned into a rout as troops, government officials, camp followers and civilians crowded the narrow escape route. The retreat never stopped until the army was safely over the border and into France. Few armies had ever been so thoroughly beaten.

Leo missed the rout. Left to themselves, the two

youngsters had loaded Leo onto one of their horses and led the horse down the mountainside to rejoin Hill's main command, still waiting on the road. Hill immediately commanded that Leo be taken off the field of battle back to where Dr. McGrigor had his hospital tents pitched.

Even on the field of battle, it still counted for something to be an earl.

Now, he was in one of the hospital tents having a ball taken out of his back. He was enormously lucky in that the bullet had not touched either of his lungs; it had broken one rib and lodged behind another. He was in much pain, but he was going to be all right.

That night, as he lay awake under the canvas tent enduring the pain, one thought kept going round and round in his mind: *I might have been killed. I might never have seen her again.*

He had never thought very much about being killed—even though he had taken a bullet once before. In the way of young men, he supposed, he had always vaguely thought that he was immortal. But that ball smashing into his back had done more than torn his flesh; it had torn his peace of mind as well.

What was I thinking, to leave her like that? Did I really think I was going to live the rest of my life without her?

What could I have been thinking?

He had gone into their love affair with the clear idea that it would be temporary. It had never once crossed his mind that he, the Earl of Branford, might marry a circus girl. But Gabrielle had turned out to be so much more than he had ever imagined any woman could be.

He pictured her in his mind: as she looked when she rode Noble; as she looked when she was petting Colette; as she looked when she was lying beside him in bed.

Slowly his mind came to accept what his heart had always known.

He loved her.

"Gabrielle." His lips moved, forming her name.

I love her, he thought. *I deeply love her.*

What am I going to do about it?

The answer came quickly. *I'm going to marry her.*

She owned a circus, he thought. She performed in public. She was not the kind of girl earls married. And did he care?

No, he did not.

If I marry Gabrielle, I can get her away from the circus and all its responsibilities. She can bring her horses to Branford Abbey, where they'll live like kings. I can take care of the boys. All of her problems will be solved.

He pictured Gabrielle's face when she saw the Branford stables, and he smiled.

We'll be married and we'll go back to Branford Abbey to live.

He thought about the important position the Earl of Branford played in the neighborhood, in the county, in the country. He thought about the kind of social life that was expected of an earl and his wife. It would be very painful for Gabrielle if she was not accepted by his peers.

We can always live at Branford Abbey and the hell with the rest of the world, he thought.

But that wasn't what he wanted to happen. He wanted her to take her full place in society as his wife. He wanted to show her off, to be proud of her. He wanted other people to value her as he valued her. And she would hate being spurned by English society.

There must be something I can do to fix this. He spent the rest of the pain-filled night cudgeling his brain to come up with a solution. The first light of dawn was beginning to stain the sky when he found an answer.

Thirty-Six

Leo returned home at the beginning of July, crossing to England on a naval ship and arriving at Branford Abbey on a beautiful day of clear skies and fluffy white clouds. Branford stood on the West Downs of Sussex, and at the beginning of the seventeenth century it had been substantially remodeled from the stone abbey it once was into a house befitting an earl. Most of the house was still the Jacobean edifice built by the first earl, from the front hall—one of the grandest in all England—with its massive fireplace and spectacular screen, its awe-inspiring staircase, to the ornate and stately rooms on the second floor with their displays of portraiture and paintings and fine furniture.

Leo loved his home, but he had spent most of his life living away from it, first at school and then in the army. As he dined in state all by himself in the magnificent dining room, he thought how wonderful it would be to make this house a home again, to bring Gabrielle here, with her laughter and her greatheartedness. They would have children to fill up the nurseries, he thought, and Albert could have a studio and Mathieu a study to work on mathematical formulas.

"Do you know if my mother is in residence at Marley Manor?" he asked his butler as one dish was removed and another one served.

"I don't know, my lord," replied the venerable retainer, who had served his mother when she was Lady Branford. "I can have one of the grooms ride over there to ascertain if she is."

"Do that," Leo said. "Have him go tomorrow morning. I'll give him a note to deliver in case she is there. If she isn't, have him find out where she has gone."

"Yes, my lord," the butler replied.

He was very tired after dinner. That was one thing about being wounded; you got tired very easily. But the bandages had come off the wound and his ribs were healing and, all in all, he was in good shape, considering how serious things might have been.

He retired to his chambers, picturing how Gabrielle would look beside him in the high four-poster bed.

Leo's butler sought him out following breakfast the next morning. "Lady Rivers is in residence, my lord, and she sent you this reply to your note."

He offered the note, which reposed upon a silver salver, to Leo. Leo took it and unfolded it. *Come when you wish, I will be home all day.*

"Henderson, have the curricle brought to the front door," he said.

"Yes, my lord."

Half an hour later, Leo was on his way to visit Marley Manor, the home of his mother and her husband, Lord Rivers. Marley was eight miles away from Branford Abbey, and Leo had never once set foot in it during all the eleven years that his mother had been re-wed.

The home of Lord Rivers was a pleasant brick building, less than a quarter the size of Branford Abbey. There was a butler to answer the door, however, and Leo was shown into the house with great reverence.

His sister was just coming down the stairs as he came in.

"Leo!" she cried. "Is that really you?"

"It's I," he replied. "How are you, Dolly? You are looking very pretty this morning."

She was wearing a chip straw hat over her blond curls and a sprig muslin dress was tied under her high young breasts. On her feet she wore serviceable boots.

"I'm going to cut flowers for Mama in the garden," she said. "Whatever are you doing here? Are you all right? We heard that you were wounded again!"

"I am fine," he replied. "I came to see Mama."

Dolly looked flabbergasted. "You did?"

"Yes," Leo replied serenely.

Lady Rivers appeared at the top of the staircase. "Mama!" Dolly cried. "Leo has come to see you!"

"Yes, I know," Lady Rivers replied. "Come upstairs to the drawing room, Leo, where we can be private."

Leo followed his mother as she led him toward a yellow-painted room off the hallway. Lady Rivers closed the door firmly behind him and looked up into his face. Her eyes filled with tears. "Thank God you are all right," she said. "We were notified that you were wounded, but you seem well enough."

"I am fine," he replied. "A little stiff in the middle, perhaps, but that will wear off."

She blinked back the tears so that they didn't fall. "Please sit down," she said. "When did you get to Branford?"

"Yesterday," he replied.

She nodded and took a seat on a gold striped sofa. He sat on a gold velvet chair facing it.

"I was surprised to hear from you," she said cautiously.

Now that he was here, it was hard finding a place to start. He nodded and said, "How did Dolly's first season go?"

"Very well. She got two proposals of marriage from very eligible men, but she informed me that she didn't love either of them, so we will try again next year."

"What was wrong with the two eligible men?"

"Nothing, as far as I could see—except the fact that Dolly didn't love them."

He frowned a little, and she added, as if she expected him to object, "After all, she is only eighteen, Leo. There is no rush."

"Of course not," he said firmly. "It's important to love the person one marries. I have come to understand that very well."

There was a little silence, then Lady Rivers said carefully, "Are you by any chance in love yourself?"

He looked at her. She was still a very lovely woman. When he had been a child he had thought her the most beautiful woman in all the world. "Yes, I am."

"Tell me about her," she said.

He took a long breath. "Her name is Gabrielle Robichon and she is the proprietor of a French circus. She smuggled gold for the army from Belgium to the south of France, and I rode with the circus the whole time to keep an eye on the money."

He paused for breath, and to try to ascertain his mother's reaction. She looked astounded. "She owns a circus?" she murmured.

"An equestrian circus. She is the best rider I have ever seen. To watch her ride is magical."

She said, "She does not sound like an...appropriate... person for you to fall in love with, Leo."

He leaned a little in her direction. "If you look at it with worldly eyes, she isn't. But she is the most beautiful, the most brave, the most gallant woman I have ever met. She's a much better person than I am, Mama. In the eyes of God, she stands miles ahead of me."

She looked down at her hands, which were clasped in her lap, then back up to him. "Why have you come to me?" she asked finally.

He leaned slightly more forward. "I want you to help her to be accepted by society. I don't want to marry Gabrielle and have her ostracized by my own people. She doesn't deserve that."

Lady Rivers changed the way her hands were clasped; otherwise she was motionless. "Leo," she said. "Tell me how you came to fall in love with this girl."

He told her how he had looked down on the "circus girl" when first they met; he told her how gallant Gabrielle was, shouldering the burden of her young brothers and of all the people in the circus who were depending upon her. He told of her kindness, of her tolerance, of her charity. "My mind was so prejudiced by the social gap between us, that I never thought of marrying her until after I had left her," he concluded. "I knew I was miserable without her, but it took a bullet in my back to make me realize that the only way my life could be important was for me to be with her. I thought and I thought about how I could marry her and make my world accept her, and finally I thought of you." He fixed her with a pleading look. "Do you think you can help me, Mama?"

She searched his face. "Leo...how does this girl feel about you?"

"She loves me. I know she loves me."

"What about this circus that you say is so important to her?"

"I'll pay them all double what they would have got for the rest of the season. That way she won't have to worry about leaving them in the lurch. And her beloved horses can come to Branford—and her brothers as well. You'll like Mathieu and Albert, Mama. They are wonderful youngsters."

She smiled faintly. "You seem to have figured this all out."

"I've figured out everything except a way to make sure that Gabrielle is accepted into the ton. I don't want her ever to feel inferior, Mama. That would be a terrible thing to do to her."

Lady Rivers got practical. "What is Gabrielle's background? Who were her father and her mother?"

"Her father was Master of the Horse under Louis XVI. I don't know anything about her mother. Oh! I remember she once said that her grandfather was a minor noble. I had forgot about that."

"That is encouraging," Lady Rivers said. She nodded slowly. "Her father was a member of the court of Louis XVI. Her grandfather was a noble. These are things I can work with."

Leo brightened. "Do you think so?"

Lady Rivers said thoughtfully, "What I might do is hold a ball in order to introduce your new wife to society. I'm sure I can get Sally Jersey to attend—she is a particular friend of mine—and if Sally Jersey comes, the world will follow."

"That sounds wonderful, Mama," Leo said fervently.

Lady Rivers went on, "I can tell people that her family lost their estate in the Revolution and that she has bravely been raising her little brothers by herself."

"That's not a lie, either," Leo interjected.

She raised an eyebrow. "I assume that she is presentable, Leo?"

"She's the most beautiful girl I have ever seen."

"Her manners are good?"

"Her manners are perfect."

"I will have to get her a wardrobe. Does she speak English?"

"Yes."

"How well?"

"Well enough. And she's very smart. She will pick it up in no time."

"Well then…" Lady Rivers straightened her shoulders. "I think we can do it, Leo. She does sound like a brave girl. Her story—if it is presented properly—should garner a great deal of sympathy."

He gave her the smile he had not been able to give her in more than a decade. "This is wonderful, Mama."

Lady Rivers smiled back. "I think you should be married in the chapel at Branford. All of the family will come. That way Gabrielle will face society as your wife, and the wife of the Earl of Branford is one of the highest positions in English society. There have been Earls of Branford at Branford Abbey since the sixteenth century. Not too many people will want to snub your wife, especially if she is introduced by your family.

"How does that sound, Leo?" she asked.

"It sounds wonderful." His voice was a little subdued and he couldn't look at her. "I have been thinking…it is very kind of you to support me like this—especially since I have scarcely been kind to you these past twelve years."

She said, with an ache in her voice, "I always understood how you felt, Leo. I have never blamed you for rejecting me."

"No. It was wrong of me." He managed a crooked smile. "Gabrielle tells me that everything can be forgiven, but I didn't want to forgive. I wanted to remember—and to hurt you, like you had hurt me. It was childish of me. Can you ever forgive me, Mama?"

"Oh, darling, of course I can forgive you." Tears started to stream down her face. "Jasper and I were wrong to do what we did, and your finding us the way you did was the worst punishment that could ever have happened to me. I would have given anything to take back that moment—anything!"

He said in a low voice, "I couldn't understand it, you see." His voice took on a painful note. "I still can't understand it."

She looked at him, her eyes full of tears. "Leo…let me try to explain. Your papa and I…our marriage was arranged by our families, and we simply did not love each other the way you love your Gabrielle. When you were still a small boy, I fell in love with Jasper. He loved me back, but for many years we kept our love in check. I tried my best to be a good wife to your father and a good mother to you children. Then your father became ill and it was clear that he would not live."

The tears fell faster. "I didn't wish it on him, Leo. Believe me that I never did that. Your papa was a good man—he was always kind to me. I took the best care of him that I possibly could…."

Her voice tapered off.

Leo said flatly, "But Papa's death meant that you could marry Rivers."

"Yes. And for one moment—the only time, Leo!—we allowed ourselves to act out the love that had always been in our hearts."

"And I walked in on you."

"Yes. Because of my weakness, I lost my son."

Silence fell in the room. Then Leo said, "I'm through with judging you, Mama. I know a little myself now about the exigencies of love. It does not always come where it is appropriate or convenient. I can only say that I hope you have found happiness in your years spent with Rivers."

"Oh, Leo." Tears clogged her voice as well as her eyes. "The only flaw in my happiness has been my estrangement from you."

"Don't cry, Mama, please don't cry." He moved to sit next to her on the sofa. He took her hand into his. "I'm sorry. I'm sorry I was such a boor for all those years."

"I never blamed you," she said.

He took a square of white linen out of his pocket and put it into her hand. She wiped her cheeks and her streaming eyes.

"I'm so happy," she said.

He smiled. "You don't look it."

"These are tears of joy."

"I missed you all these years," he said. "I missed my family. I was a fool to turn my back on everything I loved the most."

"You had reason—good reason. But I hated to see you so alone. And I worried so much the whole time you were in the army."

"I'm selling out," he said. "The biggest battle is over. Now all Wellington has to do is sweep into France from the south while the Allies—which now include Austria—invade from the east. Napoléon's hours are numbered. I think I've done my part. The others can finish it up."

"Thank God," she said. "You were wounded twice. God knows what might have happened the next time."

"I have been thinking about that—and once you start thinking that way, you had better get out. I want a long life in front of me to spend with Gabrielle. I don't want to be buried on some French battlefield."

"God bless Gabrielle," Lady Rivers said. She gave her son a radiant smile. "She has given you back to me."

"Yes," Leo said. He bent his head and kissed his mother's soft cheek. "She has."

Thirty-Seven

The Battle of Vitoria was fought on June 21; Gabrielle learned of it, and of the thorough trouncing of the French army, on June 24. From that date forward, her mind was filled with the possibility of Leo's being wounded—the possibility of his being dead.

I will never know, she thought. *No one will contact me to let me know what happened to him. He could be in his grave right now, and I will never know.*

She had thought she was miserable when he left, but the depth of despair into which she fell after she learned of the battle was anguish at its purest.

Mathieu and Albert worried about her. "This is worse than it was when André died," Albert said to Mathieu one night as they got ready for bed in their hotel room. "Then, she mourned. Now she is just—frozen. It's as if the Gabrielle we know has gone away."

"He should have left her alone," Mathieu said furiously. He kicked his boots into the corner. "He made her fall in love with him and then he just left her. I used to like Leo, but not anymore. Now I think he is a skunk."

"He could be dead," Albert said. "I think that is what Gabrielle fears the most. There were heavy casualties on both sides—and Leo was wounded once before. And there is no way of us knowing! That's one of the things that's so terrible. We have no claim on Leo—there's no way of finding out what has happened to him.''

"He was dead to us, anyway," Mathieu said angrily. He peeled off his stockings and threw them after his boots. "He befriended us and then he left. As far as I am concerned, he *is* dead."

"Don't say that, Mathieu!"

"Why not? It's true. He is supposedly coming back to take you to England with him, but even if he does show up—which I doubt—I don't think you should go, Albert. We can't either of us desert Gabrielle now. She needs her family around her."

Albert finished taking off his own boots and began to strip off his breeches. "But she said she wants me to go to England! And Leo has said he will help me to become an established artist. I can make money, Mathieu. Perhaps I can help Gabrielle that way."

Mathieu pulled on his nightshirt. "Leo said a lot of things. I wouldn't count on seeing him, if I were you, Albert."

Albert took his shirt off over his head and went to get his nightshirt out of his valise. "You don't think Leo will come for me?" He could not keep the worry out of his voice.

"I wouldn't count on it, *mon frère*," Mathieu said. "Leo is a great lord. Once he gets back among his own kind, he is likely to forget all about us."

"I don't think Leo is like that," Albert said.

"If he's not like that, then why did he break Gabrielle's heart?"

Albert began to put on his nightshirt. His voice sounded muffled from within its folds. "What could he do? He had to go back to the army. He is an officer."

"Then he should have left her alone," Mathieu repeated.

Albert's head emerged. "I think Leo fell in love with Gabrielle just the way she fell in love with him."

Mathieu got into his side of the bed. "A funny way he has of showing it."

"Maybe he will come back and surprise you," Albert said stubbornly.

"Yes, and maybe he is buried somewhere in the Spanish Pyrenees," Mathieu retorted. "He should never have gone off and left her like that. The not knowing is killing her."

Albert got into bed as well. "I am going to pray that Leo comes back," he said.

"Go ahead," Mathieu said. "As for me, I am going to pray that Gabrielle gets over him." He punched his pillow into the shape he liked, turned his back on Albert and prepared to go to sleep.

It was a month after Vitoria, and the Cirque Equestre was playing just outside of Lyons. The July day was warm and Gabrielle was hot in her velvet jacket as she put Noble through his paces in front of an appreciative audience.

The circus had been going well. After all of the disasters of the trip south to Biarritz, things had straightened out. Everyone was getting along with one another; the acts were all solid and well received; the horses were sound; even the weather had cooperated with a succession of rainless days that brought standing-room-only crowds.

Gabrielle knew that she should be happy. She tried to act happy, and she thought that she had most of the circus people fooled. But Mathieu and Albert saw through her.

She had caught the anxious glances they sent her way, and she knew they understood how she was feeling. Thank God they didn't say anything. She could just about manage if she kept her unhappiness bottled up inside of her; if she had to talk about it, she was afraid she would simply fall apart.

Leo came just after the second show of the day had finished and Gabrielle and the boys were settling the horses for the night. She had just finished picking out Sandi's hooves, and when she straightened up, he was standing there before her.

She could feel every ounce of blood drain from her face.

"Gabrielle," Leo said. "I have missed you so much. I love you. Will you marry me?"

For the first time in her entire life, Gabrielle fainted.

When she came to, she was lying on the grass outside the corral, with Leo, Mathieu and Albert bending over her.

"She's coming around now," Albert said thankfully. "Gabrielle! Gabrielle! Are you all right?"

She looked up into Leo's eyes. No one had eyes like Leo, she thought. She ran her tongue over her lips to moisten them and said breathlessly, "*What* did you say to me?"

He was watching her gravely. "I said that I missed you, that I loved you, and then I asked you to marry me."

"I *told* you so," Albert said triumphantly to Mathieu. "Didn't I tell you that Leo loved Gabrielle?"

"Shh," Mathieu said in response.

"It's Leo!" someone from behind them called, and the rest of the circus folk began to move in their direction.

"Where's your wagon?" Leo said to Gabrielle. "You and I are going somewhere where we can be private."

"I'll show you where it is," Albert said exuberantly.

Leo bent and lifted Gabrielle in his arms. "Just point it out to me," he said.

"It's there, in front of Henri's," Mathieu said gruffly.

Leo nodded and began to stride away, holding Gabrielle in his arms. She hid her face in his shoulder.

"It's a good thing you came back," a voice from behind them called. Leo kept on going.

Colette was reclining on her couch when Leo reached the open back door of the wagon. "I might have known," he said humorously. "She always seems to be there whenever I want to be alone with you."

"You can put me down now," Gabrielle said breathlessly.

"Can we get into the wagon? Everyone is staring at us and it's a little off-putting."

Leo set her on her feet and the two of them climbed into the wagon. Gabrielle coaxed a reluctant Colette off the sofa, then the two of them sat down.

Gabrielle's eyes clung to his face. "I was so afraid you had been killed," she said. "There was no way of my finding out if you had survived the battle or not. I have been so miserable, Leo!"

He took her into his arms. "I am so sorry, sweetheart. I never should have left you the way I did. In my heart I knew that I loved you, but my mind didn't understand. It was so stupid of me. It took a bullet to knock some sense into me. As I lay on the ground all I could think was *I may never see Gabrielle again.*

She pulled away to look him up and down. "You were wounded? Where? You seem all right now!"

He smiled reassuringly. "I took a bullet in the back. I'm fine now. It didn't hit anything vital. The reason it took me so long to come was that I had to go home first to see my mother.''

She didn't say anything, just continued to look at him.

''I told my mother that I wanted to marry you, and she has promised to help me make certain that you are accepted into English society.''

She stiffened a little. ''You went home to ask her *that?*''

He caught the note in her voice and frowned faintly. ''Please don't misunderstand me, sweetheart. I would have married you no matter what she said. But I thought it would be more comfortable for you to know that you would be accepted by my family and by my world. And you will be. My mother will see to that. You will have no trouble joining English society as the Countess of Branford.''

Her brown eyes were huge. ''This is hard for me to take in all at once,'' she said. ''You truly want to marry me?''

''If you don't marry me I will be the most miserable man in the world.''

A smile trembled on her lips. ''I would not want that to happen.''

''I love you,'' he said. ''And I want to make this clear. I love you as you are—Gabrielle Robichon, proprietor and chief equestrienne of the Cirque Equestre. I didn't fall in love with some high-bred lady who never did a stitch of work in her life. I fell in love with you. I love you for your bravery, your loyalty, your sense of responsibility....''

''All right, I understand.'' She was smiling. ''You love me because I know how to muck out a stall.''

He smiled back at her. ''Among other things. I don't

want you to change, Gabrielle. I want you to stay the same person you are today.''

"I love you, too," she said. "Your leaving left me utterly devastated.''

"I was so stupid," he said.

She took his hand in hers and raised it to her cheek. "You were the Earl of Branford and I was a circus girl. I didn't blame you, Leo.''

"That's what my mother said—that she didn't blame me," he said. "God, the generosity of women!''

She kissed his hand and put it down. "I am glad that you have made peace with your mother.''

"Do you know what she said to me? She said, 'God bless Gabrielle. She has given you back to me.'''

Color flushed into Gabrielle's cheeks. "Did she really say that?''

"Yes, she did.''

Colette, who had been lying on the wooden floor in front of them, decided that it was time to remind them of her presence. She got up and came to poke her nose into Gabrielle's lap.

Gabrielle laughed and petted her.

Leo said, "Did you let her back into your bed?''

Gabrielle bent to hide her face in the dog's long, elegant neck. "Yes.''

"Wonderful." He sounded partially amused and partially exasperated.

"I was lonely," Gabrielle said. "The bed was so empty without you.''

"I was lonely, too, but I didn't share my bed with a dog.''

"That's because you weren't lucky enough to have a wonderful dog like Colette.''

"You're right," he said. "I want to have a dog again,

and a family. The boys can come to live with us at Branford Abbey, Gabrielle. Albert can get the painting instruction he needs and I'll see about getting Mathieu into Oxford so he can study mathematics.''

She looked up from Colette's neck. Her smile was radiant. ''That sounds wonderful.''

''And your precious horses can come, too. Remember how you said you wished they had a place with big stalls and green pastures? Well, they can have those things at Branford.''

''Leo...Leo...you are overwhelming me,'' she laughed.

''All I want is for you to be happy,'' he said. ''It's the one thing I want most in this life, for you to be happy.''

Tears glistened in her eyes. ''That is such a wonderful thing for you to say.''

''I mean it.''

''Leo,'' she said. She put her arms around Colette and rested her cheek against the dog's deerlike face. ''What will happen to everyone if I just close up the circus in the middle of the season and go home with you? Perhaps I should finish out the season before I go to England....''

''No,'' he said. ''I will pay everyone double the amount of money they would have made if they finished out the season with the Cirque Equestre. That way, they will have plenty of money until they find work with another circus.''

''But suppose they can't find anything?''

''They are all premier acts—they will find something. You can't take responsibility for the rest of their lives, sweetheart. They are not your family, you know. They all have their own families to rely on.''

''Sully doesn't. And Gerard is too old to be taken on by anyone. And Emma helped to bring me up.''

"All right. Sully and Gerard and Emma can come with us if they want. I'm sure I can find a place on the estate for them."

She kissed Colette and released her. "Gerard can help with our horses and Emma can help me with whatever duties I may have as your wife. And perhaps—if you spoke up for him—perhaps Sully could get a job at Astleys in London. He speaks English, you know. And he hasn't been drunk once since you left, Leo. I think he did not want to do anything to distress me."

"I'll see what I can do," Leo said.

"This is wonderful," Gabrielle said. "Oh, Leo, I am so happy!"

He held out his arms. "You could try kissing me instead of Colette."

She leaned into him and raised her face. His mouth came down on hers and the world went away.

"Gabrielle!" Albert had to repeat her name several times before she heard it.

"Damn," Leo said in her ear.

"We will be alone tonight," she whispered as she pulled away from him.

His eyes narrowed and he gave her a very focused look.

Mathieu said, "I'm sorry, Gabrielle, but I couldn't keep him away." Albert had pushed the wagon door open and he and Mathieu were standing just outside, looking in.

"Is it true, Leo?" Albert said. "Are you going to marry Gabrielle?"

"Your sister has done me the honor of accepting my proposal," Leo said.

"Hurrah!" Albert cheered. "I knew you would come

back, Leo. Mathieu didn't think you would, but I did. I knew you loved Gabrielle.''

Mathieu said, "He prayed. If ever I want something badly, I think I'll have Albert pray for me."

Leo and Gabrielle laughed. "Come," Gabrielle said. "We had better give this couch back to Colette."

As the two of them jumped down from the wagon, Mathieu said, "What is going to happen to the circus? Do you want me to run it by myself?"

Gabrielle's "Of course not!" clashed with Leo's "The both of you will come back to England with us."

Mathieu folded his arms and looked at Leo, who was now standing on the ground next to him. "What am I going to do in England? The only thing I know is circus life."

"You are going to go to Oxford and learn to be a brilliant mathematician," Leo said. "You already are brilliant. The mathematician part you can learn."

Mathieu stared up at him, looking so much like Gabrielle that Leo smiled. "Do you mean that?" Mathieu asked finally in a hushed voice.

"Yes," Leo said.

"It's true, Mathieu," Albert said. "You are too smart to spend the rest of your life jumping on and off of horses."

Mathieu was very pale. "I don't know what to say, Leo...."

"You don't have to say anything," Leo said. "We are a family now, you and Albert and Gabrielle and me. We do things for one another. Isn't that what a family is all about?"

"Yes, it is," Albert said firmly.

Gabrielle said, "Leo also said that Gerard and Emma

can come with us. And he will try to get Sully a job at Astleys in London.''

Mathieu finally smiled. ''You are really taking this family idea to heart, Leo!''

''Yes, I am,'' Leo said. ''I enjoyed the time I spent with the circus. I never expected to, but I did. I didn't even mind being the ringmaster.''

''Circus life is not so bad, eh?'' Mathieu said.

''No, it's not. But it's not for any of you anymore. It's time you developed the other talents that God has given you.''

''What about Gabrielle's riding?'' Albert asked. ''Papa always said she was the most talented rider he had ever taught.''

''Gabrielle won't stop riding,'' Leo assured him. ''Don't worry about that.''

''I would feel like half a person if I didn't ride,'' Gabrielle said.

''I suppose we should go and talk to the others.'' Leo looked at the collection of people gathered in front of the corral. ''They look like they're waiting for us.'' He turned back to Gabrielle. ''They still think that we're married, don't they?''

''Yes. I told them about the supposed death of your father and that you wanted me to come to England and that I wouldn't go. We should probably just say that, now that I have seen you, I have changed my mind.''

''They won't be happy to hear that the circus is closing down,'' Mathieu said.

''Leo is going to pay everyone double for the rest of the season,'' Gabrielle told them. ''That way, they will be all right if they can't find another job right away.''

''That's very generous of you, Leo,'' Mathieu gasped.

"I like them," Leo said. "And I can afford it. Come along, Gabrielle. Let's do the deed."

"Are you very rich?" Albert asked as Leo started to move away.

"Albert, you don't ask questions like that," Mathieu said, embarrassed.

"It's all right," Leo said to Mathieu. He turned to Albert. "Yes, I am very rich. I can easily afford to educate you and Mathieu."

"Will I be able to earn a living as a mathematician?" Mathieu asked. "I don't want to live on your charity forever, Leo."

"You'll be able to find a job," Leo assured him. "You can always teach at Oxford."

"And I'll earn my living by my painting," Albert put in.

"I know you will," Leo said. "But you both are going to have to learn English."

"That will be easy," Mathieu said.

Albert skipped like a small child. "This is *formidable.* Whoever thought, when Leo joined our circus, that we would end up like this?"

Gabrielle gave her rich, deep chuckle. "Not I," she said.

Leo took her hand. "I'm a lucky man," he said.

She looked up at him, her face radiant. "We're both lucky," she said.

"Leo!" Henri called. "Have you come back for Gabrielle?"

"Yes," Leo replied. "I have."

Everyone looked at Gabrielle's radiant face. "I am going to return to England with Leo," she said. "And Leo is going to pay you all double wages for the rest of the canceled season."

A little murmur ran through the group. Then Antonio said, "Your father must have left you a lot of money, Leo."

"He left me a generous amount," Leo said imperturbably.

"I'm glad you changed your mind and are going with Leo," Carlotta said to Gabrielle. "You were miserable without him."

"Yes," Gabrielle agreed. "I was. But I feel badly leaving you all in the lurch."

"*C'est la vie,*" Carlotta said. "I will miss the Cirque Equestre, but it will be nice to have the extra money, too."

The rest of the group murmured their agreement.

"We'll have a lot of toasts to make at the café tonight," Antonio said.

Leo felt a flash of dismay. Was he never going to get Gabrielle to himself? Then he looked at all of the people surrounding her. *I shouldn't be greedy. I'm going to have her for the rest of my life. Let these people who love her have a chance to say goodbye.*

"Yes," he said heartily. "We will have a party tonight at the café."

Across the crowd, Gabrielle's eyes met his. He sent her a silent message: *Tonight, after the café.*

Epilogue

Four Years Later

Gabrielle cantered across the diagonal line of the improvised riding ring, with Noble changing his lead on every stride. A loud "ooh" came from the gathered crowd, which was comprised of Branford servants, laborers and tenants; local townspeople and yeomanry; and a goodly number of aristocratic neighbors and guests. It was the second annual Branford Summer Festival, put on by the Earl and Countess of Branford to entertain their dependents, neighbors and friends.

There were many exciting things for the guests to do on Branford's festival day. There were boats on the lake, pony rides for the children, archery contests, children's games with prizes, music and dancing, an exhibition of paintings by Albert in the house, and plenty of food set up in a blue-and-white-striped tent on the lawn. But the highlight of the day was the equestrian demonstration, when Gabrielle exhibited her Arabians and her Lipizzaners, and she and Leo did a pas de deux on Noble and Sandi.

Gabrielle half halted softly, slightly increased the pressure of her leg, and Noble began a canter-pirouette. This raised another "ooh" from the crowd.

Noble's ears were pricked and he was listening eagerly to all of his rider's aids. They cantered into the corner and began another diagonal line of one-stride tempe changes, which made Noble look as if he was skipping as he went across the ring.

When the demonstration was over, the applause was loud and enthusiastic. Gabrielle and Noble took a bow, and Gabrielle's eyes met those of Leo's mother, who was sitting in one of the chairs that had been set for the upper-class guests. Lady Rivers waved and Gabrielle smiled.

The hillside above the ring was thronged with the less socially elevated guests, but there were quite a large number of lords, ladies and gentlemen to take up the seats that had been set out for them. The person in particular whom Gabrielle was most excited about was the director of the Spanish Riding School in Vienna. Her book, *The Art of Horsemanship,* had just been published in German, and he had read it and had wanted to see her ride and talk to her about her father and some of his ideas.

When the demonstrations were over, she went back to the house to change her clothes, stopping along the way to talk to as many of her guests as she could.

She went up to the third floor where the nursery was located and looked in on her two-year-old son. Leo had taken little Peter around the festival during the morning, but he had become fretful at about midday and Gabrielle had decreed that he needed to go back to the nursery and nap.

Peter was having his dinner when Gabrielle came in, and his brown eyes, so like her own, sparkled. "Mama!" he said. "I want to go back to the fest'val."

Gabrielle ruffled his golden curls. "When you have finished your dinner I will take you," she promised, and sat down beside him.

"Did he have a good sleep?" she asked Emma, who had volunteered to be Peter's nurse when he was born.

She spoke in French and Emma replied in the same language. "He went right off, Gabrielle. He was all tuckered out."

"Being around so many people can be tiring," Gabrielle said. "I feel rather tuckered out myself."

Emma gave her a shrewd, narrow-eyed look. "You're never tired. Are you feeling well?"

"I'm fine," Gabrielle said.

"Perhaps you ought to take a nap, like Peter."

"Don't be ridiculous," Gabrielle said. "I'll sit with Peter until he finishes his dinner and then I'll take him back outside."

"Want to ride the pony again," Peter said in French. Gabrielle had been making an effort to have him grow up bilingual.

Gabrielle rolled her eyes. "Peter, you can ride your pony every day. Why not leave the pony to the children who don't have a chance to ride?"

"My pony," Peter wailed. "I want to ride my pony!"

Gabrielle looked at Emma. "My mother-in-law assures me that he will outgrow this behavior. Apparently two is a dreadful age."

Emma smiled. "He is fine," she said. "A little lordly, perhaps, but then, he *is* a lord."

Gabrielle stood up. "I am going to change my clothes and then I will come back to collect Peter. Did you get a chance to look around the festival yourself, Emma?"

"I'll go when you come back for Peter," Emma said. "Gerard and I are going to look around together."

"Good," Gabrielle said, and went to change her clothes.

*   *   *

The festival went smoothly all day, and Leo had arranged Chinese lanterns strung around the gardens so that people could stay on after dark. It was midnight when Gabrielle finally saw the last of her houseguests up the stairs and was able to retire to her own apartment, which was on the second floor with all the other staterooms.

Gabrielle had been awestruck the first time she had beheld the bedroom that belonged to the Earl of Branford and his consort. The walls were hung with Italian Renaissance paintings, the long windows were hung with antique silk drapery, and the floor was covered in two magnificent Persian carpets. The furniture was heavy Jacobean walnut.

Colette's dog bed looked distinctly out of place in such splendid surroundings. She lifted her head when Gabrielle came in, then rested it back on her paws and closed her eyes. One of the footmen was in charge of taking her out at ten every evening, so Gabrielle knew she didn't have to disturb her.

Colette was looking older these days, and spent most of her time sleeping. She ignored Leo's two dogs and went her own way. Leo called her "the princess."

I'm so tired, Gabrielle thought. She hadn't felt this tired since she was carrying Peter.

The bedroom door opened and Leo came into the room. "Thank God Endersby didn't want to play another game of billiards," he said. "I was afraid I was never going to get rid of him."

She smiled. "Most of our guests sat in the shade in the gardens all day. They are rested. You and I worked."

He came across the room to kiss the top of her head. "Your ride was splendid. The director was very impressed."

"He really liked Noble and Sandi."

"What was he talking to you about?"

She gave him a bright-eyed look. "He asked if he could send me a few horses to train."

He sat down on the bed next to her. "Sweetheart! That's wonderful!"

"I am very excited," she confided. "And very flattered. To be asked to train horses for the Spanish Riding School! It's almost unbelievable."

"Not to me," he said.

She smiled up at him. "I wish everyone thought I was as wonderful as you do."

He laughed.

"The festival went very well," she went on. "It is so kind of you, Leo, to have such a day for the neighborhood. So many people told me that they looked forward to it all year."

He shrugged. "Many people have a day for their tenants."

"For their tenants, perhaps, but not for their servants and for the whole surrounding area. We must have had five hundred people here today!"

"We fed a lot of mouths," he agreed.

She yawned, showing an expanse of pink mouth and white teeth.

"You're tired," he said. He looked toward her dressing room. "Is Francine waiting to help you undress?"

"Yes. I had better go to her before she falls asleep."

She got up from the bed and went to the door that led into her sumptuous dressing room. When she returned fifteen minutes later, clad in a snow-white nightgown that buttoned down the front, Leo was gone. The murmur of male voices from his dressing room told her that he was with his valet.

She got into bed and pulled the covers up to her waist.
What a wonderful day, she thought. *What a wonderful
life I have.*

Everything had gone so smoothly. Mathieu was work-
ing with a team of mathematicians at Oxford, trying to
do something with numbers and theories that Gabrielle
couldn't understand. But he was happy. And Albert had
more people trying to commission him than he could ac-
commodate. The circus folk she had left behind had all
found other work, and she heard from Carlotta occasionally, which helped her to keep in touch with what everyone was doing. And Leo had managed to get Sully a job
with Astleys in London.

All of this happiness is because of Leo, she thought.

Tears stung her eyes.

I must be pregnant, she thought. *I'm not usually this
weepy.*

She thought of Peter, with his big brown eyes and his
beautiful golden curls. He wasn't going to be pleased to
be knocked off his solitary pedestal.

It will be good for him, she thought. *We all spoil him
too much. It will be good for him to have some competition.*

The dressing room door opened and Leo came back
into the room wearing his black silk robe.

"I was talking to Overton today," he said. "He has
just finished an addition to his house and I was asking
him about his architect."

Leo had been talking about building a new wing on
Branford to house the family, and also adding to the
property an indoor riding arena for Gabrielle, so she
could ride all year long. In fact, he had been talking about
little else for the last few months. Gabrielle encouraged
him; it was nice to see him so enthusiastic, she thought.

"What kind of an addition did Lord Overton build?" she asked now.

She listened to Leo as he spoke, and tried to pay attention, but she was so tired.

Finally he ran out of words. He looked down into her face and frowned. "You look exhausted," he said. "You should have stopped me from prattling on."

"I am tired," she said. "But I like to hear you talk."

"You had a long day," he said. "Between the two of us, I think we talked to every single one of our guests—including the children."

She smiled. "I think we did."

He said, "I'm sorry, I didn't think—you always seem to have such boundless energy." He leaned down and kissed her. "Go to sleep," he said. "And don't worry about our guests tomorrow morning. I'll take care of them."

"You can take care of the men, and I'll take care of the women," she said. "Don't worry about me, Leo, I'll be fine."

"Are you sure? You look a little white to me."

She hesitated, then said, "I think I am with child. Remember how easily I tired when I was carrying Peter?"

His blue-green eyes lit up. "Oh, Gabrielle," he said huskily. "Oh, Gabrielle."

"I haven't seen the doctor yet, but I'm fairly sure. I remember the feeling."

He put his arm around her and drew her to his side. He felt so big and strong against her. She leaned her head against his shoulder.

"You have made me the happiest man in the world, do you know that?"

"I'm pretty happy myself," she answered.

He bent his head and buried his mouth in the silky hair on the top of her head. "Are you happy? Really?"

"How can you ask such a silly question? Of course I'm happy!"

"Watching you ride today, seeing how perfect you are, I was thinking that perhaps you missed performing."

"Leo! How can you say I am not performing when you make every guest who darkens our doorway sit and watch me exhibit Noble and Sandi? I perform constantly!"

His arm around her tightened, and she snuggled her cheek into his shoulder. "This life is much better for the horses," she said. "And we have lent the Arabians to Astleys a few times, so all of their training is not hidden away. Gerard does a good job of exhibiting them."

"Yes, he does."

"I am happy, my horses are happy, my brothers are happy. And I am going to have another baby. Life is good, Leo, and it's all because of you."

"Thank you, sweetheart," he said huskily.

"Did I tell you that I got a letter from Carlotta today and Franz is getting married?"

"To a circus performer?"

"Yes. She is a rope-dancer also."

"That's nice," Leo said.

Gabrielle listened to the beat of his heart. "That life seems so long ago," she said. "It seems like Gabrielle Robichon, circus girl, was a different person from who I am now."

"You're the person you are now because you *were* Gabrielle Robichon," he said. "And I'm the person I am now because of who I once was. Perhaps I wouldn't appreciate my family so much if I hadn't been without one for so long."

"That's true," she murmured. Her eyes were closed and the steady beat of his heart was making her feel very sleepy.

"If you feel up to it, Overton invited us to Lockwood to see his new addition," Leo said.

"Mmm," she said.

"He was able to quarry the same stone for the addition as was used for the original house. I hope we can do that, too...."

Leo's voice went on, but Gabrielle was already fast asleep.

**From the *USA TODAY* bestselling
author of *Getting Lucky***

Susan Andersen

Were things getting
too hot to handle...?

When Victoria Hamilton's "no strings, no last names" vacation
fling resulted in a baby, she knew she had to begin a new life
far from her family's corrupting influence. Now her father has
been murdered, her half brother, Jared, is the prime suspect
and Tori has no choice but to return to Colorado Springs with
her six-year-old daughter. She'll do anything to prove Jared's
innocence. But confronting her past when she opens the door
to her new private investigator and comes face-to-face with
John "Rocket" Miglionni—the former marine who rocked her
world six years ago—sure isn't what she had in mind....

**hot
&
bothered**

MIRA®

*Available in August 2004
wherever paperbacks are sold.*

www.MIRABooks.com

MSA2021

He was a man well schooled in deception,
cruelty and murder—yet she could not
entirely resist his charms.

USA TODAY bestselling author

Anne Stuart

Independent and headstrong, Elizabeth of Bredon wants only to become a
nun, but her journey to the convent of St. Anne's threatens her choice. It's
not the holy friars in the escort who tempt her, but the man they are
taking to do penance for his many sins. Elizabeth has heard whispers
about Prince William's treatment of women, yet she cannot seem to keep
her distance, even though it may cost her her life.

"Anne Stuart conjures clever, enticing tales
of romance, intrigue and passion that lure
the reader into the story and never let go."
—*Romantic Times*

Available in August 2004
wherever paperbacks are sold.

Hidden Honor